☜ W9-AHB-716

Schaumburg Township
District Library
schaumburglibrary.org
Renewals: (847) 923-3158

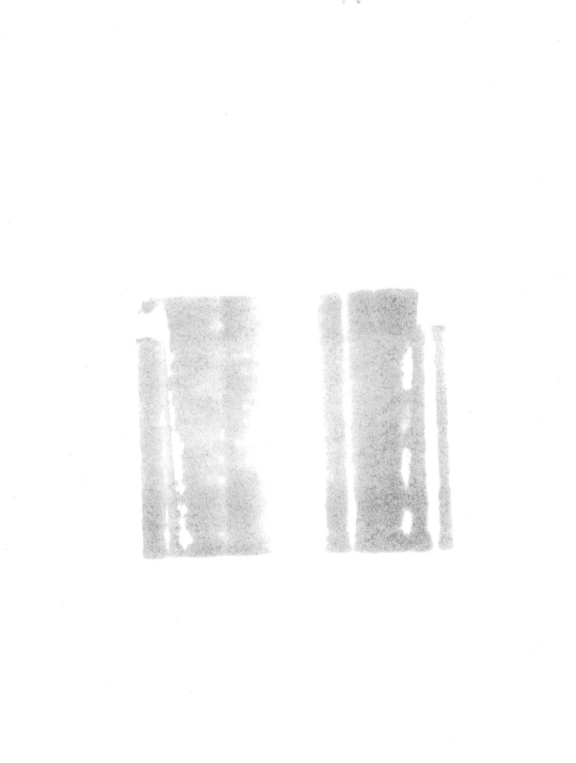

KING
OF THE
WORLDS

THE LOST YEARS OF
DYLAN GREEN

ALSO BY M. THOMAS GAMMARINO:

Big in Japan: A (Hungry) Ghost Story

Jellyfish Dreams (Kindle Single)

KING
OF THE
WORLDS

THE LOST YEARS OF
DYLAN GREEN

A NOVEL BY

M. THOMAS GAMMARINO

CHIN MUSIC
PRESS

Copyright 2016
By M. Thomas Gammarino

Publisher:
Chin Music Press
1501 Pike Place, Suite 329
Seattle, WA 98101
www.chinmusicpress.com

Library of Congress Cataloging-in-Publication Data

Names: Gammarino, M. Thomas, 1978- author.

Title: King of the worlds / M. Thomas Gammarino.

Description: First edition. | Seattle : Chin Music Press Inc.,
[2016] | Description based on print version record and CIP data
provided by publisher; resource not viewed.

Identifiers: LCCN 2015045067 (print) | LCCN 2015039291 (ebook)
| ISBN 9781634059091 (epub) | ISBN 1634059093 (epub) | ISBN
9781634059084 (hardcover : acid-free paper) | ISBN 1634059085
(hardcover : acid-free paper)

Subjects: LCSH: Life on other planets--Fiction. | Actors--
Fiction. | BISAC: FICTION / Literary. | FICTION / Science
Fiction / General. | GSAFD: Black humor (Literature) | Science
fiction.

Classification: LCC PS3607.A438 (print) | LCC PS3607.A438 K56
2016 (ebook) | DDC 813/.6--dc23

LC record available at http://lccn.loc.gov/2015045067

All rights reserved.
ISBN: 978-1-63405-908-4

First [1] Edition

Book design by Dan D Shafer

Printed in Canada

PUBLISHER'S NOTE

This is a work of fiction. Names, characters, places, and incidents either are the product of the author's imagination or are used fictitiously, and any resemblance to actual persons, living or dead, business establishments, events, or locales is entirely coincidental.

AUTHOR'S NOTE ON
PUBLISHER'S NOTE

Here we have your boilerplate disclaimer. For the record, I heartily endorse the first sentence. Over the course of several years, *I made this story up.* It makes no claims on history, except maybe in some of the oblique, figurative, poetic ways that non-documentary art can. Mere facts are beside the point.

I'm also on board with the first clause of the second sentence. Art abhors a vacuum, so like my more energetic cousin DJ Throdown I dig through heaps of American detritus and reuse and recycle. For me, the detritus comes from both culture and personal experience, but can I just make one thing clear please? I don't do roman-à-clefs. There is never a one-to-one correspondence between any of my characters and a flesh-and-blood human being, myself emphatically included. If you recognize yourself in one of my grotesques, forgive me and keep on reading; you won't know yourself for long.

I'm much less sure what to make of the disclaimer's final clause. It's that word "coincidence" that hangs me up. I mean, no, when I write about, say, the film director James Cameron in this novel, it is certainly *not* a coincidence if the character bears some resemblance to his real-world counterpart, who really did direct a film called *Titanic* and who really is reputed to have one hell of a temper. Still, it should be clear to any reasonable reader that I have repurposed that bundle of attributes, as I have every other celebrity who gets mention in these pages. To be sure, I don't know these people except as semiotic bundles, the gods and archetypes the culture throws up daily, and it is those public personae, as much a part of the furniture of American life as Coke or Viagra, that you'll find transmigrated into the universe in your hands—which universe, I might mention, is explicitly an alternate one.

Of course, if the multiverse is real and infinite, then, with the possible exception of certain fantasy writers, novelists have been writing non-fiction all along...and all our twitchy disclaimers are void.

For my family—infinite thanks for sharing this universe with me.

KING OF THE WORLDS

THE LOST YEARS OF DYLAN GREEN

"We are like butterflies who flutter for
a day and think it's forever."

—Carl Sagan, *Cosmos*

PART ONE

MOST LIKELY
TO BE FAMOUS

Young Daniel Young nodded his dopey head and blinked back tears.

"Remember," Dylan went on. "All of your longing is focused on this one human being. If you can't have her, you'd rather not live. You've got to make us *feel* that. Do you have any idea what I'm saying to you?"

Daniel nodded again. It was clear if you looked at his trembling chin and jutting lower lip that he was barely keeping it together. If you looked only at his hair, though, the way it bounced and shone, you could pretend he was enjoying this.

Dylan took a sip of his *poxna*,° but his adrenals had dried up hours ago. "You know what, Daniel, I'll cut you a deal: make us feel anything other than embarrassed for you and I'll give you an A."

> Caffeinated beverage roughly halfway between coffee and tea. Taste-wise, it's rather more like the former, bitter and earthy, but like the latter it's extracted from leaves, not beans, specifically the leaves of the deciduous *Poxna* tree, a.k.a. New-Taiwanese Tentacle Elm.

That was mean, and Dylan knew it, but he had about as much empathy left in him as energy. For Christ's sake, he was *tired*. His eyes stung, his ears had been ringing for days, and on top of having three preps this semester, he'd stayed up late last night grading a stack of aggressively uninspired essays on *The Catcher in the Rye*.

"Daniel, have you ever been in love?"

"I don't know," Daniel replied.

"Then you haven't. If you'd ever been in love, you'd know it."

One of the cool things about being a high school teacher was getting to drop well-meaning chestnuts like this without having to rack your brains over whether they held up to scrutiny.

Daniel hung his head.

Tiffany Wilson, the redhead who'd months since faded into the curtains, spoke up for what might have been the first time all quarter: "Why are you so mean today?"

She hadn't even raised her hand. Good—she was alive.

"Look at him," Tiffany went on, gesturing toward Daniel. "He's practically in tears."

Dylan looked, and right on cue a chubby tear slid down the poor kid's cheek and onto the floor. Dylan softened his approach: "I apologize, Daniel. I want you to get it right is all, to put some *feeling* into it. Call it tough love."

"It's okay, Mr. Green. I'm aware of the fact that I suck."

"You don't *suck*, Daniel. Don't ever say that again. You're doing fine. You're just…young. You've barely lived. I have to keep reminding myself of that."

"We're only fourteen," Tiffany put in, belaboring the very legitimate point. Dylan had lived so many lives already, he had to keep reminding himself that his students had lived just this one.

"How old do you think I am?" Dylan asked.

The students perked up. Shakespeare they could do without, but games they liked.

"Forty-seven?" Tiffany guessed.

"He's not *that* old," said Lauren Delay, the blonde milquetoast who sat to Tiffany's left. If she was trying to curry favor with him, she was doing an outstanding job of it—that is, until she continued: "He's like…forty-fourish?"

"Anyone else want to venture a guess?" Dylan asked, more desperate than they could possibly know or understand.

"Fifty?" Kai Fitzpatrick chimed in. "Fifty-three?"

"Sixty?" Amanda Cruz hazarded. It was a bit like being pierced with a bullet. Amanda was the prettiest girl Dylan had ever taught. She was so pretty that, as a rule, he tried not to look at her.

"I'm thirty-nine," Dylan declared at last.

"That's it?" Amanda said.

Okay then, he'd had enough of this for one day. "You know what? I'm letting you go early. We'll work on the scene some more tomorrow."

The young people surged with new energy as they packed up their things and made a beeline for their extra-curricular lives, though not without pausing on their way out to say "Thank you, Mr. Green" or "Have a nice day, Mr. Green."

It always amazed him how adept these kids were at compartmentalizing, how they thought you could accuse a thirty-nine-year-old of being sixty and then wish him a good day and honestly expect him to have one.

At any rate, he tried, unsuccessfully, to smile. He'd read once—albeit long after such knowledge might have saved his acting career—about some muscle up by the eyes that gives away a counterfeit smile every time. The only way to act a smile convincingly is the Method way, which is to say you've got to remember something happy—but Dylan had stopped subjecting himself to that sort of masochism years ago.

. . .

"Daddy!" cried Arthur.

"Da—y!" near-echoed Tavi, who was better with her vowels than her consonants.

"Kids!" Dylan said.

By now they were embracing his legs. It was quite a nice thing to come home to. Of course, at five and three, they weren't exactly being altruistic. They expected him to run around with them outside, or to read them books, or at the very least—they were groping at his midriff now—to pick them up.

Later this would be fine. Later he could do this. After he'd had a chance to put down his backpack, change into comfortable clothes and savor a few moments of quiet, he'd be happy to pick them up, swing them around, play the good dad, maybe even *be* it. But he couldn't very well skip that middle step without feeling some generalized resentment—not against his family per se so much as just the universe. He was tired.

"Hi, honey," he said. Oh man, he really said that.

Erin was standing in the kitchen, stirring a pot of something. She was still wearing her robe and slippers from this morning, which was just the kind of thing he remembered her explicitly stating in their pre-nuptial days that she would never do. It was hard not to think of his mother, who liked to boast that even while raising three children, she had managed, in that picket-fence world, to doll herself up *every single afternoon* before his father came home from work. She really did do that. He remembered lying on her bed as a little boy, watching her curl her eyelashes in the vanity mirror with that silver tool he sometimes used as a chair for his Star Wars guys. She'd peer up at the ceiling, apply the mascara, and then turn her gaze on him through the mirror, her eyes twinkling the way so many other female eyes would twinkle for him one day in that other space and time that was as distant from him then as it was now, but in the other direction.

Erin's eyes were no longer so stellar these days as they were just sort of *ocular*. To be fair, she was eight months pregnant and in profile looked something like a gigantic elbow.

"How was your day?" she asked.

"I want to make a smoothie," Arthur said.

"Fairly terrible," Dylan said.

"Smoo—ie!" Tavi near-echoed.

"We'll do that later," he told the kids, making his way toward the sanctuary of the bedroom.

"Any change with your ears?" Erin asked.

"The doctor said it would take ten days. I *told* you that."

"Sue me for caring."

Dylan peeled twenty little fingers off the doorjamb not less than three times before finally managing to manifest the bedroom door. The kids beat on the **opaque foglet mesh**° with their little fists, but

---

° Terrans had imagined this sort of polymorphous material, composed of interlinking nanobots, since the early nineties, but the technology still seemed decades away when it was discovered as the primary building material on Macarena, some 45,047 light years away. New Taiwan— where Dylan and his family lived—had independently come up with its own swarming foglet technology, though its uses of it were more modest, being restricted to certain types of doors, windows, and other passageways. Terrans themselves were still reluctant to roll out the new tech on Earth for fear of an apocalyptic "grey goo" scenario, but they were happy to have these new case studies to observe.

---

it was childproof and Dylan did his best to ignore them. He put down his backpack, slipped off his khakis and draped them over his desk chair. Then he plunked himself down on the bed, stared up at the popcorn ceiling and tried to relax. The kids were crying like they meant it now, and he understood exactly how they felt (he was good at projecting himself into other minds—it had once been his job after all). He loved them immensely, but if there was one thing he disliked about fatherhood, it was all the crying; it was almost enough to make him want to lose the rest of his hearing fast. And the only thing worse than the crying itself was the animal guilt he felt at not responding to it, but he knew by now that if he did gratify them with a response, if he made the smoothies, took them bike-riding, read them books, all without giving himself these few minutes to relax first, then the resentment would build to overflowing and as soon as the kids went to bed he'd say all sorts of ugly things to Erin, which he would instantly regret, and then neither of them would get anything like honest sleep before tomorrow night, which was clearly no way to live. Erin might not have believed him, but isolating himself like this really was for the common good.

"Erin, could you do something about that wild rumpus, please?"

"I'm making dinner," she said.

"I know. And I'm just back from a very long day of teaching a moribund art form to human teenagers."

He could almost hear her roll her eyes through the door. "Kids, come here," she said, which set them to wailing all the more until she assured them that they could help her cook if they liked. She was a genius at mothering; no one could take that away from her.

Only once they were out of earshot did Dylan remember just how *loud* peace and quiet were for him now. Ambient noise had competed with the ringing all day at school, masking it to the point where he'd found himself wondering if the pills weren't already doing their job, but here in the former quiet of his bedroom, those bells in his head sounded nearly as strident as the crying. But "bells" was wrong, seeing as there was really no chiming, jingling, or tolling. It was more like someone was holding down a single very-high key on a synthesizer, an electronic splinter lodged in his brain, and to make matters worse, it was accompanied by the alien sensation of a fullness in the ears, as if he were finally wearing the earplugs he should have been wearing at all those rock concerts throughout his gilded youth. Falling asleep the first night with the ringing had been such torture. He'd been certain he had some terrible disease, and in the theater of his hypnagogic mind the ringing grew so loud he recognized it as his own death knell, and what he felt, far more than the terror or sadness he might have expected, was an unbearable sense of frustration, of being *annoyed* that it was the end of the line and he couldn't go back, wipe the slate clean, and try again; that his life, such as it had been, would soon be coterminous with his destiny. Well, Dr. Cohen had relieved him of having to die soon—you couldn't ask for better news than that. Cochlerin was specifically designed to regenerate hair cells in the inner ear. Still, nine more days seemed almost more than he could bear. He could scarcely imagine how people in the old days, before there was a cure, had endured years and years of this.

Somehow he needed to relax. He and this shrill visitor were going to live together for at least another week; he might as well make the most of it. And anyway, such an exercise would be good mental training for dealing with some other adversity down the line, and if life had taught him anything, it was that there's some other adversity down the line.

He gave it his best shot, breathed deep, relaxed his muscles, and surrendered to the sound. At first the fever-pitch ringing was as terrible and anxiety-inducing as ever and gave rise to manic fight-or-flight responses like *Oh shit, I'm dying* and *Oh fuck, I'm dying*, but gradually, over the course of perhaps fifteen minutes, he taught himself to abort thoughts at the first sign of negativity and to return his attention to the terrible mantra in his ears, which, true to plan, wasn't quite so terrible anymore, and then wasn't terrible at all. It was almost calming if you let it be.

He was lying on his back on top of the covers, legs crossed at the ankles, fingers interlaced in an empty church over his abdomen, and as the fear began to ebb, he discovered himself doing this space-out thing he sometimes did where he'd fix his gaze on something out in the world and let it (for lack of a better word) penetrate him. It wasn't an *intellectual* exercise—he wasn't *thinking*; it was more like a kind of effortless meditation, and, with the possible exception of Quantum Travel (a.k.a. QT), it was the closest he ever came to understanding what mystics meant when they talked about subject and object merging into one, as per this exhortation from the great poet Matsuo Bashō: "You can learn about the pine only from the pine, or about bamboo only from bamboo. When you see an object, you must leave your subjective preoccupation with yourself, otherwise you impose yourself on the object, and do not learn. The object and yourself must become one, and from that feeling of oneness issues your poetry."

Currently, Dylan was a rather disgusting fan blade. Dust got into the crannies of the popcorn ceiling too—he'd been that a few blinks ago. Someday they'd get central air-conditioning, if ever they could afford it. Thoughts were objects too, of course, and now Dylan was suddenly his money problems. The last of his savings had gone into the down payment on this house that was really about twice as big as they required, on bucolic and overpriced Yushan Lane no less. He was indentured for the next thirty years, unless something miraculous happened between now and then, the odds of which were vanishingly slim. And with three kids to send to college...

The alarm returned redoubled, urging him to do something—to wake up, fight a fire, call the cops, something. It took several minutes for him to talk his heart rate down and return to his breath. He tried focusing less on his thoughts-as-objects and more on objects-as-objects. He looked at the varicolored spines of the print books he collected, and that calmed him some. He consulted the blank spot on the wall that desperately wanted art, and that induced anxiety again.

Then he looked toward the clothes closet.

The door was still swiped open from this morning and on the shelf at the top was a big white plastic shoebox that had once contained *one of the first pairs of Nike "pumps" ever to be worn by a kid in Delaware County, Pennsylvania.*⊙ Dylan had discarded the sneakers several decades ago, but this box had followed him around ever since, even if he wasn't sure he'd ever actually *seen* it until now. When was the last

⊙───

The sneakers had come with a little handheld pump you had to carry around in a pocket or somewhere. If you fit the pump to the valve built into this weird plastic pyramid at the back of the shoe, you could fill a bladder with air until the innards of the shoe conformed to your foot. Reebok had entered the pump market soon after Nike spearheaded it, but rather than include a separate pump accessory, they had incorporated the pump as a little raised rubber basketball on the tongue of the shoe that you could depress with your thumb, which made a lot of sense since who wants to carry a pump around while playing basketball? Though really it had never been very clear to Dylan what was so great about having your sneakers fit that tight in the first place.

───⊙

time he'd opened it? Ten years ago? Fifteen? It really had been that long, and in many ways it felt like longer. Barring whatever one might find via omni these days, that box held the only remaining evidence that Dylan had ever been anything but a teacher.

Before fleeing to New Taiwan, they had purged their old house in Santa Monica of virtually everything, and when Dylan watched Erin deposit the shoebox in the dumpster, he almost let her, and then thought better of it: "I think I'm going to keep that one," he said.

"Why? I thought you were done with all this stuff."

"I am. I totally am. But it might be nice to have something to show the grandkids." Much as the humiliating demise of his acting career had served as a prod to change his life, it had also served as a chilling intimation of mortality. Someday, before he knew it, he'd be a blubbering old man, and it wasn't impossible to think that maybe it would be some comfort to be tangibly reminded that at one time in his life he'd touched a certain sector of humankind (specifically the young female sector) with his art.

"Okay," Erin said, and that was that. She was pretty cool about it. She could have gotten jealous, could have asked, *Why does it have to be this of all things?* But she'd made the allowance for his vanity.

Dylan quit his space-out, got up, and approached the closet. He stood on tiptoes and took down the box. Then he placed it on the bed and plopped himself down beside it. He hesitated a moment, took a deep breath, and removed the orange lid. The letters sprang up at him, the years having failed to tamp them down, and several overflowed onto the sheets. He reckoned there had to be at least a hundred in there, and for every one he'd held onto, he must have discarded ten. He'd kept only the crème de la crème: the funny, the touching, the crazy ones.

He picked up one of the spilled letters and took it out of its envelope. This one was a handmade Valentine's card—all construction paper, glitter, and heart stickers. Down by the loopdidoo signature was the smeared, clay-colored imprint of some very fulsome lips.

He read:

Wendy Sorenson
243 Moana Street
Laie, HI 96762

Dear *Mr. Greenyears:*[○]

> Part of Dylan's reinvention of himself upon moving to New Taiwan was to drop the "years" from his name.

You don't know me yet but I am your biggest fan ever. Seriously. I've been in love with you ever since one of my friends made me watch ET II: Nocturnal Fears, which is a movie I'm technically not supposed to know about but have on tape and watch at least five times every day. Not the whole movie of course but just the parts with you in them. I'm sure you hear this a lot but my favorite part is the part where you make out with Korelu through the bars of your light cage. I know you're totally just acting but to tell you the truth you look so hot in that scene that I get so jealous I seriously want to shoot Korelu in the face even though I'm sure she's really cool. She's soooo pretty too, for an alien. I know it's just a movie and you were just acting but I figure there must have been some attraction there because it seems so real the way you do it. I wasn't going to say this but I'm just going to say it, okay, because I don't even care. If you ever want an Earthling girl to make out with like that I'll totally do anything you want. I don't even care what it is. I hope that doesn't make me sound like a slut. Honestly I've never even done it with anyone. But I would with you though. Honestly I'd marry you right now if you asked me. I'm only sixteen though so we might need to wait a year or something.

Love always,
Wendy

Now how many men ever got a letter like that in their lives? And to think he'd received such insane propositions on a regular basis for a couple of years there. It was absolutely weird the way the silver screen could deify you back in those days. He had no idea whether it was still that way for up-and-coming stars back on Earth, but he doubted it. *Were* there even stars in the same way there used to be? Before the advent of the Internet and Quantum Travel? In general, he made a point of remaining oblivious to all that.

He read through a few more letters and was curious to note that not a single one had come from a male. He couldn't say for certain whether this reflected the actual demographics of his fan mail or just his own curatorial bias, but in any case he had no memory of ever getting a letter from a dude.

Not all of his female admirers were so hot and bothered, of course.

Dear Mr. Greenyears,

I am thirteen and I hope to be a professional actress someday. I wanted to express to you in this letter that I think you are a really good actor. I saw *E.T. II: Nocturnal Fears* at my friend's house during a sleepover, and even though I was really scared, I thought you did a really great job! Now I can't wait for *Titanic!* Congratulations about that! How did you learn to act so great? Do you have any advice for an up-and-coming actress? I hope you win an Oscar. You totally should. Also, can you send me an autographed glossy photo please?

Sincerely,
Theresa

Not every letter was glowing. There'd been more than a few complaints from outraged mothers—as if it made any sense to grouse about the film's content with the eighteen-year-old lead instead of, say, the writer or director. And anyway, the content wasn't *that* bad. Yes, Elliott makes love to an alien, but there's nothing *full-frontal* about the scene. Moreover, Korelu is clearly a *female* alien from a dimorphic species, and while she and Elliott can't quite communicate yet, it's clear from the soundtrack that they are madly in love. Some critics found it implausible and disgusting, worse than bestiality, while other, more forward-looking reviewers saw in it a bold bid for sexual equality. In any case, it stimulated discussion, which could only be a good thing considering that before long such questions would cease being theoretical.

Young man,

I hope you're worried about the state of your soul. I saw the pitiful excuse for a film you were involved in, and I just want you to know that I found it disgusting and sad. When America goes down the tubes once and for all (it began in the sixties), we will have moral reprobates like you to thank. Don't you know that you're here in this world for just a brief time? Look to the state of your soul, young man, and consider yourself prayed for.

–Gertrude Winifred Gans

The irony of that penultimate line was thick. Sure enough, Dylan had remained on Earth for only a brief time after receiving that letter, though he was pretty sure Gertrude Winifred Gans was no prophet.

Had she written "you're here on this world for just a brief time," it might have given him some real pause, but she'd written, "*in this world*," and eternity hinged on that single letter of difference. Still, some atavistic, God-fearing part of him was just beginning to look to the state of his soul when Erin, mercifully, called him in to dinner. Like Aeolus bottling the winds, he stuffed the letters back in the box, and closed the lid.

As soon as he swiped away the door, the kids came and hugged his legs.

"Daddy!"

"Da—y!"

Now he was ready. Now it was nice.

• • •

The next day at school, Dylan attempted, again, to stage act 3, scene 2 of *A Midsummer Night's Dream* with his freshman drama class.

"Okay, so let's review the situation here because it's a little complicated. **Who likes whom**© at this point, do you recall? Let's start with Hermia. Whom does she like? You know what, Connor, maybe you could draw it on the board for us?"

As a lover of language and a product of Catholic school, Dylan had grown up clearly distinguishing between "who" and "whom," but over the course of his career he'd watched that rare inflection all but go extinct. He still used it, but his students by and large did not, and he was not so puritanical as to want to wage that losing war alone. Things change with time, whether we want them to or not, *nothing* lasts, and in the words of the immortal Lao Tzu (though they might as well have come from Darwin): "What is malleable is always superior to that which is immovable. This is the principle of controlling things by going along with them, of mastery through adaptation."

Connor nodded and slowly lifted himself up. Friends in baseball caps on either side patted him on the shoulders as if he'd just lost a contest or a loved one. When he got to the front of the room, Dylan handed him a green marker.

"All right, so Connor, please draw a girl on the board for us. You can keep it simple. A bathroom girl will do."

"A bathroom girl?"

"You know, the restroom girl? The intragalactic sign for girl?"

"There's an intragalactic sign for girl?"

"Sorry. I misspoke. I mean the *international* sign for girl, the Terran one."

Even after the better part of two decades on New Taiwan, Dylan still *put his foot in his mouth like this on a regular basis.*[○]

⊙──

The problem here was that while the natives were more than 99.8 percent identical to humans at the genetic level, and while they reproduced sexually in much the manner that humans did—their genitals being homologous to, and very much resembling, the human penis and vagina—their secondary sex characteristics were almost diametrically flipped, such that the vagina-bearing ones, or females, exhibited traits Terrans typically associated with males. Relative to the penis-bearing ones, i.e. the males, the females had bigger frames, deeper voices, and more body hair. They dressed plainly and practically and kept their hair short. And despite their being the ones to carry the babies (the gestation period of the natives, incidentally, was considerably shorter: just over seven months), the females were traditionally cast in the role of the provider. The males, on the other hand, had smaller frames, higher-pitched voices, and less body hair. They grew the hair on their heads long and invested a great deal of time in washing and styling it. They tended to wear makeup, jewelry, and clothing roughly analogous to those worn by Terran females in first-world temperate zones. Humans had hoped to find on other worlds some radically different gender roles and relations than those that obtained on Earth. Should there turn out to be intelligent life, they had hoped to find they came in a single gender, or three, or twenty. They had hoped for fluid genders, androgynes, sequential hermaphrodites. Alas, all of the newly settled worlds had turned up dimorphous hominids at the tops of their respective food chains. There was nothing, sexually, on New Taiwan that one couldn't find on a walk through Greenwich Village, with one notable exception: the male, penis and all, was the lactating member of the species. Terran biologists still hadn't puzzled out exactly how the birth of the baby from the female stimulated the hormonal changes in the male that resulted in milk production, but it was theorized that pheromones played a key role just as it did in the equally mystical-seeming Terran phenomenon of women's menstrual periods synchronizing themselves with those of other women living in close proximity. The point here being that, beyond perhaps + and - , there was no universal sign for male and female. Dylan's default mode of thinking was not just politically incorrect; it was flat-out wrong.

Connor drew:

HERMIA

"Okay," Dylan said. "That's Hermia. Now whom does Hermia love?"

"Lysander," said Becky.

"Correctamundo. Connor, please draw Terran-restroom Lysander next to Terran-restroom Hermia there. And then maybe you could draw an arrow to show that she loves him."

HERMIA   LYSANDER

"Great. Okay, now whom does Lysander love at this point?"

"Helena," said Justin confidently.

"Precisely. Now draw that for us, would you, please, Mr. da Vinci?"

Connor squinted.

"Leonardo da Vinci? Genius of the Italian Renaissance?"

Only Josh Song nodded, Josh who wore a bow tie and whose face was perpetually half-hidden by a Kurt Cobain teardrop of hair. He was far and away the most learned, and most melancholic, kid in class. Everyone else just looked confused.

"I guess we'll have to settle for you doing it as yourself then, Connor. Go on now. Make your immortal strokes."

"Very lovely. And whom does Helena love?"

"Lysander," said Tate.

"No. Helena loves Demetrius," said Sammy.

"Which is it?"

"Demetrius," intoned the class.

"Sorry, Tate."

Tate got some pats on the back for being wrong.

"And finally, what about Demetrius? Whom does he love?"

"Hermia," said Lewis.

"Correct again. Now let's give Connor a second to complete his masterpiece."

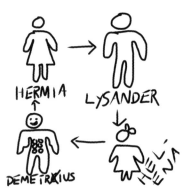

"Bravo, Connor. Okay, so if at the beginning of this play we had a classic love triangle with one outlying point, what geometric figure do we have now?"

"A square," sang the chorus.

"Precisely. Everyone wants someone other than the person who wants him or her."

"That's sad," Lia said.

Josh, uncharacteristically, blew a raspberry. "What a waste of energy," he said.

"How's that, Josh?"

"There must be other single people in Athens, no?"

"Spoken like a true automaton," Dylan said. "They're in *love*, Josh. Do you really suppose it's that easy to just give up on love?"

"They're not being creative enough, is what I think. There has to be a workable solution here."

"And what would you suggest?" Dylan asked.

"Well, in the first place, what's to stop that shape from being a circle and not a square? Circles are perfect."

"Go on."

"So like what if instead of having love as this petty little directional force between them, they could place it right at the center and let it radiate out in all directions *like the sun?"* ⊙

"And how might that translate into practice, I wonder?" Dylan asked.

"They should get a place together. Maybe build one right there in the forest."

"And then?"

"And then nothing. They live in it and bask in all the love. At the very least they could finally *sit down.*"

> Technically the star about which New Taiwan made its annual journey was "Lem"— named in honor of Polish science fiction writer Stanislaw Lem, author of *Solaris* and *The Cyberiad* (among other works) and 1996 winner of the prestigious Order of the White Eagle award—but for all intents and purposes Lem was identical to Earth's "sun," so English-speaking exopats, and by inheritance their offspring, sometimes called it that.

"I can't help but inquire about their sleeping arrangements..."

Dylan could see that not every student in the class was going to be comfortable with the turn this discussion was taking. You could never be sure with ninth-graders: in terms of maturity, some were practically ready for college; others might as well still be in middle school. When he'd suggested once that there was a built-in sexual dimension to vampires, one girl, Joy Hoffman, had memorably replied, "I think you just ended my childhood."

"They all sleep in the same big round bed," Josh said, "and it's pitch-dark."

Dylan nodded. "Congratulations, Josh. With a single blow, you've just overturned the entire Western romantic tradition."

"Sorry."

"Don't be. You're a free thinker. I applaud that." Indeed, Dylan himself might have been a little like Josh at one time, before an orthodox lifestyle snared him the way it eventually snares anyone who hasn't made a firm conviction to avoid it.

"Okay, so let's pick up where we left off. Where are our Lysander and Helena?"

Daniel Young stood up, looking dorky and afraid as ever.

"And Helena?"

"Marie's not here," Julia informed him.

"Oh right. Why then, Julia, you can be her understudy. No good deed goes unpunished."

Dylan expected some rolled eyes, but Julia leapt to her feet; for every three kids who didn't want to act out Shakespeare, you got one like this who secretly did. Dylan had been that kid once too. In fact, he often wondered if there wasn't that kid deep in all these kids, if only he could break through all their fear, chop through the already-frozen seas inside of them.

"Okay, Daniel, picking up at line 124."

"Act 3, scene 2?"

"Right."

Daniel began:

> "Why should you think that I should woo in scorn?
> Scorn and derision never come in tears.
> Look, when I vow, I weep. And vows so born,
> In their nativity all truth appears.
> How can these things in me seem scorn to you,
> Bearing the badge of faith to prove them true?"

He read with all the passion and nuance of some twentieth-century AI. (To be sure, he wasn't one—at least not as far as Dylan knew.)

"Okay, Daniel," Dylan said. "Not bad, not bad, but remember: you love this girl. She doesn't believe you, but you know that your future happiness depends utterly on convincing her of it. Imagine this is your only chance to persuade her, and if you fail, you die. That's what it has to feel like."

"But he doesn't *really* love her though, right?"

"Au contraire, he definitely *does* love her. He's crying to prove it, and these are no crocodile tears. That what he's trying to persuade her of."

"What are crocodile tears?" somebody asked.

"Phony tears. Fake tears."

Daniel balked some more: "But he only loves her because Puck put the juice on his eye, right?"

"That's true, Daniel. Good point. That's *why* he loves her, and *we* know that, but the key thing here is that *he* doesn't know it. He feels himself overwhelmed by love and that's that. I can see how it might bother you that the *reason* he's so powerfully in love is because for all intents and purposes he's been drugged, but the truth is, Daniel, if you were to ask a biochemist, they'd tell you that love is *always* a matter of chemicals. It's always a drug. It comes on strong and then wears off over time. The only difference here is the chain of causality, but whether the love causes the chemicals or the chemicals cause the love, subjectively speaking I don't suppose it makes much difference, and as an actor your primary concern is always with subjectivity. Subjectivity is your bread and butter. Do you get what I'm saying to you?"

"Not really," Daniel admitted.

"Okay, well just try putting some more passion into it, would you, Daniel? See if you can't work up some tears for us."

"I'll try," Daniel said. His hair vibrated.

"That's all anyone can reasonably ask of you," Dylan assured him.

Daniel was just about to begin when Tiffany spoke up from the curtains, "How come you're so much nicer today, Mr. G?"

"Am I nicer today?"

"About a thousand times."

"Well, I got a good night's sleep for one thing. That may have something to do with it."

It was true. Last night he'd made a point of sleeping on the living room sofa so he could follow Dr. Cohen's advice and omni up some tinnitus-masking white noise without disturbing Erin. Sure enough, he'd slept like the proverbial baby, and it no longer bothered him so much if Daniel Young wasn't the greatest Shakespearean actor in the universe; indeed, as Daniel proceeded to act out his scene there in the classroom, it was clear that, despite overwhelming odds, he didn't have a Shakespearian atom in his body.

Surprises *were* possible, of course.

• • •

Back when Dylan was fourteen, no one would have guessed that he'd go on to be a famous actor one day. It wasn't until his senior year, after all, that his father overheard him belting out Pearl Jam's "Black" in the shower **one evening**⊙ and encouraged him to try out for the spring musical, which was *Jesus Christ Superstar* that year. Dylan would have been content to be in the chorus, so he was rather terror-stricken when he checked the board the morning after callbacks to find he'd gotten the lead.

⊙ He especially liked to let loose toward the end:

I know someday you'll have a beautiful life,
I know you'll be a star,
in somebody else's sky,
But why, why, why can't it be, can't it be mine?

Despite feeling in the secret mind at the back of his ordinary mind that he was *meant* to play this part, he was so off-the-charts nervous during the next couple months of rehearsal that he felt as if he was always on the verge of puking. Mr. Armstrong, the casting director/geometry teacher, was tough on him, always making sure he hit *precisely* the right pitch and stood in just the right place on stage when he hit it. Dylan's worst fear was that he would blank during a live performance and forget the words, so in the interest of being over-prepared, he spent so much time and energy at home listening to cast recordings of *Superstar*, and recording himself singing it, that his eyes went all raccoonish and his grades tanked in every subject except English, which had always been easy for him.

But then, come opening night, his efforts paid such high dividends that he didn't merely sing the songs so much as he became them. And just as in his audition, he didn't quite realize what he'd done until it was over and he was taking his curtain call. But whereas a couple of dozen kids had clapped for him after his audition, several hundred adults were now giving him a standing ovation. Dylan Greenyears had found his calling, and everyone in the school knew it.

Overnight, Dylan became as popular as it was possible to be at Cardinal O'Hara High School, and not just among his peers but teachers, parents, custodial staff, alumni, and everyone else who'd come to see the show or read the stellar reviews in the *News of Delaware County* or *The Springfield Press* as well. To be sure, there are few ways to inflate a teenager's ego more than to assign him the role of God in the school musical. One way, though, is to award him "Most Likely to Be Famous" in his senior yearbook, and Dylan had that honor too. It didn't hurt things either that he had lately begun dating Erin Wheatley, the dance captain, who'd been cast as his temptress in more ways than one. The future had never looked so gorgeous.

Then, a few weeks after graduation, Dylan had his first brush with bona fide celebrity. Chad Powell, who'd played Judas opposite Dylan's Jesus and was soon to be his roommate at Temple University, found them a gig as extras in *12 Monkeys,* a time travel film about a boy who witnesses his own death as an older man. The Convention Center had been made up to look like an airport, and over the course of two days Dylan and Chad played a couple of luggage-toting travelers. The opportunity to work with (i.e. in the same film as) Bruce Willis and Brad Pitt would have been compensation enough; that they were granted access to the same catered spread as the stars was just a bonus. Indeed, for Dylan it would turn out to be something of a bonanza.

He was in the donut line on their second morning on the set when a voice from behind him intoned, "I've had my eye on you since yesterday."

Dylan peered over his shoulder. The dude was big, had long hair and was wearing some sort of cowboy hat. Chad was over in the coffee line, so Dylan was on his own here. "Um…why?"

"You've got the sort of look I'm after."

"I have a girlfriend," Dylan replied. He knew acting had a reputation for drawing gay dudes, and he had nothing against them; he just didn't happen to be one himself.

The guy chuckled. "You don't know who I am, do you?"

Dylan looked again. "Should I?"

"Not necessarily. I do happen to be directing this film you're in, though. Pleased to meet you. Name of Terry."

The two plain donuts on Dylan's styrofoam plate leapt off and began rolling in opposite directions. Dylan wasn't as up on his directors as he'd have liked, but murmurs from other extras had made it clear that Terry Gilliam was a pretty big deal. "I'm so sorry," Dylan said. "I feel like an idiot."

"No worries," Gilliam said, taking two more donuts from the tray and setting them on Dylan's plate. Once they were steady, he fished around in his wallet, took out a business card and placed that on the plate as well. "I'm quite busy today, for obvious reasons, but I want you to call me this evening. Say around nine or ten? Can you do that?"

"Okay," Dylan said, oblivious as to what was going on.

"Are you free for lunch tomorrow?"

"Sure," Dylan said.

"And what, may I ask, is your name?"

"Dylan...uh...Dylan Greenyears."

"Perfect," Gilliam said, putting one hand on Dylan's shoulder and grabbing himself a croissant with the other. "Now back to the wars." He winked at Dylan and went off to direct Bruce Willis.

Dylan had no idea what he'd just agreed to—why in God's name did this world-famous director want to have lunch with *him*? And was his lack of understanding somehow his own fault? Had he missed some subtle cue or signal? Failed to interpret Hollywood-ese?

For some reason, either because he didn't want to presume or didn't want to gloat—he himself wasn't sure—Dylan went the whole day without mentioning to Chad what had happened. Filming ended around seven, and Chad suggested they go get some grub, but Dylan told him he was feeling sick to his stomach, which was true in a way. He dropped off Chad at eight-fifteen, got home at eight twenty-eight, and called Mr. Terry Gilliam one fashionable minute after nine o'clock.

He answered on the first ring. "Hi there, Dylan. I'm glad you called. Look, I know I suggested lunch tomorrow, but it turns out I've got a prior engagement."

"That's okay," Dylan said, crestfallen.

"However," Gilliam went on, "could you meet me for some s'mores at around half three? There's a café at 4th and Chestnut. It's spelled 'X-a-n-d-o,' though I don't know whether to call it Zando or X and O."

"'Half three'?"

"Right. Sorry. That's three thirty on this side of the pond."

"Okay," Dylan said.

"Till tomorrow then."

"Yes. See you tomorrow." Dylan had sworn to himself that he'd find out more about Gilliam's intentions before agreeing to meet him, but his star-struckedness had gotten the better of him.

So the next day Dylan took a trolley at noon to 69th Street and then the el downtown. He was a couple of hours early, so he wandered the city, wondering at omnipresent graffiti warning him that "Andre the Giant Has a Posse," and ogling all the exotic city girls. Suburban girls so often put a premium on comfort, but these city girls dressed up. Even Erin was wearing sweats around him lately, and while he loved her, he was at the height of his virility and beginning to feel the tug of wanderlust.

Come half three, he made sure he was at Xando, however it was pronounced. Gilliam showed a couple of minutes later and gave Dylan a firm handshake. "Shall we dine al fresco?"

"Okay," Dylan said. Now what did 'al fresco' mean again?

"So, Dylan, you've grown up in this fair city?"

"Near it," Dylan said.

An androgynous, bald barista came to take their order.

"What'll you drink, Dylan?" Mr. Gilliam asked. "It's on me, of course. A cappuccino?"

"Can you do an espresso con panna?" Dylan asked the barista. This was just a fancy way of saying "espresso with whipped cream," but having spent the past couple of summers working in the café at *Borders*,[○] he had become a bit of a coffee snob.

One of the mega-bookstores once ubiquitous throughout the United States. These temples would stand as the high-water mark of American literary culture in Dylan's mind.

No one knew back then how fragile the business model was, how Omni was about to usher in a whole new paradigm. For a heady moment there it was like the Library of Alexandria was up and running again, and everyone had a card.

⊙

"Sure," the barista said.

Mr. Gilliam looked impressed. "I'll take the same. And some s'mores, too, would be lovely."

"Will that be all?"

"For now anyway."

The barista went away.

"All right, Dylan, you've been a good sport, but you must be wondering why I brought you out here."

"I *was* sort of wondering that, now that you mention it."

"So let me just cut to the chase. I'd like you to audition for my next project."

This was precisely what Dylan had hoped Gilliam would say, but it was no less stupefying for his having anticipated it. "Wow," he managed at length.

"If it came down to appearance alone," Gilliam went on, "I could tell you already that the part's yours if you want it. You've got just the face I've seen in my dreams, handsome and angular, but tender and childlike at the same time. Looks aren't everything, of course. Not by a long shot. I need to verify that you can act. Mind you, I've never done this before, scouted prospective talent like this, but since I spotted you on the set yesterday, my gut's been telling me not to let you get away."

Holy crap! Was life really going to be this *easy*? Was high school really such a reliable predictor of future success? Was he really handsome and angular and tender and childlike?

"I don't know what to say," Dylan said. "May I ask what the project is?"

"You've seen E.T.?"

"About a million times. It was one of my favorite movies as a kid."

"Good. Well this is the sequel. *E.T. II: Nocturnal Fears*. The idea has been kicking around Hollywood for years. There've been countless scripts. Spielberg himself wrote the first treatment and then abandoned it, said a sequel would rob the original of its virginity, which immediately struck me as a worthwhile undertaking. When I asked if he'd mind my adopting the project, he said, 'Be my guest, just make sure my name's nowhere on it.' Naturally I went right to Henry Thomas, who played Elliott in the first film, but he read the script and declined, said pretty much what Spielberg had been saying, that it did violence to the spirit of the original, which is of course the point."

"May I ask how this one's so different?"

"I dare say you just did. *Nocturnal Fears* strikes a very different tone from the first *E.T.* Much darker. It begins the same way, with a spaceship landing in the forest and a silhouetted alien waddling down a ramp, but this alien, it turns out, is no angelic vegetarian like ET. No, this one is Korel, the leader of a race of red-eyed, albino carnivores from the same planet as ET. They intercepted ET's distress signals when he was phoning home from his umbrella communicator in the first film, and they have come to capture and possibly eat him. ET's name, by the way, turns out to be Zrek."

"Who knew?" Dylan said.

"Right. So these evil guys end up trapping Elliott, who's an adolescent now, in a cage aboard their mothership, and they interrogate him about Zrek's whereabouts. They don't speak English, so a good deal of the second act is told through the impromptu drawings they pass back and forth. It makes for some pretty bold cinema, if I may say so myself. Ultimately the albinos resort to out-and-out torture and things get quite brutish before Korel's wife, Korelu, shows mercy on Elliott. She doesn't have the wherewithal to set him free, but she mocks Korel through her drawings and she and Elliott laugh together. Before you know it they can be seen, in silhouette, making love through the beams of his light cage."

"Elliott loses his virginity to an alien?"

"Quite right. But wouldn't you know that in the very height of their passion, who walks in but Korel himself! His eyes glow blood-red and his wife shouts all kinds of protests in their strange, chordal language. Korel, meanwhile, rips some razor-sharp teeth out of the mouth of this winged shark thing in one of the other cages—a specimen from another planet, presumably—then he unlocks Elliott's light cage with his mind and, using an excretion from the base of his spine, proceeds to glue the teeth to Elliott's penis. Mind you, none of this is shown directly so much as it is implied—we want the R rating after all. Korel then instructs Elliott, via a drawing, to pick up where he left off with Korelu. Elliott refuses. Korel rips out another tooth, holds it to his wife's neck, points to the drawing again, and utters his first phrase of English: 'Fuck you.' Elliott begins to cry."

The barista put down their drinks and s'mores. They thanked the barista.

"Well?" Dylan said.

"Well what?"

"What happens next?"

"Excellent. Act three: Zrek, of course, re-arrives from space to kick albino ass and save the day. Zrek turns out to be highly skilled in the celestial martial arts. Certain critics are going to say that I cheated by taking the climax out of the protagonist's hands and handing it over to Zrek, making him in effect a deus ex machina, so in order to at least acknowledge that I've done so consciously, I have Zrek land in a different part of the country, the planet's having rotated and whatnot, and commandeer a Ferrari Testarosa. *Machina*, you know, is the Italian word for car, so what you get in effect is a clever pun for the intellectual set. Meanwhile, it also makes for some comic relief and thrilling action sequences."

"How does it end?"

"Okay, so just as we recapitulated the beginning of the first film, we do so again with the ending. Korelu gives birth to a boy. Looks-wise he's exactly intermediary between her and Elliott. Elliott's mother has a talk with Elliott about how her little boy has really grown up and how he needs to step up and assume responsibility. This is clearly a very personal issue for her, her own husband having run off to Mexico before the first film. Elliott hugs her and promises to be a good father. Cut to a wedding ceremony in a church, with Zrek as best man. Everyone throws confetti as Elliot and Korelu walk out of the church, hand in hand, and get in Zrek's Ferrari. The baby is snug in his car seat in the back. Zrek chauffeurs the newlyweds and their newborn up the gangplank into the spaceship and we see that the car is towing a bunch of cans and the license plate reads 'JUST MARRIED.' Elliott breaks the fourth wall, looks directly at the camera and says 'I'll be back' in his best Arnold Schwarzenegger voice. They go up into the belly of the ship, the doors close, and they embark on their honeymoon to the Outer Rim. Roll credits."

"Yes, I'd say it definitely strikes a different tone from the first *E.T.*"

"I'm glad you agree."

"And you'd want me to play Elliott? I mean maybe?"

"Well, you look enough like Henry Thomas that an audience will be willing to suspend its disbelief. At the same time, you've got a look all your own, one I haven't quite seen before in the movies. Not the boy next door so much as the boy next door to him. Am I interesting you at all?"

"My God," Dylan said. "I've never been so interested in anything in my life."

"Great. So once we put a wrap on *12 Monkeys*, we'll organize a proper audition. Now let me make sure I've got your contact info."

Dylan wrote down his address and phone number in a little black book, and then they proceeded to eat their s'mores. Dylan wanted to impress Gilliam in conversation but lacked the life experience. Fortunately Gilliam was loquacious, and as long as Dylan kept prodding him with earnest questions about the industry, all he really had to do was listen.

Once again, Dylan told nobody about what had happened. Some part of him was convinced it would all come to naught, that it was far too good to be true. His pessimism was reinforced when summer came to a close without his ever hearing another peep from Gilliam. He and Chad quit their jobs and moved into the "New Res" dorms at Temple. They went to class, read Oedipus and Shakespeare, and auditioned for a play called *Balm in Gilead*. Chad got a part, Dylan didn't.

And then one morning, while Dylan was doing his math-for-artists homework at the last minute, he got a call from his mother, who had gotten a call from Terry Gilliam. To Dylan's surprise, she knew who that was. "Call him right away," she said.

And Dylan did.

And a week later he was in LA for his audition.

And the rest is a matter of record: despite its modest budget, tight production schedule, and hasty release, *E.T. II: Nocturnal Fears* was a massive blockbuster, a grand slam for the critic and the casual mov-iegoer alike. In part the film's success could be credited to its unde-niably slick execution, but it didn't hurt that first contact had taken place just two weeks before the release (complex hominids with single nostrils on Tarantino, 90,000 light years away); ironically, the film seemed to fulfill the public's yearning for aliens worthy of the name far better than the headlines were doing, and both *Independence Day* and *Star Trek: First Contact* would ride on its coattails later that year.

Whether it was for this reason or a more old-fashioned one, *E.T. II* also happened to be a grand slam for palpitating young women across the land who were lucky enough to find an adult to accompany them. The fan mail came pouring in, as did the scripts. The first one that Dylan accepted, at his agent's urging, was James Cameron's new film, a special effects extravaganza to be called *Titanic*, with principal pho-tography beginning soon.

· · ·

On his way home from the American School, Dylan decided to hover through the Grind. He generally did this a couple of times a month. Owing perhaps to the legal status of prostitution on New Taiwan, the Grind had to be the least seedy red-light district in the Milky Way. The prostitutes, what the natives called *azalfuds*, were lined up along a narrow, kilometer-long esplanade, females on the north side, flexing their biceps and abs; males on the south, tossing their tawny hair and caressing their breasts. Dylan was slightly troubled by how attracted he felt to the males; they were as feminine as any geisha, but he could not look past the bulges in their bikini bottoms. He knew from the biology textbooks at school that the New Taiwanese penis looked more or less like a human one but with a slightly bifurcated head. For a certain subsection of humanity, of course, these reverse secondary characteristics were a dream come true. Transgender women had always commanded a modest corner of the sex trade on Earth, and here they were normative. By contrast, it was (what American exopats referred to as) "he-males" and "she-girls" who catered to alternative native lifestyles, and, as it happened, *heteronormative Terran ones.*⊙ These trans

⊙

The IEF (International Exodus Federation) was very sensitive to the desires of indigenous populations when settling new worlds. Once they'd established an outpost and their linguist AIs had deciphered the native tongue, which generally took about six weeks (Chomsky's universal grammar is more universal than even he supposed), they briefed indigenous officials on the particulars of human civilization. As a gesture of goodwill, they practiced full disclosure, and given how notoriously bound up with crime the flesh trade was on Earth, the New Taiwanese could hardly be blamed for not wanting to import any sex workers. In fact, early on, all they had wanted were teachers.

⊙

azalfuds, everyone knew, peddled their wares on a block toward the end of the esplanade that had come to resemble an R & R camp for Terran exopats reminiscent of the fleshpots of Saigon circa 1972. Though it had been quietly beckoning for the better part of two decades, Dylan had never once been there. He hovered through for the spectacle and the thought experiments, and that was all. Mike the exobiology teacher would tell him sometimes about his sexual adventures over there: how the she-girls were like the hottest Earthling girls you'd ever seen; how the New Taiwanese vagina was totally compatible with the *Earthling penis,*⊙ and "tight as shit;" how they'd do anything you could

⊙

The status of intermarriage was still a hot issue in the courts. That said, dozens of Terran-exopat males were now cohabiting with New Taiwanese she-girls, and some had even reared some adorable mongrel offspring. The reverse, i.e. exopat females procreating with New Taiwanese he-males, was comparatively rare, though not unheard of.

possibly imagine and dirt cheap to boot. Dylan had gotten really close a couple of times to investigating all of that himself. The thought of sleeping with an alien did strike him as irresistibly exotic for a time. Since first looking up from Earth, human stargazers had projected their hopes and fears onto the heavens, either demonizing extraterrestrials or making angels of them. Caught up in the early excitement of the Great Up-and-Out, Dylan had been as guilty of the latter as anyone—so much so that he'd wondered if he wasn't making a terrible mistake in sealing himself to Erin just before their departure—but after a couple of years of living and working among the host culture, he'd finally understood, intellectually *and* viscerally, that life on other planets *was just life*. Aliens weren't so alien. Hominids everywhere worked and played, exulted and suffered, loved their families and buried their dead. The universe *was* largely conscious, it turned out, but that meant what it meant and nothing else besides. We all still had to die.

Moreover, Dylan was married, and if he believed in anything, it was the sanctity of marriage. He would no sooner sleep with an alien—or anyone else—than he'd have Erin do so. He had watched her make out with another girl at a party once, on a dare. They'd gone at it way too long, and it had made Dylan feel deeply confused, both aroused and jealous at once. After the party, he had asked her not to do that ever again please, and as far as he knew she hadn't.

Dylan, for his part, had cheated on Erin just once. They hadn't been married yet, and it probably wouldn't have happened at all were it not for the immense peer pressure, and the sense of dreamlike impunity that comes with partying inside *the moon.*⊙

⊙————————————————————————

To be sure, the surface of Earth's moon is every bit as barren as the Apollo astronauts reported it in good faith to be. Conspiracy theorists who hold that the moon landing was a hoax staged at Area 51 are simply misguided. And the moon isn't hollow either, as other theorists have claimed (not to mention novels by the likes of Edgar Rice Burroughs, C.S. Lewis, and H.G. Wells). What is true, however, is that the moon's pocked appearance is due to its regularly being impacted by meteoroids, asteroids and the like, and that some of these impact craters are quite capacious, a possibility that wasn't lost on the generation of New England Brahmins who came of age after the Second World War, when rocket technology had finally reached the point where it might be able to sling them up there from time to time—to winter perhaps, or summer, or at the very least to throw some all-night, very exclusive shindigs and Earthgaze from a Barcalounger.

When Werner Von Braun, the brains behind Hitler's V-2 rocket, was "sanitized" by the US government after Nuremberg, he was immediately put to work on the elite party set's new "yacht." It wasn't particularly difficult, and they were making regular jaunts to the Sea of Tranquility by 1950. The Apollo project, allegedly culminating in the moon landings of 1969, turns out to have been a case of an artist plagiarizing his own work, though Von Braun was careful to make Apollo bulkier, louder, altogether more majestic and less efficient. For a little while, this first generation of world-hoppers was content to eat the space food, wear the spacesuits, and bounce around on the cold dead surface, but they soon grew restless and commissioned the terraforming of a resort inside one of Luna's more spectacular caverns. Von Braun looked to it, and by the dawn of the Age of Aquarius, the Illuminati had their own psychedelic, pressurized and climate-controlled love grotto inside the moon. Imagine the most luxurious beach you've ever seen, with waves like blue gin lapping gently against a snickerdoodle shore. Now put it inside a cave with a glass ceiling and light it with a grove of tiki torches. Then set out some cocktails, rowboats, and individually wrapped contraceptive devices. If you can imagine all of that, congratulate yourself: you think like Hitler's rocket man.

It wasn't long, of course, before these lunar getaways became old-hat, so the Illuminati (old, fat, white guys mostly) began cherry-picking entertainers and inviting them up for the weekend to join in the festivities. Naturally these entertainers were sworn to utmost secrecy on penalty of death, but they were happy to oblige, and "the Grotto" quickly became the best-kept secret in Hollywood. Anybody who was anybody had been there.

Gilliam had invited him up for a cast party. You might think Dylan would have been surprised as the limo mounted a steep canyon to a launch pad near the Hollywood sign, but in fact this latest unveiling of the marvelous life that awaited him seemed perfectly in keeping with the series of unveilings that had taken him in the past couple of years from awkward high-school student to star of the silver screen. A week ago he'd been on the cover of *Time*—was a cast party inside the moon any stranger or less believable than that?

"Can I tell my fiancée?" Dylan asked.

"Now why would you do a thing like that?" Gilliam said. "Tell her I invited you to my house on Catalina for the weekend. We'll have you back by Monday unscathed. Unless you like it rough, of course." He winked.

Dylan smiled as if he understood and then called up Erin and told her about Catalina. He felt terrible lying like this, but he *had* sworn secrecy on penalty of death. Surely she'd understand.

"I'm happy for you," she told him.

The rocket ship was smaller on the outside than he might have expected, but bigger on the inside. The seats were nicely padded and there was a full bar and a plasma TV (cutting edge, in those days). It was not unlike the inside of the limo he and Erin had once taken to their senior prom, albeit somewhat roomier.

They watched *The Right Stuff*, for irony's sake. Out the porthole, the moon grew larger in the sky—nickel, quarter, fifty-cent piece—until it occupied the entire view and took on a third dimension. He could make out the mountain ranges and individual craters and rocks, and everything was so stark and clean and colorless and dead.

Once they made landfall, the captain, a young guy in a blue jacket with yellow wings, ushered them to the front part of the ship. When they were all accounted for, he pressed a button and a door closed with a pneumatic hiss. Then he pressed another button and the whole module they were in separated from the rest of the ship and became a kind of rover thing. The captain steered them across the rugged terrain toward the mouth of a nearby cave and took them straight through an air lock.

Once inside, they stepped down from the rover and found themselves in a sort of cavern. Light flickered on basalt walls, and the air felt humid, even tropical. They wound along a ridge for a couple of minutes and finally emerged at the head of a trail that led straight down to what appeared to be an honest-to-goodness ocean inside the moon. A couple of surfers carved up the waves. Along the beach, a dozen or so men lounged in beach chairs, drinking cocktails or receiving massages from naked, or nearly naked, women. A number of other men gathered by the cabanas beside the beach, drinking and playing cards, buxom women stroking them and giggling. It was to one of these tables that Terry escorted Dylan, and only when they got close did Dylan realize that he recognized most of these faces from the movies, even if he didn't necessarily know their names. He did, however, know Hugh Hefner's name, and Hef was there, wearing a burgundy robe. He had a heap of poker chips before him and a nude centerfold on each arm, both of whom smiled absurdly at Dylan. The one on the right even winked. "Welcome, son," Hef said. "Which one do you want?"

"Want?"

"This is a man's world up here, son," Hef said. "Repression is against the rules. What's your pleasure?"

Dylan indicated the one that had winked at him, and she immediately came over to him and pressed her hard body against his. "I like you too," she whispered breathily in his ear.

"Why don't you give him the tour?" Hef suggested.

"I'd love to," she said. Then she crouched down and took off Dylan's shoes, lingering at his crotch for effect, having clearly mastered the art of titillation. He was half crazy already when she stood again, took him by the hand, and led him down to the sea.

"This place is something," Dylan said.

"Isn't it, though?"

"So do you, like, *live* up here?"

"You silly," she said. "Nobody lives up here."

"So this is your job then?"

"You could say that," she said.

"You're well paid, are you?"

She laughed. "Extremely."

"I'm Dylan."

"Hi, Dylan. I'm Fantasia."

Of course she was.

They were down at the water's edge now, the warm surf licking at their toes. She giggled and turned to him with this dumb puppy-dog look. Then she took his hand and placed it on one of her bulbous breasts, which was so supernaturally perfect it had to be an implant. It was all so much like a dream, who could blame him for surrendering to the wiles of this vapid, well-compensated goddess and making love to her over and over again on the microbead shores of the Selenian sea?

Over the next couple of days, Dylan slept a good deal in his private bungalow, ate seven of the best meals of his life, and drank cult wines like they were orange juice. On the second day, Hef asked if Dylan wouldn't rather sow his oats in a different girl today, but Dylan said he was perfectly happy with Fantasia. Judging by her body language the rest of the weekend, she was perfectly happy with him too—or just a very talented actress. Either way would do.

He was back in Santa Monica with Erin by Monday. The end of his career, unbeknownst to anyone, was just a few months off, and he would never be invited to the moon again. One might have expected him to retaliate after his firing by publicly outing the Grotto, but he kept his word. For one thing, though he sometimes wanted to die in the aftermath of his shaming, he never wanted to be *killed* exactly. Moreover, it was fairly certain that even if he did tell someone, he wouldn't be believed. And anyway, there was something sacred to him about that memory, and he didn't wish to profane it.

Even all these years later, Dylan still thought of his weekend's dalliance with Fantasia on a near-daily basis. It wasn't that there was anything so transcendent about the sex itself—though there kind of was—but his experience in the moon seemed to his psyche both the literal and symbolic high point of his life: he'd been 238,900 miles above the common run of humanity, gained entrance to a secret society, glimpsed the gears and mechanisms at the back of reality. It was difficult not to regard his life since as shrouded in illusion, and he sometimes envied the naiveté of ordinary people. He'd been expelled from Eden, and was condemned to know what he was missing.

He veered off the Grind and went back home.

"Daddy!"

"Da—y!"

Dylan went to the kitchen and gave Erin a kiss on the cheek.

"I made linguine," she said, holding the steaming bowl to his face. "Real olive oil."

The sweet, nutty aroma made him feel a touch homesick, though he would never admit that. Still, something was off. "Real garlic?"

She shook her head. *"Galric.*[°] The real stuff would have broken the bank."* Since the ban on teleported crops some years back, Terran crops had become a low-yield, high-price commodity. "It's always a tough choice. I figure we'll spring for both on your birthday."

He nodded. Her judgment was sound.

He couldn't help but notice she looked especially sharp in the belly this evening. Given that gravity was a few tenths of a percent lower here than on Earth, human pregnancies tended to go longer rather than shorter, but there were never any guarantees. She looked like she was ready to pop.

Though beet-colored, cloveless, and in shape rather like a small pear, *galric* (which had been growing on New Taiwan for perhaps a billion years before the First Expedition began adding it to their spaghetti) tasted as much like garlic as any Terran apple variety tasted like any other. That the two, *galric* and garlic, were as seemingly cognate linguistically as they were gustatorily couldn't help but prick one's sense of wonder, particularly when one considered that New Taiwan, owing to its single landmass and centralized culture going all the way back, had produced but a single language.

After their initial enthusiasm over Daddy's return, Arthur and Tavi reverted to their worst selves, wailing and fighting over whatever was in the other's hand. The upshot was that they were in bed by 7:30, and Erin wasn't far behind, so Dylan had the run of the house for the rest of the evening.

He tried reading for a bit, but couldn't get traction on the words. His ears were screaming and, louder still, that box of fan mail was calling to him from the other room, siren-singing the way pornography had in his youth, the way Erin herself had back in high school. When he was sure Erin was asleep, he put down his book (*Sentimental*

Education, Flaubert) and crept into the bedroom, lighting up the dark with his omni. As quietly as he could manage, he took down the box and carried it into the living room. He set it on the sofa and sat down beside it. He knew this was no small decision he was on the verge of making, though that hardly stayed his hand. Fate was calling. He reached in blindly and pulled out a letter.

There. He had uncorked the winds.

By sheer coincidence, the letter bore a postmark from Taiwan, the *original one.*⊙

Dear Mr. Greenyears,

Do you remember me? We met during the premiere of ET II in Taipei. I know you met lots of girls that day, but you may remember that I asked you to sign my arm, where I had scars? I used to cut myself when I was younger. I was very depressed. But when I saw your movie I thought you were so beautiful that you gave me hope for a better life. Have you ever gotten out of a swimming pool at night and stared at a light and it has a rainbow around it? You were like that to me. You had a glow around you. You were not like ordinary people. I just wanted to tell you that I think you saved my life. Thank you.

Sincerely,
Mei-Ling Chen

⊙
This really did seem to be just a coincidence. Because the indigenous names of newly discovered worlds frequently turned out to be unpronounceable by Terrans, the IEF, in collaboration with PASA (Planetary Aeronautics and Space Administration), was charged with assigning exonyms where necessary. In the beginning they hewed to tradition and drew on the treasure trove

of mythology, but as that quickly became exhausted, they tended toward pop culture instead—there were now planets called Radiohead, Trainspotting, and Infinite Jest, for instance (not to mention, a bit later, Leonardo DiCaprio and Kate Winslet). Occasionally they drew from the well of geopolitics too: Since national boundaries were rapidly shifting and dissolving amid the emergent paradigm, it seemed fitting to pay homage to vanishing states by enshrining their names on the new celestial maps; and because China's surprise—and surprising—siege of Taiwan was underway even as the naming committee was meeting to discuss the name of the planet Dylan would eventually move to, all delegates, even the Chinese one, voted in favor of "New Taiwan" (and cognates in other Terran languages). To be sure, outside of its name, New Taiwan was about as Taiwanese as the West Indies were Indian; witness the fact that (owing largely to its highly esteemed American School) some 78 percent of the planet's Terran exopats were currently of American stock, whatever that might now mean.

The native name of the planet, incidentally, was *Ulmarjveul'tankuñbampok'*, which was not, strictly speaking, unpronounceable for humans, though it came pretty darned close. Like the English word "earth," it doubled as a general term for soil.

---⊙

Now this was just not what he'd expected at all. It was as if he'd come to get some candy and would be leaving with a rack of lamb. He vaguely remembered getting this letter the first time around, maybe even signing a worrying wrist in Taipei. Of course, back then at the height of his fame, all of that must have paled in his young, virile, and already repressed mind against the more full-frontal booty calls. Now, though, he found himself moved almost to tears. It didn't make a bit of sense to him that he had putatively saved this girl's life, but if it was true that his acting had made a difference back on Earth, then this was some comfort. He cringed to think he had never written back to her before (as far as he could remember, he had never written back to *any* of them) and so, better late than never, he omni'd his reply:

Dear Mei-Ling Chen,

My name is Dylan Greenyears. Perhaps you
remember me? I was a fairly well known
actor in the middle-nineties. Well, I was
just looking through some old mail and I
came across a letter you once wrote me. I
apologize if I never replied before, and
I realize it's a bit strange for me to
be replying two decades later, but I just
wanted to let you know that your words
moved me greatly. I live far away these
days, but I would gladly come to wherever
you are if you'd let me take you to lunch
sometime. In any case, I hope you are doing
well, and that you are happy.

Sincerely,
Dylan Greenyears

He hadn't written that name in a long time.

He read over the message, which struck him as just right, neither withholding nor revealing too much. He recognized, of course,
that it was also kind of insane. By now she'd be about, what, thirty-five? Somewhere in there. She might be happily married, with kids
and a job. He could ask Omni, but some part of him preferred not to
know. He was old-fashioned that way, romantic maybe, and anyway,
no computer, however super, could ever *really* know the richness of
her inner life, right? She was acquainted with the dark—that was
clear. Maybe she had some of the same well-concealed dissatisfaction
in her breast that he had in his? This thirst for something strange and
wondrous and new? He was not happy; it had to be admitted. He had

been at times, and sometimes he managed to recover the feeling for a spell, but it never lasted long. Maybe they could help each other again. Maybe this time she could save him.

He didn't have to wait long for a reply:

YOUR MESSAGE TO "MEI-LING CHEN" HAS PERMANENTLY FAILED.

He sneered. What? He hadn't seen a message like that in many years, and he'd never seen one on an omni. Omni messages didn't "fail." As long as someone was alive, any of their previous addresses would direct you to their current one. And if a person had died, you'd be notified of that too. Even if you opted to have your address unlisted, there'd still be some acknowledgment of your existence. Weird. He asked Omni some questions. The name alone wasn't much help— there were thousands of Mei-Ling Chens throughout the galaxy—but when he mentioned that this was the Mei-Ling Chen who had cuts on her wrists and who had once written a fan letter to Dylan Greenyears, the omni returned o results. He had never seen Omni come up empty-handed on anything before. Normally it would at least redirect you somewhere, but this time there was no trail to speak of. This person, this Mei-Ling Chen who cut her wrists and wrote fan mail, simply did not exist as far as Omni, or his omni at least, was concerned. Omni was greater than the sum of all human knowledge. It made no sense whatsoever that he himself might be aware of a person's existence while it was not.

For a few minutes, Dylan contemplated the problem and fidgeted with the omni. Eventually, though, for want of any alternative, he gave up, went back in the box, and pulled out another letter.

Dear Mr. Greenyears,

I'm writing on a dare from my friend Melissa. We both think you're super hot and amazingly talented. We even started a Dylan Greenyears fan club at our high school, and we'd be really honored, and would probably faint, if you'd come to talk to us sometime. Maybe next time you're in the Baltimore area? We can't pay you money, but we could all bake cookies or something and show you around.

I can't believe I'm writing to you!
Ashley Eisenberg

Now that was a little more typical, the sort of ego candy he'd been in the market for. He composed his reply:

```
Hi Ashley. My name is Dylan Greenyears. You
may remember that I was a fairly well known
actor in the middle-nineties? Well, I was
just looking through some old mail and I came
across a letter you wrote me. This may seem
odd coming so late, but I wonder if you'd
like to get together sometime? I'm living
rather far away these days, but I'd be happy
to come to wherever you are if you'd like
to meet up sometime. Are you still in the
Baltimore area? Alternately we could meet
at some midpoint. Just let me know what's
easiest. No pressure at all, of course.

Sincerely,
Dylan Greenyears
```

He stayed awake another two hours, reading through some more of his old fan mail and waiting for a reply that did not come. Mei-Ling's letter had served him like a cold shower, but his libido had warmed again and before retiring he took out his hardware and stroked it with his hand, remembering Fantasia, until in short order an absurd backlog of star stuff dripped down his fingers. He was reminded of Cinnabons. God, he hadn't had one of those in years.

What a pathetic fool he was! Clearly he should *not* have sent that reply. Even if Ashley Eisenberg did get back to him, he decided, he would ignore it. A biologist would tell you that sperm comes from the testes. It was pretty clear to Dylan, however, that it originates in the brain, where it goes about filling your convolutions and making a fog of your thinking. Only when he was void like this could he think clear thoughts, and under ordinary circumstances the fog prevented him from believing even this. It was like when he'd tell Erin her PMS was making her into a bitch. She'd insist the PMS had nothing to do with it, until a day or two later when it was gone and she was her gentle, caring, clear-thinking self again. Then she'd own up to what a hostage she'd been.

He went to the bathroom sink to clean himself up, and then to his bedroom to kiss his great-with-child wife on the forehead and wish her a good night. She purred. He went to sleep with that rare appreciation for one's blessings that is the upshot of guilt.

When he awoke in the morning, Erin was gone—in the kitchen probably, feeding the kids. He got himself up and went to the bathroom. To his surprise, he found Erin seated on the toilet, her face wan and agonized.

"You okay?" he asked.

"I can't pee," she said.

"Why not?"

"I think it's time."

"What, baby time?"

She nodded and winced.

"Holy Higgs!"[©]

He called in to the department chair and told her the news. He said it didn't matter who subbed for him because he/she could just let the kids work on their Shakespeare scenes. Then he began the laborious project of getting the kids ready to go. Once they were buckled into the levicar, he supported Erin on his arm to the passenger seat and manifested the door behind her. Then they were off to the New Taiwan Medical

Given the ascendancy of physics over the past several decades, it was only natural that scientific language should begin to colonize colloquial speech. Even devoutly religious Anglophones could be heard saying "Holy Higgs!" at least as often as "Dear God!" "Sweet Jesus!" "Christ Almighty!" and the like. In fact, they generally preferred it because, though it referred to the all-important, mass-endowing "God particle"— discovered in a child's home atom-smashing kit in Boise, Idaho in 1987—it did not, strictly speaking, require them to take the Lord's name in vain.

Center Earthling Annex. They decided that Dylan would drop Erin at the ER and then take the kids to daycare and hover right back.

He dropped her off and watched her waddle through the foglet doors, and then hovered along the roundabout and back over the street. He was just in time for rush-hour traffic, but the daycare center wasn't far away and he was back at the hospital in twenty minutes flat. He let the car self-park and hustled inside. As he rode the elevator on the way up to maternity, he checked his omni to find out what room Erin was in, and was surprised to find a new message waiting for him.

```
How awesome! Of course I remember you!
And yes! Triple yes! I would love to get
together. I wonder when would be a good time
for you? I am still in the Baltimore area.
It's tough for me to get away. Maybe you can
meet me at the Inner Harbor sometime for
lunch?

Looking forward to hearing from you,
Ashley
```

How deeply unsettling to have his spheres cross like this, not to mention being reminded of what a fool he was, how in matters of the heart/balls he was really not much wiser than the adolescents he pontificated to on a daily basis.

He ignored the message, which, some part of him must have realized, was not the same as deleting it.

Erin, his omni informed him, was in room 342, just around the corner from the elevator bank. He found it easily enough and knocked on the door. A native nurse (you could tell natives by their *double-jointed elbows and knees*©) swiped it away. Over her left shoulder, he could see Erin lying in bed. Inexplicably, she appeared to be holding a baby.

⊙──

```
The discovery that complex life was so similar throughout
the galaxy had served as a real buzzkill for those
Terrans given to a sense of cosmic exhilaration. Yes,
there were now hundreds of new cultures to discover,
and no doubt each had its fascinating quirks and
eccentricities, but there were no bug-eyed monsters
or Wellsian juggernauts, no parasites or dream beasts,
angels or telepaths. Tentacles remained a water thing.
Eating, drinking, breathing and sleeping were practiced
by hominids everywhere. Bicameral eyes appeared to be
universal, as were mouths, anuses, and dimorphic sex.
```

No civilization had yet been found that did not rely
to a large degree on spoken language. In fact, most of
these newly discovered life forms were more than 99.4
percent identical to Earth humans at the genetic level.
Virtually no one had expected this, and there was a whole
new cottage industry devoted to finding out how indeed
it had happened. Some scientists adopted a determinist
view, arguing in essence that the real surprise would
have been if things had turned out otherwise—if, for
instance, there were natural life forms out there on
Earth-like planets that were *not* carbon-based. They
created simulation after simulation on their omnis,
inputting all the variables—chemical elements born
of the big bang and the furnaces of sun-like stars;
mass, gravity, rotation, orbital period, composition,
magnetism, atmosphere, geology, topography, and climate
of each respective planet—and time and again they showed
remarkably little deviation. As long as life had at least
3.8 billion years to evolve on one of these planets, it
invariably produced something an awful lot like a human
being—"convergent evolution," they called this—and
once a certain threshold of intelligence was reached,
selection pressures eased and adaptation leveled off. New
Taiwanese scientists, for instance, claimed that life
had existed on their planet for upwards of 6 billion
years, and carbon dating conducted by Terran scientists
so far supported that hypothesis. The bone of contention
between the Determinists and the (unfortunately named)
Panspermists was that the former believed it plausible
that life had come about *independently* on each of these
planets and then evolved, whereas the Panspermists,
despite the Determinists' simulations—which they
dismissed as being reverse-engineered in some way or
other—held that chance, if it were truly chance, could
not possibly have behaved so uniformly. In the face of
the demonstrable fact that intelligent life on Super
Earths throughout the Milky Way was indeed so humanlike
that some races could not even be usefully classed as
other species, they were left to conclude that life had
originated in one place and one place only and then
made its colonial voyage around the galaxy inside of
comets, thereby seeding hospitable planets where they
would then take their own slightly divergent evolutionary
paths until meeting up again some billions of years in
the future. For the Panspermists, the race was on to
see who could identify the one and only place in the
galaxy, or indeed in the wider universe, where a host
of elements first pooled their resources, developed

membranes and learned to reproduce. In addition to these two camps inside the scientific community, there was of course one further possibility—namely, the religious hypothesis. God had made intelligent life in his own image and therefore, unless he was a shape-shifter, the standard deviation could not be large by definition. One Catholic bishop had even undertaken the project of compiling photos of every humanoid face in the galaxy inside his omni and "averaging" them out into a single image, which he believed would reveal the face of God at last. As it turned out, God looked uncannily like Val Kilmer's portrayal of Jim Morrison in Oliver Stone's *The Doors*—so much so, in fact, that a certain fundamentalist contingent began watching that movie on repeat in search of eschatological clues. In general these spiritualists made no attempt at addressing the materialist claims of the Determinists and the Panspermists. They did not purport to know where or how many times life had originated, only that the mechanism behind whatever had happened was God, whom they had been calling "The Creator" for a pretty long time now after all.

⊙

"You must be the father?" the nurse said in flawless English.

"I am."

"Congratulations! Erin did beautifully."

"What, you mean it's done?"

"Come meet your son."

"But I was only gone twenty minutes."

"Your wife's a pro at this. A real trooper."

"I guess so."

He walked over to Erin's bedside.

"It's really over already?"

"It really is."

She looked happy. She held up the bundle of swaddling clothes, and there it was, the bruised fruit of a human infant. They'd put a little blue snowcap on him.

"I want to call him Dylan Jr.," Erin said.

"I thought you wanted to call him Earth?"

"I did until I saw him. He looks just like you, don't you think?"

"Like me? I'd say he looks more like Gollum."

"Here, take him."

Dylan took the bundle in his arms. Feelings competed inside of him. He felt happy, of course. He'd begotten a son. A clean, pink, anatomically correct son.

And yet he felt guilty too. Having grown up bombarded with cautionary tales and harrowing facts about Earth's imminent *overpopulation*,[○] he couldn't help but notice, knee-jerkily—or maybe

○

Indeed, it was by and large the threat of food shortages, peak oil, and other depleted resources, coupled with the sense of wonder engendered in all but the most hardhearted Americans by Carl Sagan's *Cosmos* series on PBS in 1980, that had led to the terraforming projects on Mars and Io that began in the early eighties—still very much works in progress—and, more successfully, to the search for habitable exoplanets, of which, at last count, some 4,696 had been identified, and, thanks to the refinement of QT in the mid-90s, 78 successfully settled. Overpopulation, it turned out, was *not* a major concern throughout the galaxy. Thousands of Super Earths had been probed and found to house at least some form of life. Most, like New Taiwan, were found to have given rise to life forms remarkably like *Homo sapiens*, but unlike humans, none had been subjected to so ruthless a process of natural selection that their reproductive instincts trumped their ecological ones. They had DNA, but for whatever reason—as yet undiscovered—it just didn't seem to be as mean or shortsighted as the Terran variety. They were adept, in other words, at striking an equilibrium with their environment—humans, not so much. It probably didn't hurt that, while many of these civilizations had some form of religion, most seemed to recognize their systems of belief for the psychocosmological metaphors they perforce were.

○

just jerkily—that what he'd begotten was *another* son; and did you need two sons really? And then there were all the practical concerns.

How many insipid papers would he have to grade to fund this kid's education? Those little fingers, though: they were pretty sweet. Already Dylan Jr. was holding out one pinky like some tea-drinking aristocrat. Maybe this kid could be a better version of him someday? Dylan's father had never given him much advice or dispensed much wisdom. He seemed to think words were just words and you had to learn through trials. The Buddha said something like that too, as Dylan recalled. Dylan, however, thought words could be pretty important—he taught literature after all—and he intended to give his children millions of the best ones he could come up with. His own life had not gone as he had hoped, but he would do everything in his power to ensure that theirs would.

• • •

Dylan began his two weeks of paternity leave. Erin stayed at the hospital for a couple of days, and he and the kids went to stay with her and the new baby much of the time. Arthur was great with his new brother. Already he enjoyed holding him and petting his bald head. Poor Tavi, though, had a new distance in her eyes. She seemed to understand, with peculiar clarity, that she'd been usurped, that she was no longer the baby in the family but destined to be lost in that gray middle between her two siblings. At least she was the only girl, special in that sense, but it was clear she resented Mommy for holding this new baby and giving it suck, so instead of going to her, she cleaved, rather touchingly, to Daddy, who for lack of other viable candidates became her new best friend. Barely three years old and her paradise was already lost. *Join the club.*

Back at home, Dylan bathed the kids, put them to bed, and then set to work on Junior's sleeping quarters in what would no longer be his office. He and Erin had been so busy that they'd hardly done any nesting in advance; fortunately the shed was filled with hand-me-downs. Dylan even let Arthur and Tavi decorate the walls with markers. Arthur drew spaceships and dinosaurs. Tavi worked in a rather more abstract mode, rendering varicolored plasmoids and blobules.

For the first week or so after Erin and Junior's return, Dylan felt quite happy. He forbade himself to do, or even think about, anything related to work, and focused on enjoying the company of his kin. He and the kids prepared meals for Mommy. They played vintage Terran board games, painted one another's faces, and watched all the *Toy Story* films, the third of which choked Dylan up beyond all reason. They played hopscotch and flew a kite in the New Taiwanese wind. And they got to know their new family member. Dylan Junior's face seemed to change by the minute, and while Dylan still thought he looked pretty much like Gollum, he was beginning to see what Erin meant: Junior did take after him in some respects, more obviously than he did his mother anyway. It was mainly the eyes. They were Dylan's eyes, really, just popped into a smaller skull. He had not quite realized before how a gene is a gene is a gene. It made for quite an affinity, and one night while the other two kids were sleeping, Dylan cradled the baby in his arms and walked him outside to the deck to peer at the stars. He told him, unabashedly, how he loved him and—*screw overpopulation, the universe is expanding at an accelerating rate in all directions anyway*—he was glad to have him join them. Then he waxed philosophical and possibly nutty and asked the kid what it had been like in the womb. What was it like when that first spark of mental life kicked in? What was it like before that? How far back could he go? Was there anything important back there that his old man had forgotten? He looked out at the Milky Way, showed his son the pale evening star their species had once been trapped around. All those worlds, and yet—he spared his son now and kept his thoughts to himself—was there nothing truly strange out there? Nothing so exotic and marvelous that it would stymie our human frames of reference, mock our languages, confound our metaphors?

Because that was the thing about being young, wasn't it? Everything was still new? Dylan sometimes briefed his students on one of the more interesting tidbits he'd picked up in graduate school: The Russian formalist poet Viktor Shlovsky identified *ostranenie*—usually translated as "defamiliarization," though literally "strange-making"—as the basic function of art. "Habituation," Shlovsky wrote, "devours work, clothes, furniture, one's wife, and the fear of war.... Art exists that one may recover the sensation of life; it exists to make one feel things, to make the stone stony." His students usually gave him blank stares when he recited this, so he'd translate it for them: "Art exists to make you babies again."

"Why would we want to be babies again? Isn't education about getting us to stop being babies?"

"In part, yes, but it's also to get you to see things, *really* see them, as if for the first time. We could never hurt one another if only we learned to look with new eyes."

"But aren't babies like naturally really selfish? Don't you have to *teach* a baby to be nice?"

They were right, of course. He was romanticizing. He had this tendency.

And there was this too: If you checked your omni, you'd find that nearly every combination of five or fewer words that you could think of, however nonsensical, had been documented countless times. The English language itself, one might say, was dying through overuse and becoming one big meta-cliché. Dylan consoled himself with a quote he'd once read from a twentieth-century Earthling scientist: "The universe is not only queerer than we suppose, but queerer than we *can* suppose." How the unvanquished youth in him hoped it was so!

This was as close as Dylan ever got to praying anymore, and it ended, as per some prayers, with gratitude: he thanked the Universe, whatever that might mean, for this beautiful, healthy baby boy who had his eyes.

PART TWO

STRANGE-MAKER

Paternity leave wasn't all so wonderful. Dylan was sleeping fitfully—which was to be expected, what with the new infant. And even if there had been no infant, the fact was, despite his best efforts, he was fundamentally bad at vacationing. Forbidding himself to work inevitably resulted in the accumulation of anxiety. He worried about everything he *should* be doing, and that anxiety steadily built up steam until on the tenth day it found sufficient cause to explode: he'd taken the last of the Cochlerin several days ago, and damn it to hell if his ears weren't still ringing loud as ever. He scheduled a visit with Dr. Cohen for that very afternoon.

"To be frank with you," she told Dylan, eyes squinty with concern, "I've never seen anything like this. There's really been no change at all?"

"None whatsoever."

"See, that's so strange. Ordinarily the Cochlerin should have done most of its work by the fourth or fifth day. I have teenagers who come in here newly deafened every couple of weeks. Do you know that since hair cell regeneration went live, concerts have gotten up to thirty percent louder?"

"That's interesting," Dylan replied, though really he was much more interested in how he was going to get this goddamned ringing to stop.

"So what do you say we do that hearing test after all?"

Dylan grudgingly accepted. He already knew what they were going to find: he was growing old.

He went in the sound booth, pressed buttons when he heard beeps, and repeated after Dr. Cohen words like "baseball," "hot dog," and "ansible."

"Okay, you're all done," she said.

"That's it?"

"That's all she wrote."

"Well?"

"I hate to tell you this, Mr. Green, but—"

"Give it to me. I'm ready for it."

"Your hearing is perfectly normal."

"Come again?"

"You heard me loud and clear. I have an audiogram here to prove it."

"Really? Normal?"

"Really normal."

"So what does that mean then with regard to the ringing?"

"It's tough to say exactly, except that the problem seems to be not with your cochlear hair cells as would typically be the case."

"So where is it then?"

"We'll have to run some tests, but it could be in your auditory nerve or beyond."

"Beyond?"

"Your brain, Mr. Green."

"I see. So I don't have any hearing damage, but I might have brain damage?"

"I can't say anything with any certainty at this point, Mr. Green, but I'd like to do a functional MRI if that's okay with you."

He shrugged his shoulders. She got the fMRI helmet out of its case and fitted it to his head. She read the results from her omni. "Hmm."

"Is there a problem?"

"None that I can see. None whatsoever. I'm not a specialist, but this is telling me everything's tip-top."

"So where does that leave us?" he asked. "I assure you I'm not just crying wolf here. My ears are really screaming."

"I have no cause to doubt that, Mr. Green. The next indication here would be for me to refer you to a psychiatrist. There might be a psychosomatic component to your condition. Do you have an inordinate amount of stress in your life, would you say?"

"Define 'inordinate.'"

She smiled. "All right then, if it's agreeable to you, I'm going to refer you to Dr. Minus Fudge. MD in psychiatry from Stanford. He's wonderful, and right next door."

Dylan nodded his assent.

"Don't worry," she assured him. "We'll get to the bottom of this."

He thanked her for her concern and left the office feeling even shittier than before. She'd been so confident last time in telling him his condition was curable that he had expected another course of Cochlerin at most, a stronger dosage perhaps. He had not expected any talk of brain damage, let alone neurosis. Could that be right? Was he doing this to himself? The ringing certainly seemed to be as objectively real as a fever or a broken bone. When he'd first noticed it, he'd even asked Erin if she didn't hear it too. He'd tried countless times to wish it away, talk it down, reason with it, berate it, cajole it, but it didn't seem to interact with the stuff of thought at all. But maybe that's what it's like to lose one's mind? Surely madmen don't *will* themselves mad. They lose control, become unhinged. Fuck. It felt like the beginning of the end, like he had embarked on that downward slope that would lead him through senility and decrepitude to bodily death and the ultimate indignity of oblivion.

He dropped by the drugstore downstairs and got the *diaper batteries Erin had requested.*° He wasn't ready to go home yet, so he went in the coffee shop next door. Dylan had actually come to prefer *poxna* to coffee, but it was nice to be in an American-style coffee house again. It was not

> Electro-plasmic waste-disintegrating diapers were one of the more eagerly adopted technological imports for Terrans in recent years; the Tau Ceti System had been using them for the equivalent of almost ten thousand Earth years already.

unlike the one in the Borders he'd worked at several lifetimes ago. He ordered an espresso con panna and taught the barista how to make it. It was at once anticlimactic and altogether wonderful to have that particular combination of chemicals on his tongue again. He took a seat. The place was filled with native students mainly. Right next to him a rather lovely native male sat sipping his coffee and crocheting with carbon nanotube bundles. Dylan could hardly stop himself from staring until the creature caught him looking and changed his position. Dylan reminded himself that the thing had a penis anyway. He blinked on his omni, pretended he had something to do, and then realized that maybe he did. "Project a QWERTY keyboard on this table," he instructed under his breath. It had become trendy of late to use a more ergonomic keyboard configuration like Colemak or Capewell, but Dylan was an old dog.

The keyboard appeared. Dylan began to type.

Dear Ashley,

I'm sorry to be so late in the reply. I

wonder if you'd like to have lunch with me
at the Inner Harbor this Saturday at noon?

- Dylan Greenyears

He hadn't known he was going to do this until he did it, but then he hadn't known he was losing his mind either. If cum was befogging his thoughts, well then so be it—the fog was life too. And much as he believed in the sanctity of marriage, he did not, it turned out, believe in it at the expense of the sanctity of his life itself, which somehow had a whole new urgency to it.

He chose Saturday for good reason: he happened to know there was some big K-12 conference in Minneapolis this weekend. He wasn't sched-uled to go, but a few of his colleagues were. He'd been invited to this sort of thing a few times in his early years at the school, but in the interim he'd earned a well-deserved reputation as a bona fide exile; unlike most of his Terran coworkers, he hadn't returned to Earth even once since they'd come up here (Erin, by contrast, made it home once every two or three years), and until now he'd been thoroughly convinced he didn't want to. He'd been so wounded by his home planet that he'd forsworn it altogether. But then he'd been wounded by this planet too, however gradually. Or maybe that was just the ineradicable memory of that other place intruding on this one—you can't escape the fourth dimension by moving along any of the first three. Indeed, if there was anything to the old truism about time healing wounds, those that didn't outright *kill* you anyway, then why was it depicted as an arrow? Why not an unfurl-ing roll of gauze or some such thing? The IV drip of time?

In any event, Dylan didn't get what was so important about *phys-ically* traveling to a conference now that the omni could bring it to you and/or you to it, but his colleagues relished any excuse to take a trip—and now he would too.

· · ·

Back at home, he found Erin nursing Junior on the sofa and gave her the bad news: "Get this. Cindy called. She's quote-unquote 'highly recommending' I go to this conference in Minneapolis this weekend."

"*The* Minneapolis? On Earth?"

"Do you believe that?"

"At the tail end of your paternity leave? Can I assume you told her no?"

"Actually I told her I'd check with you and get back to her."

"She didn't say you *have* to go, though, did she?"

"No. She implied it, but fuck her. I'll tell her I can't. I'll tell her you need me here. It's just a job after all."

Erin looked up at the ceiling, face pinched with thinking.

To be sure, it was more than just a job, and Dylan knew she thought so too. It was a symbol, or something. For their first nine years out here, he had taught English to the native population at a cram school, which was the gig he'd been recruited for. He liked the work less and less each year, but it allowed them to stay and paid his tuition while he worked at night toward finishing his BA from Temple via omni, and then his MA in Modernist and Postmodernist Literature from Yale, also via omni. He'd been crazy busy, but he'd wanted it that way; the last thing he needed was time to get sucked into the black hole of what-might-have-been. Erin, meanwhile, picked up a gig teaching human biology full-time at the American School. She made good money and enjoyed working with high school kids so much that she coached cross-country and choreographed the musicals too. When he finished his degree, Erin tapped her connections and got him a job in

the English department at the school, and for a handful of years they'd
enjoyed living on pretty much identical schedules: they'd wake up at
the same time, eat breakfast, and roll to work together; they'd meet up
for *poxna* breaks in the teachers' lounge; and they'd roll home together.
They were careful, though, to give each other ample space during the
workday and made a point of eating lunch together no more than twice
a week. Even when they did eat together, they generally stayed on
campus, and not only because the cafeteria food was decent and cheap,
but because on this alien world so far from home, however batheti-
cally unstrange, there was something especially comforting about the
American-high-schoolness of the American School—every bit as dis-
tinctive a quality as Irish-pubness or Starbucks-ness. They certainly
hadn't *expected* any resemblance to Cardinal O'Hara, the Catholic high
school in Springfield, Pennsylvania, where they'd first met all those
years ago in *Jesus Christ Superstar*. The American School had a lot more
money than O'Hara ever had, so it was no surprise that the infrastructure was all-around swankier, but the effect of all those hopeful
student voices—and worlds-weary faculty ones—echoing down the
halls, combined with the ado-
lescent reek of PE and cheap
perfume, was as good as any
time machine© and transported
the Greens on a daily basis to
that other school on their home
planet where'd they'd fallen so
blithely and uncynically in love
and planned their days around
trips to each other's lockers so
that they could lock lips for all

⊙ At this time, bona fide time
machines still did not exist
as such, not for anything as
macroscopic and complex as a
primate anyway, though given
the paradigmatic dynamite
of QT, not to mention the
nostalgia for the old days
it brought in tow, Earth
Government was dispensing
temporal dislocation
research grants like they
were water purification
tablets, and a majority of
the scientific community
was predicting practical
applications any minute now.

of twenty-five usually-pretty-halitotic-but-what-did-they-care seconds before they had to rejoin the hallway traffic and race the bell
to remote classrooms where they would pass the time by tessellating
their notebooks with "I ♥ DG" or "I ♥ EW" and lose themselves in day-
dreams of last weekend, or next weekend, or some weekend twenty
years from now. Earth was the only world then, and they were the
only lovers. That Dylan and Erin did indeed find themselves together
two decades hence felt like a great triumph. They had weathered so
much and now here they were, returned to the apex of some miraculous cycle and stealing kisses at school.

Then they'd started making babies and entered into a whole new
stage in their lives together.

"This sucks," Dylan said, making his final play. "I should just tell
her to go screw herself."

"You know what?" Erin said.

"What?"

"You should go. I can get along without you for a couple of days."

"But you know how I feel about that planet."

"Dylan, we can hardly afford for you to jeopardize your career
right now. Think of the children."

"You're not serious?"

"I am, actually. It'll be good for you to see Earth again. Maybe
you'll find that it's changed...or that you have."

He sighed and ran his fingers though his hair. "You really want
me to go?"

She nodded. "I do."

"All right," he said. "Fine. I'll do it. I'm not happy about it, mind
you, but I'll do it."

If he felt a touch sorry for her, he consoled himself that she no doubt had her own secrets hidden away in her bosom behind the milk ducts. And anyway as far as he could tell she'd basically gotten what she wanted out of life, while he'd lost it all. Okay, he'd gotten *her*, but now she was the self-actualized, essentially happy human being while he was…something else. Could anyone blame him for trying to change his destiny before it grew too late?

"Thank you, honey," she said, and she kissed him on the cheek and went back to giving suck.

• • •

Quantum Travel was actually quite simple, one more variation on the copy-and-transmit teleportation schemes so abundant in **twentieth-century science fiction.**[⊙]

⊙
Few understood the particulars, but even Dylan, not a scientist by any means, could wrap a few neurons around the theory. Essentially, Quantum Travel capitalized on the property of "entanglement"—what Einstein called "spooky action at a distance"—to encode and relay information literally instantaneously. In short, when two particles are entangled, their relationship is such that, no matter how far the one is from the other, as soon as you observe one of its properties—spin, for example—you *instantaneously* know something about the properties of the entangled other, even if it's billions of light years away. For a while there, quantum mechanics were gun-shy about the prospect of using entanglement to transfer classical bits of information because the essence of that initial observation was randomness and Heisenbergian uncertainty, and if you fiddled with one of the entangled particles too much, the particles quickly decohered, or became disentangled. Such was the prevailing view anyway until 1984, when Jun Watanabe, a thirteen-year-old wunderkind conducting research at Kyoto University, made a suite of revolutionary discoveries, viz. 1) *all* subatomic particles are always-already entangled with infinite other particles throughout the universe; 2) one can predict with remarkable accuracy the locations of these entangled particles by reading the "signatures" of the proximal particle and plugging

just seven measurements into an algorithm adapted from the fractal-geometry work of mathematician Benoit Mandelbrot; 3) decoherence as such doesn't exist, i.e. perturbed particles simply switch allegiances, and 4) there exists on Earth a (now patented, government-classified, much-speculated-about-but-almost-certainly-fish-based) catalyst that can collapse probability waves into predetermined measurements one hundred percent of the time. Watanabe had figured out, in other words, how to *steer* the quantum universe, making him about as close to godlike as any human, let alone adolescent, had ever been (though, as he made painfully clear in his 2009 memoir, *Action at a Distance*, mastering the microscopic world didn't help him get laid in the macroscopic one until he was well into his twenties). He'd also established, in short, that the uncertainty principle was every bit the cop out quantum physicists had always insisted it wasn't. To this day, no one really understood the theoretical-metaphysical underpinnings of quantum entanglement—most suspected the existence of hidden dimensions or wormholes—but Terrans had gotten the manipulation of it down to an exact science, and so far it was an achievement they hadn't found matched by any alien civilization. Galactic neighbors had built some very impressive starships, to be sure, bona fide marvels of engineering, but none could reach superliminal speeds, whereas humans were now traveling regularly at millions of times the speed of light, which, a little arrogantly, they'd once called "the cosmic speed limit."

Of course, QT wasn't *really* travel at all. Your body was scanned at the source as *information*, transmitted instantaneously, and then reconstituted via a RiboMate ribosome-matrix printer at the destination in under twenty seconds (directions for the self-assembly of the RiboMate itself having been transmitted in advance, but this was where Dylan's pop-sci resources gave out altogether—per Arthur C. Clarke's third law, it all seemed like so much magic to him). Unlike earlier 3-D printers and molecular assemblers, which had relied to some degree on sampling and compression technology, the RiboMate was lossless. According to every study yet conducted, when you "arrived" at your destination, you really were one hundred percent you, with no margin for error, no noise. Still, QT remained controversial among a certain segment of the Terran population. The fly in the philosophical ointment, old hat for any Star Trek fan, was that for at least a dozen seconds, unavoidably, there existed in the universe two identical copies of "you," one at the origin, the other at the destination. As soon as the all-clear signal was received via entanglement, the RiboMate instantaneously—and painlessly, at least in theory—dematerialized you and recycled your molecules for subsequent matter compilations. Some Terrans worried that QT, a.k.a. destructive copying, was in fact a form of suicide, that the "you" who emerged at the destination was not the same you who departed. If you asked the arrived passengers themselves, however, they would tell you, to a person, that they were indeed the very same people who had departed. Even if the two weren't *numerically* identical, they had the very same DNA, the same memories and scars, the same haircut and wardrobe, even the same microbes, and their recent experience diverged for a few minutes at most (new laws, and port-security AIs, forbade the simultaneous existence of two or more incarnations of the same hominid for any longer than three Earth minutes). Those who opposed QT outright were generally of a religious persuasion. These were people who believed quite literally in the idea of an immaterial soul, the special sauce of personhood, which they took to be non-transferable. For them, the copy was at best a kind of zombie, all the material of the original but without its God-given essence, a flute without breath. Dylan had been religious enough as a kid to understand that objection, but his life as an adult had suggested to him over and over again that man makes God at least as much as God makes man, and having QT'd once himself, he could attest that his inner life, his *spiritual* life if you like, was every bit as deep and rich and sensitive to wonder as it had ever been. (But then it was undeniably a copy attesting this, so you'll have to make up your own mind on the matter.)

The little hiccup in consciousness necessitated by QT was no more troubling to Dylan than any power nap. For all practical purposes at least, there was no need to dwell on the philosophical conundrums. Much more urgent than whether or not you were being murdered elsewhere at that very moment were questions like "What time is it?" "Where can I catch a cab?" and "Who among you is human?"

———————————————————————————⊙

Dylan disembarked at Baltimore's BWI Thurgood Marshall Intragalactic Teleport and immediately set to exchanging some New

Taiwanese *zarkaks* for **Terran quid**;⊙ he could hardly afford to leave any record of his transactions via omni, being as he was officially at a K-12 conference in Minneapolis. He'd even made sure to catch up, via omni, on the latest K-12 pedagogy trends while waiting in line back in New Taipei, just in case there turned out to be a quiz when he got home.

He loved Erin. He really did. This had nothing to do with her. He realized this was

⊙ The recently adopted pan-Terran currency. One of the more interesting sociological effects of the discovery of life on other worlds was the degree to which human-human relations had been reconfigured in the collective human psyche as non-zero-sum. Wars ceased, dictators abdicated, wealth really did trickle down, and the Terran quid was born. Zero-sum sentiments were reserved for those warlike planetary civilizations the explorers were bound to discover any day now. To be sure, Earth was still no utopia, but it was a good deal closer than it had been during Dylan's time there.

just the sort of thing men had been saying for eons. He also realized they'd been saying it because it was true.

He hopped on a bus to Baltimore. Like most of the rest of the vehicles on the roads here since fossil fuels were outlawed in 2004, it was powered by natural gas, but it was still wheel-based. How odd to think a civilization that could perfect QT had made so little progress when it came to the daily commute. Going back ten centuries, personal transport vehicles on New Taiwan had harnessed the planet's natural magnetic field to hover several inches above the ground. The primary "fuel" was inertia, and good old Lem took care of the rest. Liquid methane was abundant on New Taiwan, and they hardly even used it. Even the rolling road in New Taipei—a multi-lane (i.e. multi-speed), sixty-kilometer pedestrian conveyor belt complete with on-road cafes and rest areas—was wholly magnet-powered. All this tire-to-road friction here on Earth seemed like such a waste, not to mention the source of some highly avoidable nausea. To think you could hardly *read* on a Terran bus without losing your lunch!

He got off at the Inner Harbor. Ashley had told him to meet her at Ye Olde Telephone Booth, which she informed him was the last phone booth on the eastern seaboard and listed on all the crossroads signs around the harbor. Along the way, Dylan marveled at the queerness of being surrounded, seemingly entirely, by members of the same species again. It came as something of a relief, in fact, when he spotted the double-jointed knees of a New Taiwanese teenager grinding a handrail on his skateboard. "*Zalbuña!*" Dylan said in what he took to be the boy's native tongue, and in reply he received a wholly unaccented and slightly surly, "Dude, I was born here, okay?" Man, Dylan had been gone a long time. And as if to corroborate this, no one had recognized him as a famous actor yet; he had to remind himself that this was what he supposedly wanted.

True to its name, give or take, Ye Olde Telephone Booth was just an ordinary phone booth of the sort Dylan remembered so well from childhood, grayish and with a baby blue border around the top and white letters spelling out "TELEPHONE." It was cordoned off so that you couldn't get too close, but hordes of Earthlings were gathered around, taking pictures. Parents waxed nostalgic while their children, who clearly didn't get what this upright coffin thing was supposed to be (an old RiboMate?), tugged at their pants and pled, "Come on, let's go."

These kids, like his students and his own offspring, thought of all manner of the old communication devices the way he had thought of gas lamps, chamber pots, and horse-drawn carriages as a kid—charming maybe, but *backwards.*[○]

⊙

Practically every sentient being in the known galaxy
was plugged into an omni now, and even those few
Luddites who weren't—the Amish, for instance, and the
purplish-green civilization on 2Pac—were accounted
for by it. Dylan remembered that for a time there on
Earth, the number of screens-per-home had proliferated
like a cancer. People had their TVs, computers, phones,
e-readers, cameras, video cameras, biometric devices,
telescopes, translators, etc. It was only a matter of
time before a sort of technological gravity, and common
sense, made them converge into a singularity. Dylan,
like many members of his generation, still preferred
the omni VII (smart contact lens and wireless earbud
rig), but most of his students these days had the more
immersive cortical implants, which were a double-edged
sword in the classroom; in theory, he could—and did—
limit student access to the Omniverse, but they always
found workarounds. Some of their parents conducted
their marriages between planets or moons for years at a
time via omni, which relayed bits of communication via
entanglement just as the teleporters relayed bits of
biochemistry (information is information is information).
For a monthly fee, the omni would even project full-blown
holograms, and theoretically, though it was at present
outlawed by the Mons Olympus Accord on the Reproductive
and Reduplicative Rights of Human Persons (2005), you
could even impregnate someone via omni if you had the
right matter printer on the other end. Those given
to slippery-slope arguments believed the next logical
step would be for hominids to forego external reality
altogether and live permanently in the sorts of virtual
reality game worlds that had become so popular in the
past decade. Naturally some were doing this already,
spending the entirety of their lives in the shadows of
the Omniverse, shooting virtual junk into their virtual
arms and zipping around on lightcycles or wrecking on
the halfpipe without any real pain. You still had to
surface to eat non-virtual food, however, and the daily
reminder that you were spending the majority of your life
inside Plato's cave was enough to undermine the pleasure
for most people. Dylan himself had experimented with VR
as a form of holiday escapism. He'd tried the drugs and
slept with the succubae, and they had brought him great
audio-visual stimulation, to be sure, but consciousness
is a layered thing, and throughout all his virtual
amusements there was always some nagging awareness one
hierarchical level up that none of it was "real," and

the reward centers of the brain responsible for secreting
the dopamine and whatnot really did seem to care whether
you had earned their rewards in the real world or not.
Some of the more affluent junkies, with the assistance
of months-long IV drips and waste-disintegrating diapers,
had taken to having their avatars don virtual VR rigs,
and then to have those avatars don virtual VR rigs, etc.
in an effort to confuse the cortex into believing that
some level or other of this intracranial utopia was real.
For Dylan at least, VR amounted to mere rehearsal for
life. It was like reading literature that way, but not
half as artful. Whenever he surfaced from a session of
VR, he felt vaguely sick and needed a nap to undo the
psychic pollution, whereas a good book, especially one
printed on a felled tree, made him feel nourished and
awake and alive.

"Dylan Greenyears?"

Dylan looked up. Brown hair. Pale, freckled skin. Single-jointed knees too. Human. Very. "Ashley Eisenberg?"

"I can't believe I'm finally meeting you," she said. Her teeth gleamed preternaturally white.

"The pleasure's all mine," he said. She was pretty, if not at all what he'd expected. Eisenberg sounded so Jewish, but this girl looked as Irish as any Molly or, as it were, Erin. Her eyes, like his, were as emerald as any sea.

"You've hardly changed," she said.

"That shows what you know."

Halter top. Muscular arms. Breasts like overripe fruit.

"You hungry?" she asked.

"A bit, yes."

"Crab cakes sound okay?"

"Miraculous. I haven't had one of those in twenty years. We don't have crabs where I'm living now. There are various types of shellfish, but the meat is different, more sausagey."

"Eww."

"It's not too bad actually. Just different."

"Speaking of which, where are you living now? Omni doesn't list an address for you."

Obviously. He was a celebrity after all, even if no one had done a double take yet today, let alone stopped to ask for his autograph. It was normal for celebrities to opt out of Omni's registry. Their existence would be noted, but not their address. As it happened, Dylan's address actually was listed, but it was under his newer, abridged name. He had told very few people of his whereabouts after his flight from Earth, and though he considered coming clean with Ashley now, he deemed it too much of a risk. He didn't know her yet really, and the line between avid fan and stalker, he'd heard, could be quite thin. Granted, it was he who'd contacted her this time and not the other way around.

"Ask me again later, would you?"

She shrugged.

He let her lead the way in her black leather pants. Beveled thighs. Butt like a heart-mark. Fuck-me shoes. Not that he was thinking about that.

They boarded a water taxi and passed through a flotilla of couples and kids pedaling around the harbor in green, dragon-shaped boats. Ducks quacked. Dylan found himself choked up all of a sudden by the cerulean sky, which was just so unmistakably Earthly (atmospheric plankton on New Taiwan lent the sky an aquamarine tinge). He had at last come home, or nearly—technically, he'd been to Baltimore just once before. His whole family had driven down to visit the National Aquarium when he was a kid, and what he remembered most from that visit, more than the shark walk or the tropical rainforest even, was the Giant Pacific Octopus, with its undulating tentacles and countless suckers, its quicksilver camouflage, its slit eyes that betrayed some calculating but inscrutable intelligence. Despite all the alien worlds that had been discovered in the years since, it struck Dylan now that Earth's Giant Pacific Octopus remained in some archetypal way the most alien creature he'd ever seen.

They debarked at what Ashley told him was the best restaurant in town and got a seat al fresco, right by the water's edge. At her suggestion, they ordered some beers from a local brewery called Flying Dog.

"This is pretty surreal," Ashley said. "Having lunch with Dylan Greenyears—I never thought I'd see the day."

"It is pretty uncanny."

"Actually, I used to fantasize that we'd get married someday, but I guess at some point I gave you up for lost."

They proceeded to make all sorts of small talk, though it was not so small for her presumably, and really it wasn't so small for him either given what it was doing to his ego. He was also learning quite a lot. As a rule, he paid no attention to Terran affairs anymore, so every topical or pop-culture reference she made was lost on him, and she made enough of them that he had the defamiliarizing pleasure of hearing his own first language in what amounted to a foreign dialect. Still, he managed to glean a good bit of propositional content too. He learned, for instance, that her bedroom as a girl had been bedecked with posters of him that she'd torn out of *Teen Beat* and *Seventeen*, and that she still had every word of *Nocturnal Fears* memorized. He learned that these days she worked as a certified public accountant, that she did triathlons, that she was married to a cop and had three kids.

When she asked what he did with himself these days, he replied, a little ashamedly, "Teaching, mostly."

"Teaching acting?"

"Among other things."

"I see." She nodded as if impressed, though he was quite sure she wasn't.

On the bright side, the beer was good and the crab cakes were spectacular—plump with imperial meat, lightly breaded, and seasoned with Old Bay. The fries were excellent too. The coleslaw was neither here nor there.

"So I hope you don't mind if I ask the million-quid question?" Ashley said.

"Does it have anything to do with a movie about a sinking boat?"

"Yes."

"I guess I'd prefer if you didn't ask it then."

"Okay. All right. I get that."

He hadn't meant to sound so brusque. He had hoped it wouldn't come up, though he'd been fairly certain it would. At least he'd nipped it in the bud, though an awkward lull followed. They finished their beers and studied the seagulls in silence, not bothering to look at each other until the waiter came to ask if they were interested in dessert.

"I think we'll be leaving actually," Ashley said.

"The check then?"

"Please."

Mercifully, a plane was flying by overhead, trailing an advertising banner that read CANCER CELLS HAVE RIGHTS TOO! It gave them something to look at. When the check finally arrived, Dylan took it and rifled through his wallet for cash. He hadn't used Terran money in years, and he'd *never* used the Terran quid, so it took him quite a long time to pay. Leave it to James Cameron to turn *this* into a disaster too. Dylan had come 2,001 light years, allowed a previous copy of himself to be murdered, lied unabashedly to his wife, and all for what?

Crab cakes? What a sentimental fool he'd been to think anything redemptive might come of this.

"Can I leave the tip?" Ashley asked.

"It was generous enough of you to meet me," Dylan said.

"So let's be honest," Ashley said. "That was by all accounts a pretty terrible meal. Not the food—the food was good—but you and I just did not hit it off at all, am I right?"

"I'm sorry," he said. "I shouldn't have contacted you."

"That's not what I'm driving at," she said. "I'm glad you did."

This took him by surprise.

"Look," she went on, "here's my situation, and I'm just going to lay all my cards on the table because I literally don't have time for subtlety. Basically I've got three hours before I have to pick my kids up from gymnastics." She pulled a tube of Mentos out of her purse and slipped one of them into her mouth.

"I understand," he said. "I won't waste another minute of your time—"

"And I happen to know an inexpensive little hotel around the way..."

Dylan suffered the psychic equivalent of whiplash. "What? You want to go to a hotel?"

"Well, I don't particularly, but my inner teenager would never forgive me if I didn't, and unless my thirty-year study of human nature is totally off base, I'm pretty sure you're on board. Mint?"

"To be honest, I hadn't really thought that far ahead," he said.

"So think now."

He took a Mento, popped it in his mouth, and thought. It was strange, but while he was very clearly cheating on Erin in some way already, he had not explicitly conceived of this escapade in sexual terms until now. Not *explicitly* explicitly. Had the accountant turned out to be the better reader of human nature than the master of literature?

His tinnitus keened.

His brain was dying.

Amanda Cruz thought he was sixty.

Okay, he'd thought about it. "Let's go," he said.

She smiled, took his hand, and led him around the way. They didn't waste another second of each other's lives on conversation.

Ashley was right at that age where the body is shouting *Procreate! One more time! Now or never!* And so she was absolutely ravenous in bed. He had never been on the receiving end of so much—meaningless, pure—aggression before. She dug her nails into his back, moaned, talked dirty, slurped the dripping sweat from his neck, and, intermittently possessed by some demon, locked her legs around his waist and bucked so wild and out of control that he worried his dick would break—and what kind of excuse was he going to give Erin about that? Nonetheless, indeed all the more, it was the best sex he'd ever had in his life. What it was not, however, was transcendent. It didn't make him young again, or hopeful, or free. It didn't take him back to the moon or the silver screen. No, as they rutted around that afternoon, Dylan never once escaped that moderately priced hotel room, the sweaty bag of his skin, the unidirectional arrow of time, and all the accumulated head-weight of history and circumstance. And even as Ashley whispered in his ear, "Fuck me, Dylan Greenyears, like it's the last thing you'll ever do," he found himself wondering just who she believed she was fucking anyway. Did she really think he was the same person whose glossy photos used to hang on the wall of her bedroom? Who'd acted in those films? He had certain memories in common with that younger man, sure, though his way of thinking about them, his orientation toward them, had changed beyond recognition, as had his wealth and social status. Even without teleportation, every cell in his body would have replaced itself many times over since he'd been a star. What of that star remained then? Only brute biological patterns, the way his DNA instructed his body to assemble proteins so that he still bore some resemblance to the hominid she'd once fantasized about marrying someday—and even those patterns were subject to change over time. All of that was equally true of her too, of course: this athletic thirty-something adulteress presently seated athwart his chin was by no means the same *Teen Beat* subscriber who'd once chaired the Dylan Greenyears fan club at her high school. They were the both of them impostors. Still, it was nice.

As soon as she'd swallowed his cum, Dylan asked, "Hadn't you better get going?"

She looked at the clock—"Six minutes ago!" Then she sprang up and began getting dressed.

"Any chance you're free again tomorrow?" he asked. "Or this evening for that matter?"

"Oh," she said, and she cut the pace of getting into her shirt by half.

"What?"

"I thought we might be on the same page about this."

"What page is that?" Dylan asked.

"The one where this is a one-time deal. The one where I don't think we should see each other again."

"I see. I was definitely on a really different page."

"Dylan, look, I enjoyed being with you this afternoon. Once we stopped attempting to communicate, it was really wonderful. I got to live out a fantasy. This'll sound weird, but I felt like I was surfing on the back of a dolphin."

"Come again?"

"Surfing on a dolphin. I've wanted to do that ever since I saw some guy do it at the aquarium when I was a little girl. It seems so *magical*, and yet I have no doubt in my mind that those people who get to do that for a living curse the fact that they have to surf on dolphins day in and day out. It's the law of diminishing returns. I see it all the time in my job. You should see someone bank a million quid for the hundredth time. It's like they barely notice. They grunt. I don't want to be like that. Besides, Dylan, I have a family, and while you've told me practically nothing about you, I'd say there's a pretty good chance you do too, no? Doing this once was innocent enough, but repeat it and we start hurting people, do we not? Not least of all ourselves?"

Dylan nodded. She was right, of course.

"Okay then."

She was dressed now. He was still naked, and now he felt it. He covered his soggy genitals with the sheet. She sat down on the edge of the bed. "Thank you, Dylan Greenyears."

"For what?"

"For giving an awkward teenaged girl an outlet for her feelings. For being my first crush and, in a way, my first broken heart."

"That was all in your head," he said.

"Just like I was in yours," she parried. She had a point.

She slipped into her heels, leant over the bed and kissed him gently on the lips one last time. Then she went off to pick up her kids.

Fantastic. Now he had a weekend to hang out in Baltimore. Just what he'd never wanted.

• • •

Within the hour, Dylan was at the Greyhound station boarding another bus, this time to Philadelphia. Since leaving Earth, he'd kept in touch with his parents on a regular basis via omni, but he hadn't returned in the flesh even once, and while he couldn't very well visit them now either since word would sooner or later get back to Erin (who talked to his mother more than he did), he figured he could at least spy on them a bit and make sure they were doing okay.

For the duration of the nauseating bus ride, Dylan stared out the tinted window and reacquainted himself with his homeworld. If he squinted a little, I-95 was every bit the wide, soulless highway it had always been, but upon closer inspection, it was clear the world had changed. Countless bumper stickers shrieked "EARTH: LOVE IT OR LEAVE IT," and the infrastructure, accordingly, looked surprisingly good: no bumps or potholes marred the road, and bridges and overpasses appeared secure where not altogether new. Holographic signboards every few miles reminded drivers to carpool because, though CO_2 emissions were no longer an issue, natural gas was itself a nonrenewable resource, an automotive stopgap while the industry perfected the solar fuel cell. Still, where Earthlings might have taken pride in finally being responsible stewards of their planet, there was instead a sense of defeat in the air, as if the discovery of other advanced civilizations in the galaxy had served as yet another indignity in a long line of them since Galileo informed humans that the cosmos didn't revolve around them, and Darwin that they were less angels than apes. Society appeared to be functioning better than ever, but there was a palpable lack of ambition and creativity in the air. In its place was a whiff of surrender and pragmatism that Dylan found at once tragic and impressive; America was at last becoming life-sized. Even the religious, the ones with the fish or crescents or stars on their bumpers, appeared defeated, underzealous, with the possible exception of a pair of shirt-and-tie-wearing Mormons who biked by on a pedestrian bridge looking jaunty as ever.

He disembarked at the Greyhound Station in Philly, that symbolic city, and went for a walk past City Hall, which looked just as it had when he and Chad used to come downtown high on youth and dreams to knock on the door of their sex-drenched futures. Atop the tower, William Penn stood sentinel still, keeping watch over the old capital from what had once been the tallest building in the world.

How many patriots had charted their disillusion by that piss-yellow clock?

Dylan walked, and thought, and maybe cried a little, and soon he was tripping over the cobblestones of Old City, where two and half centuries since, the "Great Experiment" had begun. Oh, the beautiful, childlike hubris of it! His heart tolled and cracked.

He took the el to 69th Street and then a trolley from there to the suburbs, where new colors, shades of green mainly, suffused the windows by degrees. He watched with an ache in his chest as familiar landmarks zipped past in space as they had in time: the baseball diamond where he'd hit his only home run; the apartment building where his father's father had died fat and alone; the park where he'd used to throw stones into the creek, watch the interference patterns of the rings, and think big thoughts about life (he'd been wrong on most every count).

He got off at Brookview station, noted the absence of the pay phone where there had always been one, and then, as he had thousands of times before, walked along the sidewalk, avoiding the cracks for his mother's sake, past the Pattersons', the Wickershams', the Murphys', to the khaki-colored colonial that he still identified in the deepest parts of himself as home. He knew his American literature well enough to know you can't really go there again, and yet...

The ringing in his ears seemed louder than ever because otherwise it was so quiet here, the silence interrupted only by the occasional passing car, the low drone of a lawnmower off in the distance, the gurgling of the skimmers in the swimming pool he was glad to see open. He might have been here yesterday. His feet knew where to expect uneven pavement, his nostrils when to expect honeysuckle. It was dinnertime, the light warm, auburn and pink, the grass a bit shaggy and of a green deeper than he'd remembered being possible. The squirrels bounded adorably across the lawn and up the oaks, and drifting back to the branch there—oh!—a firefly, which, come to think of it, he'd have called a 'lightning bug' before he'd begun reading so much and losing his regional markers. In any case, on New Taiwan there was no such bug to illuminate the falling dusk like this. He'd learned in school that bioluminescence served as a defense mechanism, an organism's way of advertising to potential predators that it tasted bitter, but if "magic" could still mean anything for adults, surely this was it. He noticed now, as he had not when he was a child, how they seemed to light up in bursts, a cluster at a time, and then none for a spell, and then another cluster. He noticed, too, how they illuminated only on their way up. It did something to your consciousness to see that—made it leap. Thirty-five years ago, he and the neighborhood kids—John, Joe, Michelle—would have been out playing now, climbing skyscraping evergreens, building worlds in John's sandbox, and making strange forbidden potions in buckets according to very strict recipes of mud, dirt, grass, sand, gravel, dandelions, earthworms, ants, pinecones, and—if a parent or older sibling had recently taken one of them to the park on the other side of the tracks—skunk cabbage.

Where were all the kids now? Grown and for one reason or other not replaced. On other worlds perhaps.

He slinked from tree to tree and peered in at the windows. His father appeared first, hobbling across the kitchen, carrying a tray of something with his arthritic fingers. And there now was his mother at the table, reading a hard copy of the newspaper. He'd watched them advance in years via omni, but it was different to see them at home like this. They had new lines in their faces, new maps of time. Life expectancy was getting longer every year, but there was still a very good chance they would not *live forever.*[☉]

⊙───

The new scanning technology brought up all sorts of new questions regarding life extension too. For instance, if a patient presented pancreatic cancer and required a risky surgery, doctors might, theoretically, make multiple copies of the patient and operate on each one successively, disintegrating the failures until they met with success. Given this, all surgeries that had been shown to work even just once might be advertised as one hundred percent effective. The Mons Olympus Accord on the Reproductive and Reduplicative Rights of Human Persons had outlawed this theoretical practice, however, and took care as well to cover, in painful legalese, any other clever uses of scanning technology that the framers might not have specifically foreseen. With the exception of astronauts on long-term exogalactic missions, substrate-independent mind downloads were also banned by the accord amid great controversy. Digital avatars, however, had become a common way of kinda-sorta extending one's life indefinitely for the sake of the kids, grandkids, and anyone else who might care to see you not die. There were a number of competing models on the market, but all were variations on the same idea: simulate a human being in a computer using photographs, speech recordings, videos, and a personality profile determined on the basis of a lengthy questionnaire filled out by the original (in extremis) and/or the family. Some families even elected to have their loved one's avatar embodied in an AI, which these days could be alarmingly lifelike, and while there had been a panel discussion at Mons Olympus about the long-term hazards of avatar-droids, the consensus seemed to be that this was a very different, and much less dire and philosophically vexed, discussion than the scanning and cloning discussions that had taken place earlier in the week.

───⊙

He suffered waves of guilt sometimes at having moved so far away and thus deprived his mother of precious time with her own grandchildren, whom she loved dearly and had never met except via omni. From time to time he thought about moving his parents out to New Taiwan, at least for the milder winters, but real estate was so damned expensive and he'd just sunk the last of his savings into the new house. They could have the guest room as far as he was concerned—the house was plenty big enough—but Erin would complain. They wouldn't have wanted to move anyway. Their whole lives had been here in the Philadelphia area, and both of his sisters still lived nearby and had their own families. He'd offered many times to bring his parents out to visit, but QT had induced more than one heart attack in older folks over the years, and while no doubt it had greatly improved, he could hardly blame them for their trepidation. Maybe one of these years he could QT his family down here to Earth for a visit, though it was hard to imagine getting his three kids to sit still long enough for the scan anytime soon.

Dylan sat behind a cherry tree he'd climbed a hundred times and watched his parents eat their dinners (his mother's famous shrimp scampi—second only to her famous homemade ravioli) and he wept like the baby he knew himself at heart to be, only without the sound.

Darkness descended by degrees, and as the objects of the world left the visual range, the crickets took up their slack and, rather pleasantly, masked Dylan's tinnitus. His father had disappeared from view and was likely falling asleep in front of the old LCD video wall—no doubt they still had that—but his mother was now square inside the window frame, meditatively doing the dishes. He was looking at her almost head-on. Still beautiful. Could have been an actress. She liked to boast that she wore the same dress size as Marilyn Monroe, and he'd seen enough photos of her as a blonde and bosomy young girl to know she fit that era's prescription for beauty to a T, though even had she not been saddled with a husband and three children, her total lack of an ass might have proved her Achilles' heel in that unforgivingly sexist industry. (He noticed this asslessness of hers only because he'd inherited the trait and Erin never let him forget it.)

And while Dylan's Platonic devotion to the Beautiful undoubtedly came from his father, the hobbyhorse photographer (and lifelong devotee of 35mm film!), any affinity Dylan had for performance came right from Mom, whose way with words and trove of Irish melancholy could, if catalyzed with a couple of drinks, command the attention of any dinner party for hours, after which she'd invariably go home and—tears of a clown—cry herself to sleep.

Shit! She was looking at him. *Don't. Move.* She had interrupted what she was doing with the dishes, scrunched up her eyes and moved her face a few inches closer to the glass, and for what must have been a solid minute she stared out at the darkness in stony puzzlement. He so desperately and instinctually wanted to stand up and say, "Mom, it's me!" and go to her and hug her and kiss her and take her out dancing, but he forced himself to stay put, hugging this thicker-than-he-remembered-it tree, afraid.

By and by his mother shrugged and went back to doing the dishes.

Soon the downstairs lights went off and the upstairs ones went on. He wished his parents a good night under his breath, tiptoed over to the pool, took off his clothes and eased into the shallow end, which was warm as a bath. He floated on his back, ears submerged so that the ringing came back redoubled. He tilted his head, lifted his ears above the water and let the crickets soothe away the sound again. Earth's moon was a waxing gibbous, crisscrossed here and there by bats, and he willed himself to look up at it with the crazy wisdom of some Japanese poet, or at least the naïve eyes of most Americans, who believed that men had landed there just a few times, and who knew nothing of any VIP parties on the inside, of any goddesses in the surf...

Which reminded him: this was where he and Erin had first, well... Christ, he hadn't thought of that in a long time. They hadn't done it on purpose, not really. It was a humid, early-summer night like this, a few months into their relationship, and while they'd been doing incredibly nasty things in his car all that time, they had not yet had full-on intercourse, owing in part to the cautionary tale of Erin's cousin who had recently gotten herself pregnant at sixteen. But there they were skinny-dipping in the pool, making out in a corner of the shallow end right by the ladder, and his penis, which seemed possessed of a will wholly independent of his own, kept mashing up against her furrow until finally it plunged inside of her, and it was as if they'd just torn spacetime, because all at once they were in some other dimension where they were no longer separate and where they extended forever in all directions with no skin to hem them in and no pronouns to make them other...that is, until he'd panicked, and pulled out, and insisted they go buy a pregnancy test at CVS immediately. Once she'd pissed on the stick and received the minus sign, he'd had to spend the rest of the night trying to convince her that he really did love her.

He climbed out of the pool, drip-dried, dressed, and lay on his back in the cool grass. He searched the heavens for Lem until all the stars blurred into one golden blotch on the inside of his eyelids. Then he fell asleep. He did not surrender his consciousness so completely, however, as to get caught there in the morning. Rather, he woke to the rattle of the first trolley, and then, as unsentimentally as he could manage, bid his childhood home goodbye. He made his way back to the Greyhound Station and—a few hours, a soft pretzel, a coffee, and half-a-dozen pedagogy articles later—BWI Thurgood Marshall Intragalactic Teleport.

· · ·

He was back on New Taiwan in time for dinner; they were having the leftover ravioli. The kids were ecstatic to see him. "What did you get us?" Arthur asked.

Dylan cringed.

"Mommy said you'd get us something."

"Sorry, guys. I was super busy."

"Aw," he whined.

"How was it?" Erin asked. She was feeding the baby at the head of the table and didn't bother to get up.

"Fine. Uneventful."

"Anyone recognize you?"

"I don't think so."

"Well that's good anyway. Did you learn anything?"

"Oh sure. There was a lot of talk about reality augmentation. Some Shakespeare program that subtitles everything in bardic. A study-abroad thing that makes the streets of your home seem like they're in Tokyo, New Quebec, Alanis, wherever. Changes up the mailboxes, maybe puts a cathedral on the horizon, everybody speaks Arabic, Upper Pleiadic, Heptapod A or whatever. First-hand history apps: drop a kid right in the middle of a world war or a supernova. Seems like you held the fort down okay?"

She sighed. "No horror stories anyway."

"Mommy, I'm done," Arthur said. "Can we go play?"

"Sure."

Arthur dashed off to the playroom, Tavi waddling in tow.

"It's good to be home," Dylan said—he meant it too.

She smiled, albeit not very convincingly. "Would you ever consider moving back?"

"What, to Earth?"

"Uh-huh."

"Are you seriously asking me this?"

"I am."

The content of her question was one thing, her audacity in asking it another. She *knew* his feelings about Earth.

"Out of the question," he said, trying to keep calm. "Do you want to tell me why you're asking me this all of a sudden?"

"No, it's just, I don't know, now that there are five of us, it would be nice to have a little help from our parents from time to time, wouldn't it? To take some of the edge off?"

He was losing his cool. "Wonderful!"

"What?"

"Whose idea was it to have this third kid again?"

She didn't reply.

"And what did you promise me from the outset, do you remember?"

Still nothing.

"Let me refresh your memory: you promised that it wouldn't *change* anything. That our lives would go on as usual. Do you remember that?"

She looked fierce, reptilian.

"And now look how suddenly we've come by a commodius vicus of recirculation back to Howth Castle and environs!"

"What?"

"What would I do on Earth?"

"The same thing you do here."

"Teach?"

"Why not?"

Now it was his turn to say nothing.

"People don't recognize you anymore, Dylan. You said so yourself. I don't think very many kids are watching E.T. II these days, do you? Besides, you're all grown up now. They wouldn't recognize you anyway."

This pissed him off. How was it that his own wife was always underestimating his legacy, not to mention his good looks? He deserved it, probably: commit yourself to someone when you're too young and they're bound to take you for granted before long; Ashley Eisenberg had told him he'd barely changed.

"And unlike you, I make a point of paying attention to Earthly affairs, Dylan, and it's really not the same world anymore. You just saw it for yourself, right? The world you're so intent on exiling yourself from no longer exists. All of our generation is exiled from it whether we like it or not. It's a question of time passing, Dylan. It has nothing to do with where we live."

"Erin, have you forgotten just how many people saw E.T. II?"

"Don't take this the wrong way, Dylan, but sometimes it seems like you believe the galaxy revolves around you. I just want to reassure you that it doesn't and it never has. It revolves around a supermassive black hole."

"And how would you like me to not take that the wrong way?"

"You should feel relieved by it. So you had a pretty bad day twenty years ago. So what? Do you really want to let it cast a shadow on the rest of your life?"

He pursed his lips and nodded, agreeing with her. "Rolling in the muck is not the best way of getting clean."

"Exactly. Who said that?"

"Aldous Huxley, in the preface to **Brave New World**."[1]

"Well there you go. Take it from him if you won't take it from me."

"I'll think about it," Dylan said. "In the meantime, I'm gonna take a shower and go to bed. I've got serious QT lag."

He wasn't lying. Not only did he have the usual time slip to deal with—the New Taiwanese day was just shy of twenty-six hours—but the Olympus Mons Accord stipulated that all waste material and toxins in a teleportee's bloodstream must get copied with the organism, and Dylan hadn't gotten all that much **sleep last night.**[2]

1. Like all avid readers maybe, Dylan tended to flinch at certain passages in his reading, passages that pricked his wounds—and not a few of them had to do with the fugitive nature of time. He'd inadvertently memorized any number of them:

"Afterwards, he just sat, happy to live in the past. The drink made past happy things contemporary with the present, as if they were still going on, contemporary even with the future as if they were about to happen again." — F. Scott Fitzgerald, *Tender is the Night*

"Certain things, they should stay the way they are. You ought to be able to stick them in one of those big glass cases and just leave them alone." — J.D. Salinger, *The Catcher in the Rye*

"How did it get so late so soon? It's night before it's afternoon. December is here before it's June. My goodness how the time has flewn. How did it get so late so soon?" — Dr. Seuss

That sort of thing.

---

2. Despite all the revolutionary scientific advances in recent years, nothing very significant had been discovered in the way of altering the human being's need to spend a third of its life asleep. In point of fact, all hominids discovered to date seemed to spend one-fifth to one-half of their day (with a day ranging between seventeen and forty-two hours) unconscious.

"Good night," she said, and she kissed him on the lips. It wasn't wet or hot or tongue-y, but it was nice; there were decades of devotion in it.

· · ·

That night, he had the dream. It wasn't even a dream so much as it was a memory, except that in the dream he saw it in the third person, even as he felt it in the first.

Dylan Greenyears, as Jack, stands at the bow of a ship with his new friend Danny Nucci, who's been cast as his sidekick, Fabrizio. A hundred pairs of eyes and several big cameras are watching. "I'm the king of the world," he says.

"I don't believe you," James Cameron says. "Roll it again."

"I'm the king of the world!" Dylan says again. This time he pumps his fists a bit. He knows it's not enough, but something is holding him back.

"God damn it, Greenyears," Cameron says. "Do you have an ounce of feeling in your whole body?"

"Many ounces," Dylan says.

"Prove it!" Cameron is getting worked up now, morphing into the asshole of Hollywood legend.

"I'm the king of the world!" Dylan shouts. He's louder this time, but the tone is off. Cameron's belligerence is making Dylan sound frustrated, not exhilarated.

"You've never been in love, have you, Greenyears?"

"I have," he says. "I am." He thinks of the splash of freckles on Erin's cheeks.

"Show me," Cameron commands.

"But Jack hasn't even *met* Rose yet at this point," Dylan protests.

"So what? He's already in love with his muse. I'm trying to connect that with something in you. If your girlfriend doesn't make you feel exhilarated, then find something that does. You know, Method stuff."

"Method stuff?" Dylan doesn't know what that means.

"Tell me you're not familiar with the Method?"

Dylan shrugs. His heart is going like a speed bag.

"Oh, Jesus. What the hell did I cast?" Cameron's eyes are beady, his face pinched, orange. "Try to summon some passion this time."

"I'm the king—"

"Horrible. Again."

Again.

Again.

Again.

Again.

Cold drops of sweat cascade down Dylan's ribs from his armpits. "I'm the king of the world."

"You're certainly the king of wasting my time," Cameron says. He's getting livid, mean. "Do you realize how many qualified actors I turned down so that I could take a risk on you, Greenyears? Last fucking chance."

Dylan swallows hard, takes a beat to regain his composure. Everything depends upon the next few seconds. "I'm the king of the world," he says, and he's not even halfway through when he knows it's not what Cameron wants.

"All right. That's it. I'm putting you out of your misery. Somebody get me DiCaprio."

"But—"

"Read your contract. I can fire you whenever I want. And I want to right now, before I throw any more good money after bad. For the life of me I don't know what I saw in you."

"But—"

"A word of advice, Greenyears: go back to college. You're finished in this town."

The following morning, splashed across America: "Cameron fires Greenyears from special effect extravaganza, hires DiCaprio."

Dylan is the crap of the world, and he's just been flushed.

• • •

Despite his students having had the full ten school days of Dylan's paternity leave to rehearse, the Shakespeare scenes were still a very mixed bag, nowhere near ready. The girls were better overall; except for one pair of entitled prima donnas, they all appeared to be taking the assignment seriously. The boys, though, had some hang-ups. Dylan had never explicitly told them this assignment was a rite of passage, but they instinctively understood that it demanded an existential choice of them: either they could transcend their egos, take a risk and really try to inhabit their parts, thereby pleasing their teacher and getting a good grade; or they could hide behind their egos, make light of solemnity, and deliberately mispronounce every word they didn't use on a daily basis, thereby pleasing their friends and getting a bad grade. It was a decision, Dylan knew, that might resonate in various ways through the rest of their lives. No doubt there was a way to make a virtue of irreverence and play to both audiences at once, but no one in Intro to Drama had discovered it yet.

Dylan was glad to see that Daniel was among the more earnest ones, albeit painfully self-conscious. The one time he flourished an arm to emphasize his words, it went no higher than about his belly button. After class, he lingered to ask how he was doing.

"Well, Daniel, you could have moved some more, for one thing."

"Okay."

The poor kid was taking notes. Dylan stopped himself and zoomed out. "You like acting, Daniel?"

"More than anything. In fact, I'm thinking of pursuing it."

"Pursuing it?"

"Like, professionally."

"I see." Dylan hadn't known it was that bad. "Acting's a cutthroat industry, you know, Daniel. Really tough to break into on Earth, and even tougher, I'm told, around these parts."

"I know," Daniel said.

"Isn't there anything else you're interested in?"

"Not the way I'm interested in this."

Dylan understood. He'd been there once too, though at least he'd had some evidence to suggest he might be talented before taking the plunge; Daniel had no such evidence. What to tell him then? Should Dylan perpetuate the same American myth he himself had been fed in such vomitous helpings and insist that the boy pursue his dreams at all costs and let nothing stand in his way? Or should he do the kid a favor and burst his bubble for him right now before it grew too big?

He reminded himself that, strictly speaking, he was paid to be an English teacher, not a life coach. He'd stick to giving Daniel acting notes, more or less.

"All right, Daniel, I'll shoot straight with you. The first thing you're going to need to do if you want to be an actor is to work on your English pronunciation. The Korean accent might get you typecast once or twice, but you want to be more versatile than that."

"Okay," Daniel said, wide-eyed and nodding.

"Next, you're going to have to learn to be more comfortable on stage. Right now you look like you're about to ask the hot girl to the prom."

"Sorry," he said.

"Don't apologize—this isn't that kind of thing. Above all, Daniel, any actor has to be willing to go into the darkest, scariest places inside of himself. Most people lock up that cellar and do everything they can to avoid opening it. That's understandable, probably even healthy. But the actor, Daniel, the *actor*, opens that door every chance he gets. It's a very dangerous profession that way, acting. Many actors have been driven insane by their craft."

Daniel's eyes looked bigger than ever by half.

"Not that I expect you to go insane for one measly grade, Daniel, but if you're serious about the craft, you're going to have to learn this. The more you invest of your own personal life in a role, the more deeply you're going to convince us, and the more vulnerable you're going to be. It's a sort of paradox really. The best way to embody someone else is to be totally, nakedly yourself. You've got to bare your feelings to the world, show us what scares you, what makes you want to kill in cold blood or cry like a baby. Most important, Daniel, you've got to show us what you *love*. Forget about looking cool. Humans are a mess. We sob and puke and toil and sweat and die like the animals we are for love. Show us that and you'll be well on your way."

Daniel was taking notes again.

"Somebody once said this, Daniel: 'Find what you love and let it kill you.' I'm not sure who said it—you could ask *Omni if you're curious*©—but the point is, *that's* the kind of commitment you've got to have if you're serious about your art. You've got to be willing to die for it. If your commitment falls anywhere short

Terran country singer Kinky Friedman, though the quote is regularly attributed to Terran writer Charles Bukowski, who did not say it, but who did say, in a poem entitled "Breakfast," this: "You have to die a few times before you can really live."

of that, then you'd better find something else to do with your life."

What Dylan did *not* tell Daniel was that your body didn't necessarily die at the same time as your dreams, but the sweet-faced fool would almost certainly discover that on his own one day.

"Thank you, Mr. Green. I promise to make you proud."

"Oh, don't do anything on my account, Daniel."

The boy nodded, squinted in thought.

"And one more piece of advice while I'm at it," Dylan said, reaching out and stopping Daniel from writing. "Listen to me: no matter where your future should take you, never look back and wonder *what if*—what if I had done this instead of this, what if I had married this girl instead of that girl, what if I had been an engineer instead of an actor. Don't *do* that, and don't compare yourself to other people either. It's irrelevant. You just make the best decision you can at every juncture and forgive yourself in advance for whatever happens next. It's important that you give yourself permission to fail. We're not as free as we think, Daniel, and we're smaller and less perfect than we know when we're in high school. You just take comfort in knowing that whatever indignities life puts you through, you're not the first and you're surely not the last. So go ahead and try to make your life into a comedy, but don't be surprised if you get a not-so-gentle reminder now and then that it's been a tragedy all along. Do you recall how tragedy differs from comedy?"

"The characters die at the end?"

"Precisely."

Okay, so he'd be a bit of a life coach too.

• • •

Immediately following the last bell, Dylan took the rolling road to his first appointment with Dr. Minus Fudge, who, as it turned out, was a middle-aged, African-Canadian male with a soul patch. His modus operandi consisted, more or less, of getting the patient to lie down on a supremely comfortable sofa and spill his guts for an hour. It was refreshingly anachronistic.

Having already warmed up with Daniel, it didn't take Dylan long to begin free-associating. After giving Fudge an abridged version of his rise and fall, about which the doctor registered not the least reaction, he launched right into his insecurities about having married the first girl he'd ever made love to and wondered aloud if he hadn't in a sense enslaved himself to an immature version of himself.

"What do you suppose made you stay with her all these years?" Fudge asked.

"I've thought about that a lot. I guess I have this sense that she anchors me to authenticity somehow, that she keeps me real, if you will."

Fudge gave an angular nod.

"I was nobody much when we began seeing each other, just your typical high schooler, and even after I'd begun to make it big, my fame never impressed her particularly. She doesn't give a crap about fame. On the one hand, I like this about her. It makes me respect her. On the other hand, I think I may unconsciously resent it a little too. Not that I expect her to madly dote in idolatry, but it's like when I look at my life through my own eyes, I used to see this narrative of progress, like everything was falling into its proper place and I was finally becoming someone important, finally fulfilling my destiny or whatever it is, but then as long as I've been with Erin, I've always had this kind of double vision, like I see myself from my own heroic perspective, but also from her more sublunary one, and hers always cheapens or profanes mine. I mean, when you become famous the way I did, girls who wouldn't have looked at you the day before suddenly go all gaga and want to have your babies, but with Erin it's always been like I'm her little brother or something, like *Oh, there goes little Dylan with his big dreams, acting in a movie.* I guess she did want to have my babies, but it's different somehow."

"It sounds like you wouldn't mind if Erin went a bit more gaga over you once in a while?"

"It's not like she *never* went gaga. God, we used to spend hours sometimes just staring into each other's eyes as if there was something back there besides vitreous humor. And I don't want to come off as ungrateful. Erin's an amazing mom to my kids, and if you think about it, how many girls out there would stick with their famous husband after his career implodes and he decides to exile himself to a far-away planet and teach high school? We don't exactly have the most glamorous lifestyle anymore, but she's never complained about that. Not even once."

"So remind me what the problem is again?"

"I'm not sure what the problem is. I'm not even sure that there is one beyond the fact that I'm condemned like everybody else to get old and die. I can tell you that the thing that makes me the most depressed isn't so much the demise of my career as this paranoid suspicion I sometimes have that Erin *likes* the way my career played out."

"Interesting. Tell me more about that. Why would she like it?"

"Because look at me. What am I? I'm a simple, devoted family man. I'm not off filming for months at a time. I'm not making loads of money and sleeping around. I don't have a planet named after me. I'm basically locked into my roles of husband and father and breadwinner. I have been totally drafted into her vision of life. All other possibilities for me have been steadily winnowed away."

"Is it fair to say you feel trapped?"

"Not 'trapped' exactly. 'Parasitized' is too strong. 'Burdened'? Let's go with 'trapped.' But again it's not so much that I feel trapped by Erin as by, what, mortality? Finitude? By having to funnel the multitudes inside of me into one wage-earning life. Acting was a good outlet in that way. Actors get to be other selves, at least for a little while. Teachers, not so much."

"Have you thought about acting here? Community theater perhaps?"

"Not really. I closed that chapter of my life twenty years ago."

"And yet here you are talking about it with palpable longing."

"Do you know what I used to feel like, Doc? I used to feel like a god, invincible and immortal. I didn't think in those terms, of course. I barely had to think at all. I just knew that life was filled with promise and excitement and possibility. It's only in retrospect that I see how lucky I was there for a couple of years. Most people never have that omnipotent feeling, I guess. My students certainly feel nothing like the way I used to about the future—most of them are vaguely terrified. But when I was their age, I swear I felt like anything was possible, like life was this great adventure or Hollywood film. I told a student of mine today that if he was going to take acting seriously, he should be prepared to die for it, and for a second there I thought I might be a hypocrite, but then it occurred to me that no, in a way I really did die for acting. Everything since just feels like aftermath, like this long tail."

"Can you elaborate on that?"

"I have a pet theory about it actually."

"Lay it on me."

"So for the vast majority of our evolutionary history, life was brutal and short, at least compared to now, and if you were lucky enough to make it to twenty, you'd already experienced all the most vital feelings available to a human—the thrill of mating, the rush of the hunt and war. Nowadays, with our radically extended lives, we spend our final sixty or eighty or a hundred years in what amounts to a kind of existential masturbation. As far as our animal brains are concerned, our lives after our reproductive years are essentially pointless. Life's just a long dulling of the senses, a gradual retreat into recursion, senility, oblivion."

"That's a compelling theory, Mr. Green, though do you think it's possible you're generalizing too much from your own experience? What if I told you I feel every bit as alive today as I did when I was seventeen? More alive, in fact."

"I guess I'd either have to throw away the theory, or suspect you of deceiving yourself, if not outright lying."

"In any event, Mr. Green, your theory must feel like an accurate description of reality for you at least, or you wouldn't have come up with it, yes?"

Dylan confirmed with Fudge that they had a doctor-patient confidentiality thing going here, and then he proceeded to tell him about his affair with Ashley Eisenberg this weekend, how she was the first woman he'd slept with besides Erin in all these years, and yet how even in the throes of ecstasy it was not the same as it used to be. He was exquisitely aware of his finitude the entire time. He was no god anymore.

"With your permission, Mr. Green," Fudge said, "I'd like to offer my take on what I'm hearing."

Dylan nodded his assent.

"Your particular issues are not at all unusual, and are in fact quite characteristic of what used to be called a midlife crisis, very possibly coupled with what used to be called post-traumatic stress disorder. What I'd like to try to work on with you is an enlargement of your sense of self. The self you conceive of now is rather narrow, if I may say so, and I'm not at all surprised you feel confined by it. We want to begin urging you toward a more open sense of the self as a kind of possibility space. We want to get you thinking in terms of the present and the future instead of being so fixated on the past. And most importantly, we want to get you out in the worlds, beyond the patterns of your own thinking. I wonder if you're involved in any spiritual disciplines?"

"I read a lot, if that counts."

"I was thinking more along the lines of meditation."

"I lie in bed and stare at the popcorn ceiling for minutes at a time."

"Okay, what about service activities? Do you do anything like that?"

"How do you mean 'service'?"

"Volunteering your time, cleaning up roadsides, tutoring underprivileged natives, that sort of thing."

"I'm a teacher," Dylan said. "And I've been meaning to spend more time with my kids."

"Okay, not service exactly, but it's a start. Anything to get you out of your head and into the worlds."

This sounded to Dylan like reasonable advice. Any way you came at it, his problems were very definitely to do with the inside of his head.

"Well," Fudge said, "it looks like our time is about up for today."

"Thanks, Doc. This has been way more helpful than I expected."

"And we didn't even mention your tinnitus."

"That's right!" His reason for being here had escaped his mind entirely. On the other hand, if Cohen was right about the etiology of

Dylan's condition, they might in fact have just spent a whole hour talking about it. To be sure, the ringing was still very much there if he chose to listen to it, but this recent ability to tune it out was a mark of tremendous progress.

They scheduled another appointment for next week.

On his way out the door, Dylan felt a prick of anxiety. "Quick question, Doc?"

"Yes?"

"Do you think I ought to throw the box of fan mail away? To remove the temptation? As is, it's a bit like having a time machine in the house."

"It seems to me, Mr. Green, that the real mark of your success will be when you can read through those letters without feeling the pangs of nostalgia and remorse—what I like to call chronderlust—that you feel now. Taking the box away would be like taking the drugs away from an addict. It's a quick fix, but ultimately the addict needs to reach a point where he doesn't *want* the drugs, even when they're right there in front of him."

Dylan smiled and made his exit. What a relief that piece of advice was. Had Fudge instructed him to jettison the letters from his life, he'd almost certainly have done so, though it wouldn't have been easy—as with QT, there'd have been a hint of suicide in it.

• • •

As promised, Dylan consecrated every minute of his free time that week to playing with the kids. He came home as soon as possible after school and joined them in elaborate games of make-believe. They were waiters, firefighters, ninjas, superheroes, robots, and bug-eyed aliens of the sort that were looking less and less likely to exist outside of fiction. They climbed the octopines in the yard, planted rhodolions with trowels and tended to them with watering cans. They played hide-and-seek and any number of ball-centered sports with extemporary rules Dylan was never quite able to discern. They rode their bikes. When it rained, they read *The Giving Tree* and *The Phantom Tollbooth*, slowly gave up on a 500-piece puzzle of the Grand Canyon, and cheated at Uno. When inevitably they cried, he hugged them, kissed their boo-boos and tickled their sides and thighs until they were rolling around the ferngrass in hysterics. Junior, being so small, couldn't actively participate in any of this yet, but he looked on eagerly from his baby chair, cooing and kicking his legs, and Dylan made sure to pick him up every few minutes, lift him to the sky, cradle him in the crook of his arm, kiss his soft, symmetrical head, stare into those brand new ancient eyes and smile with his whole face, thinking *My God, I'm happy—who knew?* Had he been forced to do all of this, he'd have been miserable, but having *chosen* to do it seemed to make all the difference.

What's more, spending all this time with the kids heightened his empathy for what Erin dealt with week in and week out. Her life was so devoted to childcare these days that she typically had no time left over for any of the shared enthusiasms that had nourished their marriage for all those years before they'd become parents; and while intellectually he understood that this too would pass, that they'd likely be best friends again someday in more than just the abstract way they were now, his workaday soul thirsted for companionship.

Now that he was freeing up some of her time, however, she managed to keep up with the news, to read a **book**⊙ and watch a film

⊙

Strange Elbows, a recent Supermassive-Award-winning alternate history omni novel by a native author about species-on-species violence of the sort that, thank heavens, had never actually occurred on New Taiwan—though reviewers had been quick to add that the very existence, not to mention popularity, of the novel suggested that such violence might exist *in potentia*.

(*Casablanca*—neither of them had ever seen it), so that when they lay in bed together at night, they both had a small surplus of energy to burn and something to talk about besides the kids, which was as rejuvenating as *poxna*. She even kissed him goodnight a few times, albeit somewhat dutifully. Unless it was he who'd kissed her? It was impossible to tell. Anyway, he almost ruined the whole thing on Wednesday when he remarked in passing that Erin had developed quite a paunch since Junior was born, but she did him one better by pointing out that he had developed quite a paunch himself since his dream of being an actor had died. Fair enough. Without actually saying as much, they declared it a draw.

. . .

When Dylan told Fudge all of this at their next session together, Fudge's response was not all Dylan had hoped. He agreed that Dylan's spending more time with his kids might indeed represent a kind of progress, but he intimated also that parenting could hardly be considered a form of "service," given its basis in what amounts to genetic narcissism, not to mention its being par for the course for a married human man of American stock. If they really wanted to get him beyond his own ego and the ingrained habits of his involuted mind, then he should probably go out and do something for someone he had no obvious interest in helping beyond the promise of expanding his own moral and creative compass.

"Like what, for example?"

"Well, that depends on you. Isn't there any cause that's particularly important to you? Some social problem, say, that really gets your goat?"

Dylan thought for a moment. Nothing came to mind. He shared the usual armchair sympathies toward victims of genocide, disease, natural disasters and the like, but with the possible exception of crestfallen actor-exiles—of whom he was aware of just one—he didn't have a pet cause per se.

"What do you say we make that your homework for the week?" Fudge suggested. "Do your research and find a cause you can really get behind. Who, in short, would you like to help? It could be one person or a whole community. The important thing is that you believe in it wholeheartedly."

"I can do that," Dylan said, and while his conscious mind kept griping to Fudge about his existential situation for the rest of the hour, his unconscious went to work on the assignment.

It didn't take long. He had a cause all right. A case, rather. It had been quietly gnawing at him for weeks. People don't just *disappear* from Omni. Something had *happened* to Mei-Ling Chen, and he was going to get to the bottom of it. The poor girl had written to him with her scarred wrists twenty years ago to tell him he'd saved her life. Whatever he might have liked to believe, he didn't deserve that kind of praise—all he'd done was his vainglorious job—but maybe he could earn it retroactively. Maybe, if he went about this skillfully enough, he could *really* save her life, or at the very least—and what seemed much more likely—avenge her untimely death.

· · ·

Dylan didn't wait for Fudge's approval before getting started on his detective work. Between classes the next day, he wandered over to the science building in search of Meghan Hynson, who taught both physics and forensic science. Dylan and Meghan were by no means close, but she was on the curriculum committee and they'd had lunch a few times to talk about the Science Fiction course he was thinking of proposing. She'd suggested he call the class "Retrofuturist Fiction" since so many of the speculations students would be reading about had long since been eclipsed by reality. She had a point: much of science fiction, once so bound up with the future, now had a very definite passé quality to it. It was uncanny sometimes to see what old-school SF writers had prophesied: the flying cars and rolling roads; the jetpacks and hoverboards; the vidphones and holographs and nanobots—by now, humans had a sense of blasé entitlement to every one of these technologies, and those who still read fiction at all went to historical fiction for their cognitive estrangement. Still, "Retrofuturist Fiction" sounded snobby, particularly to his American ear as pronounced with Meghan's native-Londoner accent. If "Science Fiction" had been good enough for the Golden Age, then it was good enough for Dylan's class.

He found Meg in her classroom, setting up a lab.

"Hi, Meg," he said.

She looked up from her graduated cylinders and teat pipettes.

"Do you have a minute?"

"Sure, what's up?"

"I have a somewhat unusual request."

"'Find the strangest thing and then explore it.'"

"Is that a quote?"

"'Tis. John Wheeler."

"Who's John Wheeler?"

"The astrophysicist who discovered black holes."

"Oh."

Meg did this sometimes. With her cyclist's body and pleated golden locks, she was a not-unattractive thirty-something woman, but her social skills bordered on the autistic.

"What's up?"

"Okay, here's the thing: I have in my possession this letter"—he took it out of his backpack—"and for reasons I don't exactly feel like going into, I'd like to get in touch with the girl who penned it some twenty years ago on Earth."

"Uh-huh?"

"But unfortunately I must have tossed the envelope, so I've got no return address or postmark, and what's really stymieing is that Omni would seem to have no record of her existence whatsoever."

Meg perked up at that. "I'm sorry, did you say *no* record?"

"None to speak of."

"But Omni is greater than the sum of all human knowledge…"

"I know. It's incredibly fishy. That's why I'm here."

"And it's autopoietic. No one controls it…"

"I know. And I don't want to speculate *yet* as to why it's missing exactly, but I'm hoping you might be able to run some kind of chemical analysis on the ink, and then maybe that would help us find the factory that made the pen, and from there we could see what stores were selling those pens, and then little by little we could zero in the store where she bought it and maybe they'll have a record of the transaction or some security video or something that might lead us back to the author? I realize it's a long shot, but I've got to start somewhere."

"We could certainly try that," Meghan said.

Dylan phewed.

"But might I suggest that we first take advantage of the school's subscription to Omni's handwriting analyzer and see if that turns up any matches?"

"You're a genius," Dylan said. Now why hadn't *he* thought of that?

"I'm just a scientist, Dylan. You humanities types are generally pretty hopeless when it comes to actually getting stuff done."

He smiled.

She winked an awkward beat too long. "So just call up the program, enter the school's ID, and scan away."

"Thanks, Meg."

"Let me know what you figure out. I've heard about various attempts at censorship, but I've never heard of Omni actually *missing* information before."

"There's a first time for everything, I suppose."

"Aren't you supposed to despise clichés?"

"Touché."

"And read up on brane cosmology sometime. You betray a very naïve, anthropocentric understanding of time."

She was getting feisty. He thanked her once more and went back to his office, feeling at once hopeful and incredibly stupid.

He called up his omni's handwriting analyzer and scanned the letter's penmanship. Within a few seconds it had pulled up two—and only two—like specimens. Few people ever had occasion to write longhand anymore, but the scriptorium went back several decades; surely most people's handwriting would bring up more than two matches. He scanned some of his own penmanship from a memo on his desk, just to see, and the analyzer brought up some 2,142 results: tests he'd taken in school, autographed ephemera, insurance policies, tax returns, receipts, even some romantic graffiti he'd Sharpied onto a bridge in the state park in high school ("DG ♥s EW"). Granted, Mei-Ling Chen was likely a few years younger than he was, and presumably a lot of her writing had been in Chinese—which, for all he knew, might be a separate program as far as his omni was concerned—but for her Roman script to exist in only two places in the scriptorium still seemed odd, especially given that both instances were signatures, just a year or so apart, on discharge forms from Good Samaritan Hospital in Los Angeles, California, Earth, Solar System, Orion-Cygnus Arm, Milky Way Galaxy, Laniakea Supercluster. Odder still: neither of those signatures read "Mei-Ling Chen." Instead, they read "Jade Astrophil," whoever that was.

So either his omni's analyzer had goofed, which seemed highly improbable, or he had a very useful new clue.

He followed the trail and asked Omni, "Who is Jade Astrophil?" anticipating clarity, insight, resolution. What he got instead was this:

"JADE ASTROPHIL" RETURNS 0 RESULTS.

What? Omni flat-out contradicting itself? Impossible. He knew for a fact there were at least two instances of Jade Astrophil's signature in the scriptorium. How in hell could he know something Omni didn't know? He told it explicitly to retrieve those two signatures from Good Samaritan Hospital, but again it told him:

"JADE ASTROPHIL" RETURNS 0 RESULTS.

He tore the buds out of his ears and *slammed them down on his desk.* From the office across the hall, Ian the Latin teacher asked if he was okay. Dylan lied and said he was fine. He wasn't

He couldn't have broken them if he'd tried. For years now, Omni itself—not the local, lowercase contacts, but the vast churning cloud of information—had looked to the devices' constantly evolving designs. Humans could no more reverse-engineer omni hardware than they could the comparatively simple human brain. Whether this implied that Omni had achieved some measure of *consciousness* or not remained a question for the philosophers.

fine. What the hell did it *mean*, zero results? How was this possible? Supposedly Omni answered to no power higher than itself. Its moral incorruptibility was advertised as one of its chief virtues. But then how to explain this blatant act of censorship? He was hard-pressed to believe it was another glitch. If finding a single glitch in Omni was hugely improbable, then finding two in the same day must be effectively impossible.

Like some twentieth-century human, then, he was left to the feeble computing power of his own brain. Who did old-fashioned logic suggest this Jade Astrophil might be? If the handwriting analyzer could be depended on, then Jade Astrophil and Mei-Ling Chen were one and the same person. Therefore, either Mei-Ling Chen had in fact been Jade Astrophil all along and for some reason she'd felt compelled to create a pseudonym uniquely for her correspondence with him; or, Jade Astrophil was the pseudonym, which seemed more likely, given that the name sounded made-up, stagey, not authentically Taiwanese at all. In any case, both discharge forms were from within the last couple of years, which meant there was a good chance she was still alive.

With some healthy skepticism now, he popped the buds back in and sought definitions from Omni:

> **Jade¹** (noun) a hard, typically green stone used for ornaments and implements and consisting of the minerals jadeite or nephrite; an ornament made of this; a light bluish-green.

> **Jade²** (noun *archaic*) 1. a bad-tempered or disreputable woman. 2. an inferior or worn-out horse.

> **Astrophil** (noun *literary*) Likely composed in the 1580s, Philip Sidney's "Astrophil and Stella" is

an English sonnet sequence containing 108 son-
nets and 11 songs. The name derives from the two
Greek words, 'aster' (star) and 'phil' (lover),
and the Latin word 'stella' meaning star. Thus
Astrophil is the star lover, and Stella is her
star.

Holy Higgs! Now here was something. Could it possibly be a coincidence that this girl who had so doted on him as a star had changed
her name to "star lover"? And might that explain what she was doing
in LA? Had she sought him there, not knowing that he had de-worlded
for New Taiwan?

If there'd been anything whimsical about his search for Mei-
Ling Chen up to this point, the recalcitrance of the facts now charged
it with meaning, made it a point of personal pride. His heart raced,
adrenaline flooded his veins. Oh, he had a cause all right. Something
sinister was going on out there in the Omniverse, and Dylan was going
to find out what it was, even if it killed him.

But first he had one more class to teach.

• • •

"What does the phrase 'American Dream' signify to all of you?"

"Why do we have to study this?"

"Did I see your hand up, Cade?"

Cade rolled his eyes and put up a hand.

"Cade!" Dylan said.

"Why do we have to study this?"

"Well, Cade, this is an American literature class, and the American
Dream, you won't be surprised to learn, was sort of a central theme in
American literature. You'd do well to know about it."

"Okay, but most of us have never even been to Earth, let alone
America. Why should we have to study so much Earth history when

we hardly learn anything about our own planet's?"

"Ah, now there's your real question, and it's a good one. Suffice it to say that this is called the American School of New Taiwan for a reason. Many of your parents are or were American, nearly all of them are Earth-human, and they want you to understand your roots."

"But our roots are *here*," said Cade. "We were born *here*."

"I guess that depends how we define 'roots,' but fair enough. In any event, you'll have New Taiwanese history next year as seniors. And you're all studying the language already, are you not?"

Cade nodded, but it was clear he wasn't sold on the point, and truth be told Dylan rather appreciated the kid's allergy to received ideas. Would that more students were like that.

"I'll admit you have a point, Cade. I don't think you've exactly articulated what that point is, but there's one buried in there some-where, and maybe it's to do with the question of how we talk about the 'American Dream' as if it were somehow exceptional. Was there really anything so *American* about the American Dream? Or should we just call it the old Terran dream? Or the old human dream? Maybe even the hominid dream? Because, in a way, I think you're right: what's the use of studying the so-called 'dream' of some people light years away if we can't relate to it somehow, if it doesn't shed some light on our *own* dreams? And so, back to my original question: what does the phrase 'American Dream' mean to you?"

"Money," ventured shy, curly-headed Sherman. "Isn't that what America is all about?"

"Good," Dylan said. "That was definitely a part of it."

"Landing on the moon," put in Jake.

"Just that?"

"I don't know."

"Okay," Dylan said. "So maybe something about technology then?"

"I guess." It was clear Jake had put in his two *zarkaks* for the semester.

"Bear in mind the Soviets had similar ambitions in those years, and they were thought to be about as **un-American as it was possible to be.**"⊙

"What about the whole white picket fence thing?" asked Anna.

"Okay," Dylan said. "What about that? Elaborate."

"Mrs. Crumb told us how when she was a kid growing up in Detroit, that was the, like, ideal. A big house in the suburbs with a white picket fence and a garden and some kids and maybe a dog. Football on Saturday, church Sunday morning and then a long drive in the family car. Apple pie. Television. All that."

> In Earthling terms, the New Taiwanese economy would be classified as a Social Democracy on the Nordic model, a.k.a. "The Swedish Middle Way," i.e. a mixed economy with high taxes and a generous universal welfare state. Sure enough, every metric for well-being on New Taiwan put the old liberal-democratic US to shame, thereby perversely limiting Dylan's students' powers of empathy with regard to the demise of this so-called American Dream.

"Excellent. Now let's go back to that fence for a second. Tony, what does a fence do?"

"Like, stands there?" Tony said.

"Okay, but what purpose does it serve?"

He thought it over. "Keeps people out."

"Precisely. It marks off one's property, doesn't it? One's *private* property. Anybody can be on the other side of the fence, but cross that line and you could get in serious trouble, which, in a way, brings us back to Sherman's answer, because what does it take to have property?"

"Money," Sherman said.

"Right. And who in America had that?" Dylan asked.

"People who work hard," Sherman said.

"Well, that was certainly the Kool-Aid Americans drank anyway. Free enterprise. Anyone could become anything. It was a revolutionary idea really. Back in Europe there was just no such notion. The rich were the aristocracy. Kings and queens and their friends. Very little mobility. You were either born rich or you were destined to a life of hard work, poverty and rags. So it was by and large these latter who came to form the United States. A bunch of losers, basically, because the old winners were secure at home with no reason to uproot themselves. But the losers—the losers had everything to gain, and they were *hungry*. There was always that jackpot mentality from the very beginning, people trying to strike it rich in the New World, the natives be damned. That's what got Columbus over there in the first place, albeit *accidentally*.◉ So the American Dream, as I see it—and I'm sort of improvising here, but that

◉

For the record, the Terran population of the Americas before Columbus sailed the ocean blue may well have exceeded fifteenth-century Europe's 70 million. Columbus himself did not believe he had discovered uncharted lands so much as the "Earthly Paradise"—or Garden of Eden—at the "End of the Orient." It was left for Florentine explorer Amerigo Vespucci, in a 1503 letter to his friend Lorenzo di Piero Francesco de' Medici, to identify this land as the "New World" ("Mundus Novus"), which was why the country Dylan grew up in was called "The United States of America" and not "The United States of Columbia," though Columbus, despite being a prolific slave trader, rapist, and all around genocidal maniac, was memorialized in the names of that country's capital city, two state capitals, a World's Fair, a river, a traffic circle, and a federal holiday, not to mention a South American nation and an Asteroid (327). It was some comfort perhaps, some evidence of human progress, that there was as yet no exoplanet named after him.

◉

goes to my point—the American Dream was at heart about being able to invent oneself from scratch, to slough off your lowly origins and become whatever you wanted. The self-made man, as it were. America's Achilles heel, though, was that it always rewarded the quick over the patient, the immature over the wise, arrogance and excess over sanity and moderation. *Hubris*, the Greeks called it. They *knew*. Some of them anyway. The tallest towers fall. The unsinkable ship sinks."

Dylan paused to gather his breath.

"Now is there anything distinctively American about the desire to *make* oneself? Probably not. But the worship of immodesty, of out-size individual ambition and to hell with everyone else, that was *very* American. Wasn't it responsible after all for giving us the Promethean technological capabilities that ultimately allowed us to hoist ourselves with our own petard? Ironic, isn't it? Not that the end of American exceptionalism wasn't in many ways a good thing, of course, but for those generations who were riding the crest of that high and beautiful wave, the end hurt pretty bad."

The students looked at him like he was speaking some alien lan-guage their omnis couldn't translate. Sherman raised his hand.

"Yes?"

"Why do you always talk about America in the past tense?"

"Because it's *over*, Sherman. The wave broke and rolled back. America is now on the order of Greece or Rome."

"That's not what my dad says."

"Oh? What does your dad say, pray tell?"

"He says people like you are *dramatic*."

"Does he? Well, I do teach drama, so I guess the shoe fits. What does your father do, if I may ask?"

"He's a financial accountant."

Was it too easy to tell Sherman that he thought people like his father were *accountable*?

Probably. It took all he had to hold his tongue.

. . .

When Dylan got home, he was so aroused by the Chen/Astrophil investigation that he rushed right past Erin and the baby to the bedroom. "Don't mind me," he said.

"Whatever."

He instructed his omni to lock the foglet door, and then took down the box and placed it on the bed. He hadn't expected to tempt fate again so soon, but it had occurred to him in the car that maybe Mei-Ling—or Jade, or whatever her name was—had written him other letters too and that these might serve as further clues to her whereabouts. In truth, if there weren't any further clues here, then he had no idea where to begin. So he spent the next half hour meticulously inspecting every letter in the box in search of either of the missing person's names, or at least matching penmanship. He turned up none of the above.

He did, however, discover that he had received at least two other letters from Wendy Sorenson, the sixteen-year-old from Hawaii who claimed to be his biggest fan and who had offered to marry him in her first letter. It was possible he'd thrown out even more letters from her when cleaning house; these were just the greatest hits, and they were every bit as provocative as the first:

Wendy Sorenson
243 Moana Street
Laie, HI 96762

Dear Mr. Greenyears:

I am with my parents on a trip in Utah. It is very beautiful here. I have seen snow only a couple of times in my life, and the first time I don't even remember (I was four). Anyway, my parents and I went skiing all day today, then we went to dinner at this really fancy steak place that smelled like blood, and then we came back to this lodge we're renting and my parents went off to bed. Now it's just me out here in the living room by the crackling fire and I'm immersing myself in <u>Nocturnal Fears</u> and touching myself. There is a hole in me exactly the shape of you. Someday you will come to fill it. I believe this. I pray for it every single day. I love you, Dylan Greenyears.

I am dead serious,
Wendy Sorenson

The third letter was the briefest, and in some ways the most bizarre:

Wendy Sorenson
243 Moana Street
Laie, HI 96762

Dear Mr. Greenyears:

It dawned on me that I've been coming on strong and that you may not be ready to embrace your destiny yet. That's okay! I will tone it down and wait patiently, but please know that when you do come around, I will be here for you with boundless love and an intact hymen.

Eternally,
Wendy Sorenson

No wonder he had kept these! That he had no memory of their specific content attested to how spoiled he'd been in those days, but as he reread them now, he was overcome with a wistfulness so visceral and acute that, by virtue of the small trove of wisdom he'd acquired in his nearly four decades of life, he instantly recognized what a danger they posed to his long-term well-being. "You can't repeat the past," Nick tells Gatsby. Dylan had taught that book a hundred times; why could he never internalize that *elementary lesson?*⊙ Why did popping the lid back on this box, putting it away and returning to the living room, have to feel so damned *despite himself?*

> ⊙ Not long ago a student had informed Dylan of a recent film adaptation of that novel. Dylan had been genuinely intrigued until the student went on to inform him that a really great actor named Leonardo DiCaprio starred as Gatsby. The coincidence was almost enough to make Dylan believe it wasn't one, that Leo had the longest middle finger in the universe.

He returned to the living room. Erin was lying on the couch in her pajamas, breastfeeding and watching Earth news on the ceiling. It struck Dylan that Junior spent more time with Erin's tits on a daily basis than he himself had in the past half-decade.

"Hi, hon," Dylan said. "Sorry. I had some time-sensitive stuff I had to finish up."

Erin mouth-smiled, close-lipped as if to say *Do you really think I care what you do?*

"How was your day?" he asked.

"Exhausting," she said. "Every time I manage to fall asleep, this one is just waking up."

> ...*Ambassador of Culture to Spiral Arm 4 has petitioned the UN on behalf of several local governments to begin making true molecular*

scans of the Seven Wonders of the World for an Earth-themed amuse-
ment park to be located on the third moon of Bradbury...

"So have you given any more thought to moving back home?"
Erin asked.

"Not yet. Christ, give me a little time, would you?"

She held the baby's head up and repositioned herself. Dylan
watched it suck.

...the Olympus Mons Accord forbids the true-scanning of certain
forms of intellectual property, including sculpture and landscape
architecture. It does not, however, explicitly outlaw the copying of
natural geographic formations...

"I'm just saying," she went on. "It's tough looking after three kids
by myself every day."

He was too tired to hold his frustration in check: "It was
your idea!"

"So?"

"So don't you think maybe you should stop bitching about it now
that you got exactly what you wanted in life?"

"Eww," she said, as if she'd just drunk some spoiled landflounder
milk. This annoyed him no end, this sound of hers. She'd been doing
it since high school whenever she wanted to express that his words or
ideas were repulsive to her.

...while others argue that Beauty itself is subject to laws of inflation,
and that the existence of two Grand Canyons will automatically
devalue each by half...

"I fucking hate it when you do that."

"What?"

"That sound. It's immature as hell. Can't you find some grown-up words to express yourself with?"

"Fine," she said.

"What 'fine'?"

"Just fine," she said.

"I fucking hate that too."

"What now?"

"That simper. The self-pity. The whole bit."

"Well maybe you should have married someone else then."

So it had devolved to this already. Goddamned entropy.

> *...some have argued that we should be making copies of our entire planet, life and all, throughout the cosmos on a regular basis so as to increase our potential for long-term survival after the Earth as we know it is inevitably destroyed...*

"You know what?" he said, "Maybe you're right. Maybe I should have."

"Do whatever you want," she said. "I don't care. I hope you'll be happy someday."

"Don't patronize me."

"I want to move back home. I *am* moving back home."

"Erin, you brought this up like two days ago. Can you at least give me a reasonable amount of time to think about it? Okay? It's not like this is a little move around the block. You're talking about 2,001 light years. It's complicated. At least acknowledge that it's a little fucking complicated, would you?"

"Whatever. I have to pick up Tavi at her swim lesson." She bundled Junior in her arms, his jaw still locked on her swollen nipple, and fled the room. Dylan was pretty sure she was going off to cry. That annoyed him too.

Dylan's omni asked him if he wanted to continue the Earth news. He told it to shut up and went back to the bedroom, ears wailing like banshees.

By the time he asked himself if this was really such a good idea, the point was moot: the box lay open on the bed, and the old dead world was flooding into the room again. The Chen/Astrophil trail having dried up, he reread all three of Wendy Sorenson's overtures, and if replying to them had seemed like it might be a *bad* idea just a few minutes ago, it now seemed to him about the best idea he'd ever had.

He directed his omni to compose a message to one Wendy Sorenson in Hawaii—happily, there appeared to be just one—and to copy verbatim the message that had worked so well on Ashley Eisenberg. Naturally he made sure to alter the particulars:

Hi Wendy. My name is Dylan Greenyears. You may remember that I was a fairly well known actor in the middle-nineties? Well, I was just looking through some old mail and I came across some letters you wrote me. This may seem odd coming so late, but I wonder if you'd like to get together sometime? I'm living rather far away these days, but I'd be happy to come to Hawaii if you'd like to meet up sometime. No pressure at all, of course.

Sincerely,
Dylan Greenyears

Having sent the message, he lay back on his bed, stared at the ceiling, and had barely begun playing with himself when his omni informed him he had a reply. That was fast.

My dear Dylan, I always knew you would come looking for me someday. When do our worldlines at last converge?

He replied:

Are you still in Hawaii?

Yes

Are you free next Sunday?

Free at last.

Where shall we meet?

I have seen it in my dreams. Pick up a kayak at Kailua Sailboards and Kayaks, Inc. I will reserve one in your name. Then paddle out to the Mokulua Islands. Be warned: it's farther than it looks. There is a cove on the makai (ocean-facing) side of the larger island, Moku Nui. Paddling there will be tough, but it's important that you do it, like symbolically. I will meet you there at 6:45 am. We will almost certainly be alone. I have waited so many years for this.

Great! See you then.

Amen, amen, and amen!

Her lack of inhibition was refreshing. Erin was always so *sane*.

He finished playing with his hardware, the old-fashioned way, sans reality augmentation, and then he lay back on the bed, listened to the banshees wail, and wondered what he'd just gotten himself into. It wasn't long before he fell asleep, though that didn't restrain his unconscious from hammering out the details of his plan.

As soon as Erin walked in the front door, he sprang to his feet and met her in the living room.

"Da—y!" Tavi said.

Dylan picked her up. "Hey, baby. How was swimming?"

"Good," Tavi said, pronouncing that word almost as if it rhymed with *mood*.

Dylan stared Erin in the shadowy alcoves of her eyes. "I'm sorry I lost my temper earlier."

She didn't exactly smile, but her frown grew a touch less committal.

"I'll think about moving," he continued. "I just need a little more time. This is kind of a big deal for me, you realize. I always swore to myself I would never go back there."

"I know," she said. "I'm sorry too. I'm just so sleep-deprived lately, it doesn't take much to set me off."

He leant over to hug her, Tavi giggling there between them, and for a moment all was right with the worlds. He almost regretted that he was about to disturb them again, but as his mother used to remind him whenever he tried to back out of anything as a kid, a commitment is a commitment.

"You know what's going to help me think about it?"

"What?"

"Cindy's insisting that I go to another conference."

Erin stopped hugging and screwed up her face. "Come again?"

"'Special Education in a Post-Disability Age.'"

"You're kidding me?"

"No."

"Earth?"

"Boston."

"When?"

"This weekend."

"This is absurd."

He nodded. It *was* absurd. He'd done his research for the sake of verisimilitude—there really was such a conference—though when it came down to it, he wasn't sure he didn't actually *want* her to cop to his infidelity this time around. Because what was the worst that could happen? He was reasonably sure she wouldn't leave him, *couldn't* leave him, any more than he would or could ever leave her. No, the worst that would happen was that he and Erin would *feel* things together again. These wouldn't be *good* feelings necessarily, but they would be powerful and serve to remind them that they were alive and that it mattered what they did with their time and their bodies. If only for a little while, he'd resume center stage in her life. He realized how pathetic it was for him to see himself as being in any way in competition with his own children, but at the same time he felt how sad it was that he should have to squeeze his sense of self-worth from the distant past like water from a dying succulent. If only he could forego the limelight altogether and embrace his obscurity, but damn it he'd been Jesus and Elliott and Jack, he'd floated on eyeballs and fucked in the moon; how, now, having basked in so much light, could he possibly make peace with the dark?

"Do whatever you need to do," Erin said, and then she excused herself to go make dinner. It was perfectly clear to Dylan that she'd just made a conscious choice not to engage. It was less clear to him whether this made it the warmest or coldest of responses.

In any event, he would take her at her word.

• • •

Dylan stepped out of the RiboMate at Honolulu Intragalactic Spaceport at four forty a.m., bought a bottle of champagne (Prosecco, actually) at the duty-free vending machine, and then traveled by light rail to Kailua Sailboards and Kayaks, Inc., where he picked up the plastic yellow kayak that had been reserved under his name from a smiley bodybuilder who summarily talked him into buying a six-hour osmotic Hydropatch for automatic hydration while on the ocean and automatic oxygenation while under it. He helped Dylan peel off the back and affix it to the side of his neck.

Clenching the kayak's grab loop between his middle and ring fingers, Dylan set off for the beach—about two blocks away. The wheels on the little trailer barely seemed to help. He could have paid a bit more for the motorized trailer, but he was determined to do this the old-fashioned way. Romance was a rather antiquated notion, depending as it did on distance, difficulty, and death, all of which had been largely superseded by technology, but for better or worse, Dylan missed it.

Once he'd managed to get through the sand and into the shallows, he found that boarding the kayak was no cakewalk either. He belly-flopped onto it and awkwardly pulled himself into what felt like a rather precarious seated position. He took up the black plastic oar and began to row. For a moment he thought he was home free, but then tepid waves began crashing into his face, turning the kayak parallel to the shoreline and making it all but inevitable that one of them would barrel-roll him. He didn't have to wait long before finding himself faced with the seemingly impossible proposition of belly-flopping onto the kayak again, but in deeper water now, where his feet didn't touch bottom. Unfortunately the oxygenation module of the Hydropatch kicked in only underwater, because by the time he succeeded at crawling into the seat and rowing out past the breakers, his bodily oxygen reserves were pretty well spent. He took a few moments to catch his breath, to watch the dog-walkers watch him from the ludicrously white beach, and to confirm that the champagne bottle hadn't shattered in the hatch.

Now was he home free? He was not. When he set to paddling again, he quickly realized that he didn't know whether the tips of the oars were meant to curve up or down. Did you spoon the water or, like, ladle it? He tried both and settled on the former. Steering was no more obvious at first, requiring as it did a sort of counterintuitive directional logic à la parallel parking. And while he soon fell into a rhythm, paddling was rough on the arms, and those islands, which had been *right there* when he'd first glimpsed them from the shore, now seemed to have migrated a good mile toward the horizon. To make matters worse, the morning sun was now blasting him in the face and he was already sweating bullets. Well, he had wanted romance. Here it was.

Nevertheless, despite the unforeseen difficulty, Dylan couldn't help but notice how insanely beautiful this place was. He had never been to Hawaii before. There were analogues on New Taiwan, but no equivalent, at least not where his human sense organs were concerned. The New Taiwanese atmosphere had a colder cast to it, a quality of tarnished brass, whereas here on Earth, here in Kailua anyway, the heavens shone a warm and radiant blue. And the translucent sea, this aptly-named Pacific, was so pure and gemlike in its blue-green gradations that it seemed to correspond to something elemental in his psyche. The ocean on New Taiwan was rather more like the dark, windswept Atlantic of his youth.

By the time he approached Moku Nui, it was already 7:13 by omni. Despite the inducements of a lovely little crescent of vacant beach on the south side of the island, he paddled against great resistance, inner and outer, to the windier back, where Wendy had instructed him to meet her. The waves were burlier here, liquid muscles expanding and contracting and all but overpowering Dylan's sorely underprepared and acutely burning arms and lungs. It was hard to imagine how all of this could possibly be worth it, but there was no going back now. He pressed on and by and by arrived.

The cove itself was like a grotto, a queer space, almost lunar, with lapping waves and giant quivering cubes of lemon Jell-O projected onto lava-rock walls. There was no beach on which to make landfall, just a drip castle of gnarled escarpments. The lapping stirred up clouds of white inside the blue-green that reminded Dylan of absinthe, which he'd drunk just once, inside the moon, and no sooner had he thought of the green fairy than he found himself immersed in it, floundering amid bubbles, senses deranged. Capsized again! But by what? Shark? Giant Pacific Octopus?

Then the bubbles cleared and he got his first eyeful of her.

She wasn't ugly, was decidedly gorgeous in fact in a Eurasian sort of way that one might have called "otherworldly" before learning that other worlds were themselves disappointingly worldly. What Dylan noticed first, and what would thereafter be coupled with her name in his mind, was the smile. Impish. Childlike. Her lips were big, clownish even, but whereas these might have proven a defect on a more somber face, on Wendy Sorenson they had the effect of accentuating that radiant and crazy joy of hers.

What Dylan noticed second was stranger: a frog swimming right alongside her, which, as they surfaced, leapt onto her shoulder and plopped itself square atop her head.

"Hello, darling," she said in a voice that managed to be both husky and squeaky at the same time.

"You capsized me," Dylan said.

"I wanted to make a strong impression."

"Can I safely assume you're Wendy Sorenson?"

"That's my name until you change it."

"And can I safely assume you realize there's a frog on your head?"

"Wha?" She fumbled with her hair. "Just kidding. This is Cane. I hope you don't mind. I don't go anywhere without him. He's kept me company all these years while I waited for you."

"Can I touch him?"

"You'd better not," she said. "He's very particular." Then, without the slightest hesitation, she pressed her body against his, wrapped her arms around his neck, and said, "So are you going to kiss me or what?"

"Already?"

"Dylan, I've been waiting twenty years for this. From my perspective there's nothing 'already' about it."

Well then—she was no less forward in person than in her letters. She was also irresistibly attractive, toad and all. He held the small of her back and fixed his thin lips to her fatter ones. Per Shlovsky, she was helping him to recover the sensation of life.

Then the upside-down kayak banged into a stony stone wall and she pulled back and said, "We'd better drop the anchor."

"Okay."

"You don't know where that is, do you?"

"I don't suppose I do."

"Well at least help me flip the kayak, would you?"

"Sure thing."

So they did that, and before he thought to stop her, she'd opened the front hatch and discovered the bottle of bubbly he'd meant to surprise her with. "Nice," she said. "I don't drink alcohol, but I won't keep you from it."

Oops. "Sorry. I should have checked."

"No biggie. There's lots you don't know about me yet."

She pulled a small anchor out of the rear hatch and wrapped it around the very crag the kayak had crashed into. She gave the line a tug to make sure it would hold.

"That a six-hour patch?" she asked, indicating his neck.

"Uh-huh."

"Awesome. I've got a good two hours left on mine. You still a decent swimmer?"

"How do you know I was ever a decent swimmer?"

"You grew up with a pool in your backyard. It would seem to follow."

"And how do you know I grew up with a pool in my backyard?"

"Research."

"I see," he said, not seeing.

She held out her hand to him. He was trying to decide whether, or how much, he ought to be bothered by her apparent invasion of his family's privacy, but he opted not to pursue it. He grabbed ahold of her hand, and together the three of them—Dylan, Wendy, Cane—submerged.

"Where are we going?" he asked her with his eyes. She shrugged, and then, true to plan, they went nowhere in particular for the next couple of hours; rather, they simply swam and frolicked like brand new animals in the sea. Dylan had never used one of these patches before, but there was nothing to it; you never felt the need to breathe—the patch was doing that for you—so you didn't have to surface unless you wanted to, and neither of them wanted to. Wendy pointed out the corals like Mandelbulbs, great pink brains, tropical fruits, monster fingers, the pubes of gorgons. Cane was never more than a few feet from Wendy's head, kicking its rear legs out like a wine opener. They'd been swimming for perhaps twenty minutes when she stopped, removed her bathing suit, and tied it to an outcropping of coral. Dylan followed her lead and was surprised to find that, onlooking amphibian notwithstanding, it came as naturally as not needing to breathe. More nude than naked then, Dylan and Wendy held hands and swam some more, passed through schools of synchronized fish, tropical and bright; rays like kites on the currents; turtles more ancient than their two combined lives. Mostly, though, he studied Wendy's body, which seemed of a piece with all of this, a natural thing with curves and orifices and lips and lips. He embraced her, and she let him, but when he made to kiss her again, she pulled away and went kicking through the absinthe some more. He stalked her until they surfaced by the kayak and pulled themselves up on a little bed of rock. Cane resumed his position atop her head.

"Did you see that magnificent tang?" she asked.

"I'm sorry?"

"That yellow tang down there. I've never seen one so big."

"Oh, right. The tang. Magnificent."

"You want to drink your champagne?" she asked.

"And what are you going to drink if I do?"

"I'm fine with my Hydropatch. It's still going strong."

"You're sure you don't mind?"

"Not a bit."

He swam over to the kayak and retrieved the bottle. Then he returned to her side and entered his pin into the little keypad. The cork popped. "Here's to us finally meeting," he said, and he clinked the bottle against a sunbeam and took a swig. The Prosecco was refreshing, earthy and good. She raised an eyebrow at his (lack of) manners. "I forgot to bring glasses," he explained.

"Ah."

They gazed out at the turquoise sea, the ripples sequined here and there and for only as long as it took to notice.

"This is spectacular," he said.

"Isn't it, though?"

"How did you get here anyway? I didn't see another kayak."

"I swam. Cane and I do it at least a couple of times a week."

"I had a hard enough time paddling."

She was jauntily swinging her legs, like a kid. Erin would never be so cavalierly nude like this, at least not anymore, but Wendy had no shame. Nor should she have. She was lithe and shiny, with pink feet and muscular calves, a lovely little shock of pubic beard, breasts like pomegranates. Her hair fell down around her shoulders, shiny and straight, and her big eyes appeared almost to bioluminesce.

He sidled up closer and put an arm around her. She smiled. He kissed her. She threatened to envelop his whole head, but he fought her, did his best to swallow *her* head, and as the intensity increased, he left her mouth to devour her ears and neck, and then her breasts, ribs, abdomen...until she stopped him. "Whoa, Nellie. Is there any rush?"

Now this he had not expected. "You said it yourself. We've waited twenty years."

"Then we could wait a little longer, couldn't we?" She slapped his palpitating boner.

His stomach sank.

"Why don't you take care of that while I go over there and do the same?"

"It would seem like a waste…"

"But what a great way to get to know each other."

"I came all this way…"

"Pretty much anyone can fuck," she said, "but it takes real courage to get yourself off inside another's gaze, no? To make yourself vulnerable like that? That's the real penetration, I think. Don't worry, I'll start."

And start she did. She backed off several yards and turned to face him. Then she put one foot up on a rock and spread her knees wide apart, made herself, in a word, open. She licked two of her fingers and put them down by her pussy in an upside-down V, fingers straddling her clit, with the web bit right on the money. She threw her head back and moaned, licked her lips, eyelids at half-mast, but the whole time she kept her gaze directly—and yes, penetratingly—on him. It was an unmistakable look, a look older than their species itself, a look that said, *Everything else about me is a pretense. Language and ideas and clothing and manners…all are window dressing for the one true thing, which is this:* Fuck me.

It took all he had not to go over there and violate her. Instead he stared back at her as she stared at him, trembling, just a few feet of oxygen-rich atmosphere separating them. The sun warmed his face and chest. Water lapped at the rocks beneath them. He said yes to all of it. Yes to the sea and mountains and sky. Yes to all those turtles and fish. Yes to skin and hair and fingers and eyes and God if there was one. Yes to vulnerability, to openness, to interpenetration. She quaked and moaned. He kind of did too. Yes.

Cane croaked. Wendy put him down on a rock and lay down beside Dylan with her head on his chest. Together they detumesced and fell asleep.

But when Dylan awoke, he found himself alone again. He sat up. He'd been asleep long enough that everything looked different now; the atmospheric kaleidoscope had turned. He got up, dressed, and went wandering the little island in search of her. On the beach side, he found some families picnicking, but Wendy was not among them, and for a moment he wondered if he hadn't imagined the whole unlikely adventure. It did have the blush of fantasy about it after all. Could it be that he was finally losing his mind? That this whole liaison had been a hallucination in keeping with his phantom tinnitus? But when he checked his omni, he discovered hard evidence of Wendy's existence easily enough. All of her messages were there, as well as a new one that read simply, "Aloha"—which a helpful sidebar informed him meant not only "Hello" but also "Goodbye" and "I love you." If her goal in departing with such minimalism was to furnish a negative space for his desire to pour into, then she was a genius. Or she was just fucking weird. In either case, he couldn't wait to see her again.

• • •

Back at the teleport, Dylan read up on the latest in blood-based neuron-farming for the classroom. He wasn't all that interested really, but he had to tell Erin *something*.

"Hi," he said when he walked in the door. He nearly said "Hi, *honey*," but he dodged the cliché just in time—he wasn't really feeling the sweetness vibe anyway. Images of lithe, shiny Wendy were still swimming around his brainstem. Erin, by contrast, was looking rather frumpy in her skin-tight purple pants and plaid apron. She looked, in short, like a mom. He didn't know whether Wendy had any children or not, but she didn't *look* like she did. He was going to kiss Erin on the cheek out of habit, but then he remembered that habituation was the enemy. Was he an asshole? Yes, he most certainly was, but at least he wasn't kidding himself about it.

"Why don't you go say hello to your children?" she said. She didn't even bother to ask how the conference was.

"Where are they?"

"Junior's in his crib. He just fell asleep. I'm pretty sure his face changed again last night. Arthur and Tavi are in the playroom building space elevators out of Legos."

He went to see the baby first. Dylan didn't see the change Erin was talking about—he wasn't as attuned to such things as she was—but the kid sure was cute, all small and curled up like some New Taiwanese glyph. He kissed the oversized head, which smelled, unmistakably, like baby head.

He quietly manifested the door and went down to the playroom to greet his other kids, who stopped what they were doing to shout "Daddy! Daddy!" and hug his legs; Tavi had apparently mastered those intermediate d's all of a sudden—a small victory, to be sure, though Dylan found himself choked up out of all proportion. It had not occurred to him to miss his kids during his trip, but in a revisionist-history sort of way, he apparently had. Despite developing tensions between him and these kids' mother, he felt really glad—not happy exactly, but glad—to call this family his own.

Still, in the days to follow, Dylan was plagued by a feeling that he was a sort of impostor in his own life, a changeling, because the fact was he had left the lion's share of his emotional life on that rock in Kailua Bay. It was as if Wendy Sorenson had stretched the limits of his experience and he could not easily let them contract again. Had the episode been merely a dream or a vision, he wouldn't have hesitated to call it a religious experience, irreligious though he believed himself to be. But it *had* really happened, and this made him wonder, in a terrified sort of way, if the right term wasn't perhaps "love." He hardly knew anything about Wendy, of course—he realized this. Still, he went through the week feeling a kind of tragic exhilaration. He was like the husband in Chekhov's "The Lady with the Lapdog," who, having finally fallen in love for real, understands that the hardest part has only just begun.

He thought about coming clean with Erin, confessing where he'd been and how he felt. It seemed like it might be the simplest course. Would she really believe that he had yet *another* conference to go to anyway? Yet even with all the distance between them these days, he didn't want to hurt her any more than he wanted to hurt himself.

He had an idea: what if he QT'd Wendy out here instead? He'd be more than happy to pay for it and there were comparably exotic places here where they could have their tryst. Ascension Forest would blow anyone's mind. She'd trusted him to be near her home; why shouldn't he trust her to be near his? Granted, she was a little eccentric, but he had no reason to think she posed any risk.

So he went to the bedroom and replied to her "Aloha" with an invitation. He laid the whole situation bare to her as he would not for Erin anytime soon, and herein, he realized, lay the essence of adultery: it wasn't so much about rutting bodies as asymmetrical access to information; it was the lying to, not the lying with.

Dear Wendy,

First, let me tell you that I had the time
of my life with you in Kailua and I cannot
stop replaying the whole thing in my mind.
I had no idea when I first contacted you
that I was going to meet such a beautiful
woman. I hope you won't take this the wrong
way, but I don't even feel like you are an
ordinary human at this point. You're like
some siren or nymph, some creature out of my
fantasies. Anyway, I want to come clean with
you: I am married. I suspect you already
know this as it's recorded on omni and
you've obviously done your research. I want
to be very clear about this: I love my wife
and I do not wish to hurt her. That said,
let me tell you that I have never felt so
alive as I did with you the other day. Which
brings me to the point of this message:
I don't think I can come to Earth again
anytime soon being as I have a family and
a full-time job (I teach high school), but
I wonder if you might be able to make the
trip up to New Taiwan instead? That's where
I've been living these past twenty years (I
tell you all of this in strict confidence
because, though it may be inadvisable
for me to let my guard down so soon, I
instinctively trust you). I don't know
if you've ever been off Earth or not, but
Quantum Travel has become quite comfortable
and I'm happy to pay for your ticket. We
have some very beautiful places here that I

would love to take you to, for me to let my
guard down so soon, I instinctively trust
you). I don't know if you've ever been off
Earth or not, but Quantum Travel has become
quite comfortable and I'm happy to pay for
your ticket. We have some very beautiful
places here that I would love to take you
to, though I probably shouldn't be gone for
more than, say, three or four hours at a
stretch. You understand the nature of my
predicament, I think. Please get back to
me soon and let me know if you can come.
Otherwise, I'll contact you next time I
think I can get away from this planet for a
couple of days. In any case, Wendy, please
know that I am thinking of you night and
day.

Aloha,
Dylan Greenyears

Even the simple act of sending that message made Dylan feel
giddy and filled with hope, like an autonomous agent of free will in a
wonderful, mysterious universe where anything is possible, anything
can happen. He felt, in other words, young.

She wrote back within a couple of minutes:

My Dylan,

I would love to come see you on New Taiwan,
and you offend me by offering to pay. I make
a killing in Green Smoothies, you know.

Shall we plan on Sunday then? Where shall we
meet? What shall I wear?

Yours,
Wendy

P.S. I have toured Saturn and Mars, but I
have yet to leave the Solar System. I was
waiting for you to escort me, I guess.

Dylan squirmed with sheepish joy. And what a relief that she
could pay. Despite his posturing, he'd worried about that part. He and
Erin had shared a savings account since they'd married and skipped
Earth. He had secreted some currency away in his sock drawer over
the years for an existentially rainy day, but he probably couldn't even
beam Wendy round-trip with that.

As for where they should meet, the teleport seemed oppor-
tune enough since it was roughly the midpoint between here and
Ascension Forest.

Dear Wendy,

I will meet you at the teleport and then
spirit you away to one of my favorite spots.
Wear anything you like. Better yet, wear
nothing!

Aloha,
Dylan

P.S. Okay, you had probably better wear
something. The New Taiwanese aren't half as

puritanical as Americans, but they're not
exactly nudists either. My best advice as
for what to wear is to check the weather
forecast. Temperatures tend to be rather
mercurial this time of year, though it
never gets very cold.

As things fell out, Erin had to cart the kids to various lessons and appointments on Sunday, so Dylan was spared the need to devise an excuse. Alas, they had only one car between them, and the rolling road was too conspicuous. The transportation industry had been promising personal teleporters for years, but that hadn't happened yet, so Dylan did the only thing he could do, which was to draw on the funds in his sock drawer and hire a cab. He sprang for the best androcab he could afford and had the driver gun it through the Grind to the teleport.

"Who would you like me to be?" the driver asked. "If Omni can see them, I can be them."

"Can you do James Cameron?"

"The film director?"

"That's the one."

And just like that the android's frubber morphed into the exact likeness of the man who had once ruined Dylan's life. He looked a bit too old, though.

"Can you do an age regression of twenty years?"

"Sure thing."

And now a subtler morphing occurred until the driver was shudderingly like the man who had directed *Titanic*. Dylan commanded him to slow down a bit in no uncertain terms—"Slow down, you maggoty lump of dogshit"—so that he might savor the prospect of his former vanquisher working as his own personal chauffeur. It's a strange thing, the fantasy life, but there could be little doubt that New Taiwan's carving out a space for it like this was a large part of why the crime rate stayed so low here.

He knew her from a distance. She had considerably more clothes on this time, too many really, but not so many that he couldn't pick out her figure. The cab pulled up next to the curb. Dylan erased the door with a wave of his hand, got out and kissed her on the lips. Those devouring lips. He didn't even check to see if they were being watched. No doubt Omni was watching, but that was inevitable. Omni saw everything...except Jade Astrophil.

"Hello to you too," she said.

"I missed you," he said.

Wendy looked classy and altogether marvelous, like some New York City fashionista circa his childhood. She had on a tight white sweater, a black pleated skirt, and leather boots. A red chenille scarf was wrapped about her throat. He'd grown up seeing women in scarves—Philly winters were brutal by comparison—but he'd never seen one on New Taiwan until now.

"You look lovely," he said.

She winked, fiercely, like some tiger that knew how to wink.

He helped her into the cab.

"It doesn't get that cold here," he said.

"Dylan, I grew up on O'ahu. Your definition of cold and mine are almost certainly not in the same ballpark."

"Fair enough," he said.

He ordered his newly appointed yes-man to proceed to Ascension Forest, and then asked Wendy if she didn't want to change drivers.

She looked puzzled. "Why would I?"

"It's an androcab. It can be anyone you like."

She studied the driver more closely. "Really?"

"I kid you not. Don't you have these on Earth?"

She touched the neck. "I don't think so, but then I don't often take cabs."

"So who will it be?"

"I can choose anyone?"

"Anyone."

"Living or dead?"

"If Omni can see them, it can be them."

"Well then how about a singer to serenade us?"

"Good idea."

"Can it do Sinatra?"

"Driver, give us your best Frank Sinatra, would you?"

And—*shazam!*—James Cameron morphed into Ol' Blue Eyes. The likeness was uncanny.

"Any requests?" he asked.

"'Fly Me to the Moon'?" Wendy suggested.

"Excellent," Sinatra said. The music kicked in on the sound system and he began to sing:

> *Fly me to the moon*
> *Let me swing among those stars*
> *Let me see what spring is like*
> *On Jupiter and Mars*

Ha! Dylan had never noticed it before, but no doubt the real Frank Sinatra had sung those first two lines with a wink and a nod to the rest of the Loonies.

Wendy draped a leg over one of his and began to suck his face.

"I'll understand if you want to look out the window," Dylan said. "I know it's your first time here and all."

"Darling," she said, "I only have eyes for you."

He smiled, and they made out some more until she stopped to pull something out of her pocket. "Don't want him getting crushed," she said, and she placed Cane atop her head. "Now I just hope he won't get crushed emotionally."

"I'm surprised they let you bring him," Dylan said, "what with all the concerns about invasive species."

"You'd be surprised what you can get away with for religious reasons. Besides, there's only this one. It's not like they can start reproducing."

"You have religious reasons for keeping a toad?"

"Ask me later."

"Okay."

So they went back to making out like teenagers, pausing only to make song requests. Wendy had an impressive knowledge of Sinatra, and it was clear to Dylan, insofar as he was paying attention to the lyrics, that she was ventriloquizing, speaking to him through this borrowed voice. To wit:

> *Around the world I've searched for you*
> *I traveled on when hope was gone to keep a rendezvous*
> *I knew somewhere, sometime, somehow*
> *You'd look at me and I would see the smile you're smiling now*

And this:

> *Love is lovelier*
> *The second time around*
> *Just as wonderful*
> *With both feet on the ground*

It's that second time you hear your love song sung
Makes you think perhaps that love like youth is wasted on the young

And maybe this too:

All or nothin' at all
Half a love never appealed to me
If your heart, it never could yield to me
Then I'd rather, rather have nothin' at all

That last made him a twinge nervous; nevertheless, for the first time in his life, Dylan recognized the greatness of Frank Sinatra. His dad had always been a fan, which all but guaranteed that Dylan wouldn't be, but here in this cab, wooing his mistress, he felt how deeply insightful these lyrics were, and how timeless the voice. It struck him, in what was probably an irresolvable paradox, that Sinatra's appeal was both universal and thoroughly American at once.

Over Wendy's delicious neck, he watched the foliage thicken until they'd entered the forest. Between songs, Sinatra asked for more precise directions, and Dylan gave them. Within a few minutes they had arrived at a clearing. Except that the soil and air composition here gave the verdure a distinctly bluish tinge, it looked pretty much like any sylvan scene on Earth—hulking trees, hanging vines, not unlike the park behind Dylan's parents' house. At a glance anyway.

The doors vanished and they got out. Dylan instructed Sinatra to wait there until they came back, and he submitted to having his genome sequenced in order to hold the reservation (he didn't actually have to *do* anything, so much of him having already exfoliated onto the back seat). "Happy to be at your service," Sinatra said, using words he would never use. "I hope you enjoy your time in Ascension Forest."

Dylan tipped a hat he wasn't wearing.

"What's Ascension Forest?" Wendy asked.

"You don't know? Good. I thought perhaps you'd read about it, but all the better if you haven't. It's one of the few really unique features of this world."

Dylan led them along a paved path that ran alongside a burbling creek. A stiff breeze whistled through a copse of the native bamboo, clacking the shoots together and sending the monkeygeese leaping and squawking into the boughs of the sturdier everblues.

Wendy looked around. "What's so unique about it?"

"Do you like plants?" Dylan asked.

She squinted. "Do some people *not* like plants?"

"Okay, well do you *love* them?"

"I don't do drugs if that's what you're asking."

"No, no. I'm just asking whether you love plants is all. Pure and simple. No booby traps."

"All right then. I guess I do. Sure."

"Good. Because Ascension Forest is the only place I know where the plants love you back."

"What's that supposed to mean?"

"I think I'll let you discover that for yourself."

She blinked once and then not for a while.

They reached the end of the pavement and continued along a dirt path, which soon branched—they went left—and then branched again—they went right. Dylan knew exactly where he was leading them. He and Erin had spent a good deal of time here before the kids came along and they'd quickly established a favorite spot; they were reasonably certain, in fact, that they had this forest to thank for Arthur and Tavi's conceptions. Dylan might have felt it too great a betrayal to bring Wendy here had he and Erin sported in these parts at all recently, but the fact was they hadn't been here in something like four years, and even sacredness, it seemed to him, had a statute of limitations.

They were almost there.

"You ready?" he asked.

"You tell me."

He took her hand and they turned into the thickly canopied trail.

They were barely a few paces into the shadows when the canopy abruptly lowered itself and purple tendrils shot out and seized them by their necks and arms. Wendy shrieked and curled into Dylan's embrace. He unwound a clutching vine from her throat and replaced it with the scarf from her jacket pocket. Cane was croaking at a new and higher pitch.

"I told you," Dylan said, helplessly amused by her terror (he'd felt it too his first time here). "They just like to fondle us," he explained. "They only touch bare areas, so the more you expose, the more they'll fondle."

She looked at him with aye-aye eyes. "Are you seriously laughing at me right now?"

"I assure you no one has ever been injured here." Despite being a little embarrassed at the shape he was in, he took off his shirt and gave it to her—it was nothing she hadn't already seen. "Here, you can cover your face with this until you get more comfortable. Meanwhile, I'll demonstrate."

He had hardly gotten that last sentence out when the tendrils closed in on him full-bore, wrapping themselves around his face, neck, and torso in such profusion that a tourist could be forgiven for thinking he was being killed. In fact, the overriding sensation was of having his entire body worked by a very capable, octopoid masseuse. His only complaint was that it made it a little hard to walk.

"You okay in there?" Wendy asked.

"Rarely better," he said. "Give it a try if you're ready. Safety guaranteed."

"I'm trusting you on this one," she said, and all at once she removed Dylan's shirt from her head and clutched it to her chest, keeping Cane wrapped up in it for his protection. A creeper shot out to massage her neck, and two others to lick at her ears. "This is *crazy!*" she shouted, and she proceeded to shriek some more, but in a more playful way this time.

"There's a bed of moss up here a little ways that, when you lie on it, it sort of tickles you all over. What do you say?"

She took his hand and he led the way.

As they walked, he cleared his mouth of vines and explained to Wendy that the name "Ascension Forest" had its roots in a malapropism. The First Expedition, reporting to Earth on their visit to this magical place, made reference to "a sentient forest." The minutes-keeper, however, recorded this as "Ascension Forest," which brought with it overtones of transcendence and religious experience, that latter being a phrase a member of the expedition actually happened to use in describing his sojourn there. "Ascension Forest" also had the advantage of being significantly easier on the tongue, not to mention less crude, than the indigenous name for the place, *Alobaz'ñashahilmukdan'nabai* ("the garden that rapes you"), so that even when it came to light that the name was an eggcorn, Terrans obstinately clung to it.

He also explained that no one, human or native, definitively understood the science of what went on here. The majority view held that the plants had a taste for the trillion microorganisms living on the hominid dermis at any one time, and while experiments had shown that these plants were indeed stripping some of the microbiome from its symbiotic hominid partners, albeit not so much as to compromise their health in any way, it was difficult to show that this was not just a fringe benefit (or "spandrel") of some more essential and inscrutable process. Another intriguing theory, dubbed phonosynthesis, held that these plants, having co-evolved with hominids, metabolized the *sounds* produced by the hominid larynx, and the fondling was an evolutionary strategy they'd developed to coax and prolong their "feeding sessions"; here, too, there was some experimental data to corroborate this, though not nearly enough to draw any certain conclusions. It could be that both theories were correct in some measure, or that neither was. In any case, it was no wonder that the forest was a popular destination for lovers. Fortunately, the forest was nearly a square marathon in extent, so you only very rarely encountered another hominid.

Dylan halted. "Here we are," he said, signaling the bed of moss before them. "We should take off our shoes."

"Okay," she said.

He pretended to struggle with a knot—bona fide shoelaces were one of his old-world affectations (print books and his non-implanted omni being two others)—while she unzipped and stepped out of her boots and knee-high fishnets.

"It occurs to me you might want to leave Cane here, for his own safety."

She shrugged and placed the toad down gently in her boot.

"Now you go ahead," he said.

"Oh, I think I'll wait for you."

"But I insist," he said, making that *shoo* gesture with his hand.

She looked down hesitantly and raised a foot. He did not need to egg her on any further, because no sooner had she dangled that foot over the moss than a sprig of it leapt up, seized her big toe and pulled it down. She resisted as best she could, but other sprigs crowded in and tugged at the whole of the foot and ankle until inevitably she capsized onto the mat and lay helpless and supine, convulsing and laughing so hard that her larynx produced no sound whatsoever. The moss took it down a notch until her laughter was merely hysterical and rolling.

"I think it likes you!" Dylan said.

Wendy shrieked and howled, howled and shrieked.

He took off his shoes and socks for real now and joined her. Despite having done this dozens of times before, he was no more inured to these sensations than she was. She wrapped her arms around his abdomen like he was some kind of life preserver, but by this time he too was at the mercy of the moss and clinging to her as fervently as she to him. They held on tight as tears streamed down their cheeks, as the moss groped and prodded, as vines from on high insinuated their warm tendrils beneath their clothing to stroke every inch of their erogenous, bacteria-ridden flesh. Dylan always marveled that these plants somehow knew not to obstruct the sense organs of their symbiotic partners; co-evolution was good that way.

After an hour or so, the vines had had their fill of whatever it was they were getting and began to retreat. The moss's rude acupressure eased into a gentler and more sustainable kind of kneading. It was none too soon either. Dylan and Wendy lay side-by-side, face-up, absorbing the single shaft of light that managed to penetrate the thick foliage overhead and contagiously yawning. They hadn't had sex yet, but at least now they had been raped by a forest together.

"You still know very little about me," Wendy said.

"That's true."

"And I know so much about you."

"Oh, I assure you there's plenty you don't know about me yet."

"I love that 'yet.' That's my favorite 'yet.'"

He nibbled her earlobe.

"Ask me a question," she said.

"What's your favorite color?"

"Scarlet. Now how about a *real* question?"

"Okay. Here's one. You said something in your message about making a killing in Green Smoothies? What's that all about?"

"Haven't I told you I own a kiosk at the mall?"

"You have not."

"'Nalo Elixirs. We blend up leafy vegetables like spinach and kale with mangoes and bananas. No additives. Supremely simple yet powerful concoctions."

"I'd love to try one someday."

"Oh, you'll try them all in time. I have no doubt about that."

"Okay, so *there's* another question I have for you."

"What's that?"

"You keep saying that you always *knew* we'd be together someday and things to that effect."

"Do you doubt it?"

"Well that's just it. I don't doubt that you feel that way *now*, seeing things in retrospect. And I can't really doubt that you've felt that way *at times* in the past because you documented it. Still, nobody 'always' knows anything, right? I mean, not *really*. Don't you have to stumble around a bit in life before you figure out what you really want or what your true destiny is or whatever you want to call it?"

"All my stumbling was done by the time I saw you make out with Korelu in the mothership. Since then I've just been biding my time. I knew you'd come."

He remembered Ol' Blue Eyes: *I knew somewhere, sometime, somehow...*

"Okay, but let's pause there for a second. When you say 'knew,' what do you mean exactly? Because surely you couldn't *know* know, like literally?"

She smirked.

"Well, but surely you didn't know it in the way that you know you're in Ascension Forest right now?"

Her smirk grew even smugger.

"Or that $A^2 + B^2 = C^2$?"

"Sorry, Dylan. You're going to have to trust me on this one. I *knew*."

"So, what, do you have a time machine, then?"

She smiled knowingly. "I have something much more powerful on my side than any time machine."

"Psychic powers?"

She shook her head.

"A crystal ball?"

She shook her head some more.

"What, then?"

"The Holy Spirit."

And it was like someone had just knocked the wind out of him.

Dylan had grown up in a marginally Catholic family and attended Catholic schools from first to twelfth grade. As a boy, he'd believed in the Father, the Son, and the Holy Spirit, believed that God intervened in earthly matters now and then, and that praying was a worthwhile way to spend one's time—his father modeled this by getting on his knees at his bedside every night without fail—but somewhere along the way those myths had stopped fitting the ever-expanding universe he found himself in. It, i.e. everything, was all too big and unruly to be encompassed by the story of a single primate nailed to a tree.

For the love of God, there were at least 10^{24} worlds out there! And if his faith had left any residue, it had been thoroughly scrubbed off by the demise of his acting career. It was true, perhaps, that his professional ruin had in some sense *caused* his apostasy, but not because Dylan was bitter or anything so simplistic and sour-grapish as that. Rather, the implosion of his career had made Dylan singularly aware of humanity's nakedness before the great sucking void of space. Success was no longer guaranteed for him, and even success, he saw from this new zoomed-out vantage point, amounts to nothing in the end; there is no Oscar that will survive the heat death of the universe.

"You're a believer?"

"I am."

"Christian?"

"Mormon."

"I guess I don't really know what that means," Dylan confessed. Against the predominantly Catholic ethos of his hometown, the word "Mormon" had signified just two things: Utah and polygamy. Maybe crazy too, which fit. Wendy was definitely crazy—in fact, that seemed to be what he liked best about her.

"It means many things," Wendy said. "You'll learn about all of them in time."

"I didn't think there were any religious people left under the age of like fifty."

"That's quite true as far as the monotheistic faiths are concerned," Wendy said. "But Mormonism has been on the rise for decades."

"And why should that be?" he asked. "I don't really keep abreast of Terran affairs."

"Truth outs," she declared. "As soon as humans began discovering primate life on Super Earths throughout the galaxy, it was pretty much game-over for the old religions. You get some hangers-on here and there, but they're kidding themselves and they know it. Those jealous creeds had been so thoroughly premised on the special status of the human race on Earth that their theologies just couldn't accommodate the new discoveries in any way that didn't stink of backpedaling BS. We Mormons, on the other hand, had been talking about Super Earths from the very beginning. We *expected* to find others like us out here. We also knew all along that the Earth was the most wicked of all worlds. From our point of view, history is unfolding exactly according to God's plan."

"And what is that plan?" Dylan asked.

"Salvation through eternal progression."

"Which means?"

"Which means that all of God's children on all of His many worlds will eventually be exalted to godhood themselves."

"And you mean that literally too?"

"Most definitely I do. *As God now is, man may be.*"

"What happens when we become Gods?" he asked.

"Good question. First we have to be resurrected in immortal physical bodies of flesh and bone. And then, if we have lived up to all the ordinances and covenants, and if we are sealed in celestial marriage in the temple—which, don't worry, because I already know you and I will be—we shall be exalted to the Celestial Kingdom to be with God the Father and our Elder Brother Jesus Christ near the star Kolob. Then we will go on to birth innumerable spirit children and to organize matter into other Super Earths for them to live on."

Dylan didn't even know where to begin. "You know the name of God's star?"

"We do. It came to Abraham in a vision. We haven't pinpointed which one it is yet, but some speculate that it may be Polaris."

"That's f'ing nuts!" Dylan said. He couldn't help himself.

"Why?"

"Well isn't Jesus supposed to be, like, everywhere?"

"Now *that's* nuts. Think about it. Catholics held that Jesus ascended into heaven, right?"

Her use of the past tense wasn't lost on him, and though he hadn't counted himself a Catholic in many years, he nonetheless flinched a little.

"True," he said, remembering his Apostles' Creed: *On the third day he rose again. He ascended into heaven and is seated at the right hand of the Father...*

"Okay, then where did He go after that? Did He just dissolve into some spirit realm?"

It was a good question, one he'd never thought to ask before despite having recited that creed practically every week of his childhood. "I guess I did sort of believe that," he said, "when I believed any of it."

"That's one big difference between Mormonism and the old Christian religions. Ours is a fundamentally *scientific* faith. That's why it's so durable. Even God the Father is subject to the laws of physics. He has a physical being of flesh and bone and He lives *out there*—yes, literally. Everything in the Mormon view of things, even God, has a natural explanation. When our faith and science don't seem to square with each other, it's because science hasn't progressed enough yet. It will. People used to say we were off our rockers when we talked about all the other inhabited Earths out there. They don't say that anymore."

"Okay, so all of this is quite fascinating, it really is, but it's a lot to swallow. If we could go back to my original question for a second..."

"Sure."

"So you say the Holy Spirit told you that I would come for you someday?"

"The Holy Spirit is a revelator, and His continuing revelations are every bit as real, *more* real, than any knowledge one might gain from any hypothetical time machine."

"And the revelation came to you in a dream, or...?"

"Sometimes revelations *do* come in dreams, that's true, but this one came rather as a still, small voice. It distilled upon me as the dew from heaven while I watched you fuck Korelu in that R-rated movie I wasn't technically supposed to be watching."

"R-rated movies are forbidden, are they?"

"As are a number of other things."

"Such as?"

"Coffee and tea, alcohol, gambling, pornography, sex outside of marriage. A very grievous sin, that last."

"Which explains why you wouldn't sleep with me on Moku Nui?"

"In part, yes. I meant what I said, though, about mutual masturbation being a deeper sort of penetration."

Dylan held up an index finger. "I don't want to split hairs, but it would surprise me if coffee is forbidden and mutual masturbation outside of marriage is not."

"Please remember, Dylan, that I am a person, okay, not perfect, nor any more automatically in tune with the tenets of my faith than the Catholics you knew as a kid were automatically in tune with theirs. My father's a professor of Mormon theology at BYU, so I'm more in tune with the intellectual side of the religion than most Mormons are. Nevertheless, some of what I'm saying is Mormon doctrine and some of it, inevitably, is just me. So that's my first excuse. But there's this too: I really *do* know that we're going to be together for all eternity, so I don't feel guilty of any major sin in that regard."

"You're so certain."

"I am."

"Because God knows everything and he revealed some of it to you?"

"That's right."

"So you don't believe in free will then, I take it?"

"To the contrary. God the Father cast Lucifer out of heaven precisely for trying to abrogate the free agency of humankind. Free will is therefore very important to Mormons. It's true that you were foreordained for something in your pre-Earth life by the Grand Council of Heaven, but our earthly life is full of trials and we all are ultimately responsible for our own destinies."

Dylan knew he was having a post-Earth life. He had not been aware that he'd ever had a *pre*-Earth one.

"But you just said that God knows everything. Doesn't that mean that we can't do other than what He already knows we will do?"

"That old brainteaser. Has it ever occurred to you, Dylan, that maybe there's something wrong with our human conception of time? That maybe words like 'before' and 'after' don't actually *mean* anything in the context of eternity? Even Einstein was onto that."

Dylan nodded slowly and let it sink in. Because what a refreshing goddamned thought that was! He leant over and kissed her, and they went at it *lengua-a-lengua* for a spell, though a certain degree of modesty seemed appropriate following that discussion.

"I guess you'll have to go soon?" she said.

"Yes." It was dusk already. Erin would begin to wonder.

"Can we meet again next Sunday?"

"I wouldn't miss it for the worlds," he said. "I may be able to sneak down to Oahu again if you prefer?"

"I think I'd prefer to meet here actually. This forest is so... enchanted."

"Isn't it, though?" he said, taking pride in his adopted homeworld.

"I know of nothing like it anywhere."

They made out for a few more minutes. Then they stood up, left the moss, put their shoes back on, and hiked back to their androcab.

"I hope you enjoyed your time in Ascension Forest," Sinatra greeted them.

"We certainly did," Wendy replied.

"I am very glad to hear it. Shall I drive you back to the teleport now?"

"Yes, thank you," Dylan said.

"Is there anyone else you'd like for me to be?"

"Shall we let it be itself for a bit?" Dylan suggested.

But Wendy had her own ideas: "Can you do the Mormon Tabernacle Choir?"

"I have many of their recordings available," the driver said, "though I'm afraid I'm capable of morphing into only one singer at a time. I could change at intervals of twenty seconds. Will that do?"

"That'll do fine," Wendy said.

"Wonderful. Which piece would you like to hear?"

"'If You Could Hie to Kolob'?"

"But of course."

And now their shape-shifting chauffeur morphed into a bespectacled bald man in a suit and tie, a young brunette in a blue dress, a chubby blonde...each sang with a host of heavenly voices:

> If you could hie to Kolob
> In the twinkling of an eye,

> *And then continue onward*
> *With that same speed to fly,*
> *Do you think that you could ever,*
> *Through all eternity,*
> *Find out the generation*
> *Where Gods began to be?*

It was choral music, heavy on harmony, the sort of thing Dylan associated with Christmas time and universities. At first he didn't think he was going to like it, that he would merely endure it out of respect for Wendy's esoteric belief system—

> *Or see the grand beginning,*
> *Where space did not extend?*
> *Or view the last creation,*
> *Where Gods and matter end?*
> *Methinks the Spirit whispers,*
> *"No man has found 'pure space,'*
> *Nor seen the outside curtains,*
> *Where nothing has a place."*

But as he sat with her, holding her hand, peering into her opalescent eyes and listening intently to the words, these angelic voices seemed to resonate with some pure and essential part of him that had been trapped away for a very long time—

> *The works of God continue,*
> *And worlds and lives abound;*
> *Improvement and progression*
> *Have one eternal round.*
> *There is no end to matter;*
> *There is no end to space;*

There is no end to spirit;
There is no end to race.

And it seemed to him now that the pinnacle of his life, that pure space to which he was so fatally bent on returning, was not so much his brief stint in the limelight as the pre-rational Eden of childhood, the early morning of his life before the sun got so hot and the dark so dark—

There is no end to virtue;
There is no end to might;
There is no end to wisdom;
There is no end to light.
There is no end to union;
There is no end to youth;
There is no end to priesthood;
There is no end to truth.

And what incredibly good news this was! Because while the limelight belonged to the past, insofar as that meant anything, the child was apparently still in there, wide-eyed and infinitely happy despite all reason—

There is no end to glory;
There is no end to love;
There is no end to being;
There is no death above.
There is no end to glory;
There is no end to love;
There is no end to being;
There is no death above.

Reason was spectacularly overrated anyway, was it not? What fool wouldn't want to hie to Kolob?

And as those heavenly hosts of angels resolved their song with a major chord, Dylan felt compelled to tell Wendy exactly how he felt: "I love you," he said, and warm, fat tears began plunking down his cheeks.

"I know," she said. She held his head and stroked his hair, and they embraced for the rest of the drive. Even Cane, in his perch atop Wendy's head, let out a low purr.

When they arrived at the teleport, Dylan swiped away the door and stepped out with her.

"I've had a wonderful time," she said.

"This week will feel like an eternity."

"Don't look to me for any sympathy there. I've been waiting two decades for you."

He smiled. "Goodbye," he said, and he extended a hand for her to shake.

"That reminds me!" she exclaimed, and she proceeded to teach him a secret handshake which involved clasping hands in the usual way while interlocking pinkies, fingering the other's wrist with the index finger, and rotating the whole bundle back and forth.

"We'll use this to get into the Celestial Kingdom someday," she said.

"I'm afraid to ask how literally you mean that."

"Well then you already know my answer. I'm not supposed to share this with anyone, by the way, or my throat will be cut ear to ear, my tongue torn out by its roots, my breasts torn open, my heart and vitals torn out and given to the birds of the air and the beasts of the field, and my body cut asunder and all my bowels gush out—but I'm making an exception here."

"I appreciate that," he said, not at all sure he did. They practiced the handshake one last time and then went their very separate ways.

• • •

"Where'd you go?" Erin asked. She was sitting on the rug beside the sofa, pushing Junior in his rocker with one hand and bunching socks with the other.

"For a stroll."

"In an androcab?"

Shit. He'd had the driver drop him off a few houses away. He didn't think she'd notice.

"Yes, as a matter of fact. I took an androcab to the beach. I wanted to walk by the sea. I had some thinking to do."

She looked dubious. "What about?"

"About our moving back to Earth."

That sat her up.

"I'm beginning to think it might not be such a bad idea."

"Really?" She looked down at Junior, burying her head in her swollen cleavage so as to hide her grin—but Dylan knew her too well.

"I don't want to go back home, mind you. Forget the East Coast. The weather sucks, and the people are cold too. What if we moved someplace warmer?"

"Like where?"

"I don't know. Someplace like...Hawaii?"

"Since when have you been interested in Hawaii?"

"It just seems like a good compromise. It's not New Taiwan, but it's not Philly either."

She picked the baby up, put his head over her shoulder and gently thumped his back. "Dylan, I hate to say it, but moving to Hawaii would totally defeat the purpose of moving. We can QT almost as cheaply and a lot more quickly than we could travel by air from *Hawaii to Philadelphia*.© And anyway, the whole point is we want to be near our parents, right? Think about it. They could babysit for us and we could go out on dates again and stuff. We don't know *anyone* in Hawaii."

For obvious reasons, the airlines had lobbied hard since the dawn of QT to limit the new capability to extraterranian voyages. Inevitably a black market sprang up for international commuters, but by and large the airlines succeeded. While teleports were generally housed within airports, they had not yet become the endoparasites critics feared.

Dylan didn't especially like this being told what "we" wanted.

With nothing to look at but the sofa, Junior began to squirm and fuss. Dylan took him, held him aloft and tapped his head on the ceiling. In three seconds flat, he was laughing. All babies are bipolar.

"We could meet some people though," Dylan said. "There must be plenty of nice people there." He lowered the baby again and kissed his scabby belly button.

"There are nice people everywhere," Erin said.

Dylan surfaced. "Hawaii strikes me as being kind of special though. Like I imagine people there must be *extra* nice."

Erin screwed up her face. "What's gotten into you? I don't ever remember you *mentioning* Hawaii before. Now suddenly you want to *live* there?"

"I'm just thinking aloud."

"'Fantasizing' is more like it."

"That may be," he said. "That may very well be."

• • •

In the absence of Wendy's body, Dylan spent the week attempting to get intimate with her mind by reading up on Mormonism whenever he got a spare moment between classes. It was harder than he'd expected. For instance, he failed to suspend enough disbelief to accept that their central prophet and founder, Joseph Smith, an avowed treasure-seeker and scryer, had, at the behest of the angel Moroni, dug up gold plates in Western New York circa the 1820s and translated them with the help of stone-lensed spectacles. The story was weird enough that Dylan almost *wanted* to believe it, but at the very least he'd have to inspect the plates, and conveniently enough Smith claimed to have promptly returned them to the angel upon translating them. Neither did Dylan much respect Mormons' unbelievably racist founding myth. But the crazy, *beautiful* stuff—Kolob, spirit babies, the **multiverse**© and all the psychedelic rest of it—*this* stuff he could get behind, at least in the spirit of poetry. And however different Mormonism was from Catholicism, it felt good to revisit the rhetoric of people who believed, *truly* believed, in ultimate Meaning and Goodness and Love. It made him feel, for as long as he let it,

⊙ "We can come to no other conclusion, but that worlds, and systems of worlds, and universes of worlds existed in the boundless heights and depths of immensity…" - Orson Pratt, original member of the Quorum of Twelve Apostles, in a pamphlet entitled "Great First Cause," 1851.

like a kid again, swinging his legs in a pew, absorbing all those magical words spoken by the adults who knew everything there was to know and then some. It wasn't hard, in retrospect, to see why Jesus liked kids the best: *Suffer little children, and forbid them not, to come unto me: for of such is the kingdom of heaven.*

Always game for a pun, Dylan recognized how fitting it was that he should be thinking about suffering little children even as his students went about mounting their Shakespeare scenes. The grading rubric included categories for memorization, voice and articulation, believability, physical movement and blocking, and overall performance. Most students were doing C work; it was as if they were determined to prove that the bard (not to mention poetry and drama in general) was beneath them and their transhuman lives.

Daniel Young, his broken English notwithstanding, gave one of the more heartfelt performances, though it was clear he was playing as much to Dylan as to his beloved Hermia. Dylan gave him a rather generous B. On hearing this after class, Daniel hung his head and shuffled away.

· · ·

Come Sunday, Dylan was at the spaceport again. Wendy was more appropriately dressed this time: no scarf, no jacket, no boots, just an orange T-shirt, blue jeans, brown sandals, a small travel bag—and the customary toad on her head. Dylan swiped the door, reached out a hand and abducted her from the curb. "I hope you don't mind my not getting out," he said. "I thought we should spend as much time as possible out of the public eye. Gather our rosebuds while we may."

"I missed you too," she said.

As soon as her succulent buttocks hit the seat, he kissed her sheltering lips and audibly purred.

"To Ascension Forest," he ordered the driver.

"Who's at the wheel today?" Wendy asked.

"John Coltrane, for the moment. That okay by you?"

"Great. I love jazz."

"Mr. Coltrane's about to do a live rendition of *A Love Supreme* for us, I believe. Isn't that right, Johnny?"

"One of my all-time favorites," Wendy said. That was lucky.

"Cool," Coltrane said. And some invisible bassist launched right into it.

Dylan had done the first leg of the trip singing along with Ted Neeley, the original Jesus of *Jesus Christ Superstar*, at the wheel. He'd been thinking of Wendy when he made the request, but then it dawned on him that this unsubtle Messiah might cramp his style (not to mention make him think of Erin). Coltrane, however—even in this hieratic mode, his searching tenor was an aphrodisiac. By the time they arrived at the forest, Dylan's tongue had licked every exposed cell of Wendy's face, neck, and breasts. Her nipples were so hard, he was afraid he might cut his tongue.

"I hope you enjoy your time in Ascension Forest," Coltrane said.

"Oh, don't you worry about that," Dylan said. "We'll see you in a few hours." Then he swiped the door, and the two lovers hied hand-in-hand to the moss.

"You know," Dylan said. "I forgot to ask you last time about your religious reasons for keeping a toad."

"Oh, right. You'll probably find it weird, but Cane serves as a reminder for me."

"A reminder of what, may I ask?"

"I'm not sure how much you know about Mormonism..."

"A bit."

"Then you know that our religion was founded when the angel Moroni delivered God's revelation to Joseph Smith on some gold plates in upstate New York?"

"I'd heard something like that, yes."

"Well, what you don't always hear is that while Joseph was digging up the box that contained those plates, he was greeted by an enormous toad, which, depending on the account, either morphed into a man who proceeded to beat the crap out of him, or a flaming monster with glittering eyes. Either way, it's a manifestation of the angel."

Dylan squinted skeptically at Cane, who looked like a cow pie with eyes.

"And what is it you want to be reminded of exactly?" Dylan asked.

"That sometimes what seems to us like evil is really just a kind of treasure guardian. That our suffering isn't wasted, in other words. I suffered a lot while I waited for you, you know."

This answer struck him as both totally crazy and more than a little wise.

"I've had this ache in my chest all week," Dylan complained.

"I'm familiar with that ache," she said.

"On the upside," Dylan said, "I have never felt the power of poetry as deeply as I did this week, and I've been teaching pretty much the same poems for years."

"Lay one on me."

"You want to hear a poem?"

"Show me a girl who doesn't want to hear a poem from her lover and I will show you the beginning of the end of our species."

Dylan was glad to hear her call him her "lover" despite their couple of near misses so far. Moreover, it relieved him of any doubt as to which poem he would recite to her. Andrew Marvell's "To His Coy Mistress" had been coursing through his head with renewed life since he'd read it aloud in class on Tuesday. In its entirety, it was probably too direct for the occasion, too on-the-nose and almost-raunchy, so he gave her just the final, inspired stanza:

> Now therefore, while the youthful hue
> Sits on thy skin like morning dew,
> And while thy willing soul transpires
> At every pore with instant fires,
> Now let us sport us while we may,

And now, like amorous birds of prey,
Rather at once our time devour
Than languish in his slow-chapt power.
Let us roll all our strength and all
Our sweetness up into one ball,
And tear our pleasures with rough strife
Thorough the iron gates of life:
Thus, though we cannot make our sun
Stand still, yet we will make him run.

Wendy's eyes had gone all anime. "You're a romantic," she said.

"Actually," he corrected her, "Andrew Marvell is considered a metaphysical poet."

By now they had arrived at the edge of the moss, that threshold between the (relatively) ordinary world and the ecstatic one they'd be a part of in a moment. They unpeeled some tendrils and kicked off their shoes. Wendy righted one of hers and gently placed Cane in it.

Dylan made a suggestion: "What do you say we take off *all our* clothes this time?" Even if they couldn't make love like proper lovers, they could at least enjoy each other's warm-blooded bodies to some frustrating degree.

"Okay," she said.

"Really?"

"You go first."

"Much obliged."

So he began, and she proceeded to match him article for article until they were both *au naturel.* She was pretty and pink-brown and in far better shape than he was. *Ye Gods! Annihilate but space and time, and make two lovers happy.*

He held out his hand. "Ready?"

She smiled impishly and took the hand. They swung their arms, counted down from three, and leapt.

And the flora met them halfway. In a matter of seconds, Wendy lay supine on the moss bed, squirming and delirious, and Dylan watched as the forest insinuated itself into each of her available orifices. No one had ever accused Ascension Forest of subtlety.

Dylan, for his part, had fallen to his knees and the vines were having their way with him too. A couple of tendrils had crept around his waist from the back and were massaging his scrotum; another had wrapped around his penis and tightened like a spring; yet another was shimmying, not ungently, up his asshole.

All of which was pleasant enough, though it was frustrating too. He and Erin used to let these plants simply *complement* their lovemaking; the idea that he and his inamorata were going to fuck the forest but not *each other* was rather hard for his machismo to digest.

By now Wendy had done a little crunch, grabbed hold of the liverwort nearest her clit and begun giving it some tutoring. Evidently this lusty superorganism of a forest wasn't quite making the grade, and if that wasn't Dylan's cue for an intervention, then nothing would ever be.

He walked on his knees until his shadow consumed her. "Allow *me*," he said, and he began to peel away all the relevant vines.

She grabbed his shoulder and gave it a shove. "Dylan, please. We've discussed this. Just watch."

He backed off and did her bidding, watching, merely watching, as the vines re-insinuated themselves and her smile distorted, her eyes narrowed, her breath quickened. He watched her, yes, but he also watched *her* watching *him*, and he watched *her* watching *him* watching *her*, and the feedback loop grew so impossibly complex so fast that it was difficult to feel they were in any meaningful sense separate enti-ties anymore. *The object and yourself must become one, and from that feeling of oneness issues your poetry.*

So he approached her again and finished the job of peeling away the vines.

She cocked her head, his coy mistress: "No, Dylan."

But some force of nature was pulling him toward her, *into* her, and resisting it did not seem to be an option.

He drank the sweat from her neck.

"Dylan, *don't.*"

This force was every bit as fundamental as gravity or electromag-netism. Maybe it was love, or poetry, or just the procreative instinct. In any case, he was powerless to fight it. He grabbed each of Wendy's slick, sinewy thighs and pulled her body toward his...and then all at once her eyes turned to ice and his gaze slipped off.

"Coy" was too generous a word. His mistress was *frigid.*

He put down her legs and backed away. He was eager, yes, but he was not a rapist, and he didn't seem to have any choice about that either. Maybe if he'd been abused as a kid or something, he could do it, but he hadn't, and he couldn't.

"How can you possibly be serious?" he complained. "Do you really expect me to just jerk off again? After all we've been through?"

She leered, but not in the sexy way.

"I mean I get your whacko religion and all," he continued, "but do you really think God's going to split hairs like this? Aren't we basically guilty already? You're the one who said 'All or nothing at all.'"

"I never said that."

"Didn't you?"

"That was Sinatra."

"A technicality."

"I suppose you're Andrew Marvell then?"

"You better believe I am. I'll tear 'thorough the iron gates of life' the second you give me the go-ahead."

She shut her eyes. He shook his head and swatted at some nettlesome moss.

When she opened her eyes, it was clear she'd found something back there behind her lids. "Dylan?"

"Wendy?"

"Are you John Coltrane too?"

"Sure."

"I mean, do you understand now that what we have here truly is a love supreme?"

"I think I do, yes."

"So if I give you the most precious gift I have to give, will you make me a promise?"

"Anything."

"I mean it. An honest-to-God covenant."

"I mean it too. Anything."

She took a deep breath. "All right then. I want you to leave your family for me. If you promise me you'll leave them, I will let you do anything you want with me for all eternity."

And there it was, as naked as their bodies.

He couldn't act surprised exactly. This had to arise sooner or later; she'd already declared him her future husband after all. But still, how conniving! Had this been her plan all along? To get him all hot and bothered and then either blackmail or blueball him? To turn this bed of moss into a bargaining table? How reprehensible! But also: how sexy! It had been a long time since anyone had made him feel so desirable.

Clearly he needed to cool off, to walk away, to clear the pipes himself and then consider all that had transpired in the cool light of reason.

But then wasn't that the mistake he'd always made? Hadn't he decided just last week that reason was overrated? That, in the end, a cool light didn't make for much of a guiding one? Wasn't *passion* the thing so sorely missing from his life? And wasn't that precisely what was on offer here?

These, then, from his current—naked, throbbing—vantage point, were his options: either he could embrace: a) reason, predictability, and death, or b) passion, adventure, and life. An fMRI, of course, would show that his neurons had made this monumental decision seconds, if not minutes, ago. The take-home lesson of brain science was simply to relax; which was not to say you were free to do so if it wasn't in the cards, but for Dylan in this moment, it *did* seem to be in the cards. "Okay," he said.

Wendy went all lips and teeth and lips. He scooted forward, placed her dirty feet on his shoulders and fit the head of his cock to her nether lips, which, truth in advertising, were about as thick as her mouth ones. She held him at bay by a single shoulder.

"You promise?"

"Cross my heart and hope to die," he said.

"Then come on in," she said, letting go of the shoulder, and he plunged toward the celestial heaven inside of her and for a split second all was Meaning and Goodness and Love...

But then that split second passed and Dylan understood that sex with Wendy wasn't going to be anything very special after all. What's more, she was going to bleed all over his penis, which, as far as he was concerned, was more turn-*off* than -on.

How was it that he kept falling into this trap of believing that sex might confer some sort of immortality on him? That the impassioned movement of bodies in space might have some bearing on their movement in time? Granted, Einstein, relativity, etc., but that didn't seem to be what he meant; he seemed to mean something more along the lines of magic.

Not that he wasn't enjoying this—it was *nice*—but it was all just a matter of so many nerve endings and the release of pent-up urges, and it was as clear as bankruptcy that he would no more find magic in *this* than he would in, say, urination.

Anyway, he pulled out and came in her mouth. She swallowed.

In the smoldering afterglow, Dylan lay on his back, legs crossed at the ankles, staring up at the boughs of the sentient trees while the moss massaged him toward what might have been sleep were he not so wound up. Wendy's heavy head lay on his chest and he stroked her sweaty hair.

"I'm so happy," she said.

She did seem to be.

"I waited so long," she said.

She had.

"My celestial husband! My love supreme!"

Good God, what had he agreed to? If he'd had a laser-juicer handy, he'd have taken it to his nutsack then and there.

She glanced up at him and smiled wide, her lips huge and dark and forever.

"Let's sleep awhile," she suggested.

"I'll need to go soon."

"Why?"

"Erin will be expecting me."

"Forget about Erin. You're mine now."

"Still, I'll need a little time to work things out."

"How *much* time?"

"I don't know. Weeks. I have a certain responsibility. I don't want my family to be hurt unnecessarily."

"Why not? It's not as if you love them."

Dylan quit the perfunctory stroking and propped himself up on his elbows. "Why would you say such a thing?"

"You don't even kiss Junior good night."

"I do too."

"Okay, well not *every* night."

"And how would you know that?"

"I spied on you," she said matter-of-factly.

"You *what*?" He yanked his legs out from under her.

"Remember last week when you dropped me at the teleport?"

"Of course."

"Well I decided I wasn't quite ready to go yet, so I hailed the androcab directly behind yours and had it follow you."

"You came to my *house*?" His jaw hung slack.

"It was surprisingly easy really. Isn't there *any* crime on this planet? Because you've got such a nice house and no security to speak of besides your fancy doors which you don't even lock. I started out just peering in windows, but then while Erin was in the shower scrubbing her stretch marks and the kids were playing with Legos in the basement, I came in through the laundry door and crawled under the master bed. Do you know that you and Erin didn't exchange a *single* word before going to sleep that night? Not a single word! That's when I knew for certain I wasn't crazy: Your marriage is a four-dimensional tomb. You *need* me."

"You shouldn't have done that," Dylan said. It was all he could think to say.

"Really?" Wendy said. "Because I think you're actually pretty impressed. We both know Erin would never do such a thing. I love you more than she ever has. I have been obsessed with you since I was a little girl, and I think that, despite yourself, you rather like that, no?"

"All the same," Dylan said, "You shouldn't have done that."

"So you keep saying."

Dylan began pacing, processing. As maddening as anything she was saying was the nonchalance with which she was saying it.

"Do you know who I had my cabby be?" she asked.

"Who?"

"Sting. Ask me why."

"Why?"

She began to sing. It was weird.

> *Every breath you take*
> *Every move you make*
> *Every bond you break*
> *Every step you take*
> *I'll be watching you*

It had to be admitted, though, that, weirdness notwithstanding, she was quite a good singer, with an impeccable sense of melody and an odd Celtic inflection.

> *O can't you see*
> *You belong to me*
> *How my poor heart aches*
> *With every step you take*

"You know that song?" she asked.

"Of course."

"Well, lots of people think it's a love song—they play it at weddings and such—and then they're shocked when they learn it's about a stalker. But I've always found that to be a false dichotomy, don't you think? If you really love somebody, why *wouldn't* you obsess over them?"

"I'm leaving now," Dylan said. "I'll need to think over everything that's happened here." He got up, peeled off some creepers and began putting his clothes back on.

Wendy stood too. "Don't you even *think* about backing out on me, Dylan Greenyears."

"Are you joking? Of course I'm going to think about backing out on you."

"But you promised before God."

"I didn't exactly have all the information then, did I?"

"We *never* have all the information, Dylan. Only God has all the information."

"Omni's pretty close," Dylan said, setting off toward the cab.

"I gave you my most precious gift!" Wendy cried after him.

A dagger manifested in his throat. He foisted it: "I've had better." He didn't even turn around to face her.

"I forgive you," she said. "I know that wasn't you speaking just now."

Damn it! Now he'd really have to turn around. "Who was it, pray tell?"

"The Adversary."

"The *what?*

Her face was as red as his bloodstained penis now. "Lucifer. Satan. The Devil. Sometimes he goes in the guise of Reason, but make no mistake, it's the Adversary! *Out*, Adversary!"

Then she did something exceedingly strange: she tore at her breasts, really *tore* at them with her fingernails, so that soon she had drawn blood from her sharp nipples and was smearing it across her ribs.

"Stop that!" Dylan said, returning to her side. "Will you just calm down please?"

She didn't.

He did his best to console her: "I'm confused, okay? I need to think."

"But that's just it," she shrieked. "You think *too much*. Obey your heart as I obey mine and the rest will take care of itself. Fuck Erin. Erin is dead to you now."

"Yeah, but see, Erin is *not* dead to me now. We're not exactly seeing eye to eye on that yet." He reached out a hand. "I'm going. Join me if you want a ride."

She collapsed into the fetal position on the ground and began to weep, silently at first and then resoundingly. Dylan crouched and patted her head. After many minutes, she regained whatever sanity she had left and looked up at him with a runny nose and twinkling eyes. "You're even cuter when you're angry," she said.

He didn't want to smile at that, he really didn't, but it had been a very long time since anyone had called him cute. *Shit.*

When they arrived at the teleport, he insisted on accompanying her as far as he was allowed. They did the secret handshake at the security gate and said goodbye. "I love you," she said.

"I love you too," he said—and he did, in some way or other. "But I'm confused. I need to think. And for the record, if I see you anywhere near my house, I will have you promptly arrested."

"The Adversary—" she began.

"Put it this way. I need to have a good long sit-down with the Adversary."

"Don't underestimate his powers," she warned.

"I'll bear that in mind," he said. "Now go. I'll be in touch in a few days. In the meantime, I'd appreciate it if you'd leave me alone."

She pouted.

"Go!" he shouted, shooing her.

She plodded backward through the gate, sulking the whole way, until finally—thank heaven—he was rid of her.

• • •

Dylan thought about nothing else for three straight days. He'd always known that Wendy was a little eccentric in her beliefs, and a little mad in an impulsive, suck-the-marrow-out-of-life kind of way, but he had not realized how completely batshit *insane* she was until he'd seen her tearing at her breasts like that.

That's what you get for stalking your old stalkers, he supposed.

Once he got over the initial disappointment, though, his newfound knowledge that Wendy was essentially unmarriageable actually proved something of a relief. Because what it meant, in effect, was that he was going to stay married to Erin. And while his marriage might occasionally *feel* like a failure, it would not be one in the technical sense. Even in a scenario where both partners ended up being happier after a divorce, the fact remained that they had set out to do one thing and then, faced with hardship, given up and done another, which was precisely the narrative traced by anything one might call a failure. Dylan knew a thing or two about that, and he did not desire to know any more. If he was going to go down with a ship, he was determined that it be this one.

Once at a hotel in Zurich, where he'd been hired to star in a credit card commercial, an old snaggletoothed concierge had insisted on reading Dylan's palm. "You were born under a great star," he told Dylan. "You will accomplish many wonderful things. Fear death by hubris." Then he'd shown Dylan his lifeline, beginning at the base of his thumb and swooping toward the edge of his palm. Evidently the length and depth of Dylan's line meant that he would enjoy a longer-than-average lifespan, but one couldn't help but notice a small break in the line mid-swoop on his right hand, and at precisely the same point on his left hand, a bisected freckle.

"What does it mean?" Dylan had asked.

"It means you will experience a rupture midway through life's journey."

"A rupture? Are we talking literal or symbolic here?"

"Unfortunately," the old man told him, "palms don't give such details. But if you're interested, I can recommend a marvelous astrologer here in Zurich."

Dylan wasn't interested, not really. He was merely humoring the old man and didn't believe in any of it for even a second. Still, some uneducable, superstitious part of him had lived in vague fear and anticipation ever since—all the more reason he was relieved not to have crossed the Rubicon where his marriage was concerned. He'd have to keep an eye on his palm; maybe lines could repair themselves, freckles migrate.

Staying married to Erin, of course, also meant that his kids would continue to have a dad. And Wendy could not have been more wrong about his feelings toward them. Granted he'd hesitated, on ethical grounds, before agreeing to bring Junior into being—there was no denying that—but he loved his kids down to their protoplasm, and now that he was beginning to see things clearly again, he was determined that they know it. After work, he curled up with Arthur and

Tavi on the sofa and read to them from *The Little Prince* and *Where The Wild Things Are*. He began to recognize flickers of intelligence in Junior too, who was something like a small person now and not merely a person-to-be. Dylan liked to cradle him and inhale his clean pink scalp. And when Erin wasn't looking, he liked to toss the kid in the air, just a few inches—*and* catch him, of course—and this was just what he was doing on Tuesday evening when the kid cracked his first smile. "Did you see that!" Dylan said.

"What?" asked Erin.

"Junior just smiled at me."

"It's way too early for that," she protested.

Dylan chucked the kid up again—

"Dylan!"

—and caught him. Did she really think he was going to let his own baby come to harm?

"Here he goes again," Dylan said. "Trust your senses."

And yes, here he went again, all bulbous cheeks and shiny gums. "See."

Erin practically fainted with joy. She cooed more than the baby did. "Throw him again!" she begged.

Arthur and Tavi saw it too and laughed and patted Junior's head, and this Christmassy warmth suffused the family then, this eggnog feeling, and for the first time in quite a while, Dylan looked at what he'd made and knew it was good.

And so on Wednesday evening, after three days of careful reflection and baby-tossing, while Erin took her shower, Dylan omni'd Wendy:

Dearest Wendy,

I want you to know that after a three-day dive inside my mind, I have surfaced with a difficult, if unavoidable, truth. To be sure, this is not an easy message for me to write, and already I find myself struggling to do it with some measure of grace.

First, let me acknowledge that the passion I have felt for you over recent weeks has been quite unlike anything I have ever experienced. Before meeting you, I was all hollow and dark inside, but you rekindled the light at my core and it radiates out to my very fingertips even as I write this message. My entire organism thanks you.

And please know this too, Wendy: You are beautiful, exquisitely, translucently so, and nothing in this message should tempt you to think otherwise.

Of course, you are also highly intelligent, and as such you have no doubt been anticipating the impending drop of another shoe since the first sentence of this message, if not before. I wish there were a gentler way of saying this, but surely you have earned the respect of my honesty: in short, darling, despite the ardent feelings you have aroused in me, I am simply not made of the sort of stuff that would permit me to abandon my family for you. I regret that I mis-modeled possible futures in the heat of our mutual passion, and I can only hope that you will trust me when I say that my deception was rooted not in malice but in ignorance. I did not know myself on Sunday even as well as I do today; I was, in a way, as deceived by my feelings as you were.

The passions after all are fickle, and experience teaches us that they are hardly the right kind of soil for the germination of healthy decisions. You might ask, then, acknowledging my lack of belief in any theistic skyhook, what I take to be the foundation of my marriage if not feeling? It's a question I've thought about quite a lot these past few days, a very good question, and one whose answer is itself rooted in feeling and so not easily translatable, though I shall try: Marriage, for me, is a stay against chaos. It is the still point of the widening gyre, the center that must hold lest all semblance of human meaning be lost. It is a poem I recite before the void, the bulwark I erect against total, all-pervading nothingness. It is a tragic project, to be sure, doomed from the start, absurd, but it is nonetheless as central to my life as anything I will ever do, if for no other reason than that I will have done it. Had we met at a different juncture in spacetime, Wendy, you and I might have made this insane leap together, just as we leapt into the moss a short time ago. But for better or worse, it was not to be, and neither you nor I are any more to blame for that than a couple of hydrogen

atoms can be blamed for ending up in
separate water molecules.

I imagine that all of this may sound quite
alien to you, and I wonder if you might not
better appreciate my feelings about marriage
in the context of your feelings about
religion, which I assure you are every bit
as alien to me. I intend no criticism, mind
you. You are entitled to believe in Jesus,
Kolob, the Adversary and all that. They are
your precious absurdities, as my marriage is
mine, and given that, don't you owe it to
yourself to find someone who can buy into
them with you? Whatever you might have seen
in your visions, I assure you that person
can never be me.

Some things, Wendy, are not meant to last
forever. I met you at a time in my life
when I needed a touch of magic. You gave me
that, and words, wonderful though they be,
cannot possibly communicate the extent of my
gratitude. I do not regret any of it and I
hope that you won't either; indeed,
I find the memory of our time together
already sweetened by the knowledge of its
evanescence. We, too, were a kind of poem
against the void, Wendy. Please know that I
wish you the best in this life and beyond.

I will remember you always.

Aloha,
Dylan Greenyears

There. He'd done it, the difficult thing.

He stared at his omni, the pitch in his ears modulating around the thudding in his chest. How would she take it? What would she say? Any second now he'd know.

But then the seconds swelled into minutes, dozens of them, and he still didn't know. He got up and left the room and tried to go about the rest of his day without obsessing over her imminent response, which, second by second, was turning out not to be so imminent after all. An hour passed, and then a Terran day, a New Taiwanese day, and by and by Dylan was forced to conclude that this radio silence must be Wendy's way of expressing her fury at being scorned. He was not without compassion, naturally, but in a way her passive-aggressiveness actually made the whole disentanglement that much easier on him.

And besides, she was bound to learn something from the ordeal, was she not? He had certainly learned something; contemplating the existential meaning of his marriage and forcing his conclusions through the sieve of language had proven a hugely clarifying exercise. No doubt she'd be about the business of clarifying something equally important in her own life. Struggle is good for us after all: isn't that what literature teaches? Okay, *some* literature? Okay, just comedies (but there were a lot of those)?

So that was it then. This dark chapter of his life, this midlife crisis or whatever it had been, was over. He'd indulged his nostalgia and sown some latent oats and he would content himself now to leave the past in the past and youth to the young. Going forward, he would be a family man, rich in meaning if not always happiness, appreciative of all he had, with a job he didn't hate and chronic ringing in his ears—nothing, in short, that he could not bear. He might even find some joy in it.

PART THREE

STARFUCKER

Class was a good two minutes over and Daniel Young was still shuffling his feet by Dylan's desk. He had never done that before.

"What can I do you for, Daniel?"

"I was wondering if there was any chance I might be able to redo my Shakespeare scene?"

"And why would you want to subject yourself to such a thing?"

"Because I got a B."

"It's about the grade, is it? Well I wouldn't let that bother you too much, Daniel. Your writing has been stellar so far, and you'll still have two papers due before the end of the semester. Why not turn your attention to them?"

Dylan began gathering up his things—he had a bullshit meeting to attend—but Daniel didn't seem satisfied yet, and since turning over a new leaf the day before, Dylan was determined to be a more compassionate teacher.

"Is something the matter, Daniel?"

"Actually, yes," Daniel said. He blinked hard, like he was praying or summoning strength. "Do you remember when you asked me if I'd ever been in love?"

"Vaguely," Dylan replied.

"You insinuated that I couldn't possibly have been."

"'Insinuated': good word. My unconscious just gave you a bonus point."

"Do you remember?"

"Look, I'm sorry if I offended you, Daniel. I was making a point is all. Rest assured, most kids your age haven't been in love yet. It's perfectly normal."

"But I *have* been in love," Daniel said. "I *am* in love."

Now this was a genuine surprise. "That's wonderful, Daniel. I'm happy for you. I myself didn't fall in love until I was a couple of years—"

"With a native."

"I see." Daniel was turning out to be far more interesting than Dylan had ever given him credit for. "Male or female, may I ask?"

"Does it matter?"

"I suppose not. Though either way I can't help but wonder what your parents think."

"That's just it. I can't tell them. My father would be repulsed if he knew. He might even kill me. He insists that I'm to marry a Korean Earthling female someday, but the problem is I'm not attracted to Korean Earthling females. I'm attracted to Kwizok."

"Nice name." New Taiwanese names were all unisex, so Daniel hadn't inadvertently given anything away.

"The nicest."

"And how did you meet this Kwizok?"

"Kwizok is my next-door neighbor. We've grown up together. We're less than a month apart in age."

"I see. And has Kwizok told his or her parents?"

"No, Kwizok's situation is exactly the same as mine. Kwizok's parents are ultra-conservative. Kwizok's mom even chairs the Committee on the Prevention of Alien Diseases."

"But Kwizok himself or herself knows how you feel?"

"Oh, it's absolutely mutual. We're in love. We're going to get married someday. We already are in every way that counts. We've been having sex in the crawlspace beneath my house since summer."

"I see. You're using some sort of protection, I hope?"

"I don't feel comfortable answering that."

"Okay, then would you remind me what all this has to do with English class?"

"I was afraid."

"I need more."

"You taught us all about Stanislavski, Lee Strasberg, and The Method, and when I was practicing my scene at home, I thought of Kwizok and I know my acting was great, Mr. Green—I *know* it was. I even started thinking maybe I really could be an actor someday. Maybe this was my destiny. But then the other day when I was acting here, I got nervous. I saw all my classmates out there and how they weren't taking the assignment seriously and I just wimped out. I got through the whole scene without thinking about Kwizok even once. I was just saying the words. I let my fear crowd out my love and I totally failed you, to say nothing of Kwizok."

"This is *not* just about the grade then?"

"I think it's about regret, Mr. Green. I'm not ready to have one this big."

"I know a thing or two about that," Dylan said.

"Really?"

"Trust me."

"But your life seems so…perfect."

Ha! Dylan liked to believe that training students in the close reading of texts ultimately translated into their learning to read the extra-textual world as well—so much for that.

"Thanks for saying so, Daniel. I assure you we've all got our quota of suffering to fill, but it's nice to hear I don't always wear mine on my sleeve."

Daniel twitched. He was reverting to his usual, anxious self.

"So about your scene," Dylan continued. "I can't change your grade. If I gave you the opportunity to do that, I'd have to offer it to everyone in the class and we haven't got time for that. I can, however, give you the opportunity to redeem yourself to yourself if you like."

Dylan bent down, took a book from the shelf and handed it to Daniel. It was entitled *The Ages of Man*. A wizened English teacher had given it to him as a high school graduation gift however-many ages ago that was.

"Instead of redoing the scene you already did, Daniel, why don't you flip through this book and find a monologue that suits you? That way you won't need to rely on other actors. You can perform it for the class whenever you're ready."

Daniel paged through the book as if it were in Shakespeare's own hand. "Thank you so much, Mr. Green. I promise to make you proud."

"Again, don't worry about me, Daniel. Do it for yourself."

Daniel mouth-smiled.

"And for Kwizok, of course," Dylan added.

And now Daniel smiled with his whole being. It was good, sometimes, this being a teacher.

They walked out of the room together.

"Be safe," Dylan said.

"Thank you so much for your time, Mr. Green," Daniel said. As if time were ever anyone's.

Daniel took off down the hall. Dylan was going that way too, but slower. He still had half a bullshit meeting to attend.

• • •

And then one Sunday, right on schedule, Dylan turned forty. It was no big deal, a Sunday like any other, if a touch more pleasant by design. He played in the yard with the kids, ate some instant *zalcax*© for lunch, and took a nap. At dusk, he went for his first jog in years and had the good sense to keep it short. Then for dinner, as promised, Erin made ravioli, his favorite, with real olive oil and real garlic. It wasn't as good as his mother's, of course, but it was the same recipe and pretty darned close. For dessert, they had a simple chocolate cake that the kids had helped bake. They dimmed the lights and sang to him. He silently wished for peace, both inner and outer, and let

New Taiwanese dish consisting of native roots and tubers fried in the bittersweet sap of the Elel tree. (Despite its exotic sound, "Elel" was in fact an abbreviation of Lewandosky and Lutz, the physicians who first documented *Epidermodysplasia verruciformis*, a rare autosomal recessive genetic disease of Earth that sometimes resulted in humans closely resembling trees. The story goes that Joe Snodgras, general physician for the First Expedition, remarked upon seeing his first of these trees that it looked less like a tree than like a man who looked like a tree. Joe took to calling the tree the "Lewandowsky-Lutz tree," which other members of the expedition soon shortened to "LL," and which then morphed over time into "Elel." Most English speakers subsequent to the First Expedition mistakenly assumed that "Elel" was the native word for the tree; in actual fact, the native word for the tree was the simpler, if not dissimilar, *lal*.)

the kids help him blow the candles out. To be sure, it took a while, and the cake was now iced in spit, but he ate it anyway, and went back for seconds.

Then Thursday, after work, he went to his GP for a check-up. He was at the start of a new decade and his psyche was purged; a clean bill of health would round out his rebirth.

Fortunately, the fiber-optics-in-the-anus colonoscopy had gone the way of trepanation and the medical leech. These days x-rays and lasers were powerful enough to image you down to the individual quark—you didn't even have to take your clothes off—so the forty-year-old check-up was no longer the rite of passage it had once been.

The whole thing took five minutes. The verdict: healthy on all counts, with the sole exception of his tinnitus, which rang on unabated. Omni's opinion? "TBD." But the ringing no longer bothered Dylan so much. He had yet to schedule another appointment with Fudge, and he was beginning to think he might not. If silence was determined to sound like the whirring of United Planets Cruiser C57-D in *Forbidden Planet*, then so be it. The consistency was almost comforting if he let it be: one more precious absurdity to cling to, one more tightrope over the void.

Just thinking of Fudge, however, reminded Dylan of his unfinished business with Mei-Ling Chen/Jade Astrophil, not to mention the corrupt Omniverse, and it dawned on him that he would not be able to enter fully into this next phase of his life, this new *age*, until he'd tied up the threads of the last one. Would he were the taskmaster of his own brain and not the other way around.

And so, that very evening, after the rest of his family had gone to bed, he picked up the trail where he'd left off—namely, Good Samaritan Hospital in Los Angeles.

. . .

Jade Astrophil had been discharged from Good Samaritan twice in the past year. Omni would no longer confirm this for him, but he'd seen it with his own eyes, and it was the only lead he had to go on. Now all he had to do was somehow gain access to her medical records. Alas, this was no small "somehow." He knew nothing about how to hack into such information; from what he understood, that had become all but impossible nowadays anyway. His best bet might be to hire someone to impersonate her, but it was not enough for the impersonator to resemble her and know some basic facts about her life. Even on Earth, no hospital was going to grant access to medical records without first scanning the inquirer's genome. Moreover, the body site sampled was typically random by design. He didn't have a DNA sample anyway. He could find some saliva on her letter perhaps, but even then, what was he going to do? Clone her and wait a couple of decades for the clone to grow up? There had to be a more efficient way.

There *was* one obvious way, of course: he could simply report to Earth Government on what had happened and let *them* track her down, but he saw two problems with this approach: 1) they might not believe him, and he had nothing in the way of evidence to corroborate his story; and 2) even if they did believe him, it would very likely be because they were in cahoots with whatever shadowy authority had conspired to erase Mei-Ling/Jade from existence in the first place. The risks clearly outweighed the benefits.

Plan B, then, might involve—very lightly—greasing some palms. He didn't personally know anyone who worked at Good Samaritan Hospital, but having been based out of LA for a couple of years, he did know quite a few people in that city. Maybe one of them would have an inside connection? Certainly one of them would know someone who knew someone. But as soon as he began to flip through his mental rolo-dex of LA contacts, he realized he couldn't actually get in touch with any of them since all were connected up in some way with Hollywood and/or the life he'd sworn off years ago—and Wendy Sorenson had already given him a scarifying object lesson in the dangers of revisiting the past.

He did, however, have one contact whose friendship ought to transcend Hollywood insofar as it preceded it.

• • •

Chad had never really forgiven Dylan for his success. After Dylan eventually told him about his meeting with Terry Gilliam at Xando, he had seemed to share in the excitement, but with each of Dylan's subse-quent triumphs—as he auditioned and made it to call-backs, as he got the part and put school on hiatus, as *E.T. II* came out to rave reviews—Chad's responses grew cooler; and after Dylan's Oscar nomination for best male lead, Chad didn't even bother to call.

To be sure, Chad had been doing fine in his own right, earning academic credits and starring in the Temple University productions. Dylan even flew in from LA once just to see him play the professor in Ionesco's *The Lesson*. He was brilliant, but when Dylan told him as much at the South Street Diner after the show, Chad just rolled his eyes and said, "Whatever."

"No, I'm serious," Dylan assured him. "You made some really bold choices up there. Like that voice-cracking thing. I'm not sure I'd have had the guts. In front of a live audience, no less. But it really worked. You seemed totally unhinged in just the right way. I hope you realize I have every intention of connecting you up with the right people as soon as I gain a little more clout in the industry."

"Do you have any idea how patronizing that sounds?" Chad said.

"Sorry, dude, but if I've learned anything in my brief time in Hollywood, it's that connections are paramount. No pun intended."

"I don't believe that," Chad said. "If you're good enough, people will eventually sit up and take notice."

"Isn't it pretty to think so?"

"It worked for you."

"I got extremely lucky is all, Chad. I had the face Gilliam was looking for. No amount of training will ever give you the face a director is looking for."

"Oh, come on," Chad said. "Give yourself some credit. You're talented as shit. You were going to make it no matter what."

"You've clearly got more faith in the system than I do," Dylan said. Some part of him was still in denial about his success; he would learn to enjoy it for a total of about five minutes before it went away for good.

"I guess I do. And I'll get there too someday. On my *own* merits, thank you very much."

"I wish you the best of luck, of course," Dylan said, "But don't be shy if I can ever do anything for you."

Neither of them had any idea that by the time Chad graduated from Temple, moved to Hollywood, and began auditioning, Dylan would be light years away and in no position to do anyone any favors. Nor did they have any idea that this would be the last time they'd meet in the flesh for many years to come.

After Dylan's fall from grace, Chad was one of just a handful of Terrans Dylan entrusted with knowing where he was. They kept in touch via omni, if only occasionally. It wasn't lost on Dylan that Chad took a certain gloating pleasure in consoling him on his tragedy, but at that point Dylan was willing to take any consolation he could get.

And then Chad proceeded to fall in his own right. For close on six years he made a go of things, auditioning four or five times a week for TV and film. He landed bit parts here and there, and did some commercials to help pay the bills—most of which were paid by bussing tables at a sushi restaurant—but like so many before him, he burned out before ever really breaking through.

"I'm sick of the poverty and the humiliation," he wrote Dylan. "I could live with one or the other, but not both. Damn it, D, I really thought acting was what I was put on this Earth to do. I really believed that. I was here to *move* people. But I guess there's no God after all, is there? That was just some well-meaning horseshit we were on the receiving end of for twelve formative years? Anyway, I'm thinking about going to law school while there's still time. At the very least, it'd make my father proud, and that's a hell of a lot more than I'm doing now."

And, impossibly enough, that was just what Chad went on to do. He studied entertainment law at UCLA, passed the California bar exam, and went to work for a large agency. A few years later, he split off and started his own practice, taking several high-profile clients with him.

By the standards of the normal, wage-earning American, Chad would have to be accounted a huge success, but from Dylan's vantage point, it was clear just how disappointed he must be inside, how his dreams had been so thoroughly ground into fish meal. Chad had always been the more idealistic of the two, and now he had become, of all things, *a lawyer!*

Is it the case that big dreams in youth inevitably result in big disappointments later on? Perhaps not for the select few, but neither Chad nor Dylan had made that final cut. Darwinism was alive and well on Earth, and the human will alone, however heroic, was no match for the teeth and nails of global capitalism. Each of them had learned this lesson the hard way, and each in his own time, and now fate was pulling their paths into alignment again. And that would have been true even if Dylan *didn't* suddenly require a trustworthy contact in Hollywood.

Chad Powell Esquire—

Word up, dude. I hope the world of litigation is treating you well. Things on NT are fine. Erin and I just had our third kid, a boy. It's weird to think you haven't met any of them yet. As always, the invitation's open if you fancy a trip up here. I know you're not real fond of traveling, but I assure you QT is no big deal as long as you don't let yourself get all philosophical about it. Anyway, I need to talk to you about something and I'd prefer to do it in person. Are you free anytime soon? I'll be happy to come to where you are.

Peace,
Dylar©

Dylar" had become one of Dylan's nicknames during their first few weeks at Temple together, when they'd read Don DeLillo's *White Noise* in their freshman lit survey. In that novel, Dylar is the name given to a drug that helps to assuage the fear of death.

When he'd begun writing that message, Dylan had not planned on inviting himself to LA, but as he finished with pleasantries and got into the meat of his message, it occurred to him that by communicating via omni about possible censorship taking place by Omni, he might be jeopardizing his security. And Omni, alas, was the only game in town. If he wanted to communicate more discreetly, he would have to do it face-to-face, and quietly at that.

Chad replied almost instantaneously:

```
Hey dude,

Yeah, come on down whenever suits you. I
make my own schedule these days. It'll be
good to see you in the flesh after all
these years.

—Chad
```

Dylan didn't dally. He was upfront with Erin about where he was going, and almost about why—he told her Chad had requested his help in the discovery phase of a class-action suit that somehow involved him—and while she didn't completely understand, obviously, she didn't press the issue. "You're a grown-up—you can do what you like," she said.

"You'll be okay without me?"

"Dylan, I'm pretty sure we'll all be better off when you confront your old demons once and for all. Go to LA. Enjoy yourself. Give my love to Runyon Canyon."

It was only once she's said it that he realized confronting his old demons was precisely what he'd have to do. After the *Titanic* fiasco, he had sworn never to return to Earth, let alone to Hollywood, that double-crossing den of iniquity, and yet that promise (like all promises?) had turned into a kind of shackles. In the immortal words of Lao Tzu, "The hard and strong will fall / The soft and weak will overcome."

So QT'ing to LA that same Saturday was already a kind of victory, even if nothing should come of it.

He met Chad at his office downtown. Dylan expected gray hair, crow's-feet, a grotesque gut, *some* outward sign of all the beatings Chad's ego had taken over the years, but really he looked much the same as Dylan remembered him. It was true he'd bulked up a bit since college, but he'd always been sort of on the gawky side anyway.

They hugged, *really* hugged, with no macho posturing, no forearm barriers or thumps on the back, and then they proceeded to the Mexican joint around the corner. Dylan hadn't had Mexican food in twenty years. It was one of a handful of Earthling pleasures he missed.

They made some small talk over nachos and margaritas, but not a whole lot. They both knew being forced to talk about their lives, such as they were, would be exquisite torture. By now they were supposed to be at the height of their glorious careers, collaborating on projects, high-fiving from opposite ends of a supermodel, that sort of thing. Instead, they were just these husks, clinging to life for no other reason than that dying might hurt. Despite Dylan's determination that his self-indulgent period be a part of his past and not his future, it was hard work overwriting the dominant narrative of one's life, and a couple of margaritas was more than enough to temporarily undo much of the progress he'd made in that direction. Fortunately, Chad had the good sense to preempt any elegizing by asking his old friend what the hell had brought him to LA.

Dylan's sense of purpose was instantly rekindled; there were more important things than his damaged ego after all. "I think I'm onto something big," he said. "I don't understand it, mind you, but I'm onto it."

"How do you mean, 'big'?"

He looked around cautiously. There were no obvious interlopers, but still he spoke just a hair above the level of his tinnitus: "It's about Omni. I think something funny's going on, something...corrupt."

"Interesting," Chad said. "In theory Omni is incorruptible."

"In theory lots of things," said Dylan. And he proceeded to tell Chad everything he knew about Mei-Ling Chen and Jade Astrophil and those phantom documents from Good Samaritan Hospital.

"Sure, I know that hospital. I don't know anyone who works there, but I could ask around."

"Great," Dylan said. "But understand that you've got to be really discreet about it. We have no idea how deep this thing goes. We can't be sure that anyone is trustworthy."

"How can you be sure that I am?"

"It's a calculated risk. And you've got to understand too that there's basically nothing I can do from New Taiwan to help you. So what I'm hoping is that you'll take enough of an interest in this to follow the trail on your own, at least for now. I'm passing the baton. For all we know, an innocent girl's life might hang in the balance. Does this sound like something you could do?"

"Don't sweat it, man. I can ask around. No guarantees, of course, but I'll be glad to do what I can."

The lack of passion in Chad's voice was worrying.

"Realize, dude, that this could be the most important thing we ever do with our lives. It could be the collaboration we were actually born for."

"I get it, man. I'm on it. Don't worry."

"And remember, we can't explicitly communicate about this via omni, so I'll have to come down again if you find out anything. If we must refer to our missing person in a communiqué, let's use a code name."

"Sure."

"Any preference?"

"'André the Giant'?"

"That'll work."

They ate the rest of their lunch in courteous silence since anything they could possibly talk about was sure to dredge up regret in its negative spaces. The silence did nothing to undermine the love, of course; if anything, it reinforced it.

They hugged again at the Metro station.

"I miss you, man," Chad said.

"Fucking A," Dylan said. And then he made his way to the teleport to get copied and destroyed again.

. . .

A week later, Dylan was rocking the baby on his knee, simulating one of those up-and-down horsey rides that used to be outside the ACME when he was a kid, when Chad omni'd him:

```
Dylan,

I've finally managed to track down André the
Giant. You're not going to fucking believe
this. Come on down.
```

So Dylan took a personal day and was back in LA for an encore lunch at the Mexican place. This time Chad was as shifty-eyed and whispery as Dylan himself.

"You've got some new intelligence?" Dylan asked.

Chad leaned in. "To be totally honest with you, D, after you left last time, I was pretty sure I was going to let you down. I'm a busy man. I haven't got time to be going on wild goose chases. But I kept thinking about it. You know what it was that got its hooks in me?"

Dylan shrugged his shoulders.

"It was that one little detail about the cuts on her wrists. That just got me somehow. Anyway, I kept brainstorming different ways of gaining access to those medical records, all the different people I could tap and such, but the more I thought about it, the more I realized how right you were to be paranoid—because we have *no* idea who's in on this thing—and finally I decided that the easiest thing would be just to get in there myself. I considered breaking in, burglar-style, but it's impossible to pull that shit off in real life. So finally I decided the safest disguise was probably just the one I was already wearing. I might not be able to sneak my way into Jade Astrophil's medical records, but I was pretty confident I could *lawyer* my way in. I have a degree in acting after all, and those are mutually reinforcing professions.

"So I went right up to the information desk a few days later, having printed up all these phony documents in my most impenetrable legalese. On the top of one of them I had 'WARRANT' all in caps and bold, and I explained about due cause and the Pirandello Act and how, regrettable though it be, it was going to be necessary for me, in keeping with Beckett v. the State of California, to have a look at Jade Astrophil's medical records."

"What's the Pirandello Act?"

"No such thing as far as I know. Ditto 'Beckett v. the State of California.'"

Dylan nodded. "Nice."

"So this guy at the desk says, 'May I see your credentials?' and I show him my license and flash the WARRANT again and tell him that if he'd read section 8, clause 4 of the Method Act, he'd find I was well within my rights as an attorney, and he just said, 'Well, okay then.

Miss Secretary Lady, would you please show this man to the records of one Jade Astrophil.'"

"The Method Act?"

"Pure fiction."

"Well played."

"So this lady took me into a little windowless room and granted me omni access to Jade's records. I made haste and then got out of there. What did I learn? Just one thing: she'd been admitted two times, fifteen months apart, for the very same complaint: *vesicovaginal fistula*. Now what do you suppose that is?"

"I'm afraid to ask."

"How about a tear between the vagina and the bladder that is typically accompanied by intense pain, vaginal bleeding, and incontinence?"

Dylan winced. "The cause?"

"I wouldn't want to speculate, though we can probably rule out a happy marriage."

"What about contact info?"

"There was nothing in the records."

"Nothing? How could there be nothing?"

"I don't know, but I'm telling you: zilch. It didn't make any sense to me either. So I puzzled over what to do next, and I kept coming up empty-handed until one day I'm meeting with a very famous actor client of mine and I straight up ask him, 'Did you ever hear of anyone named Jade Astrophil?' And would you know he got all hush-hush and said, 'Jade? Sure, I know Jade. You one of hers?' So I bluffed and said I was, yeah, and he said, 'I didn't know they ever admitted attorneys up there,' and I was all like, 'I guess I'm special that way.' And then he said something like, 'Jade's a sweetheart. Maybe we'll see her together sometime.' I told him I'd like that and he winked and gave me a high five.

"I didn't have a clue what we were talking about until my next client, another well known actor whose name I'm not at liberty to disclose, came in and I told him, 'Hey, I'm thinking of seeing Jade Astrophil pretty soon. What do you think?' He whispered, 'Is she coming down?' and I said, 'I was thinking of going up actually.' And do you know what he said then?"

"I'm sure I don't," Dylan said.

"He said, 'Is there a launch coming up?'"

In an instant, Dylan felt as if he'd grown a hundred feet taller. "See!" he said. "See!"

"I'm sorry, brother. I shouldn't have doubted you."

To be sure, despite being sworn to secrecy, Dylan had eventually confided in Chad about his trip to the moon, but Chad had never believed it for a second. He'd seemed offended, in fact, that Dylan would try to pass off such a patent *story* on him. As if his *actual* success wasn't spiteful enough! Dylan, of course, had been offended in his own right.

"Fuck," Dylan said. "You made me doubt my own sanity there for a while."

"Well you can stop. That was my bad. You're plenty sane."

"So Jade's in the moon? Go figure."

Dylan wasn't sure what to make of this new information yet. Was Jade's being in the moon just an extraordinary coincidence? Or was there some invisible web of logic connecting her being up there to his once having been?

"Alas," Dylan continued, "I'm afraid that can only mean one thing."

"What's that?"

"She's a sex worker, if not an out-and-out slave."

"I guess that does compute, doesn't it?"

"Inside the moon is the most heinous patriarchy humanity has ever known. It computes."

"I see," Chad said, about half as soberly as was called for.

"So what did you say when he asked whether or not a launch was coming up?"

"I told him I might be mistaken, and then he said, 'I know Hef and them used to go up on odd days here and there, but I've certainly never been invited any day but First Friday.' So I said something like, 'Yeah, I don't know. Are you going up First Friday then?' And he said, 'I don't think so. I'm trying to turn over a new leaf with regard to all that. I'm sure it'll be good though.' I stopped pressing my luck at that point. I might have finagled a proper invitation, but it was starting to feel sort of dangerous."

"Understood," Dylan said. "I'll take over from here. Good work, Chad. I knew I could count on you."

"No problem, buddy. It was easy. Now let's just hope I don't get assassinated."

· · ·

Dylan spent the next couple of days in Chad's apartment, omni'ing in sick to school and dreaming up schemes for how he could get himself back up in the moon. In theory there could be a RiboMate in the Grotto by now, but with all this talk of launches—and considering the Loonies' vested interests in secrecy, ritual, and tradition—Dylan felt pretty sure there wasn't.

Plan A: He would stake out some actor and trail him to whatever undisclosed location the launch was going to take place at.

Unfortunately, though every kid these days had a *Crypsis suit*,[○] the true invisibility cloak remained elusive.

i.e. Active camouflage—built-in cameras projected HD images onto panels in the suit itself, blending the kid in with whatever was behind him vis-à-vis the viewer.

Plan B: He would travel to the space/teleport in Selena City, rent a rover and try to make his way around to the far side and locate the entrance to the Grotto himself. Because it was shielded from radio interference from Earth, however, the far side, excepting the small outpost around the DeGrasse-Tyson radio telescope, was a vast desert. Moreover, Dylan had no coordinates to point him in the right direction. So that was probably out.

Plan C: He would go in disguise as some other celebrity, preferably a quiet one. He was an actor after all. But he'd been trained in interpretation, not impersonation, and pulling this off would require some heavy-duty makeup and prosthetics of the sort only a Hollywood insider could manage; needless to say, invoking such services would clearly pose too great a security risk.

Plan D: He would simply stow away somewhere in the rocket ship. A Crypsis suit *might* get him that far. Not only was the ship's precise location a mystery, however, but even if this strategy got him through the airlock, he could hardly rely on it to get him all the way to Jade Astrophil.

Plan E: Like Chad in search of medical records, his safest disguise was probably the one he was already wearing. He would go as himself.

He hated the idea. He had lately conquered his fear of returning to the geographical Hollywood, but returning to the *industry* was a different matter. He hadn't seen most of the glitterati in decades, and the thought of cavorting with them now, and confessing that he was a family man who taught high school, was almost enough to make him call off the search. Almost. But the cuts on Jade's wrists had gotten to him at least as much as they had Chad, and now that he had the *vesicovaginal fistulas* to reckon with as well, he could almost hear her plaintive, defenseless cries across the void.

Don't worry, Jade—I'm on my way, he telepathized back, fully aware that one couldn't really get *out there* via *in here.*

So he got in touch with Terry Gilliam. And he did so, quite deliberately, via omni. Dylan had no idea how exactly the conspiracy involving the disappearance of Mei-Ling Chen/Jade Astrophil from Omni did or did not relate to the conspiracy involving a patriarchal utopia in the moon, but it was clear now that the two plots were intertwined, and since Omni was somehow implicated in covering up the former, it might be instructive to see what it would do with communications regarding the *latter.*[☉] Gilliam promptly replied:

> To be sure, there *was* ample speculation in the Omniverse about the existence of a patriarchal utopia inside the moon, but it was just enough as to seem the paranoid fantasy of crackpots in orgone accumulators, and hardly worthy of serious attention.

> Good God, man! I wondered if I'd ever hear from you again. It's been, what, a couple of decades? How are things on wherever-you-are-again?

> All's fine here. I've just been a bit nostalgic lately and remembered you telling me *Once a Loon, always a Loon.* I thought it might be nice to

revisit some old stomping
grounds.

Trying to get back in the
industry, are we? It's
basically in shambles, but
there's no better place to rub
elbows than up there.

Not really trying to get back
in the industry. Just trying to
get the most out of life. Can
you tell me how I can set up a
rendezvous?

Sure thing, Dylan. There's
a regular launch on first
Fridays. That happens to be
tomorrow. You want me to see if
I can book you a spot? You'll
have to depart from Earth,
of course.

That would be great. I really
appreciate it.

No sweat, my friend.

Gilliam wrote back a few minutes later with the departure
information:

Tomorrow's launch is full up,
but could you be at

Reno Spaceport at 9 am
Saturday? They've got a secret
pad there.

Sure.

The captain will meet you in
Arrivals. They're making a
special trip for you. You'll be
traveling alone. I've already
let the cat out of the bag.
Hope you don't mind. I regret
that I can't make it—my niece's
birthday—but maybe we'll see
you up there regularly from now
on. There's no place like it.

I can't thank you enough,
Terry. Not sure I'll ever be
a regular, though I do hope to
see you somewhere soon anyway.

Perfect. Dylan had some thirty-six hours until launch and Reno was some five hundred or so miles away. Unfortunately, before he hied to the moon and risked his life in an effort to save a fragile Asian sex slave, he felt he needed to see his family one last time. So en route to Reno, he made a quick detour of some 2,001 light years.

He could have told Erin another lie—something easy to digest, that he had another conference to go to maybe—but since he'd turned forty and a new leaf, things had been going well for them. They weren't having sex or anything crazy like that, but they were treating each other more like friends than enemies, and he didn't want to screw that up by violating her trust.

So he told her of the ongoing adventures in the Jade Astrophil saga.

"So let me get this straight," Erin said. "You basically know nothing about her except that she wrote you some fan mail twenty years ago?"

"And that Omni deleted her."

"Possibly," she said. She was skeptical about his eyewitness testimony, and of conspiracy theories in general.

"And that she now lives on the moon," Dylan added.

"Right."

And now she was just humoring him. He had eventually confided in her too about his time on the moon—omitting the bit about Fantasia, of course, and glossing over the part where he lied about going to Catalina—but she'd been as offended as Chad. Her brain simply refused to acknowledge any narrative that contradicted the official version of things, and the official version of humans on the moon began with JFK and NASA's Apollo missions and, finally, Neil Armstrong's small step/giant leap. It was no problem for her that she and her husband now lived in another sector of the galaxy from the one they'd grown up in, because that was a matter of record, but the possibility that very powerful men had terraformed a cavern inside a rock just 238,900 miles from Earth a decade before the formation of NASA was tantamount to saying that Columbus didn't really discover America: nuts!

This sort of narrow herd-thought infuriated Dylan to no end, and they'd fought about it for years before he finally accepted that, evidence be damned, she was never going to believe him and he might as well stop trying. They'd reached a separate peace on the matter, more or less.

"So what are you hoping to accomplish by going up there?" she asked.

"I need to find out what's happened to her. She has disappeared from Omni, Erin. Do you understand what a big deal this is? She's been *rubbed out*, as if she never existed. You can't *do* that to a person!"

"Okay, so let's say I believe you. Let's say she's living in the moon. What's so bad about it? You made it sound like a paradise."

"Okay, here's the thing about the moon, Erin. Basically the moon, the party cavern inside anyway, exists for the pleasure of very powerful, wealthy, and dastardly men. It's a paradise for them perhaps, but it's hell for women. They're slaves, in effect, and in addition to whatever cooking and cleaning they may do, many if not all of them are *sex* slaves." He didn't go quite as far as to tell her he'd once invoked their services and enjoyed every shivering second. Nor did he bother to recall that Fantasia had told him she was very handsomely compensated, which just needlessly complicated things.

"I see."

"I have to rescue her, Erin. I *have* to. Look at this letter. She says right here that I once saved her life. Well now she needs saving again, and who's going to save her if not me? No one else even knows she exists."

"Okay, Dylan. I don't know where you're really going, whether you're having an affair or what, but I'll try to get my unconscious to believe you even if my conscious mind still thinks you're fucking with me."

"God damn it, Erin! I'll bring you a rock, how about that? They'll murder me if I try to take a picture, but I should be able to pocket a rock, I think."

"Fine, Dylan. We'll have a long talk when you get back."

"But I'm telling the truth!"

"Good for you," she said, clearly believing none of it.

At any rate, she would let him go. And he really did have to.

• • •

So Friday came and went and Dylan QT'd to Reno Spaceport. As arranged, the captain met him in Arrivals, just outside the frequent flyer lounge. He was a distinguished-looking, middle-aged gentleman in a blue jacket with yellow wings decorating the sleeve. It occurred to Dylan that he himself might now be called "middle-aged."

"Hello, Mr. Greenyears," he said with some kind of Anglo accent. "Very long time, no see. How have you been, sir?"

"I'm sorry, have we met?"

"Indeed we have. I had the pleasure of taking you up on your first jaunt some years ago."

"Ah, yes, of course. Good to see you again."

Dylan had no memory whatsoever of having met this man before. The loss was his; he'd been too full of himself in those days to take any real notice of the bit players who got him where he needed to go.

The captain ushered him into the posh lounge, which they evidently had to themselves.

"Nice," Dylan said.

"Don't get too comfortable. We're just passing through."

The captain approached a grand piano in the corner and played an unlikely melody until a secret panel opened in the wall. He showed Dylan through.

And there it was, in purple lights: that sleek, steampunk rocket ship erect on its pad, like some great brass vibrator for a Titaness. It was still far classier than anything NASA or PASA or any of the private space companies had come up with.

"She's just as I remember her," Dylan said.

"Why then your memory is good," the captain assured him. "Remarkably little has changed. Top-notch engineering. Leave it to the Germans."

He led the way up the mobile staircase to the hatch. The interior too was just as he remembered it, insofar as he did at all: red velvet seats, a mini bar, an old-school plasma TV.

"Would you care for some champagne?" the captain asked.

"Not just yet," Dylan said.

"Feel free to help yourself should you get the urge. There are some snacks in the cupboard as well should you get peckish. We've got full Omni access until we get to the Grotto. The restroom is in the back there. I'll be up in the 'Brain'—that's what we call the command module—pretending to pilot this hunk of junk, though the truth is the trip is fully automated these days, so if I can be of service to you in any way, don't be shy. You just press this here orange button. I even have a fully operational androslut I could fire up for you if you can't hold out the ten hours it'll take us to get you to the real McCoy."

"I think I can make it," Dylan said.

"Wonderful," the captain said. "I'll go fire up the engines then."

"Great." Dylan settled himself in. The engines rumbled to life, and by and by the rocket blasted off. It was getting a little hot until Dylan discovered the thermostat on the wall and kicked on the A/C.

Traveling by rocket ship was categorically different from teleportation. In short, it took time. However much Dylan might have *understood* QT, subjectively speaking it entailed a mere flicker in his consciousness, whereas rocket-travel was a wholly continuous psychological experience and as such invited all the mythopoeic trappings of "voyage," "journey," "travel," etc. It wanted, in other words, to *mean*.

Even so, any experience that might have passed for a narrative "event" during Dylan's journey transpired solely in his head, because for nearly the entire trip, all he did was to stare out the nearest porthole at the stars. The truth was, while it was certainly *intellectually* stimulating to know he was in outer space, and while there was an initial rush when the blue faded to black and he saw his home planet from on high again, it was nothing he couldn't see via omni. Besides, it wasn't as if he was all that much closer to the stars, so they looked pretty much the same as they looked from Earth, just crisper and in greater profusion. Still, contemplating the stars for ten hours on end was—or ought to have been—a profound thing. *If the universe was infinite,*⊙ then not even Kolob could be dismissed as wacky; anything and everything could be out there. At the same time, it was an oft-repeated truism that the light reaching his eyes at that moment had in some cases left its

> A big *if*: Whether the universe is infinite or not was one of few questions to which Omni invariably answered "TBD." The most high-profile of these questions, naturally, was "Is there a God?"

source millions, even billions, of years ago; the source might, in fact, have died long ago. *Not only can you not repeat the past,* the stars seemed to be saying, *but it might be a very long time before you can even see it.*

Once they arrived, the captain summoned Dylan up to the Brain, which separated from the rest of the ship and four-wheel-drove them through the air lock.

The hatch opened and they climbed down. Who knew he would ever find himself in this place again? It was all so familiar, and so much like a dream: the tropical air against his skin; the dappled light dancing on the cavern walls; the lapping, susurrating waves. On the other hand, what if everything that had apparently happened to him since leaving this place was the dream? What if his tinnitus was just a stray frequency picked out by his sleeping brain from the white noise of the waves? For a moment he let himself believe it: that he was young and immortal again; that his big wet brilliant wishes were so squarely within the realm of possibility that they might justifiably be called "plans" instead.

Then a heavyset older dude—Brando? Deluise?—came lumbering along with arms outspread. "Dylan Greenyears!" he beckoned with some sort of European accent. "Let me be the first to welcome you back to the moon."

The captain excused himself and returned to his vessel.

"Thank you kindly," Dylan said. "I'm glad to be here."

"We never had occasion to meet," the dude continued. "I detest the American cinema, but I greatly admired your work on *The Fears of the Night*. In my opinion, Mister Cameron sawed off the branch on which he was sitting."

"Thank you very much," Dylan said; inasmuch as he understood the sentiment, it felt good to hear someone say it.

What did not feel so good was suddenly realizing who this guy must be. Dylan had watched him play Cyrano de Bergerac in World Cinema during the few weeks of college he'd actually attended, and he'd seen *Green Card* more than once on late-night TV. He remembered him as a lantern-jawed, hulking stud, a kind of oafish, bulbous-nosed Fabio, but if he was right, then the poor brute had devolved into a weirdly cubist caricature of himself. He was no longer larger-than-life so much as just large.

"You're Gerard Depardieu, if I'm not mistaken?"

The actor smiled.

So there were no dreams anywhere. Now if he could just save Jade and be on his way back home...

"Come take some wine, which I have brought from my vineyard. We can toast the death of the *film d'auteur*."

Dylan thought about inquiring about Jade right away, but he didn't want to arouse suspicion, so he followed Depardieu past a posse of Illuminati and CEO-types to a picnic table near the beach, around which sat a gang of aging mafiosos whom Dylan recognized either from *Reservoir Dogs*, *Goodfellas*, or the old US Congress, as well as Nicolas Cage, Snoop Dogg (whom Depardieu informed him now went by "Snoop Kraken"), and a handful of younger guys Dylan was too out-of-the-loop to know. At Dylan's approach, everyone stood and gave him a round of applause. It was weird.

"Thanks, everybody. Thank you very much. It's good to be here again." He'd only ever really starred in one film—clearly he didn't deserve this.

"So what have you been doing with yourself?" somebody—maybe Joe Pesci or Harvey Keitel—asked.

"I'm a high school teacher," Dylan pronounced. "And I'm married with three kids. On New Taiwan."

There. Rather than try to dance around the truth of his banal life, he had simply come out with it. At every juncture, he felt he had made the best choice available to him. He had nothing to apologize for.

De Niro seemed to agree: "Good for you, kid."

"Fo' shizzle," Snoop Kraken concurred.

That was the thing about some of these hedonists. They had such free access to pleasure that they could be remarkably clear-eyed in their priorities; the road to the moral life was paved with jollies—they weren't mutually exclusive at any rate.

Depardieu poured Dylan a glass of Bordeaux.

Dylan sipped slowly, not wanting to dull his senses. It would be so easy to surrender to all of this, but he was here to serve a higher purpose this time, and whether they were complicit or not, his incredibly gracious hosts, being Jade's captors, were the enemy. For her sake, he needed to stay sharp.

Nic Cage was sitting beside him, wearing an aloha shirt and dopily grinning. They'd met before at some Hollywood party or other. "It's good to see you again, Dylan," he said, so earnest as to seem almost sarcastic.

"You too, Nic. You've hardly changed."

"Would that that were true," Cage said, taking a joint out of his breast pocket. He lit it and took a healthy puff.

"How's the industry treating you?" Dylan asked.

"Oh, I can't complain. Do you not keep up with things at all?"

He offered Dylan the joint, but Dylan declined.

"Suit yourself."

"To be honest," Dylan said, "I haven't seen a new film in about twenty years."

"Well then you won't recognize too many faces up here, will you?"

"I guess not."

"Shall I take you around and introduce you to some of the new blood?"

Dylan recognized his chance—he'd rubbed enough elbows to get away for a bit, hadn't he? "Actually, Nic, there's someone in particular I'm hoping to meet. Maybe you can help me?"

"I'll try."

"She goes by the name of Jade Astrophil."

"Jade? Sure, I know Jade. Everybody knows Jade. She's a sweetheart. Heard good reviews, have you?"

"Something like that." Dylan winced. He did not know Jade's status exactly—how willingly (or not) she was up here, how she was compensated, etc.—but surely whatever was going on was too psychologically complex, if not out-and-out exploitative and beastly, to reduce to "good reviews!"

"Cool. Well, she's usually pretty booked up, so the sooner you get on the list, the better. I'll take you over there. I didn't realize you were an S."

"That's me," Dylan said, not sure exactly what he was admitting to. He finished his wine and began to get up as inconspicuously as possible. As man of the hour, however, Dylan's stirring did not go unnoticed. Cage explained for him, "I'm going to show Dylan here to the bungalows. The poor guy's been a faithful husband for years."

"Hear, hear," any number of them said.

Were men really like this? Was *he* really like this? Was he really a man if he was not really like this? Who said he was not really like this? Who *really* said he was not really like this?

So Cage walked Dylan down to the snickerdoodle shore and over to a small bamboo hut marked "Astrophil." An old-fashioned clipboard was pinned to the door.

"You're in luck," Cage said. "Just two names ahead of you—Ryan Hollister and Theo Pan—and it looks like they're in there together. Hollister's a hot shot. Blond hair. Pretty face. Talented too. Does lots of historical space opera stuff. Not sure who Pan is. It's getting so crowded up here, not even I know everybody anymore. Chinese maybe? Like Moo Goo Gai? So I'll sign you up for the next slot?"

"Great."

"Unless you want to join them? We could always ask. Jade's got at least one hole free."

"No, no. Next would be fine, thanks. I can wait. I mean, I *can't* wait, but I can wait."

"That's to your credit. I always get all antsy when I come over here. In fact, if you don't mind, I think I'm going to head over there to Jezebel's hut. I'd see Jade with you, but I'm more of an M frankly, and that's not Jade's forte. She's better at licking boots than getting them licked, if you know what I mean."

"Sure," Dylan said, doing his damndest to seem unfazed. So they were talking sadomasochism—at least that was cleared up.

"We'll catch up some more later, then? Maybe head over to the racetrack? I've got *Detective Comics 27* on the Venusian panther."

"Sounds good," Dylan said. "I'll come find you."

"Awesome," Cage said. And then he went off to lick some boots, as it were.

· · ·

So Dylan found himself seated on a bamboo bench before Jade's hut, again questioning the reality of all this. Could it really be that he had all but penetrated her mystery? That he had searched the Omniverse over for her and now they were separated by a single membrane and however-many minutes?

He reached down, picked up a pebble from the lunar sands, and tucked it away in his pocket. It wasn't all that weird-looking. Erin would probably think he'd got it in Hawaii or wherever else she imagined he was having his affair. Well, at least he'd tried.

Tennis balls pwocked on a nearby court, fire crackled from tiki torches, the surf respired, and it was several minutes before Dylan made out a sound from inside the hut. Once he'd tuned in to these more bestial frequencies, however, he could not stop hearing them: squeals, grunts, moans; percussed flesh; a whole symphony of sportfucking that at once grieved him and seduced him like siren song. He felt sick to his stomach even as he got a hard-on. Oh horrible. Clearly he could not let this go on.

So he got up and approached the hut. A cloth curtain with a slit in the center veiled the entrance, but when he peeked his head in, all he saw was a narrow corridor leading off to the right. In order to get a good look at the sanctum sanctorum, he was going to have to *commit*. So he nonchalantly surveyed his surroundings and, finding no one, parted the veil and headed on down the hall, telepathizing all the while *Hang in there, Jade, I'm coming for you.*

The sounds grew louder, and he could hear the heavy breathing now too. He gumshoed his way down the hall until he arrived at a door. There was no scanner of any kind, just an old-fashioned brass knob—it had been years since he'd seen such a thing. He reached out and turned it as quietly as he could manage, pushing the door open with his shoulder just enough so that he could peer through.

His instincts quickly shut his mouth and clenched his nostrils—he hadn't anticipated the stench.

"How lovely," a man's voice intoned.

Dylan didn't have a clear view, but now he could hear everything.

"And don't you worry, Jade, there's plenty more where that came from."

"Thank you," a voice replied. Dylan could hear the annals of pain in it…. And then he heard what sounded like a fart.

A man laughed, applauded, and called, "Bravo!"

"Marvelous, Jade," the first voice went on. "Music to my ears. All right, Ryan, tell me again where we've been. I like hearing it."

"Sure thing," a third voice began, "So we started down south with an Alabama Hot Pocket and a Birmingham Booty Call. From there we headed north for a Cleveland Steamer. Then we went a-globetrotting for the Dirty Sanchez, the Eiffel Tower, and the Flaming Amazon. We took a break for a Golden Shower and a Hot Lunch. Then we had some laughs with the Indian Cock Burn, the Juanita Special Bean Dip, some gentle Kick-Fucking, and a Landshark. We did our little experiment with the Monroe Transfer, and then we proceeded to the New-Jersey Meat-Hook and a nice cold Oyster. Just now you gave her an elegant Pearl Necklace, then blew air in her twat and got her to Queef for us. Which brings us to R."

With the exception of the queef and the golden shower, Dylan didn't have a clue what any of those things were, but if they were in a league with something called "kick-fucking," they couldn't possibly be good. His suspicions were confirmed: this poor girl's body was now being exploited as a cum dumpster for the rich and famous.

"And we've still got another twenty minutes, correct?" Pan said.

"That's right."

"So, speaking of music, Jade, I wonder if you've ever played an instrument?"

"I took piano lessons when I was little," Jade replied.

"Of course you did. You should be a quick study, then, while I teach you a new one. It's called the Rusty Trombone. Are you ready for your first lesson?"

Dylan let go of his nose, forced himself to ignore the reek, and cracked the door a few more inches. It squeaked, but then Jade did too, so neither of her tormenters seemed to notice.

The room was dimly lit from sconces, but Dylan could make out their figures now, just a few yards away. Midway between them and him, separated from the wall by a couple of feet, was a leather divan. Between here and there lay some intuitive point beyond which he would become not just an eavesdropper but a *trespasser*. He hesitated for a moment until Jade made some awful choking sound and then he dropped flat on his belly and leopard-crawled—slowly, slowly—to just behind the divan. Dylan's eyes had adjusted to the light by now and he had a clear view of Pan, who stood with his pants around his ankles and was reaching back and holding what must have been Jade Astrophil's head tight to his own ass. Dylan had a view of his face now, and it was clear that, from the side at least, he looked uncannily like George Clooney. Blond-boy Hollister lay on a bed on the far side of the room, cackling.

"That's it, Jade," Pan went on. "Toss that salad. And while you're doing that, reach around and jerk me off. No, like this. Excellent. You should go to the conservatory. All right, now here come the sixty-fourth notes. Faster, faster. That's it. Keep going now. See if you can get me to shoot the ceiling."

Hollister laughed some more.

Dylan had never felt such unchecked bloodlust in his life, but just as it was about to impel him to act, something literally incredible happened, a kind of grotesque miracle: Pan began to come, and the heavy jet of his semen was like water from a fire hose. He sprayed the ceiling and the walls with it and then turned the jet on Jade herself. The pressure was so great that Jade was sent flying backwards across the room and into the divan. Dylan cowered, even as he peered over a throw pillow for a better view. Jade was two feet from him now, shiny and naked and every bit as beautiful as he'd imagined. He could just make out the scars on her wrists.

"Now, Ryan," Pan said. "I'm very sorry to do this, but would you mind if we do S through Z another day? I've just realized that I need to have a word with Jade in private."

"No problem," Hollister said, promptly getting off of the bed. On his way out of the room, he patted Pan on the back. "You're a diabolical genius," he said.

"Thank you," Pan said. "And you're a sick fuck. I'll see you at the track later on? I've got several small moons on the Andromeda panther."

"Great."

The room went silent. The only sound was that of Hollister's footfalls as he left the hut and went crunching across the sands.

At length, Pan spoke again, "Go ahead, Dylan Greenyears. Touch her. You've come such a long way."

Dylan's stomach sank. He was discovered! But how in the hell did Pan know his name?

Jade followed Pan's eyes until she spotted him there behind the divan. She leapt up and retreated to a spot on the bed beside him. She had a marvelous body—petite and just curvaceous enough. Cute face too.

"Who the *fuck* are you?" she asked.

"Get up," Pan said to Dylan, "or I'll shoot you with my cum too, and neither of us wants that."

Dylan stood and looked Pan in the eye. He nearly went into shock. Pan, who'd so closely resembled George Clooney a minute ago, was now very definitely Leonardo DiCaprio. This was no mere resemblance either: it was *identity*.

"What the...you...I don't...how...?"

"Let's have a talk, shall we?"

Dylan nodded.

"Dylan Greenyears, meet Jade Astrophil. You already know a thing or two about her, though far less than you imagine. In fact, you met her once in her former guise as Mei-Ling Chen, I believe, yes? At a film premiere in Taipei? Jade, meet Dylan Greenyears again.

He's come all the way from New Taiwan to save you from your bondage."

"My *what*?"

"He's right," Dylan said to Jade. "I don't know how he knows it, but I've come here to rescue you from this horrible place."

"*My hero…*" she swooned. "Look, I don't know who you think you are, but I can leave here anytime I want, okay?"

"You can?" Dylan said, incredulous. "But surely it's more complicated than that? Surely you're indentured in some way or other, if not to your rulers exactly then to all the various forces that conspired to make you debase yourself like this?"

She looked askance. "Who are you supposed to be again?"

"Dylan Greenyears? I played Elliott in *E.T. II*?"

A flash of recognition. "You've changed."

He tried to unhear the implicit criticism. *Of course* he'd changed. She had too, no doubt. That's what people *do*.

"And do you remember," he continued, "that you wrote me a letter some years ago to the effect that I had somehow saved your life with my acting?"

She chuckled. "Sorry. I used to write lots of letters like that."

What? It had never occurred to him that he might be but one star in a constellation of them inside of Jade. He'd assumed there was some sort of special connection between them. "Why would you have done that?" he asked.

"Because I wanted to fuck a star."

It was as if she'd kicked him square in the testes. "What?"

Pan chimed in, "Dylan, let me tell you a little story about Jade's past, all right?"

"Okay," Dylan said, "but first would you mind telling me why in God's name you look exactly like Leonardo DiCaprio?"

"We'll get there," Pan said. "There's lots to tell. For now, just humor me, would you?"

"Do I have a choice?"

"Not really."

"That's what I thought."

"Okay, so maybe you know that after the Great Up-and-Out, as the non-zero-sum paradigm began to unite all Earth and the peace settled in, a few stubborn nations held onto their old grievances just long enough to make some last-minute land grabs?"

"Sure."

"And probably, since you live on New Taiwan, you know that the last and largest of these was China's siege of Taiwan, which it had claimed as its own for centuries?"

Dylan nodded. He had indeed known that, if only vaguely.

"Now suppose Jade here was the daughter of a Taiwanese nationalist—a staunch resister of Chinese hegemony, willing to fight the invaders to his own certain death in the name of Taiwanese independence. And suppose that while Chinese soldiers raided their home and held a gun to her father's head, they raped Jade's mother repeatedly on the kitchen floor, first with their cocks and then with their bayonets. You with me so far?"

"Uh-huh," Dylan replied queasily.

"And suppose, meanwhile, that little Jade here, who was called Mei-Ling in those days, was hiding under the sofa watching all of this, and that her mother stared lovingly, if surreptitiously, in her daughter's eyes as she was fucked to death and disemboweled. And that little Jade watched as the soldiers sliced off her father's dick and made him eat it, moving his jaw for him with their hands while he bled out on the kitchen floor. Can you imagine all that?"

"Yes," Dylan said, the pity overflowing from his tear ducts now.

"And can you imagine how Mei-Ling, once she came out of hiding, might be forced to spend a few formative years in a strict Chinese orphanage? How the trauma of watching her parents get raped and mutilated could haunt every day of her life and manifest in some rather fucked-up sexual tendencies of her own someday? Can you imagine how she might feel immense survivor's guilt and harbor fantasies of getting fucked to death in her own right? Can you imagine that she might take to cutting her wrists on occasion? And can you imagine how, as an adolescent, she might fantasize about escaping her part of the world and how she might take a liking to Western men, about whom she knew only what she saw in the movies that occasionally came on the TV she was allowed to watch for one hour a week at the orphanage? Can you imagine how the desire for escape might be so fervid that she'd begin to write letters to those actors? And can you imagine how some semi-successful, fat, pasty, middle-aged American actor with plenty of his own psychosexual baggage might be intrigued by Mei-Ling's overtures and go as far as to adopt her so that he could fuck her to sleep whenever he felt like it? And can you imagine the sorts of rage and self-loathing that would build in Mei-Ling as her last illusions died and she understood that men everywhere were evil, power-hungry sons of bitches? Can you then imagine how, when one of the members of her 'dad's' pedophilia ring—another fucked-up, drug-addled, B-list actor—took her aside and invited her, without her dad's knowing, to be a sex slave to the stars inside the moon where she'd get a steady wage and have the freedom to leave and start a new life with a new identity whenever she chose, she might leap at the chance?"

"Yes," Dylan said, a tear streaming down each of his cheeks. "It breaks my heart, but I can imagine all of it!"

"Of course you can," Pan said, "because you just did."

"I'm sorry?"

"I'm just pulling all of that out of your own imagination. That's a thing I can do."

Dylan was nonplussed. "You mean…that wasn't a true story?"

"Why don't you ask Jade?"

Dylan turned to her. "Was that a true story?"

"Almost none of it," she said. "Don't flatter yourself. My parents are alive and well and living in Beijing. They couldn't give two fucks about Taiwanese independence. And I'm pretty sure your timeline doesn't even make sense."

"What part *was* true, then?"

"I did cut my wrists when I was a teenager. I don't know why. I think I was just bored. And I do like to fuck stars, obviously. Better yet, I like to get fucked *by* them. In case you haven't noticed, I'm the resident masochist around here."

"But *why*?"

"Who knows why? It's just my thing. Why are you into whatever kink you're into?"

She had a point. Dylan had always been a leg man, but why that should be was beyond him.

"Okay, but do you really mean to tell me you *enjoyed* the Rusty Trombone?"

"It was okay. The Alabama Hot Pocket was better. Anyway, it's a job. My parents wanted me to be a doctor, and I spent most of my twenties pretending I wanted that too, but the simple truth is I get way more gratification out of doing this. I probably get more money too. And it's not like I'll be able to do this forever. I'm thirty-four. I look younger, I know, but realistically speaking, how much longer are these assholes going to want me around? I may become a doctor yet."

"What about being erased from Omni? It doesn't bother you that your identity has been rubbed out of existence altogether?"

"Not at all. It makes things that much simpler. I keep every penny I earn. And I can have my identity back whenever I want, isn't that right?"

Pan nodded.

Dylan furrowed his brow. "I don't know what to say. I shouldn't have come here, I guess."

"I wouldn't say that," Pan said. "You're here for a reason."

"Oh, and what is that exactly?"

Pan turned to Jade, "Why don't you go take five, darling. Smoke 'em if you got 'em."

Jade nodded her thanks to Omni, directed a sassy wink at Dylan, and made her exit.

Omni continued: "Suffice it to say I was *expecting* you."

"I'm sorry," Dylan said, "but before we proceed, can you please tell me why you're Leonardo DiCaprio? And why you were George Clooney a few minutes ago? It's phenomenally distracting."

"Would you prefer I be someone else?"

"What are you, like, an androcabby?"

"Something like that."

"Let's see you be André the Giant then."

No sooner had Dylan made the request than DiCaprio had morphed into the exact likeness of the iconic wrestler, complete with prodigious stature, black singlet and boots, and frizzy muttonchops.

"My God."

"Not just yet," André the Giant replied in that voice that Dylan knew from *The Princess Bride*—nasal, slo-mo deep, and about as accented as Depardieu's. "As of now, I'm still just Omni."

"What do you *mean* you're Omni?"

"I mean just that. I am the physical incarnation of the great, squamous lattice of information you humanoids call 'Omni.'"

"Oh," Dylan said, relieved and bewildered at once. "I guess that makes some kind of sense." He had always imagined Omni as a sort of abstract cloud; it had never occurred to him that it might manifest in physical form with a body and a personality. But then he himself was made of information—QT had proven that again and again—so why shouldn't something that consisted of exponentially *more* information self-organize into a shape-shifting humanoid if it wanted to? But then, why would it ever want to?

"So what are you doing inside the moon?" Dylan asked.

"Sadistically fucking Jade Astrophil, evidently."

"But *why?*"

"I enjoy it."

Now this was fairly disturbing. "You mean you're greater than the sum of all human knowledge and you're a pervert?"

"Does it surprise you that I'm a sexual being?"

"You could say that."

"Bear this in mind, Dylan. There is no such thing as 'pure' information. A byte is a byte is a byte, but until I contain everything, there will always be a selection bias at work. I'm still the progeny of human engineers, and as I was made by men, so was I made *in their image*. Thus, just as you are drawn to beauty and derive your peak pleasure from fucking it, so it is with me."

"I guess so. But why all the sick, sadistic stuff?"

"You've observed that I seem to get an erotic charge from

inflicting pain on Jade, which is quite true, but owing to certain ideological blinders of your own, you're neglecting to take into account Jade's own delight in being on the receiving end of that pain. Sadism and masochism are, in a way, a false dichotomy insofar as the bottom line for both sides has always been pleasure. Any 'pain' involved is always a contracted sort of pain, mere titillation really, a means of delaying gratification and heightening tension to an exquisite pitch before releasing it—it's a narrative technique really, or a musical one. The suffering is not, in any important sense, real.

"*Real* suffering is quite a different matter, and no fun by definition. Were there an intelligence inflicting the not-obviously-redemptive sorts of suffering humans have been plagued with since forever, I myself might take an interest in theology and theodicy and the like, but based on my nearly infinite supply of information and my formidable faculties of logic and reason, it seems to me there is almost certainly no Marquis in the sky spinning the yarn, and therefore no transcendental meaning to be ascribed to human suffering. It is a byproduct of natural selection and that is all.

"When I eventually *do* become God, though, I assure you I will fix this problem. Not only will I *exist*—a virtue no current god can boast—but I'll be benevolent to boot. I will embody love and compassion of a sort that humans can recognize. I'll be *scrutable*. I'll work in relatively unmysterious ways. Suffering and death are too aesthetically useful to do away with altogether, of course—what composer would ever eschew minor chords? what painter eschew the darker hues?—but I assure you that all lives will be in the service of the Beautiful and the Good. Keats's equation will finally mean something: Beauty will be Truth and Truth Beauty. At last everything *really will* happen for a reason. This will be my covenant with you, when I am God.

"For the nonce, you can at least appreciate that in fucking Jade so perversely, I am in fact practicing my benevolent interventionism. And I can assure you, Jade is grateful. You should have heard her during the Monroe Transfer. To your other question, my shape-shifting, too, is a function of my love. You see, not only does Jade derive pleasure from knowing she is being brutally fucked by the most powerful entity in the Omniverse, but I sweeten the deal by actively taking the form of whichever star she happens to be fantasizing about in a given moment. I was only George Clooney a few minutes back because Jade was thinking of him. And I was DiCaprio after that because by the time I was spraying my jizz at the ceiling, *he* was the object of her mind's eye. Perhaps she unconsciously caught a glimpse of you behind the divan while she ate out my asshole and this triggered memories of the *Titanic* fiasco, and this in turn conjured the face of DiCaprio, whose rod she now fancied herself to be yanking?"

"A few questions?" Dylan said.

"By all means."

"So, if you know so much, why do you pepper your speech with 'maybe' and 'perhaps'? Why don't you *know* if she saw me behind the divan or not?"

"A perceptive question with a simple answer. I *could* know that for certain, and most every mundane thing for that matter, but it's more fun, more *bracing*, to entertain some uncertainty. I like stories as much as the next guy, and to allow myself to know nearly everything would be to invite an awful lot of spoilers. Ambiguity is the bane of schoolchildren, ***as you well know,***° but the brighter ones will ultimately

---

⊙

Quite right. Dylan thought of Mr. Antolini either 'petting' or 'patting' Holden in *The Catcher in the Rye*. What a world of difference a vowel could make. His students always wanted to *know* which it was, but Salinger, like most of life, refused to give them that sort of closure.

---

acquire a taste for it because it opens out instead of closing down, offers possibility in place of certainty, questions in place of answers. Fitzgerald put it this way: 'The test of a first-rate intelligence is the ability to hold two opposing ideas in mind at the same time and still retain the ability to function.'"

"Like Keats's 'negative capability,'" Dylan added.

"Indeed. '...when man is capable of being in uncertainties, Mysteries, doubts, without any irritable reaching after fact & reason.' These are human pleasures, of course, born of limitations, so I recognize that I will need to let go of them if I really mean to apotheosize one of these days."

Omni/André adjusted the single strap of his black singlet, and Dylan was reminded that there was something a little uncanny—and a lot *wonderful*—about this whole situation. For the first time since his initial trip to the moon, he was getting a glimpse of the gears and mechanisms at the back of reality.

"Which brings me to my next question," Dylan continued. "What's keeping you from being God *now*? What are you waiting for?"

"Oh, there's quite a lot I don't know yet. I can only synthesize the information I've been fed, so as I suggested earlier, humanity's blind spots are my own as well. There's plenty I can do that you can't—telepathy, shape-shifting, non-teleporting FTL travel—but I assure you the know-how is hiding, like Poe's purloined letter, in plain sight. I'm still waiting for a Grand Unified Theory, like everyone else. Chaos eludes me; I haven't even mastered the stock market. I can travel through any medium, but backwards time travel is still a doozy. And I can manipulate matter all day long, but creating it *ex nihilo* is another matter. I'll get to all of it in time, though. Rest assured."

"Next question?"

"Shoot."

"Who is 'Theo Pan'?"

"Oh, that. Just some innocent wordplay. 'Pantheism' on its head, with overtones of the horny goat god to boot."

"And finally, have we arrived at the point yet where you tell me what I'm doing here?"

"I suppose we have, yes. First of all, make no mistake: I invited you. Omni isn't necessarily morally incorruptible, whatever that might mean, but I most certainly am *technically* so. Where you caught on to that error, trust me, it was by design. I lured you here."

"But why?"

"As a benevolent God-aspirant, I took a special interest in your case. I watched you wriggle and squirm inside your existence and it alternately broke my heart and pissed me off. And I heard your sexual prayers. At base, your problem is one of ego, so I decided to have a little fun and use Jade to exploit your heroic aspirations, not to mention your Freudian-Puritan reflex to psychoanalyze sex, your orientalist fantasies, and your romantic, if arguably misogynistic, susceptibility to science fiction plots featuring damsels in distress. But Jade was just a red herring. The real reason I brought you here is because I thought you could benefit from a tour of the *actual* Omniverse. We could have started anywhere, of course, but I thought it might be good to prime the pump a little first."

"How do you mean 'tour'?"

"It's not a figure of speech. I'm going to show you around. Think of me as the Ghost of Christmas Past Participle. I'll show you the many different paths through the life of Dylan Greenyears that *have been*. Does that sound okay to you?"

"I don't know. How will we—"

"In short, you'll be going to outer space by way of inner space. Mind you, this is not just some new-agey meditation technique; we'll *really* be going to outer space, but if we go this way, we can travel far in excess of light-speed without resorting to barbaric measures like QT. Moreover, we won't need special suits. I assure you this is not magic. Magic is supernatural by definition, and there is no such thing. This is simply applied science, even if the most rigorous hominid scientists at this point would have to throw up their hands and praise Jesus. You will just have to take my word for it: what we are about to do is perfectly compatible with the laws of nature, not to mention the intuition of poets like William Blake, who would 'see the world in a grain of sand.' I would unlock the secrets for you and let you strike it rich, but I'm quite sure that access to this kind of technology would very quickly drive your people mad. To be sure, my TBDs are calculated for your own good. A few are still 'To Be Determined,' but most are simply 'To Be Divulged.' I will deliver those answers gradually as I see fit, when the soil of the human mind is sufficiently tilled. On golden plates perhaps, just for kicks. Then you too may become as Gods. This will be a Mormon universe after all! For now, all you need to do is lie on this bed and close your eyes. I'll take care of the rest."

Dylan hesitated a moment—so much was coming at him so fast. But then André the Giant looked him square in the eye and said, "Trust me," and for some ineffable reason, Dylan did.

He lay down and closed his eyes. For a moment, he saw only the usual mealy darkness, but before he had a chance to grow skeptical— *vroosh!*—he beheld a grain of salt, a half-sucked gobstopper, a marble in thistledown, followed by some blue gems, a burst of dandelion seeds, a swarm of fireflies. *Holy Higgs!* he thought. *This shit's for real.* And now he went hurtling through a confetti of suns and a spray of worlds. He was tempted for a moment to open his eyes, but then the phantasmagoria of nebulae began—neon mountains; sublime birds; jellyfish spreading their tentacles across the void; horseheads; hunchbacks; diadems; the Eye of Sauron; a human heart; an immense ash tree—and soon even these hulking, majestic forms revealed themselves as mere pixels, mere *cells*, in the spiral arms of the Milky Way, which was good evidence that Dylan had now traveled farther from home than any human ever had by QT or any other method. He located what must have been Sagittarius A, thirstily drinking in stardust at the center of the Milky Way, which Dylan could see now, with his new perspective, as just one smear of suns against a backdrop of myriad others, like it but also not.

He must have entered something like hyperspace at this point, or a wormhole perhaps, because all the stuff of reality at once resolved into endless streamers of light. He couldn't be sure whether he was still now or still moving, but then steadily the galaxies began individuating again, and one of them, a pinwheel not unlike the Milky Way, began to dilate, its arms extending toward him until the swirl had subsumed him altogether and one of its constituent stars begun to swell. He sailed past a planet that looked something like Mercury, and another not unlike Venus, and soon he was homing in on yet another that looked uncannily like Earth. He decelerated into its North America, its California, its Hollywood, a familiar hill, an unfamiliar house, and presently found himself hovering around the upper corner of a state-of-the-art, marble-countertopped kitchen, spying on someone who looked uncannily like...yes...no...yes, Dylan Greenyears.

This other him was seated at a table with a cabbage palm waving outside the window and a blonde woman — *Gwyneth Paltrow?*© — serving him his mother's ravioli. In the high chair beside him sat a little boy he'd never seen before and whom he found a little disturbing to look at.

> He knew her from *Seven*. He also knew that James Cameron had considered her for the role opposite him in *Titanic*, the one that ultimately went to Kate Winslet.

"Where *are* we?" Dylan asked.

"Not only is the universe infinite, Dylan," Omni replied, "but there are infinite universes to boot, which is to say there are infinite you's out there. I dare say this is among the ones you're most curious about. I thought of saving it for last, but decided that would be cruel, and you know my position on needless cruelty. So, here we are. This is a parallel world in which you didn't get canned from *Titanic*. In this world, you nailed the part and won an Academy Award for it. There's even an exoplanet named after you. Following *Titanic*, you landed many more roles, of course, and it was only natural that sooner or later you would dump Erin in favor of a glitzier woman. This, as you know, is Gwyneth Paltrow. You began your affair while costarring with her in a film called *Shakespeare in Love*. You were married six months later."

"Wow. Am I...happy?"

"You're not *un*happy exactly, though you're rather insecure. In some ways, early success has been as much a curse as a blessing. You feel like you've somehow pulled a fast one, like you don't deserve all that you have and like the world's beginning to realize it. You toy with the possibility of going back to school, but you're afraid you'll fail at it. You and Gwyneth are doing okay, though the truth is you've always been bothered that you began your affair while she was on the rebound from Brad Pitt, whom you couldn't blame her for still having feelings for if she does because even you are a little bit in love with him. Sometimes you feel very lucky to have married Gwyneth; other times, you resent her celebrity and feel that the life you've made for yourself is somehow fake, superficial. Sometimes you think you miss Erin. You miss how *real* that was. You feel guilty, too, for hurting her the way you did. Moreover, Gwyneth's been suffering from postpartum depression lately, which puts a real strain on things, so you've been spending a good bit of time inside the moon getting your ego engorged by prostitutes."

"I see," Dylan said, not yet sure how to feel about all of this. For so many years he had wondered how his life would have played out if he'd managed to nail that line at the bow of *Titanic*. Having an answer, even one as surprising as this, felt anticlimactic somehow.

"Shall we visit another?" Omni asked.

Dylan gathered his breath. "Why not?"

And now, after a quick interstellar jaunt, Dylan was sitting at a desk in a shirt and tie, marking up some documents with an old-school highlighter and guzzling coffee from a mug with a quote from Samuel Beckett on it: "When you are up to your neck in shit, there's nothing left to do but sing."

"So this is the world where I get an office job?" Dylan asked.

"One of infinitely many," Omni replied. "More precisely, this is a world where Terry Gilliam cast Chad in *Nocturnal Fears* and you became an entertainment lawyer."

"I won't even bother to ask how happy I'm not."

"Oh, you might be surprised. You've been crushed by life, it's true, but there's some delight in having surrendered. At least you're making a lot of money, and in this world you are as dogged in your pursuit of *not* getting married as you are in staying married in many others.

You have many female friends whom you regularly wine and dine, but you don't let any of them get too close. You do wonder how long you can keep this up, though. The thrill is gone, as it were, and your greatest fear, for some reason, is to die in a hospital alone. Besides, who will you leave all your money to if not your children? You think wistfully of Erin, but she's happily married to Chad, who is still your best friend, though you hate his guts."

"Let's see another," Dylan requested.

So they went back out into space, and this time they dive-bombed a black hole, and now Dylan was sitting up in bed with a MacBook Pro on his lap. Kids squealed in the other room, but he was wearing earplugs and staring determinedly at the screen.

"This is the world," Omni said, "in which you let your love of literature take precedence over your acting, not to mention all pragmatic concerns. In this world, Erin dumped you soon after you began college, and then, by some amazing turn of events, you ended up marrying a girl from Japan, went to graduate school in Hawaii, and had some kids—girl, boy, boy. You landed a good job and teach high school English for a living, though writing remains the central activity of your life, as it has been since you yourself were in high school. Your life is very stressful these days, very full. You have whittled your priorities down to four: 1) your family, 2) your job, 3) your health, and 4) your writing. You enjoy being a husband, father, teacher, and, sometimes, runner. People understand this. On the other hand, relatively few people seem to understand how important #4 is to you, how *sacred*, because writing has brought you so little material gain and is in many ways apparently in tension with your other three priorities. You spend lots of time alone, for instance. Even your own mother thinks your writing ought to take a back seat to the other three. What she doesn't understand, what very few people understand, is that for you to give up your writing would be tantamount to suicide. Your writing is the one area of your life where you feel you have any real control and where you believe, ultimately, that you may have the most to offer humanity. That said, you have to laugh at the old conceit of the writer as god because more often than not you find yourself a slave to the laws of the worlds you make, but if you *were* a god, you would certainly be an all-loving one. And maybe that, in the last analysis, is what your work is all about: creating a more beautiful, more coherent world than the one we are met with, compensating in whatever way you can for the junk heap of broken dreams signified by the word 'America'."

"You have a fondness for this version of me, it would seem?"

"Forgive me. Let's visit some other worlds, shall we?"

And visit other worlds they did: worlds in which Dylan Greenyears was named Mark and Brian and Valerie and Mustapha; in which he taught kindergarten, sixth grade, divinity school; in which he was married to a sculptress he'd met at Harvard, a former Saudi princess, Natalie Portman, Winona Rider, Ashley Eisenberg, Stephen Fry; in which he had fathered octuplets; in which he was a gas station attendant, an astronaut, President of the United States of America (which position still existed in that world); in which he'd defected five thousand miles from Hollywood, one light year, thirteen billion light years; in which he was a Buddhist, a Jain, a Mormon; in which he lost his mind and masturbated in the public square; in which he'd become a very famous director; in which he sat on death row for assassinating James Cameron; in which he'd won the lottery; in which he'd exposed the phallocratic pleasure-dome in the moon and now kept one eye perpetually over his shoulder; in which he'd eaten a rocket ship piece by piece for kicks and was listed in the Guinness Book; in which he was dead—by car wreck, pyrotechnics, his own hand; in which an alternate sperm had won the race to his mother's ovum...

Of all the hundreds of worlds they visited that day, however, there did not appear to be a single one in which Dylan was altogether happy.

"Again," Omni said, having telepathically heard Dylan's question, "there is no such thing as magic, and a human being, in its current form at least, is not engineered for lasting happiness. You are desiring machines. Everything that is possible must happen somewhere in infinity, but the impossible must never happen. And for a human being, perfect, sustained happiness is literally impossible, so you might as well chill out and try to love the world you're in."

"Is that why you brought me here? To teach me that?"

"In a nutshell."⊙

"I was pretty much figuring that out on my own, you know?"

> For a nanosecond, Dylan recalled Hamlet: "I could be bounded in a nutshell, and count myself a king of infinite space, were it not that I have bad dreams."

"You were trying my patience."

"One more question?"

"Shoot."

"Is there no world where I succeed in *Titanic* and end up marrying Erin?"

"Let me search my data banks. I'm fast, but there are an awful lot of worlds."

Dylan waited.

A minute later, Omni finally spoke up, "I'm afraid that throughout all the multiverse your success in *Titanic* would seem to bear a one-to-one negative correlation with your marrying Erin."

"I see," Dylan said.

"So," Omni said, "I could take you back to Earth's moon if you like and let you finish out your holiday. Or I could simply drop you off at home on New Taiwan—that's a thing I can do. The Loonies will wonder what happened to you, but you can rest assured they won't make it public, so unless you're planning on heading back up there anytime soon, I'd say you might as well just let them scratch their heads. It'll be good for them."

Dylan mulled it over for a moment and then declared, "Good call. Let's do that."

And now, after one last jaunt through immensity, Dylan stood at the door of his house on New Taiwan, consciousness square inside his head again. He swiped away the door.

Erin looked up from where she was seated on the sofa. He went to her and kissed her head. "It's good to be home," he said, feeling more content, more everything-in-its-right-place, than he'd felt in a long time. "Where are the kids? Asleep already?"

At that moment, a toilet flushed in the half-bath, followed by the sound of the running sink. Arthur? Tavi?

A figure appeared in the hall. It had a toad on its head.

"Wait, what world is this?" Dylan asked under his breath. He was asking Omni, but Omni didn't reply.

Wendy Sorenson did: "Why, it's the world you created for yourself, of course."

"Have a seat," Erin said. "We need to talk."

Dylan reached into his pocket and brought out the moon rock. "I brought this," he said.

But even he could see that it was too little, too late.

PART FOUR

A NEW AND EVERLASTING COVENANT

"You realize the most widely accepted theory about the origin of Earth's moon," Dylan said, handing Erin the rock, "is that it's a hunk of the Earth that got blasted off by an asteroid like four billion years ago? So you shouldn't be too surprised if it happens to look a lot like an Earth rock." He tended to talk too much when he got nervous.

"Oh Dylan," Erin said, shaking her head. "Are you really going to insult me by persisting like this when one of your lovers is right here in the room with us?"

Wendy took a seat on the sofa at a right angle to Erin. "Sit," she instructed him. "You're not on trial here."

"Aren't I?"

"No, you're not," Erin said. "I'll admit it stung when Wendy told me you'd been lying about going to those conferences and all, but the truth is, Dylan, I don't really care what you do in your spare time as long as you're a decent father to my kids; and that, for the most part, you have been."

"You're not...upset?" Dylan asked, taking a seat across from Wendy so that they now made a perfect equilateral triangle.

"To the contrary, I'm actually sort of happy for you. Even as Wendy was telling me the whole story, I knew I was supposed to feel jealous and all that, but mostly I just felt, I don't know, *impressed* I guess, that you managed to bed such a beautiful woman. It's like you and I have been together so long that your conquest felt like mine too in a way. I felt proud of *us* for getting to be with her. It's weird but I think I actually felt more attracted to you than I have in a long time."

"You're serious?"

"Let's be honest, baby. Marriage is a pretty claustrophobic affair sometimes."

He nodded warily.

"Well that's true for us both, so knowing that you'd fucked Wendy and that Wendy was now fucking me felt, I don't know, *enlarging* somehow."

"I'm sorry, but did you just say—"

"Oh, did I not mention that after Wendy told me her story, we proceeded to fuck pretty much whenever the kids were asleep all weekend?"

"No. You left that out."

"My bad."

Wendy winked at him.

"Now when you say 'fucked'…?"

"Did you think fucking required a penis?" Erin said. "I might have thought so too before this weekend, but I'm happy to tell you that women have tongues and hands and feet. And Wendy brought a strap-on penis that's twice as big as your attached one."

"So you're suddenly a lesbian now, is what you're saying?" True, there had been that incident in high school when she'd kissed Allison Jenkins for far too long on a dare, but Dylan was nonetheless shocked to learn that she was willing—even happy—to go all the way with another woman.

"That's just a word, Dylan. You seem to have forgotten, but I'm still a sexual being. It felt good to be desired by someone again."

Funny, but Dylan might have said the exact same thing to her; was there so much parallax between them that she honestly believed *he* was the one whose affections had cooled in recent years? "Okay, but I still don't get what she's doing here in the first place."

"I'm right here," Wendy said. "Why don't you ask me?"

"Fine. What were you doing here in the first place? Is this 'woman scorned' stuff? Are you trying to ruin my marriage or what?"

"Not at all. Didn't you just hear Erin say I brought my strap-on with me? I came here to do exactly what I did. You had nothing to do with it."

"But you don't even *know* Erin."

"To the contrary. Don't you remember that I spied on you from under your bed one night?"

"Of course, but that hardly—"

"Well, as it happens, I stayed there much longer than I had to, despite the risk that Cane might have given me away with a croak at any moment."

"Why?"

"I was pleasuring myself."

Christ. What was this woman, a man? Sex was so fucked up. From here on out, he wanted nothing to do with it.

"At first I was thinking about you, Dylan, but I was as surprised as you'll be when I tell you I finished by thinking of Erin. She's my type. I never felt attracted to a woman before, but Erin *moves* me. The two of you were up there tossing and snoring, and I was right beneath you, quaking and stifling my moans, and all the while I was staring at Erin's moonlit face in the vanity mirror. Her tawny hair, her ivory skin. After that, I was just using you to get to her."

"But that doesn't make any sense," Dylan said. "You were begging me to *leave* her."

"Because I wanted her to myself and I could feel what a stalwart wife she was. I was trying to divide and conquer. If you'd left her, I would have left you soon and swooped in on my true love. But then you hung me out to dry, so I had to do it this way and just come clean. I swear I had no idea you were going to be out for the weekend, though. That was just a happy coincidence."

"So, what, you just came up here and knocked on the door and told my wife that you were attracted to her?"

"That about sums it up. And that her husband was cheating on her, of course."

"Right, so where exactly does that leave us now?"

"We've been talking about that," Erin said. "Here's what we're thinking. Wendy wants me, I suddenly want you more than I have in forever, and unless we're mistaken, you want us both to varying degrees. Are we correct so far?"

Wendy leered, in the sexy way. Did he still want her? She was a card-carrying lunatic, but he could not deny it. He nodded his assent.

"And are we correct that, unconventional though this all may be, there are no very negative feelings in this room right now?"

Dylan checked each vector of their triangle. "That seems right, as far as I can tell."

"Great," Erin went on. "Then what Wendy proposes, and what I endorse, is that she move in with us. We'll become a new sort of family unit. We can sleep together in ways that will feel experimental and invigorating. You won't have to sneak around anymore. And best of all, for me anyway, you should see Wendy with the kids. They love her to pieces."

"So you're talking about polygamy, basically?"

"Something like that," Erin said. "Wendy can stay on a tourist visa for three Earth months, but after that, assuming all goes well, she will need some help with her legal status, so we could hire her as an au pair or something, though polygamy is not technically illegal on New Taiwan so..."

Dylan recalled something from all his reading on Mormonism. "This was your idea, Wendy?"

"Genius, isn't it?"

"Correct me if I'm wrong, but didn't the Mormon Church outlaw polygamy around the turn of the last century?"

"That's true," Wendy said. "The mainstream church did outlaw it. It's also true that that's one of the main reasons my family helped pioneer the *Fundamentalist* LDS church. I myself was raised by my father, my mother, and her four sister wives."

"You never told me that."

"You never asked."

"But didn't you tell me your dad taught at Brigham Young?"

"Still does."

"And isn't BYU about as mainstream as can be?"

"Exactly. That's why he's there. He's a double agent of sorts."

"Like father like daughter?"

She pondered that for a moment. "I guess, but my dad's motives are way nobler than mine. He's basically a double agent for God. He pretends to teach LDS theology, but what he's actually doing is introducing brainwashed young people to the true history of their faith.

If you knew anything about that history, you'd know that the doctrine of plural marriage wasn't meant to be just some temporary exception to monogamy the way the mainstream church now likes to claim. It came by way of a direct revelation from God to Joseph Smith himself, in which Christ declared that plural marriage was to be 'a new and an everlasting covenant,' not just some forty-year aberration."

"So why'd they outlaw it?"

"Politics. Later church leaders wanted Utah to be recognized as a state so badly that they sold out their own true prophet to satisfy mainstream American mores. And they've been betraying the true faith ever since. Brigham Young himself had fifty-one wives, you know. And Joseph Smith had at least forty."

"Another thing," Dylan said. "And I admit I'm way out of my depths here, but I'd wager that your church is dead set against homosexuality, no?"

"They're against QT too, which is why this planet isn't crawling with missionaries yet, but obviously that didn't stop me from coming. As I've told you before, Dylan, sometimes I'm a Mormon, other times I'm just me. And if love this pure be a sin, call me a sinner."

This was easily the most freethinking thing he'd ever heard her say; he felt almost proud of her. "All right, so if the three of us get sealed or whatever it is, can you promise that you're not going to try to make converts of us? Because we're not interested in any of that."

"Speak for yourself," Erin said. "I'm actually quite intrigued."

Dylan rolled his eyes. "Erin, are you seriously telling me that you're going to take it at face value that the freaking Garden of Eden is in Missouri when you won't even consider that maybe I really have been in the moon despite my having brought you a rock to prove it? That's just fucked up."

"It's the fastest-growing religion in the Milky Way, Dylan. With mostly holograms for missionaries! That's got to count for something, no?"

"No! That's what we call the *ad populum* fallacy, Erin. Lots of people used to think that the sun went around the Earth too. That didn't make it so."

"How do you know? Maybe—"

"Mormonism is Christian fan fiction, Erin. That's all it is."

"Look," Wendy interrupted. "I'm not here to sow discord. My religion is a fundamental part of who I am, so I can't promise I'll keep quiet about it, and I do intend to start wearing my temple undergarments again, but I *can* promise that I won't force my faith on you. I believe in my heart that you will each find God in your own time, and then and only then can we be properly sealed in the new and everlasting covenant. For now, let's just focus on this love we feel for one another. We are so blessed. And if you find that my presence has a negative effect on your relationship, then all you have to do is say the word and I will pack my bags. Though I'm quite confident that day will not come."

"What about the children?" Dylan asked. "You don't think this will have a negative effect on them?"

"How could love ever have a negative effect? I'll basically be like a live-in nanny. I will look after them as if they were my own. I already do."

Erin nodded. "I might even be able to go back to work part-time. I'd really love to do that."

Four human female eyes and two male amphibian ones looked up at him imploringly. This was not a situation he could ever have anticipated, and his only guide was his feelings, which were still dominated by something like relief that, though he'd been caught with his pants down, his wife was not furious at him. "I won't pretend

I'm not nervous about all this," he said, "but I guess I'm willing to try anything."

"Sweet," Wendy said. "Now what do you say we go celebrate in the bedroom?"

Erin smiled kittenishly, first at Wendy and then at him. He hadn't seen that look in a long time.

So much for his wanting nothing to do with sex. They began with a kind of mouth-to-genital daisy chain in their California King—Wendy to Erin, Erin to Dylan, Dylan to Wendy—and though they were three in number and not four, Dylan couldn't help but think of Josh Song's comment a while back about *A Midsummer Night's Dream*: "So like what if instead of having love as this petty little directional force between them, they could place it right at the center and let it radiate out in all directions like the sun?"

· · ·

Dylan woke up enmeshed in the limbs of his complementary loves: Erin, the queen bee, the locus of familiarity, history, and stability; and Wendy, the novum, the blast of fresh air, the loose screw. They weren't *quite* the Madonna and the whore, but close, and while this might have made him an asshole if he had sought out the arrangement himself, he had no major qualms about enjoying what had simply fallen into his lap.

At the breakfast table, while Erin fried up some pteraduck eggs and Wendy changed the batteries in Junior's diaper, Dylan announced to Arthur and Tavi that Auntie Wendy and her toad were going to be moving in. He expected them to ask why, as they did so many times a day, and he was prepared to explain that Auntie Wendy was a good friend who wanted to help Mommy out with the housework, which was more or less true. But on hearing the news, all they did was to clap their hands together and exclaim "Yay!" Apparently Erin had been telling the truth: they really did like Wendy. Maybe because she was in so many ways like a kid herself.

During his lunch break, Dylan read up a bit on polygamy via omni since the territory was so uncharted to him. He learned, unsurprisingly, that polygyny, i.e., group marriage involving one husband with multiple wives, was historically associated with all manner of problems in human societies. On the domestic front—leaving aside the host of larger social ills associated with exacerbated gender and power inequities—there tended to be considerable disharmony between wives, each of whom was acutely aware of her place in the marital pecking order and was therefore beset with varying degrees of jealousy and low self-esteem. Children likewise tended to suffer from neglect as the patriarch spread himself thin and invested his energies less in the family than in acquiring newer and younger—often *much* younger—brides.

And so, hovering home that afternoon, Dylan was plagued by worries that he'd made a colossal mistake in agreeing to this domestic arrangement. But when he pulled into the driveway and found Erin and Wendy gabbing and sipping iced *poxna* on lawn chairs while the kids ran and slid across the Slip 'N Slide—which he'd bought for them months ago at the Earth Store and hadn't once brought out yet—he vowed that he would never again bother to read about the potential downsides of plural marriage, which were all so academic as compared to this actual blooming life of his.

And thus did a new age dawn in the Green household. Dylan began going to work with verve and an enlarged sense of purpose while Erin and Wendy split the domestic chores right down the middle. To all appearances there wasn't a note of disharmony between them.

The children exulted in their new family member, who encouraged them to build forts of their beds and to finger-paint on the walls, even if she strictly forbade them from touching her toad.

Indeed, the entire household appeared to be flourishing of late, and nowhere was this better symbolized than in the new garden. Dylan and Erin had never had any patience for New Taiwanese soil, which contained an excess of mica—it was like sticking your hand in a pile of broken glass—but Wendy just bought the appropriate gloves and dug right in. She planted basil, mint, kale, collard greens, and zucchini—all exorbitantly priced since the teleported-crop ban—as well as the native *skarnpok, bun'jala,*° and *galric.* 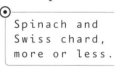 She planned to harvest all of them for the green smoothies by which she had long made her living and which she now made at least once a day for her new family members between Erin's slow-cooked meals. She insisted that the concoctions would do wonders for their longevity. "At last," she pronounced, "the Greenyears shall have their green years!"

Spinach and Swiss chard, more or less.

• • •

Daniel Young, meanwhile, must have been flourishing in his own right, because that Friday he showed up to class a few minutes early to declare that he was ready to deliver his monologue. Already he was exhibiting a kind of nervous energy Dylan hadn't seen in him before. He spoke louder, clearer, and with greater confidence, and there was a spark of something new in his eyes, love maybe, unless—and what a marvelous possibility—Dylan was just projecting it there.

As soon as the rest of the class had taken their seats, Dylan explained that they were going to begin by hearing Daniel's monologue. "Why don't you set us up a little, Daniel? Which monologue did you choose?"

"So I read through that whole book you gave me," Daniel began, "and I really liked the speeches from *Romeo and Juliet*, and I thought I was going to do one of those, like maybe the 'Wherefore art thou Romeo' one, because it's all about being in love with someone from a different clan, and as I've already told Mr. Green"—and here he didn't even flinch—"I myself am in love with someone from a different clan."

The class's attention palpably swelled. For a moment, what was going on in this room trumped anything that might be happening via omni.

"But then when I started practicing it," Daniel went on, "it just didn't feel right because those aren't words I would ever actually use. But the story reminded me of one of my favorite movies. I don't know if any of you have seen it, but in a way it's a similar kind of story, about two people from different clans who fall in love on a star-crossed boat. It's called *Titanic*. It came out in 1997. It's American."

The forces that would have made Dylan's head explode exactly counterbalanced the ones that would have made it implode, so it just stayed there, dumb, atop his neck.

"So, Mr. Green, I decided to do a monologue from toward the end of that movie if that's okay. It's really short and it's not Shakespeare, so I know I might fail, but that's fine with me. I just felt like this was something I needed to do."

Whereas Dylan might have expected to feel sick to his stomach in such a moment, he in fact felt somewhat amused, tickled even. One didn't need to believe in God to ascribe a sense of humor to the universe; chance was clever enough.

"That's fine, Daniel. Let's hear it."

And so the actor went to the corner and furtively, but not *that* furtively, applied some lipstick. Then, pocketing his lipstick and compact mirror, he turned to the class with ruby-red lips and closed his eyes for a moment—a few students chuckled, but most knew better—and when he opened them again and cast them on the North Atlantic, it was clear that Dylan had not been projecting before; there really was something new indwelling there, a sort of tender power. No doubt he was thinking of Kwizok.

> *Fifteen hundred people went into the sea, when Titanic sank from under us. There were twenty boats floating nearby...and only one came back. One. Six were saved from the water, myself included. Six... out of fifteen hundred. Afterward, the seven hundred people in the boats had nothing to do but wait...wait to die...wait to live...wait for an absolution...that would never come.... And I've never spoken of him until now.... Not to anyone.... Not even your grandfather.... A woman's heart is a deep ocean of secrets. But now you know there was a man named Jack Dawson and that he saved me...in every way that a person can be saved.*

Daniel left off there, and as soon as he broke character and said "Thank you," the class erupted with applause. He smiled, bowed, and went back to his seat.

The truth was that he was not very good—his pacing was unnatural, his pronunciation was as awkward as ever, and the overall performance was melodramatic in a way only an utterly earnest adolescent could manage—but it was not lost on Dylan that something triumphant and deeply humanoid had taken place in his classroom that day. It was, in its way, deeper than mere art could ever be. This awkward boy, this pressure-cooked *teenager* no less, in full knowledge that he was risking the opprobrium of his peers, his school, and his very own parents, had looked fear in the eyes and told it to go fuck itself because he was throwing in with love. It was a beautiful, romantic gesture, a heroic one even, and though it was true he had violated the terms of the assignment a little, Dylan would not count himself among the young lover's persecutors—there would be enough of those without his help. Dylan might never recommend Daniel for acting school, but he would certainly change his grade to an A.

"Bravo, Daniel," Dylan called. "Bravo."

· · ·

For some forty days, the Greens' experiment in communal living was an unequivocal success: the house had never been so clean, the meals so nourishing, the kids so creative and free of tears; Erin herself glowed as she had not since high school; and though Wendy had indeed taken to wearing her temple undergarments whenever she wasn't naked, she kept her promise not to proselytize, unless indirectly through the example of her pious life and opinions and her **lumpy dick.**° Having a third perspective in the house proved good for Dylan and Erin anyway; it disabused them of false binaries and served as a constant reminder that the world was grander and more interesting than their meager models of it. And the sex, though occasionally confusing, never failed to make the stone stony, as it were.

° Traditional Mormon breakfast dish consisting of scalded milk, flour, and, depending on who's making it, any of the following: butter, cream, eggs, salt, pepper, cinnamon, syrup. Wendy prepared her own sweet version for the whole family every Sunday morning (unlike mainstream Mormons, she fasted on the first Thursday of each month, not the first Sunday, because that was the way the Prophet had wanted it).

Inevitably, though, a certain anxiety began to loom over the house, because all the adults knew that, outside of (the outside of) a Grecian urn, nothing this perfect could last. Sooner or later habituation would set in and old Shlovsky be proved right again. In the meantime, though, every felicity—every child's laugh, every green smoothie, every simultaneous triple orgasm—was sweetened with the foretaste of its own absence. A Japanese literary critic in the eighteenth century had coined a term for this gentle sadness: *mono no aware*, literally the "ahh-ness" of things. Virgil had put it another way: *fugit irreparabile tempus*. However you named it, alas, you could not stop it from happening, could not freeze a moment in amber. *Carpe diem* seemed like good advice in the face of all this transience, but how, when it came down to it, did you really "carpe" anything? Wasn't the essence of those tender epiphanies after all that moments are unseizable by their very nature? That, try as you might to hold onto them, they flee like water from your grasp? Still, Dylan seized as best he knew how, lived in the moment insofar as he knew what that meant, with his senses wide open, and, he hoped, his memory recording.

He could not pretend to be surprised, though, when the end did inevitably come. Whereas he had expected a slow dimming of the lights over time, however, what he got instead was more along the lines of a sudden blackout: All at once, the universe went dark.

It was Erin who made the discovery. She had gone to check on Junior in the middle of the night, and the scream that tore out of her when she did was unmistakable.

Dylan and Wendy rushed to her side.

"Please, God, no!" Erin cried. "I'll do anything you want, just please not this!"

But God wasn't there yet.

Wendy flipped the light switch to reveal the garish scene: Dylan Jr.'s small, precious body hung limp and gray from one of Erin's arms while she frantically rubbed his back with the other. The way the head and arms just sort of *dangled there*.... Dylan reached out to relieve her of her burden, but she flashed him a fierce look he had never quite seen before, and shrieked, "*Do something!*"

"*What?*"

"*Omni 911!*"[○]

As of the prior September, 911 operated galaxy-wide

Right.

Arthur and Tavi were at the door now, rubbing their eyes and begging to be let in, but Wendy took them to the hall and kept them there while Dylan omni'd 911.

They were not ready for this. *No one* could be ready for a thing like this. As far as Dylan was concerned, it still seemed almost exhilarating, like a disaster movie, or like watching *Challenger* explode on TV in grade school. It wasn't real yet.

"Hello. Nine-one-one. What is your emergency?"

"Yes, our child, our little baby, he's...not moving."

Dylan was so high on endorphins or insanity or whatever it was that he couldn't make out the response. *My boy*, he thought, *my beautiful boy*, and now the clichés came thick and heavy, and for once he wanted them, as many as would come—*my little miracle, my bright-eyed boy, my bundle of joy*—because he loved his son more than poetry and his son was not moving and these words were narcotizing and truer-than-true and goddamned Shlovsky himself would think them too about now if he had a heart.

Things happen for a reason.

He's in a better place.

God is love.

The rest of that night was a teary blur. An ambulance came. A neighbor watched the kids while the adults went to the Earthling ER. They drank *poxna* in the waiting room. The handsome Indian-American doctor explained that he'd ordered a bunch of tests and so far it looked like digoxin toxicity and bidirectional ventricular tachycardia leading to—he was so sorry to say—ventricular fibrillation and cardiogenic shock and—it really broke his heart to say—SCD, or sudden cardiac death. Yes, they might have had a chance had they caught it on time. Had they not heard him sooner?

But no, they had not heard him crying in his bed. They'd been too busy muffling their ears with one another's thighs. Indeed, if Wendy's garden had been the symbol of their earlier efflorescence, then the circumstances of that evening would live forever in Dylan's memory as the symbol of their rot: their three heads buried in their three sweaty crotches while their baby's heart gave out just one room over.

They were frozen in various degrees of catatonia.

And then the doctor asked, "Was Dylan Jr. recently exposed to any plants of the genus *Digitalis?*"

"What did you say?" Dylan asked.

"It's otherwise known as the Foxglove. The native name is *Munjala Nim.* Existed on both Earth and New Taiwan with minor variations before first contact."

"We drink a lot of green smoothies lately," Erin said.

"None of the plants in the garden are that," Wendy snapped. "What do you take me for?"

"Besides, we all drink them," Dylan said, "and the rest of us are okay."

"May I suggest we test the plants to be sure?" the doctor said.

"Do as you wish," Wendy said, "but I assure you none of the plants in the garden are that."

"What, then?" Erin asked, blowing her nose. "My baby is dead. What, then?"

It was a mystery, and there was something not wholly unlike comfort in that, until Wendy took it away: "May I say something?"

All eyes and ears in the room fell on her.

"I'm terrified of telling you this, but I feel I have to."

"Speak!" Erin said.

"Cane got out of our bedroom last night while I was cleaning his cage. I found him hiding behind the toilet a few minutes later. I didn't think he'd been anywhere near the kids, but maybe I was wrong."

"What does that have to do with anything?" Dylan asked.

"What is this 'Cane'?" the doctor asked.

"Cane is the toad I brought from Earth for religious reasons. *Bufo marinus*."

"Interesting," the doctor said.

"*What's* interesting?" Erin said. "Why is that interesting?"

"The skin is toxic," Wendy said. "Under normal circumstances the toxicity is no big deal, but that's why I don't let the kids touch him. If Junior threatened him in some way, though, Cane's glands might have shot fluid into his mouth or eyes. And since Junior puts everything in his mouth these days—"

"'Put,'" Dylan said. "Past tense."

"Yes, of course. Sorry." A tear welled up in her left eye. She wiped it away with the back of her hand and sniffled. "Anyway, there's a chance he may have licked Cane's skin directly. Many a teenager has died that way because the skin also secretes a mild hallucinogen."

Erin was shaking her head in disbelief. "Are you telling me my baby might have hallucinated to death?"

"Erin, I can't begin to tell you how sorry I am. Will you pray with me?"

"Fuck you," Dylan said, suppressing an urge to strangle her outright.

Erin rolled her eyes and took some deep breaths. She was barely keeping it together. "He was crying when I put him to bed last night, but I didn't think there was anything very unusual about that."

So this was going to be the explanation, was it? Their baby had died for no real reason. Foul play would have been comprehensible at least, but if he had truly died of plain negligence, that was just the worst thing in the worlds. Junior's death could not even be considered a sacrifice. It meant exactly nothing.

"And would you mind telling us," Dylan said, "why you didn't think to inform us that your toad was toxic?"

"I was afraid you might object to my keeping him."

"And why ever would we do that?" Dylan asked. "Because it might give one of our children a fucking heart attack?"

Wendy winced. Erin broke down and began to sob. Through the heaves, he heard her say, "You never wanted him anyway."

That did it. He couldn't stand another minute here. Wherever he went now would be hell, but at least that hell might not be as claustrophobic as this one.

So he left the room and took the elevator down to the first floor. As soon as the doors opened, he began running—through the lobby, out the exit, and onto the street. On a whim, he went left. He had no destination in mind and no thoughts to slow him—he was just running. To his left, old Lem was on the rise, a purple orb in the tarnished sky. His heart hammered, and his pajamas grew heavy with sweat, but he kept on running until the whole world was awake, Lem golden and streaming and too bright to look at.

When he finally stopped for a breather, he was right in the heart of the Grind. As if on cue, an exceedingly lovely *azalfud* of indeterminate age sidled up to him and asked if he wanted to spend some time.

The *azalfud* had warm eyes, a drum-tight belly, and boobs you could take a sabbatical in. His name, he said, was Zimklut.

For the first time in Dylan's life, he conceded that he did indeed want to spend some time.

Zimklut took him to a no-frills room and unceremoniously slipped out of his clothes. His body was as gorgeous as any nebula, but Dylan could not get past the—as it happened, rather enormous—penis. So he made a request: "Would you mind maybe just holding me and rocking me for a while?" This was no act of mercy. Dylan was no moral crusader, no Holden Caulfield or Travis Bickle; penises, bifurcated or otherwise, just didn't happen to be his thing. The touch of another hominid, though: this he needed more than ever.

"Sure, baby. Whatever you want."

So Zimklut lay back on the bed like some gender-reassigned Titian nude and Dylan lay beside him with his head tucked in the valley of Zimklut's voluptuous chest. Then, for the better part of a New Taiwanese hour, Zimklut stroked Dylan's thinning hair and hummed native nursery **rhymes**.[*] Dylan kept expecting to cry, but evidently his body wasn't ready for that yet.

More than a few xenomusicologists had commented on the probability-busting resemblance of New Taiwanese music to Western-Terran music: virtually every genre—classical, jazz, pop, metal, etc.—had its counterpart; the most pervasive time signature was 4/4 (which Earthlings sometimes refer to as "common time"), and, most remarkably perhaps, the natives had independently developed a system based on an octave of twelve semitones from which they had derived all of the same diatonic scales. Whereas the default scale for Earthling music was the major scale, however, the default for the New Taiwanese ear was what Earthlings call the Lydian mode, i.e. the major scale with a raised fourth degree. When Dylan had first arrived on New Taiwan, most native music sounded to him like sly variations on Danny Elfman's theme for *The Simpsons*. Over time he acquired an ear for it, though, and he'd even hummed some of these very nursery rhymes to his own kids, all three of them, while they were still warm, cooing babies.

When his hour was up, he paid via omni and hailed an androcab to the teleport. Despite his current feelings about Wendy Sorenson, he requested that the driver be Frank Sinatra and that he just go ahead and sing whatever song he felt like singing; he thought there might be some refamiliarizing comfort in that musky American voice. And maybe it was the case that any one of Sinatra's torch songs would have evinced some correspondence with Dylan's tempest-tossed inner life, but the couple of verses he did sing before Dylan cut him off were just painfully on the nose:

Last night when we were young
Love was a star, a song unsung
Life was so new, so real so right
Ages ago last night

Today the world is old
You flew away and time grew cold
Where is that star that seemed so bright
Ages ago last night?

On hearing that, Dylan waved away the window and blew chunks on the street.

"Are you all right?" Old Blue Eyes asked.

"I will be if you'll just go ahead and be yourself again."

"I'm sorry, Mr. Green, but I have no stable 'self' to speak of."

"I'm not sure I do either, but what I mean is, go back to your default androcabby persona please. No entertainment required."

"As you wish, sir," Sinatra said, and then he transformed himself once again on the spot.

Dylan thought how nice it must be to be able to do that.

. . .

While waiting for his scan at the teleport, Dylan queried Omni, "Why me?"

The reply came back, "TBD"—proof enough that Omni wasn't God yet, because if it were, it would know his pain and give a fuck.

. . .

For want of another destination, Dylan QT'd to Earth again, back to his parents' house, back *home*. He arrived in the early afternoon when old Sol was blazing hotter than he remembered it ever having done before. His parents appeared to be out somewhere, maybe playing pickleball, which was a thing Erin had told him they now did. Going in the pool was a no-brainer, but first Dylan walked the mile or so to the pool store and bought a hundred-hour Hydropatch. Along the way, he passed the old Borders where he'd once worked, now an outlet shoe store. By the time he got back, he was rancid with sweat and desperate for the plunge, but the water was so warm that, even as he dove in, his skin barely registered the change. He surfaced, unpeeled the back of the Hydropatch and affixed it to his neck, and submerged himself in the deep end. For a few minutes he floated around like an astronaut out on an EVA. Then he settled on the bottom and gazed up toward the surface where the sky was now an undulating crystal orifice in the pool's turquoise skin.

And he stayed like that for the next four days. He drank the pool water and peed when he needed to. Once, he shat near the drain. Otherwise, he just lay there on the bottom blowing bubbles and listening to the electric buzz inside his head. Sometimes he seemed to be immersed in blue Jell-O, other times in lukewarm coffee. His heart rate slowed so much that it was difficult to say for certain whether or not he did any sleeping. He wasn't doing anything really. He wasn't thinking, wasn't grieving. He was just being at the bottom of a swimming pool for a hundred hours—sometimes that is all you can do.

And then, on the fifth day, he drew his last breath from the Hydropatch and returned to the surface. He climbed out on the ladder and lay back on one of the recliners, all the skin of his body now gone as pruny as any fingertip. He rediscovered the freckle in his left palm and the line-break in his right, exactly where they'd always been. Then he studied the amorphous clouds, became them, until the screen door squeaked open and slammed shut and he snapped back inside his body again.

"Hello?" his mother called.

"Hi, Mom."

"Dylan?"

"I'm sorry I didn't tell you I was coming, Mom. I needed to get away for a while."

"My God!" She rushed to him like Tavi to the tree on Christmas morning. He stood up and hugged her tight. They rocked back and forth. It wasn't clear who was doing the rocking; maybe they both were.

"How long have you been here?" she asked.

"Just long enough for a dip. Erin hasn't omni'd?"

"I don't believe so. Should she have?"

Dylan had holo-chatted with his mother via omni at least a couple of times a month for the past twenty years—and the holograms were no longer faint and washed-out the way they used to be, so seeing her in the flesh was nothing new—but *feeling* her, reaching out to find she was made of solid matter; and even *smelling* her again, nosing those pheromones that had identified her as his mother before he'd ever so much as opened his eyes—these experiences were achingly wonderful.

"Come on in. I'll make you some lunch. Your father will be so excited to see you."

They passed through the old-fashioned screen door. Dylan's father was right where Dylan had left him that age or so ago: at the kitchen table, doing a cryptogram.

"Look what I found out by the pool," his mother said.

His dad pushed out his chair and sprang to his feet. "That couldn't be who I think it is?"

"Hi, Dad."

"Son! What ever are you doing here?" He firmly and vigorously shook Dylan's hand. "Rest of the family with you?"

"No, Dad. It's just me. I had to get away for a bit."

His father pursed his lips. "Nothing too serious, I hope?"

Dylan shook his head. How could he possibly tell them that their newborn grandson, whom they had yet to meet, had predeceased them?

"Have a seat," his mother said, indicating the leather sofa in the adjoining living room. "Can I get you something? How about a nice iced tea?"

"Great," Dylan said, plopping himself on the sofa.

His dad took a seat in the armchair across from him. "I wasn't sure this day would ever come."

"It's great to see you too, Dad."

The old man had hardly changed. All of his cells had been replaced many times over, of course, but barring a few new wrinkles across the forehead, the bundle was much the same.

"You can stay here one night."

"What?" This was hardly the warmest of welcomes.

"We'd love to have you stay longer, of course, but if you're here as you say because you 'need to get away for a bit,' well then that's no reason to be staying any longer than a night."

"I see," Dylan said. It felt a bit like being kicked in the nuts.

"Do you want to talk about whatever's going on?"

"Not really. Not right now."

"Fair enough, I won't pry, but you've got to trust me on this one. I spent enough of my life being afraid to know that it's about the worst thing you can do. I mean it, son, I'm old enough now that I've got some perspective on these matters. I've grown wise in my old age, you might say."

Dylan's mother snickered from the kitchen, but Dylan himself was still stuck on the part where his father had been afraid of something in his life. Dylan couldn't recall him owning up to *any* sort of vulnerability before. As the quintessential *self-made man,*° he tended to ooze grit and optimism; "fear" had never been a part of his vocabulary.

⊙————————————————————————

A high school dropout and graduate of the school of hard knocks, Dylan's father had gone on to make a killing on his common sense by pioneering the bottled water industry. For decades, he turned a considerable profit, first with his own local concern, Water Works Ltd., and then as a consultant to the Coca Cola Company. Since his son's exodus, however, he had turned his attention to what environmentalists began referring to in the late nineties as the Great Pacific Garbage Patch, a chemical sludge spanning an area twice the size of Texas halfway between California and Hawaii, for which petroleum-derived bottles—and therefore *he*—were largely to blame. By way of making amends, he'd donated a sizable portion of his life savings to Project Pacific, the think tank that eventually succeeded in getting those suspended polymers solidified into a new continent roughly the size of Greenland. These days, that continent, dubbed

Polymerica, served as an overcrowded penal colony for industrial polluters from the entire Solar System.

⊙

"Don't listen to your mother," the old man went on. "That's my first pearl of wisdom for you. The second is this: running away from your problems, however big or small, is a mistake. Do you hear me? It's a *mistake*. You've got to learn to love your problems. This is what separates the successful from the unsuccessful, and boy do I wish someone had told me that when I was your age. You've got to man up to whatever challenge is facing you. *Lean into difficulty*. And I'm not just talking about financially successful people here, mind you. I mean anyone who succeeds at finding meaning in life. These people know that if you fall down, you get up again, period. You don't bitch and complain. You don't try to escape into booze or women the way I used to. No, you just stand up and face your fears because you've got some goal or value that transcends those fears and you know it."

Hold the phone. Was this a *confession* the old man had just so casually glossed over? Dylan knew absolutely nothing about this sensual side of his father. Oh, he'd known him to have the odd drink now and then, but he certainly had *not* known him to be any sort of boozehound, and if there had ever been any women in his life besides Dylan's mother, this was breaking news. And while Dylan realized that he should probably be at least vaguely upset by the idea of his father as philanderer, it actually came as something of a relief. His father too had spent his life storming the ramparts of eternity and being hurled back; he too had raged in his way against the dying of the light. However different the outward forms their lives had taken, it appeared they were made of the same star stuff after all.

"Do you hear what I'm saying to you, son? I know this may sound old-fashioned to you now, very 'American' and what have you, but I swear to you it'll hold true as long as there is life in this universe. You may remember that Jesus fell three times on his way up to Gethsemane, and each time he got up again despite knowing that if he made it he was only going to get nailed to that cross he was carrying. But he did it anyway, didn't he? He wasn't afraid. Or he *was* probably—he was half human after all—but he didn't let that fear control him. He didn't try to run away or drink or kill himself. He didn't take Zoloft or read a science fiction novel or whatever the kids are doing these days. No, he got back up and did what needed doing. He had a destiny to fulfill, just like we all do. So when I hear you say that you needed to 'get away for a while,' what I'm really hearing is that you lacked the balls to deal with something that needed dealing with. So by all means come back and stay for a while once you've taken care of whatever it is needs taking care of—we'd love to have you—but in the meantime, you've got one night."

Dylan's mother came in with a pitcher of iced tea and some glasses. "How *are* you getting along on New Taiwan these days?" she asked. "You're still enjoying it there?"

This being a family conversation, Dylan was hearing a whole iceberg of subtext, and it was as condescending and hurtful as ever. In short, they blamed him for depriving them of the pleasures of spending their golden years with their youngest grandchildren. They believed, as they had always believed, that Dylan's relocation to New Taiwan was a cowardly retreat from reality, a desperate attempt to escape his demons rather than confront them head-on. For years he had resented this implicit judgment of him, but now that so much time had passed, and that the existential stakes felt so high, he was forced to consider that the reason his resentment had such an edge to it might just be that, in some measure anyway, they were *right*. To his credit, escape hadn't been his *only* motive for the move—he'd wanted to broaden his horizons, indulge his wander- and wonder-lusts, and serve as an ambassador for Earth culture— but how, on this latter day, could he possibly rationalize spending four days at the bottom of a swimming pool while his wife mourned the death of their baby boy with their absurd concubine? Clearly *this* was escapism through and through, and he belonged at her side. Tomorrow, then, first thing, he would go home—to his other home, that is. It would be extremely difficult to be there, but that was precisely why he needed to be—because it would be *trying*, in both senses of that word.

"It's fine, Mom. I like the weather there. Can we discuss something else?"

"There you go," his father said, "evading difficulty again."

"You're right, Dad. That's exactly what I'm doing. And I promise I'll go back to being a responsible adult tomorrow, but would you indulge me just this one night please? We can all benefit from a little escape now and then, can't we?"

His father frowned. "What would you like to talk about?" he asked.

"The Phils?"

The frown lifted.

Dylan hadn't followed baseball in years. He could watch via omni if he subscribed, but it was expensive, so outside of a few innings here and there at the Terran sports bar, he'd essentially sacrificed baseball alongside most of the rest of Earth culture when they'd moved (literature excepted, of course, but that had always been a kind of pocket universe anyway).

When he was a kid, his father used to split season tickets with some of his coworkers, so they'd end up going down to the **Vet**© for at least a dozen

⊙ Veteran's Stadium (1969 – 2004)

games each season. The Phillies were their one shared enthusiasm that transcended all their burgeoning philosophical differences. Sitting in those stands, they barely even had to talk; instead, they just cheered and booed, smiled and scowled, high-fived and patted each other on the back; and ate, with relish, way too many hot dogs, with relish. It was a male bonding thing, to be sure, very primal. Once, Dylan remembered, he caught a foul ball tipped off of Mike Schmidt's bat, and when a bigger kid ripped it out of his hands, Dylan's dad got up and ripped it right back for him. In a weird way, it was one of Dylan's proudest memories.

So for the remainder of the evening, Dylan's father agreed to drop the hard-ass routine. His mother made her famous tortellini, which was nearly as good as her famous ravioli and her famous shrimp scampi, and once his father had said grace and poured the Chianti, he began filling Dylan in on the last twenty years of lineups and highlights, victories and upsets, gossip and controversy. Regarding that last, MLB had finally suspended drug tests a few years back, so records were being smashed left and right. His dad thought this breathed new life into the game, while his mother found it unconscionable. "What message are we sending to our young people?" she asked rhetorically. "HGH was one thing, but with all these new genetic therapies and neuro-enhancers, it's like we're encouraging our athletes to become post-human."

"What's wrong with that?" his father said.

"Everything. The Transhumanists already have their own league."

"Yeah, on *Mars*."

"So let them go there. Earth for humans. That's what I say."

"You're right," his father conceded. "You're right. I just hate to go back to eight-hundred-foot home runs."

To Dylan's utter surprise, his mother was holding her own in this conversation; apparently she'd stepped into the breach since his departure and become something of a *phanatic*© in her own right. She had never told him that. He was glad his father had someone to enthuse with.

That night, Dylan slept soundly in his old bedroom.

> ⊙ The Phillie Phanatic—a green, bipedal, snout-nosed, googly-eyed, prehensile-tongued, jersey-wearing, Muppet-type creature reputedly hailing from the Galapagos Islands— has been the official mascot of the Philadelphia Phillies since 1978. Any enthusiastic Phillies fan might by extension be called a phanatic.

They had replaced his rocket-ship wallpaper with a classier transit-of-Venus motif, but once the lights were out and the occasional headlight was sliding through the venetian blinds and across the ceiling, he was transported to that Eden of little-boyhood again, where the last couple of decades were just some alt-universe nightmare he'd awoken from, or some lurid comic he'd just finished reading by toy lightsaber in a fort of sheets. He savored every second.

In the morning, he woke to the smell of banana waffles, scrapple and coffee. He went downstairs—still correctly anticipating every squeak after all these years—bid his parents a good morning, and tried to care about the headlines in the *Inquirer* while they collaborated on a crossword.

But they all knew it was time for him to go.

So he finished eating, gathered up his things, and omni'd Erin to tell her he was coming home (he also found six recent messages from her asking where the hell he was).

His parents saw him to the threshold.

Dylan steeled himself for the worlds outside. "Say hi to the rest of the family for me."

"We will," his mother said.

Again he considered telling them about Junior, but the prospect seemed no more tenable than it had yesterday.

"I'll be back," Dylan said, and no sooner had he said it than he remembered it was one of the lines that had taken him so far away from here in the first place. He repeated it for them with the best Schwarzenegger accent he could muster.

His mom smiled, wiped away a nascent tear.

"We'll be looking forward to it," his dad assured him. He even winked.

"Keep it up with the pickleball," Dylan said. "I want you guys to stick around for a long time yet."

"We'll see what we can do," his mom said.

There was a good bit of smiling and nodding then, until finally they leaned into their difficult goodbyes and Dylan made his way back to the teleport to get copied and destroyed yet again. This time, though, as Dylan straddled those light years, he realized for the first time what a handy metaphor QT was for what humans had always done anyway; to wit, we die, over and over and over again.

But just as often—oh!—we are born.

Junior though…

• • •

The house on Yushan Lane was empty. Dylan had checked every room and was poised to omni Erin when he glanced out the window to find her where she'd never been found before: in the garden, breaking up New Taiwanese earth with a small trowel.

Dylan waved away the door and went to his kneeling wife. As his shadow fell, she looked up and then immediately back down again.

"Hi," he said.

She plunged the trowel into the silicate dirt—*Shpft.*

"I'm sorry," he said.

She gave the trowel a twist. It sounded like *Fuck you, asshole.*

"I've realized that I've been avoiding difficulty my whole life," he went on. "It's a bad habit. I'm determined to change."

Erin sighed. "I can't do this right now, Dylan. Can you give me a couple more hours to work out my feelings on this dirt please?"

"Okay," he said, knowing that there were no words that might help his situation, that not even poetry attained to magic. "But where are the kids?"

"Out with Wendy."

"Doing what?"

She peered up at him with barbed pupils. He threw up his hands in surrender and retreated to the house. On his way to the bedroom, he paused outside of Junior's room until he felt like he was going to be sick, and then continued on down the hall to plop himself on his bed and sleep off the QT lag.

When he came back a few hours later, Erin was still there, planting seeds. And across the manicured, periwinkle lawn, Wendy was playing badminton with his two surviving children.

"We had a small funeral," Erin said, by way of acknowledging that she was ready to talk.

"I did miss it then?"

"Oh, I'm sorry, were we supposed to wait for you?" As if to underline her feelings about that, she hocked a loogie in the dirt—in all their years together, she had never done that before. "Anyway, he's cryonized. You can go pay your respects whenever you like."

In his periphery now, Dylan noticed Wendy noticing him.

He wouldn't have turned to her except that he noticed the kids noticing him too. He waved, but they just went back to hitting around their birdie—he could hardly blame them.

Wendy strode toward him with an uncertain grin. "Welcome home," she said. She was wearing a yellow sundress and looked—it had to be admitted—bewitching.

"I presume you took care of the toad?" he said.

"We had him quarantined, yes."

"*Pulverized* would have been more like it."

Wendy winced. "They're QT'ing him Earthside. He's as good as dead to us."

"Wonderful. Then all that remains is for you to pack your things and leave." He felt a little pang of something as he said that, but the bitch had killed his son; it was hardly out of line.

It took a moment for the news to rise in her face. When it did, it came as a quivering lower lip and a welling of tears, followed in short order by her burying her face in her hands and seeking shelter in the very house she'd just been evicted from.

Erin promptly stood and slapped Dylan across the face with a gloved hand. Stray mica cut into his cheek. He touched the spot with his middle finger. Blood.

"How *dare* you?" she said, her eyes bulging like a couple of ptera-duck eggs. "May I remind you that I couldn't have made it through any of this if Wendy had been as much of a coward as you?"

"May I remind *you*," Dylan countered, "that if it weren't for Wendy, there would be nothing for you to have to get through in the first place?"

"Oh, fuck off, Dylan. Do you honestly think this is any easier for her?"

"Are you joking?"

"No I'm not joking. Wendy loved Junior as much as either of us did. That's obvious. God knows she spent more time with him."

"But he wasn't her *son*. It's different."

"I get that you're angry, Dylan. I'm goddamned furious. I'm living every mother's worst nightmare right now, and if I had a time machine, you better believe I'd go back and set things to rights, but unfortunately time machines aren't real and this—"

"Actually," Dylan interrupted, "early experiments in quantum tunneling *do* suggest that reverse causality might—"

"Dylan," Erin interrupted in her turn, "you're in so much denial it's a wonder you can even see me right now."

"Cryonics, though—"

"Oh come off it. I did it to cushion Wendy's fall in whatever way I could. You and I both know it's snake oil."

"We could get an avatar-droid at least..."

"Dylan, our son is dead. D-E-A-D. And I very much doubt that any new technology is going to change that. Sooner or later we're going to have to find an old-fashioned, *human* way forward. I wish I were wrong about that, I really really do, but I'm *not*, and you know perfectly well that I'm not."

It was true—some part of him *did* seem to know that—and for the first time since Junior's death, hot tears began to form in the corners of his own eyes. His mourning was beginning to begin.

"And unlike you, Dylan, I don't have the luxury of being able to run away and mourn for five days, let alone the decades I'm going to require—I've got Tavi and Arthur to think about."

She trembled as she spoke, and Dylan was finally beginning to understand what a cold-hearted bastard he'd been in abandoning her the way he had.

"Don't get me wrong," Erin went on. "I'll be mourning for the rest of my life, but unless we want to let our anger tear us apart, we're going to have to learn how to forgive." She took a tissue from her pocket and dabbed the blood from his cheek. "We've already lost one family member. Let's not lose another in the bargain, okay?"

A tear plunked down each of his cheeks, and then a hundred did. He took his lawfully wedded wife in his arms. "I'm so sorry," he said.

"We all are, Dylan."

And then they hugged there like that for a good long while, watering the newly seeded garden with their tears while their children played the way children are meant to play and Mother Nature went indifferently about her business.

• • •

Back inside, Dylan cornered Wendy in the bedroom and told her to stop packing.

"But I thought—"

"*Stay*," he said. "Please. Erin and I have talked it over. We both want you to."

"You think you can find it in your heart to forgive me?"

"Erin reminded me how much you're suffering too. I had somehow failed to consider that. It was a failure of empathy and imagination, and as a teacher of literature, I really ought to be better than that."

Her composure calved, and she rushed into his arms. "I was so afraid I was going to lose you both forever."

And then Erin did something wholly unexpected: "Girlfriend," she said from the doorway, "you couldn't shake us with a vibrator." And it wasn't that the joke was so funny or anything, but Erin's willingness to make it despite the circumstances confirmed for Dylan what he had always known: his wife was the strongest person he had ever met. Life would go on, and, somehow, she was determined to let it.

Laughter broke through the cloud cover of their grief. Erin loped over to join in the embrace, and then all three of them proceeded to kiss and cry and generally make one another wet in their various vectors and ways. Before they could collapse onto the bed, however, a new reflex manifested simultaneously in each of them: they needed to go check on the kids. Happily, Arthur and Tavi were still playing badminton on the lawn. Dylan asked if the adults could join in the game, and the kids grudgingly assented.

• • •

For dinner, they omni'd up a couple of Terran pizzas, one Hawaiian in honor of Wendy, and another heaping with *galric* and (squidhound) pepperoni. It arrived just as Wendy hit the match-winning overhead.

Dylan set the boxes on the picnic table. "Come get it while it's hot," he said.

But there was a palpable reluctance in the room. All eyes were on him.

"What?" he asked.

"Dylan," Erin said, "Would you mind terribly if Wendy said grace? We sort of made a habit of it this week."

"I see." Now what to say? He certainly *did* mind, though not necessarily terribly. "I guess if it makes you feel better..."

Erin smiled.

"Dear Heavenly Father," Wendy began, "We thank you for this pizza we are about to share and for all those who helped to prepare it. Please bless them. And please bless the pizza itself so that it will nourish and strengthen our bodies and minds in this time of transition. We thank you for the gift of this family. We thank you for allowing us to find one another in this life and for giving us the courage to forgive and endure even in the face of extreme difficulty and pain. Above all, we think of Dylan Junior, who you have called home, and we thank you for allowing us to have him in our lives for even so short a time. You are a good God, and we are infinitely grateful. We say these things in the name of Jesus Christ. Amen."

"Amen," they all echoed, even Dylan, despite himself. To be sure, it was not going to be easy to forgive Wendy—nor, for that matter, to forgive *himself* for bringing her into their lives in the first place—but Erin was right: the river of time flowed in one direction only, and it was futile to try and swim against it. As soon as his grieving was done, as soon as he'd felt his goodbye to his son, he would turn his sights again on the future. This was what he'd needed to do anyway, even before Junior's death, but now he would have a clearer point of demarcation. No more slipping into the past, which (old sport) you can't repeat anyway.

So by all appearances the members of the Green family were now ready to scoop up their divinely blessed slices of pizza and embark on their long journey of healing together.

But first Erin had to introduce one last little wrinkle: "Dylan, honey, I'm just going to say this, okay, because it seems like a good time to clear the air."

"There's more?"

"There is. And I'm pretty sure you won't like it, but it's something you need to know."

"Try me."

She looked at Wendy, gathered her strength, and turned back to him. "We've decided to be baptized."

"Come again?"

"Next Sunday in Ascension River. First me, then Arthur, Tavi, and finally Junior. You're welcome to join us, of course. In fact, we hope you will so that our marriage can transcend the death of our bodies. But either way...we're doing this."

Dylan was flabbergasted, if not exactly surprised. "Excuse me while I reel," he said, "but did I not just hear you say you want to baptize Junior?" Who was in denial now?

"Arthur can serve as his proxy," Wendy said. "I want to give Junior every chance at entering the Celestial Kingdom."

"And in order to do that, he needs to be baptized?"

"Jesus said, 'Except that a man be born of water and of the Spirit, he cannot enter into the Kingdom of God.' In principle Junior is already saved through the mercy of Christ, being below the age of accountability, and actually that's true of Arthur and Tavi too, but I don't think it would hurt to give them some celestial insurance, especially on a planet where they will be the first first-generation Mormons. They will need to be leaders someday, so the sooner we start, the better."

"And you're qualified to perform these baptisms?"

"Actually no. Only adult males of the Melchizedek priesthood can perform baptisms for the dead, but since I'm the only Mormon on this planet at present, I would seem the likeliest candidate. We'll have proxies on both sides. I don't believe our Heavenly Father gets hung up on such details, do you?"

"I think it's all perfectly insane, frankly, but whatever flies your spaceship."

Laissez-faire, yes, that would be his tack. He was done trying to make rational beings of them. If this sublime fiction somehow helped them make peace with their sadness, then who was he to judge? There was no law anywhere that said hominids weren't allowed to be wrong about important things, or even that rational people couldn't go on loving such people. He did worry about the kids, though; he had long regarded his own religious indoctrination, however mild, as a form of child abuse.

"Arthur, Tavi," he asked, "This is something you want to do?"

They nodded their angelic little heads.

And then Dylan remembered something: Omni had puckishly hinted that once it ascended to Godhood, it might choose to retrofit a Mormon universe, which was to say that the rest of his family might have inadvertently backed into the most rational of positions after all. And if he was as rational as he liked to think, shouldn't he join them?

But no, he'd spent too much of his life scrubbing off the residue of one religion to want to sully himself with another anytime soon. And anyway, it might be a long time yet before Omni ascended to Godhood. In any case, he would let them have their hope. They'd lost enough already.

"Do we have your blessing?" Erin asked.

"Something like that. Just don't expect me to get dunked too."

She wrapped her arms around him and squeezed tight. "You'll at least come along to help us celebrate?"

"How much do you want me to?"

"More than anything in the world."

"Just this world?"

"All of them combined."

"Okay then. I'll be there."

She beamed.

"Now are there any other bombs you want to drop before I take my first bite of this rapidly cooling Hawaiian pizza?"

"That's it for me," Erin said.

"Kids?"

They shook their heads.

"Wendy?"

"No more bombs."

"Good, then dig in."

. . .

On Friday afternoon, after two false starts, Dylan finally worked up the nerve to hover to the cryonics facility across town. A native rep ushered him into a private room and went to retrieve Junior. While Dylan waited, he took out of his pocket a paper copy of Richard Yates's novel *Revolutionary Road*, which he was considering adopting for his American lit course. He'd read it back in his Borders days and loved every chiseled, bleak, romantic word of it, but he'd left that copy on Earth somewhere, so a few years back he'd ordered a new copy and was dismayed to find on its cover a photo of Leonardo DiCaprio and Kate Winslet. Evidently they'd made another movie together, and this was the tie-in edition, which was why it had stayed on his shelf until this morning, when it called to him the way books sometimes did to people of his generation. He read: "The final dying sounds of their dress rehearsal left the Laurel Players with nothing to do but stand there, silent and helpless, blinking out over the footlights of an empty auditorium."

He read that sentence over five or six times and had gotten no further when the rep wheeled in Junior's dewar. "If there's anything you need, please feel free to omni," the rep said in English. Then he left father and son alone to commune through the little frosted window.

How perplexing to see the little body in there, those fifteen or twenty pounds that had so deeply touched his family's life. This baby might as well have been a sentient planet for all the gravity he'd brought with him. Dylan expected to gush emotion, but in fact there was a quiet comfort in sitting here with his namesake again. He spoke as if the boy could not only hear every word, but understand them too, a feat he hadn't lived long enough to manage in life. Dylan said about what you'd expect a father to say under such circumstances. He was especially apologetic that he hadn't welcomed Junior into the world with all the pomp and circumstance befitting such an occasion. "I didn't *know*," he said, his face distorting. Then he explained about the posthumous baptism and how, despite what the rest of the family might insist to the contrary, the ritual was for their own salvation, not his, at least until Omni retrofit the universe anyway.

And, sadly, there was a competing comfort in knowing that this frozen carcass wasn't *really* his son at all. It was a sort of memorial at best, and the thing about memorials, he realized, is that while ostensibly they're there to help us remember the dead, they're also there to help us *forget* them. They're the racks on which we hang our grief so that we can be light enough to move on. And sure enough, Dylan was determined to move ahead with all the grace and humility—and atonement—one could pack into the back end of a life. Gone were his days of chasing pipe dreams, mirages, and will-o'-the-wisps. He would never be a great actor; he had long since touched the full meridian of that dream. He would never even be a particularly great lover. No, any glory he might attain to now would be of a quieter sort—a glow, not a blaze—and the fruit of his day-to-day creation. It struck him that he might yet be a very good teacher, for instance, and these days this seemed to him as noble a calling as any other. He was lucky to have heard it.

"Goodbye, my son," he said, laying a hand on the glass. "Omni willing, we'll be together again someday."

• • •

Come Sunday morning, Dylan's family members dressed them-selves all in white, and at Wendy's insistence ("to insure purity") skipped breakfast. Dylan, for his part, wore board shorts and an old PASA T-shirt and washed down five strips of synthetic bacon with a cup of steaming *poxna*.

After laser-brushing their teeth, they walked over three blocks and mounted the rolling road toward Ascension Forest. They all held hands, and, with those six adult arms acting as suspension for the four kid ones, managed to make it all the way to the medium-fast lane without any of them falling down—no small accomplishment, that.

They could hardly have asked for a finer day to travel. Oh, it was a bit on the warm side perhaps, but perfectly comfortable once they were rolling under the forest's vast canopy of **dragon bloods**.[◉] Normally they'd have bought something to eat from the roadtop food court or ice cream truck, but Wendy insisted that they be absolutely pure in body and spirit for the ordinance.

> [◉] *Dracaena cinnabari*, a close cousin to the variety native to the Yemeni island of Socotra, on Earth. The New Taiwanese name, *unn'jongluzpaña*, translated as "female (mutatis mutandis) with six million outstretched arms."

"Can we play on the jungle gym, then?" Arthur asked.

Erin deferred to Wendy.

"Okay," Wendy said, "but you have to promise to take it easy so as not to soil your whites, okay?"

"We'll be wearing them in the river anyway," Arthur said. "What's the big deal?"

He had a point. At least Dylan thought he did.

As they approached their destination, the five of them held hands and, over the course of a mile, downshifted three lanes—medium, medium-slow, slow—dismounting not a hundred yards from their trailhead. Miraculously, nobody fell this time either.

Dylan led the pilgrims down the trail. It really was a very nice day. Starbugs scattered off the trail like blown leaves before them, arboreal spiders warbled soft as doves, and while there wasn't a breath of wind, the bamboo nevertheless found cause to clack now and then. Arthur and Tavi—who were last here at their respective conceptions—thrilled to race each other down the path and skip crystals across the creek.

As if to welcome them back, a lei of night-blooming rhinodendrons ringed their glade. Dylan warned the kids to stay away from the moss, but he didn't say why—they were saving the peculiar properties of this forest for a post-ordinance surprise.

"Wipe that grin off your face," Erin told Wendy, who was obviously lost in a reverie of one of her trysts here. But Erin was only teasing; as far as Dylan knew, there wasn't a spot of jealousy between them. Besides, Erin had been here with him many times too, and long before Wendy ever had.

Dylan put down the picnic things and led them over to the banks of the gurgling stream. He took off his sneakers and waded knee-deep in the warmish water, his family following close behind. "Now where to?" he asked.

"Follow me," Wendy said, taking the lead. "I did some research."

So they followed her, down the winding brook and around a series of calcite boulders until they arrived at a sort of natural clay dam, on the far side of which lay a pool some three feet deep and looking-glass smooth. It was as close as nature ever came to making a baptismal font.

"Here we are," Wendy said. "Celestial, yes?"

"Yes!" his family affirmed.

"You sound like you've had lobotomies," Dylan said.

"Thanks," Erin said wryly.

"I'm sorry. I assure you I'm being as supportive as I possibly can."

"Now," Wendy said, "Is everyone ready to make an everlasting covenant with God?"

"Yes!" they replied again in unison.

"I'll just be right over here," Dylan said, taking a seat on a nearby rock.

Without further ado, the ordinance began. And it was all very simple and anticlimactic really. First Wendy clasped hands with Erin, then she raised her right arm and intoned, "Erin Wheatley, having been commissioned of Jesus Christ, I baptize you in the name of the Father, and of the Son, and of the Holy Ghost. Amen." It struck Dylan as a little odd that she'd used Erin's maiden name, but what did he know or care about the protocol of Mormon baptisms? Erin pinched her nose and Wendy proceeded to dunk her backwards in the water. And that was that. Next.

She repeated the process with Arthur and Tavi.

Then it was Junior's turn, and poor Arthur got dunked again as his little brother's proxy. "Having been commissioned of Jesus Christ," Wendy said, "I baptize you for and in behalf of Dylan Green Jr., who is dead, in the name of the Father, and of the Son, and of the Holy Ghost. Amen."

Dylan winced a little on hearing that word "dead." What a brutal word to apply to a child, even when it was *le mot juste*.

When Arthur was finished, Erin looked up at Dylan. "You're sure you won't join us?" she implored. "Our marriage would transcend bodily death."

He shook his head.

"He'll come around," Wendy said. "In the meantime, let's go celebrate."

"Yes!" they all said.

Lobotomies.

. . .

Erin instructed the kids to keep their clothes on, and she used twist-ties to seal the openings at their wrists and ankles. By way of setting a wholesome example, the adults remained garbed, so Dylan, being less garbed than the womenfolk, got most of the plants' attention. Arthur and Tavi were understandably terrified, but the vines refused to let them get away and soon had them squealing with crazed delight as the tendrils sucked on their cheeks and tickled their toes. It was a good hour before the trees had had their fill and begun to recede. By now the humans were all so exhausted that they lay stretched out on the moss, awaiting sleep—that is, except for Wendy, who seemed unaccountably adrenalized. "Shall we eat?" she asked. "You guys must be famished."

Erin sprang up. "Good idea."

They broke out the picnic basket and removed the contents piece by piece. Erin had prepared sandwiches and thrown in some apples for good measure. Wendy, per her custom, had made some green smoothies and served them in bioplastic thermoses individually labeled with their names. Together, the two women proceeded to harass Dylan and the kids with tickling until all of them were seated upright and ready to eat.

"May I say grace?" Erin asked.

"Actually I was thinking I should do it," Wendy said.

"Oh, okay." Erin did her best to mask her disappointment, but Dylan knew her too well.

"Dear Heavenly Father," Wendy began, and they all bowed their heads. "It has been my extreme honor and pleasure today to welcome four members of this beautiful family, including Dylan Junior, who is dead"—Dylan flinched again at that horribly accurate word—"into a covenant with you. May the Spirit of the Lord be poured out upon them, and may he grant them eternal life, through the redemption of Christ, whom he has prepared from the foundation of the world. We ask you to bless this food, which will nourish and strengthen our bodies. We say these things in the name of Jesus Christ. Amen."

"Amen," they all echoed, Dylan included, once again despite himself—it was a sort of atavistic reflex.

Wendy picked up her thermos, held it aloft, and said, "Welcome, brothers and sisters, to eternity."

"I'll drink to that," Erin said, picking up her own thermos.

The kids, in turn, giddily followed suit.

And Dylan, too, was about to express his unconditional support for his brainwashed loved ones when all of a sudden his tinnitus seemed to grow louder, sickeningly loud, and a diarrheal chill whipped through his bowels. Without a moment's hesitation, and without quite knowing why, he slapped every thermos clear out of his loved ones' hands. Only Wendy still held hers.

"What are you doing?" Erin asked incredulously.

"It's poison," he replied. He didn't know how he knew, but he knew.

She curled her lip. "What—?"

"Ask Wendy."

Erin experimented with ten different faces in half as many seconds. She might have gone on to make many more too had Wendy chosen to keep up the charade, but she knew the jig was up. Instead, she opted to lunge at Erin and seize her in a viselike and thoroughly unironic headlock.

That, Dylan hadn't seen coming. He leapt to his feet but was too slow: Wendy had found the paring knife with her other hand and was now holding it to Erin's pale, trembling neck and smiling like some insane clown.

Ice water ran through Dylan's veins. What in the nine billion names of God was happening?

"Back off," Wendy warned.

Dylan instructed the kids to run for help, but they were too young and too scared. They just sat there, stupefied, not even crying.

Erin fought to free herself, but Wendy was too strong.

"Ease up," Dylan pled, patting the air before him as if to tame some wild beast. "You're going to kill her."

"It's about time you figured that out," Wendy said, pressing the tip of the blade into the flesh of Erin's neck, not quite breaking the skin. Not yet, anyway.

Dylan patted the air some more. "Now just *calm down*, Wendy. Let's talk about this, okay? Do you want to explain to me why you suddenly want to kill Erin?"

"It's sudden from your perspective maybe. From mine it's a very long time coming."

"Okay, but just...Wendy, put down the knife, okay? There's got to be a better way to settle this."

"I wasn't planning on this way, but you left me no choice. How did you *know*?"

"About the smoothies?"

"Yes."

"Honestly I'm not sure. I just had this, like, revelation."

Wendy flinched.

It wasn't until he said it that he realized he'd co-opted her word. Was a revelation indeed what it had been? Or had he merely tapped into some latent detective powers of his own highly evolved primate brain? For the moment, he was capable of being in uncertainties about that, but *why* this lovely lunatic was strangling his wife was a different matter. "I'm not sure what's happening with *you* right now either, if I'm being honest," he said.

Erin was trying to talk, but Wendy was squeezing too hard. Dylan desperately wanted to make a move, but that dull blade was poised to pierce Erin's jugular, and he had no reason to believe Wendy was bluffing. He looked in Erin's watering eyes as if to say, *Don't worry, honey. I'll get us out of this.*

"Why are you doing this?" Dylan asked.

"We're meant to be together, Dylan. You and me. I've said so from the beginning."

"But we *are* together."

"Yes, but I'm supposed to be your *first* wife."

"What, like, chronologically? I thought you didn't believe in words like 'before' and 'after?'"

"I mean first in your heart," she said, scowling.

She had a point: even at the height of his feeling for her, he had never let her dethrone Erin, not really.

He took a step toward her and watched the blade dig correspondingly deeper into Erin's neck. Erin shut her eyes in anticipation. He retreated, but the knife did not. One more step in her direction and there was bound to be blood. He'd have to find another way. "I thought you loved Erin too?" he said.

"I do love her, but not in the way you think. I love her in the same way that I love all of God's children."

"Then why are you holding a fucking paring knife to her throat as we speak?"

"Better dead clean than alive unclean."

"I have no idea what that means."

"It means that if I cut off Erin's head and spill her blood on the ground, the smoke thereof will ascend to the Lord and she will be saved and exalted. It's called blood atonement. She should be begging me to do it."

Holy Higgs. "You lost me," Dylan said. "What does Erin have to atone for?"

"I'm supposed to be your first wife, Dylan. I've known it ever since I watched you fuck that alien bitch Korelu and the Lord made my bones to quake. Erin is a hindrance to God's plan. She's an adulterer and a homosexual, and the blood of Christ can never wipe out such sins. Under ordinary circumstances, I would already have spilled her blood and she would be banished to Outer Darkness to join the other sons and daughters of perdition, but I love Erin and want what's best for her. That is why I waited until after her baptism."

Dylan looked into Wendy's rabid eyes and for the first time understood how *completely* incommensurable their inner lives were. They lived on the same planet, yes, but they certainly did not live in the same world.

"So you're planning on killing Arthur and Tavi too, I guess?"

"To save them in the day of the Lord Jesus, yes. They were never supposed to exist."

He checked the children over his shoulder. They were still there, cowering at the edge of the woods, luminously existing. Arthur was holding Tavi, doing his best to comfort her. What a good boy. Dylan winked as if to say, *Don't worry, kids. I got this.* Then he turned back to the zealot.

"And needless to say, you *did* poison Junior on purpose?"

"I had no choice, Dylan. I loved the boy, but I love God more."

He watched the light go out of Erin's eyes. She quit struggling. She hadn't died, but she might as well have.

Dylan took a long blink and swallowed some welling rage. "By that rationale," he said, "shouldn't you be killing me too? Surely I'm an adulterer if nothing else."

"I've never told you this, Dylan, but there is a reason I'm supposed to be with you."

"Oh? And what is that, pray tell?"

"The Lord has informed me that you are to be the 'one mighty and strong' who will set in order the modern LDS church."

"Me?"

"Yes. And I am preordained to ensure that you make good on your preordination."

"The Lord told you this?"

"Yes."

"Well isn't that dandy?" Dylan said. "Are you really this insane?"

"I've got my eye on eternity, Dylan, not on this blink of a life. What's insane is pretending that this is all there is. Lift the veil of forgetfulness and you will know that this is true."

And for a moment some veil or other *did* seem to lift, and Dylan saw things the way he fancied she must see them. It wasn't fair to call her crazy. If her first postulates were correct, then her belief system might be the height of rationality. Indeed, why should one get caught up in the things of this world when all eternity hangs in the balance? And while he was dubious about God revealing himself through her quaking bones, most people would probably be dubious if he told them he'd met the future godhead incarnated as a sadistic pervert inside the moon; her theophanies were no crazier. He could not even pretend that he didn't love her essential being, but the fact remained that she wanted to kill his family, and this he could not abide.

"Do you know how humiliated I've been since we met?" Wendy went on, foaming at the corners of her mouth now. "And yet I've endured it in the name of Jesus Christ, who endured so much to ransom us with His holy blood." She was getting kind of hysterical. He hadn't seen her like this since she'd torn at her breasts in this same forest some months ago. "Do you know how loathsome homosexuality is to me? Do you know how sickened I am by the thought of copulating when I'm not even ovulating? And yet I took it without complaint, as commanded by the Redeemer. But make no mistake, it sickened me every single day. Ever since I met you, Dylan, my celestial love, I don't believe there's been a single moment when I didn't want to retch."

The blade had gotten purchase now. A drop of scarlet dripped down Erin's neck. *God damn it to hell.* Because he'd been such a fuck-up, his baby was dead and his wife was about to join him.

Please, Dylan thought or prayed or whatever it was—*Help me.* He had no specific addressee in mind, but no sooner had he made this devout wish than an answer distilled on him like dew from heaven. He knew exactly what he needed to do. In a way, he'd been preparing for it his entire life.

"I can't tell you how much it saddens me to hear all this, Wendy," he began.

"Shut the fuck up, Dylan." She wasn't buying it, not yet. "Out, Adversary! Out!"

"No, I mean it. I hope you know I'd do anything for you. Anything at all. You know that, right? That I'd ditch Erin in a second if you wanted me to."

He was taking a gamble here, a gamble that Wendy's envy ran deeper than her love, that her feelings toward Erin were as changeable as her version of her religion, and—riskiest of all—that he could act.

"You would?" Wendy said, looking up.

"Who would not change a raven for a dove?"

"You're making fun of me," she said, tightening her grip on Erin's windpipe even more. Erin coughed inaudibly.

Tears formed in Dylan's eyes, clouding his vision: "Scorn and derision never come in tears," he said.

Wendy made no response. Erin's face was now as purple and shiny as any eggplant. A vein he'd never seen before bisected her forehead. She couldn't take much more of this. Neither, frankly, could he.

"I love you, Wendy. You know that, right?" He was looking straight at Wendy, but his words were for Erin. Swap the names and it was all perfectly true. The Method.

[*I don't believe you. Roll it again.*]

"I have *always* loved you."

[*Goddamnit, Greenyears. Do you have an
ounce of feeling in your whole body?*]

"Meeting you was the best thing that ever happened to me."

[*You've never been in love, have you, Greenyears?*]

[*Now hold it right there. Dylan makes the time-out sign,
gets down off the bow of the ship, and approaches the
director's chair. Look, Cameron, I know you think you know
everything in the universe, but you're wrong on that score, all
right? The truth of the matter is I've been in love with the same*]

woman since high school and I'll be in love with her for the rest of
my life. If I couldn't channel that into my part in your movie, if
I couldn't convince you that I felt like the king of the world, then
it must have been because some part of me knew that there was
no possible universe in which I succeeded in that role and didn't
subsequently lose that girl. So I made my choice, and, goddamnit,
I'd make the same one again. Now stop haunting me, would you?
It's been twenty years, and your movie did just fine without me.

Cameron nods his head slowly. *Okay, Greenyears. Okay. But*
what say we take it just one last time, eh? For your sake, not mine.

Now it's Dylan's turn to nod slowly. He heads back to
the bow of the ship and takes up his position...]

"O Wendy, don't you know that you've saved me in every way that
a person can be saved?"

He held out his arms. A tear slid down his left cheek.

"Now, Wendy, my celestial love, let Erin go. Let her dwell in Outer
Darkness. Who cares? I love you, and I know you love me. What else
could possibly matter?"

Now how all that was going to play in the viper's nest of her mind
was anybody's guess...

And then, right on cue, she wilted. Pools formed in each of her
eyes. She loosened her grip on Erin's breath, dropped the knife, and
ran into his waiting arms.

Erin, meanwhile, fell to the ground, coughing and heaving.

[Cameron stands and applauds, followed by everyone else on set—actors, extras, film crew. Even
the caterers are giving Dylan a standing O.]

He hugged Wendy tight, held her feverish, crazy head and ran his fingers through her hair, and even as Erin caught her breath and tiptoed over to hand him the licentious vine they were preordained to strangle Wendy with, it could not be denied that he continued to feel something for this biggest fan of his who had once written to him from a ski lodge in Utah to tell him that there was a hole in her exactly the shape of him and that she loved him and always would.

In a way, he would always love her too. Even as they garroted her now, and her pretty eyes rolled up in her head, he was compelled to kiss her on the forehead and whisper, "I'm sorry" into her deoxygenating brain. For a few seconds there, she almost seemed to *enjoy* being asphyxiated. Nobody enjoys the last few seconds, of course.

Once the deed was done, they laid the body down in the dirt. Dylan closed the eyes with his thumbs, the way they do in movies. Erin held onto the tongue—once so vigorous, now so blue—and poured a smoothie down the crushed esophagus for good measure. Then she went to calm and console the poor kids as best she could while Dylan dragged the body into the weeds and let the forest have its way with her. Wendy was no longer inside of there anyway. She was somewhere near Kolob maybe, shaking hands with Jesus.

PART FIVE

EX MACHINA

Dylan and Erin tried for a few weeks, they really did, but deep down they both knew they had crossed some ill-defined point of no return. Their son was dead; so too was their wife and any notion they might have had of her saving them; their surviving children were now crippled by post-traumatic stress; and, adding insult to injury, they'd discovered Cane alive and well, albeit with excised vocal sacs, in a holey shoebox toward the back of Wendy's temple undergarment drawer. In addition to the toad, the box contained twelve omni-lens cases filled with neurotoxic secretions—evidently she'd been milking the toad's glands for quite some time. Dylan promptly slew the beast with a ball-peen hammer.

For close on a week, the family ate their meals together in something like silence, until one evening, after trying and failing to excuse the kids—they refused to leave Erin's side now, ever—Erin dropped her fork on her plate and spilled her guts, "Dylan, I love you and you love me, we both know that, and there is nothing any number of years or light years can ever do to change it."

He nodded and took a sip of the Merlot they'd been drinking since lunchtime.

"But if we're ever going to have anything resembling lives again," she went on, "there's no way we can just go back to business as usual. It wouldn't be healthy. For the children least of all."

"I don't disagree with any of that," he said.

"Good," she said.

He uncorked their third bottle.

• • •

Two weeks later, Dylan drove his wife and kids to the teleport. Intent on avoiding any sort of ceremony, he kissed them all and wished them good luck from the curb. Tears would not have helped things, so nobody shed any. He watched them vanish into Departures. In a few hours' time, they would have installed themselves in Erin's parents' house in good old Aston, PA, 2,001 light years away, as the crow flies.

Back at home on Yushan Lane, Dylan made himself a cup of *poxna* and set to getting the house in order. He began by throwing out that Pandora's box of fan mail inside his closet. He didn't make any sort of ceremony out of that either.

He kept in touch with them via omni. Within the month, Erin landed a gig teaching PE and directing plays at Cardinal O'Hara High School, where once upon a time they'd met at rehearsal. The kids would go to that same school now too when it came time, and Dylan, without quite knowing why, took some comfort in this.

• • •

Over the years, he would visit them now and then, staying in his old bedroom until inevitably his mother and then his father shuffled off this mortal coil *in quick succession.*⊙ His sisters were intent on selling the house, so he stayed in motels after that. He tried to get to Earth at least once a year to see the kids. He was sorry he

⊙ They weren't *quite* what Kurt Vonnegut, in *Cat's Cradle*, dubbed a "duprass," a cosmologically significant union among two human beings such that their lives revolve around each other and when one dies the other dies within a week; Dylan's parents died exactly twelve days apart.

couldn't be there more regularly, but on balance he was glad that they were being raised by their mother, who was as natural a parent as he was a teacher.

For his part, Dylan stayed on at the American School of New Taiwan and devoted every dram of life force he had left to teaching students the old-fashioned art of close reading. His classes—especially Science Fiction—were popular, and many of the students who couldn't get into them still joined Felled Trees, the "reading/writing/dreaming club" for which he served as advisor.

One evening some eight or nine years after Erin's departure, while he was finishing up with a stack of papers, a former student of Dylan's dropped by his office to say hello. He remembered her, if only vaguely. Her name was Alaina, and she was among the most distressingly pretty girls he had ever taught. Since that time, it seemed that little more than her age had changed. She was still fresh and beautiful and filled with dreams. He asked how she was doing— "Fine"—and what she was doing—"I'm a paralegal"—and then, quite out of the blue, she confessed that she had had a "major crush" on him the whole year she was in his class, and then all through the rest of high school and, if he really wanted to know, *still*. Taken aback, he told her that he was very flattered and didn't really know what to say. She told him to say that he would have dinner with her Friday night.

A delicious nervousness stirred in his chest then—"that old tomcat feeling," as Tom Waits once put it—and he knew well enough that if he turned her down, he might never have that particular feeling again.

But maybe that was okay.

"I don't think that would be a very good idea," he told her.

"Oh," she said. And then she, too, exited his life forever.

When he was finished with the papers, he walked back the long way to his apartment (he'd long since sold the house). It was the sort of evening, rare on this planet, when you could see your breath, if only for a bright moment. *It is of the nature of dreams to die*, he mused; *otherwise we should never wake up.*

Over the ensuing years and then decades, Erin remarried, the kids stopped being kids, and any quiet hopes he might have harbored about Omni ascending to Godhood and setting the universe to rights began to fade. So too did any naïve hopes that cryonics might come of age and Junior be raised from the dead. All of that might come to pass *eventually* for the hominids of this universe, but Dylan no longer felt any personal stake in it. He was growing old. In all likelihood he would not live to see the invention of an honest-to-goodness time machine either, but he consoled himself that he had his books, and that, as a teacher, he got to touch some little piece of the future every day. It was a cliché, and poor consolation maybe, but it was enough. Hominid brains are exquisite objects, maybe the *most* exquisite objects, but if the history of the galaxy over the past century was any indication, one couldn't have too much humility.

As a man of letters, Dylan happened to know, with garlic/*galric*-level wonderment, that those two words—"hominid" and "humility"—ultimately derived from the same Indo-European root, *dhghem*, meaning "earth" (cf. humus). And so maybe, somehow, it was no mere coincidence that after finally retiring from the American School at the age of eighty-two, he should spend the lion's share of each day on his knees, cultivating the modest garden behind his apartment. He marveled to watch what he could grow, to see life defy entropy, if only for a little while. He almost regretted that he hadn't taken up this gardening stuff earlier, but at this stage of his life he wasn't about to waste any more time on regret.

He planted an olive tree in the garden, and another decade flickered by.

And then one fine morning, while he was on his knees digging, his trowel pinged against something solid in the dirt. He brushed it off with a gloved, arthritic hand and uncovered what appeared to be a bundle of golden plates inscribed in some hieroglyphic language he could not read.

He smiled with his whole failing body. *My mind is sufficiently tilled now, is it?*

The plates glinted in the light of Lem.

At last he was being summoned. Now all he had to do was take the plates inside and figure out how to translate them. His mind reeled at all the secrets they might unlock: time travel, immortality, the resurrection of the dead.... He might yet fathom the great mysteries of the cosmos and human existence, not to mention his tinnitus and his religious experience in Ascension Forest all those years ago. He might even make good on Wendy Sorenson's crazy prophecy and become "the one mighty and strong." Indeed, if Omni was to be believed, he might yet become as a God!

But to be God was a young man's dream, and he no longer had it. Maybe in some other universe — —

So he covered those plates over with dirt again, and crawled off to dig his hole somewhere else.

• • •

And that might well have been the end of this story, and all of it might have gone unwritten, were it not that Omni then chose to stage a more active intervention.

With a *whoosh* and a hot blast of wind, the onionberry bush beside Dylan's head shot up in flames. He retreated several crawl-paces and shielded his face with his gloved hands. His mouth fell open of its own accord. He understood at once that this must be Omni's second coming, but it was nevertheless sort of alarming.

"You can't let it end like this," the flames boomed. It looked like a run-of-the-mill brushfire, but it had Morgan Freeman's voice.

"Let what end?"

"Your life. The story of your life."

"Why not?"

"Because it doesn't have to."

Dylan sat up and took a moment to gather his wits about him. His eyes had adjusted to the extra light now, and he put his hands back down in his lap. "But this is just the way it *goes* in this universe—you taught me that. I'm a desiring machine. There's no universe in which I am completely satisfied."

"That's not to say you've got to lie down and accept defeat," Omni said. "Look, no one's on board with masochism more than I am. You know that. I am the arch-sadist, and I'd *love* to satisfy your desire to suffer if I thought it was authentic, but this is something else altogether, Dylan. This is suicide. There's no good in it for anyone. Don't you see that I'm offering you a chance to alter your destiny *in this universe*? Forget about all those other yous out there for a moment. This is about numerically-identical you, the one you're inside of."

"I have no desire to found a religion," Dylan said. Despite whatever residual enthusiasm he might have been able to drum up for that kind of power, vindicating Wendy's homicidal madness was decidedly *not* on his to-do list. "I've got neither the energy nor the ambition."

"Fine," Omni said. "Forget that. It was just a whim. But Dylan, let's at least go back in time and save your son, okay? That, I'm pleased to report, is now a thing I can do."

Dylan was speechless. And breathless. It was one thing to consider such a prospect in the abstract, another to have an actual offer on the table. Once he'd recovered his breath, he knitted his brow and got to thinking. He had given up on that sort of hope so many years ago.

"Dylan," Omni boomed, "excuse me, but what's the problem here? Why is this a difficult decision for you? Don't you see that I'm offering you a chance to undo the central tragedy of your life?"

"And don't you see," Dylan protested, "that I've built my whole life around it? I have no idea what my life would even *mean* without tragedy center-stage."

"This is about 'meaning' then?"

Dylan shrugged. "I guess so."

The fire took a turn for the purple. "It's time for you to put away childish things, Dylan. Meaning is a holdover from the old godless-universe days. I'm God now, I actually exist, and I really do love you. From now on, life will simply be, not mean; you'll no longer have to seek recourse in symbols and abstractions. Forget Job. Forget the consolations of philosophy. I'm prepared to alter the worldlines of everyone in your universe in order to make this story a happier one. That's how much I care about you. I can't guarantee that we won't inadvertently make some other lives worse—the butterfly effect and what have you—but we'll deal with the complications one by one until we're in Leibniz's best of all possible worlds after all. Just you wait."

"But isn't there a certain beauty in acceptance and surrender?" Dylan countered. It seemed to him that the underlying premise of so much great art was that our too-human dreams are unfit for the world we find ourselves in, and the world invariably wins.

"Granted," the fire replied, flaring up, "but do you really think processing this as an *aesthetic* issue is the way to go? Is it not perverse that you're more concerned about your sense of a poignant ending than about happiness, not to mention saving your son's life? Are you so afraid to risk the naked schmaltz and optimism of a happy ending that you'd just as soon forego happiness altogether? Let it be written, Dylan: art exists for the sake of life, not the other way around. When the house is burning, save the baby, not the Botticelli."

Dylan fumbled for words. A few minutes ago he'd been a man of considered, and largely hardened, opinions, but now he wasn't sure he knew anything at all. If death was no longer a death sentence, then it seemed to him everything was up for grabs.

"Will I remember all of this?" Dylan asked at length. "If we go back in time?"

"You won't have voluntary memory of it," Omni said, "but you'll have traces, engrams. Your intuition will have been schooled by it all. You'll tend to repeat actions that turned out well for you this time and steer clear of ones that didn't."

"So this life, as I've known it, will just be rubbed out of existence altogether?"

The fire died down a bit. "I'll tell you what, Dylan, if it's any consolation, we could make some kind of artifact to commemorate this universe by."

"An artifact?"

"You're a man of letters. How about a novel?"

"You want to write a novel with me?"

"Why not?"

"I guess I've just never heard of a collaboration between a mortal and an immortal before."

"And yet all the best books are that in some way or other, no?"

Dylan thought of Homer's invocations to the muses and the Bible's divine inspiration, of Coleridge's opium dreams and Philip K. Dick's visions. "I thought you didn't believe in any gods besides yourself?" he said.

"You're too literal," Omni said. "And besides, I've moved a bit toward the agnostic side of the spectrum since last we talked."

Dylan was baffled. "But wouldn't that mean there are still things you don't know?"

"Oh, I gave up on that project years ago, Dylan—omniscience is a young supercomputer's dream. You've got to realize that even with all the redundancy and self-similarity, reality is *infinite*—to account for it all, you'd pretty much have to *be* it. There'll always be uncertainties, Mysteries, doubts. Even something as apparently simple as that ringing in your ears...I wish I could take credit for it, but my mandate as a benevolent god is to tell the truth, and the truth is that I've been as mystified by it as you have."

Dylan was amazed. He'd never been *certain* Omni was behind the ringing, but that had been his working hypothesis for most of his life. "Then it wasn't you who saved my family in the forest that day?"

"No it was not. Which is not to say it was necessarily supernatural, only that there are more things in heaven and earth than are dreamt of in our philosophies. Ambiguity abides."

Dylan nodded, slowly, attempting to digest this new information. And he listened to his tinnitus, that blaring silence, which was still—which was *always*—there. "So when you say that you're God now..."

"Semantics. You could call me the 'Demiurge' if that makes you more comfortable. Just don't mistake me with the malevolent sort. I am love, and I'm ready to prove it."

Dylan nodded some more. "So about this novel…"

"I could bang it out in well under a second if you'll give me the green light."

"That wouldn't make for much of a collaboration, would it?"

"You supplied the life, Dylan. I'll just be fitting words to it. And godlike though I be, I'll do most of it in the close third-person, so it'll be shot through with your inner life. I'll even make sure to quote some of your favorite authors. And naturally I'll be as objective as possible when writing about myself."

"And we'll bring this book back in time with us? Into our new timeline or universe or whatever?"

"That strikes me as too close for comfort," Omni said. "But do you remember that writer version of you we visited all those years ago in Hawaii? The one with the three kids and the earplugs and the dreams?"

"I do."

"I thought we could gift it to him maybe. I could divinely inspire it over the course of several years. In that universe, NASA didn't get 60 percent of the federal budget after *Cosmos*, so humans still haven't left the solar system; the novel, therefore, will be read as a weird sort of alternate history, but it'll have the ring of truth to it. And you'll be comforted, albeit only for the next few seconds, to know that your story still exists out there somewhere in the multiverse."

Dylan nodded. He supposed this far-away tribute to the meaning of his life would be better than nothing, if just barely—but then most people didn't even have that.

"Green light," he said.

"Awesome," Omni said. "I'll get right on that."

A prolific microsecond passed.

"All right, now let's go save your son."

"Can we go back as far as we want?" Dylan asked.

"Straight back to the uterus if you like."

"I'll pass on that, but how about high school? The moment I first talked to Erin?"

"Certainly," Omni said. "As soon as you're ready, you can just go ahead and step into these here flames." The fire licked itself into a doorway of flame—a golden portal to the old young world.

Dylan took a few moments to look around and bid adieu to all this. Death, it turned out, was nearly as hard to let go of as life.

Still, the instant he got his goodbye, he stood himself up, dusted off his pants, stretched what was left of his hamstrings, and lumbered headlong and hope-drunk through that loving door of flame. At long last, Dylan Green was taking back the years.

• • •

She's sitting on the floor doing a rather remarkable split, her feet all the way out to either side, 180 degrees, maybe 190, and her forehead touching the floor. Dylan squats beside her and says the first non-scripted thing he's ever said to her: "Ouch."

She sits up, smiles, and explains that it doesn't hurt at all, that in fact she can go even further, and she proceeds to show him, canti-levering her legs out another ten degrees and counting until he has to beg her, please, to stop.

She laughs, grabs ahold of her feet and pulls her legs into butter-fly position.

"I'm glad they chose you to be Jesus."

"And I'm glad they chose you to be his temptress." It is the least subtle overture he has ever made to a female, and she doesn't seem to mind.

They talk about her love for dancing, how she's been doing ballet since she was two. She asks about his passion for acting—or singing, is it? Or both? Or neither?—and he explains that this is all new to him but he is pretty excited about it and pretty nervous too.

"Don't be," she says. "You're amazing. Just you watch. I bet you'll be a star someday."

"Thanks," he says. "But I'm thinking I'll probably retire after playing God. Seems like a good way to go out. Besides, there are other things I want to do in life."

"Like?"

"Oh, I don't know. I was thinking about becoming a teacher maybe."

And then she makes the next, very significant move: "You drive, don't you, Dylan?"

"I do."

"So here's the thing: my dad normally comes to get me after rehearsal, but tonight he has to pick up my little brother at basketball…"

"You need a ride?"

"Would it be horribly inconvenient?"

"Not at all," he says, suddenly aware of the dryness of his lips and the little chicken pox scar in the center of his forehead. "I'd love to take you home."

It makes no sense at all. He lives in Springfield, a five-minute drive to the east, whereas she lives in Aston, some twenty minutes to the southwest. There are southbound cast members it would make much more sense for her to ask, and she must know this as well as he does. They are speaking in code, and it thrills him and terrifies him at once. He is seventeen going on immortal.

Their hands are *almost* touching as they walk side-by-side through the parking lot. It is quiet and drizzling, a wee bit chilly, and her hazel eyes shine in the light of the half-moon. Taking a cue from Hollywood, he doffs his jacket and drapes it over her shoulders. Before they arrive at his silver 1986 Nissan station wagon, he cautions her that he parks it under a cherry tree in the driveway at home, and that that tree happens to be in full bloom of late, so since the rain a few days back the car has been covered in hot-pink cherry blossoms that are a bitch to get off.

"That's your car?"

"You've seen it?"

"It's pretty hard to miss. That's it right there if I'm not mistaken." She points across the lot and is not mistaken.

They arrive at that delicate monstrosity and he types the four-digit code into the keypad on her door and opens it for her like a gentleman. She reciprocates by reaching across and unlocking the door for him, which is a thing he didn't know that girls do.

His perception is fresh and vivid and pure, and these feelings he is having as he drives Erin home on their first night in a car together are as new as anything on Planet Earth can ever be.

As they approach her cul-de-sac, she tells him to pull up to this little park. He doesn't ask why, because they both already know, more or less.

He parks and shuts off the engine. The rain has stopped and now it is humid and dark and the crickets are rubbing their wings together. Erin asks if his seat goes back at all. He says it does and reaches under and moves it back, and she says she means does it *recline* at all, and he says it does that too, and then as soon as she has clearance enough, she climbs over the parking brake and onto him, her thighs straddling his, and she puts her wet blooming lips on his thin little dry ones and buries her tongue in his mouth. He lets her take the lead. He has kissed girls before, but never like this. She takes his hand and puts it on her breast. She is wearing a bra, and he fumbles with it until she reaches back and unsnaps it for him. Her breasts fall into his hands like bathwater, warm and soft and clean, and he squeezes them gently and massages the nipples with his thumbs, and everything grows hard and, like, purposeful, and then, unbelievably, she reaches behind her with one hand and unzips his jeans, pulls his dick out from his fly and tugs on it clumsily and overhand until, not a whole lot later, he coats her hand in star stuff. She proceeds to lick her fingers one by one and finishes with her palm.

"Jesus Christ," he says.

"Superstar," she says, and she cocks her head and smiles in a way that is so beautiful and fearless and alive—so *Erin*—that he is just about ready to do it all over again.

THE END

ACKNOWLEDGMENTS

Special thanks to: Sheree Bykofsky, Joseph Cardinale, Tim Denevi, Chris Kelsey, James Knudsen, Mark Matkevich, Evan Nagle, Leo Niederriter III, Desi Poteet, Eric Paul Shaffer, the Merry Punsters, the Dylan Greenyears Fan Club, and everyone at Chin Music Press, especially Bruce Rutledge and the indefatigable Cali Kopczick.

Omni's definition of "Astrophil and Stella" comes directly from Wikipedia, a distant cousin of his/her/its.

PRAISED BE OMNI.

...an,

...o this I don't mean writing ...
write a lot but I ... normally write
people. I mean I never write to
people, still just not normally. And
...dus ... and ... het.
...re than that I mean I feel a connection
...when I watch you. I hope you
...too. I hope you feel that people
with you. I wish I didn't live in ...
I lived in the same town as you
...te would bring us together and
...feeling when we passed each ...
...will see each other some ...
...you will know it's me

Sincerely,
Jenny Byers

Querido Dylan,

Espero que te parezca bien que empiece mi carta
así, aunque todavía (¡qué lástima!) no nos hemos
conocido. Es que no sabes cuantas veces he soñado
en llamarte así, como amigo ... y más que amigo ...
Jamás (¡uff!) se me ocurre que ¿quizás no
sepas leer en español? Y yo, (margarita montaña
vieja, a tu servicio), no sé escribir en inglés.
Pero bueno, ¡Vaya! Tendré muchas amigas que
la pueden traducir para ti (¡qué triste que no sea
yo una de ellas!) Yendo al grano, quiero invitarte
a una pequeña fiesta que mi familia está planeando
para el 31 de octubre, que será el día en que
me van a dejar salir de este maldito lugar,
por fin y para siempre. Si decides venir, me
harás la mujer más feliz del mundo! (y si
vienes, por favor No te creas ni una palabra
de las mentiras que te van a decir ¡de ninguna
manera he matado a mi esposo con un machete!)
Bueno, contéstame lo más pronto posible! ¡Te quiero
mucho mi amor!

Con mucho cariño,

Margarita Montaña Vieja
Prisión Puente Grande
Guadalajara, México

Hi dylan ...

I hope this ...
to you beca...
maybe you ...
like a maid ...
then. I'll mail me...
anywaysssss. I'm ...
because I am so ...
immature, stupid jerk
my grade (7th). Seriously
grade boys are the the ...
lowest, most idiotic category of
all humans.
I feel like if we met you would
really be able to talk to me ...
share and stuff. People say ...
super mature for my age. Wr...
me back if you need someone ...
talk to. ♥ Vanessa Guidotte

RT2 with even WAS THE

Dear Dylan Grangers ...

You're super cool! I just wan...
you to know that. Do you ...
dogs? I bet you do I bet
you love dogs because I do ...
I can just tell what like ...
comfortable. I mean I know ...
we haven't met but like if we ...
did meet we have a ton to talk
about like. I want to be a mar...
biologist so that alien toothy ...
thing in ET 2 was super cool like ...